THE RAGE COLONY

THE COLONY BOOK 2

THE RAGE COLONY

SHANON HUNT

NARROW LEDGE
PUBLISHING

First published by Narrow Ledge Publishing 2020

First edition

ISBNs
978-1-7338212-5-4 (Hardback)
978-1-7338212-4-7 (Paperback)
978-1-7338212-3-0 (Ebook)

Power is in tearing human minds to pieces and putting them together again in new shapes of your own choosing.

George Orwell, *1984*

Remains of missing fugitive found outside Black Canyon City
March 6, 2024
By Nicholas Slater

Phoenix, Arizona—Phoenix police say authorities have found the remains of a body uncovered by a flash flood 40 miles east of Black Canyon City, Arizona. DNA analysis has reportedly identified the body as Dr. Austin Harris, ex-CEO of biotech company Quandary Therapeutics. Harris, then 42, had turned fugitive after being charged with identity fraud and conspiracy to commit securities fraud in August 2019. He was never found.

Because decomposition of the body was limited by the relatively arid conditions of the environment, the medical examiner was able to establish that the approximate timeframe of death was near the time of Harris's disappearance. Phoenix police declined to comment on the possibility of reopening Harris's case or its relationship to the now permanently closed Vitapura Wellness Center, where the remains were found.

Connected to the Harris case is the disappearance of Allison Stevens, Harris's colleague and alleged lover. Stevens, then 29, vanished three weeks after Harris went missing, the same night a DEA agent was killed near her apartment in Paramus, New Jersey. Stevens, the primary suspect in the death of the agent, is still at large.

1

L ayla had a keen eye for insidious poison, and right now it was glaring back at her.

She eased into the chair next to Isaac, careful not to bang her protruding belly into the edge of the glossy cherrywood table, her gaze locked onto Keisha Marx, the fourth recruit—fifth? she'd already lost count—of today's busload to arrive at the Colony.

Keisha was over six feet tall and muscular with a smoothly shaved head and heavy eye makeup that was too excessive for her dark skin. But that's not why Layla couldn't stop staring. It was the woman's piercing gray eyes that drew her in, and the seething resentment in her expression—no, more than that, outright hatred.

Layla was good at intakes. She'd been interviewing recruits for two years now, and she'd mastered the skills necessary to establish trust and encourage openness. She could quickly evaluate recruit's suitability, and most that came through her found a home somewhere on the extensive campus, even if it wasn't in her purification program. But this woman made her wary. That burning stare was unnerving, a bit intimidating even, but there was something else. If she had to give it a name, she might even call it something evil.

Layla broke eye contact and nodded at Isaac, who she'd asked to lead the interviews today. She was ready to get this one over with.

Isaac didn't seem affected by Keisha's penetrating stare as he opened the folder and pushed it toward Layla so she could see it. "Keisha, it's a pleasure to meet you. Welcome to the Colony. I hope Michael and his team made your trip from the States comfortable. My name is Brother Isaac. This is Sister Layla."

His eyes lit up with compassion and genuine tenderness. That was Isaac.

Keisha's eyes darted to her and back to Isaac. She didn't speak or even move.

"Keisha, I understand from our recruiting team that you've expressed an interest in joining us here at the Colony. Is that right?"

"Yes." Her voice was a growl.

"Can you tell us a bit about your background?"

Keisha recounted her background with the tone of a bored teenager. "I was born in Tampa, Florida. Grew up in various cities across the US. My dad was in the military, and we lived on base. We moved around every couple of years. I left home when I was sixteen."

"Why did you leave home at such a young age?"

"I wasn't a big fan of military discipline."

It was an interesting answer and Layla wanted to hear more about that, but Isaac simply noted the response and moved on. "And why are you interested in the Colony?"

"I need a change."

"A change from what?"

"My old life."

"What was it about your old life you feel you need to change now?"

Her gaze shifted to Layla.

"Keisha?"

"I'd rather not say."

The woman's posture had changed. She sat up straighter and looked tense. Layla held her stare and tried to relax. God, there was something about this woman that chilled her. She flexed her fingers under the table.

Isaac's tone was far too empathetic for this recruit. "Well, I'm afraid this isn't going to be a very fruitful interview if you don't want to discuss your situation."

Keisha looked back at Isaac. "I don't want to say in front of her."

"And why is that?"

She didn't answer.

Layla remained silent out of respect for Isaac. Maybe it was the pregnancy hormones, but she was growing ever more irritated at him. He was so conflict averse that he tended to ignore signs of a poor fit. If he couldn't recognize the obvious hostility pouring from this woman, perhaps this wasn't the best assignment for him. The Colony had high standards of excellence, and this recruit was far from meeting them. She couldn't afford mistakes like this woman just because Isaac didn't have the guts to say no.

She could feel her blood beginning to boil and breathed slowly to calm herself.

Finally, Keisha answered. "I don't talk to white bitches."

That was it. Layla bolted up, knocking her chair over, and leaned over the table as far as her round belly would allow. "Is that so? Well unfortunately for you, the Colony is filled with white bitches. And black bitches, and Asian bitches, and Latino bitches. Our world is built on love, not hate, and certainly not on racism. So perhaps you should go back where you came from."

The woman didn't flinch. "Get out of my face."

Layla forced her anger aside and regained her professional tone. "Tell us why you're here."

"Get the fuck out of my face," Keisha hissed again.

She saw the fist clench and the woman's body tense up for the swing long before it came at her. Plenty of time to reach up and catch her wrist; she didn't even need to break eye contact. Her agile response startled Keisha, who immediately leaned back. A small sign of deference. Maybe there was hope.

She released her grip on Keisha's fist and carried her overturned chair to the other side of the table next to Keisha. She slowly eased herself into it, careful to avoid any sudden movements. Keisha was trembling, her adrenaline pumping, and Layla regretted her explosive reaction. The woman was acting out of fear; anger was just how it manifested.

The psych team would have a field day with this one.

"I'm not your enemy," she said gently. "I'm the same as you. I came here to escape something, too. The Colony helped me. It changed my life, actually, and it gave me purpose. Now I'm making a greater contribution to society. Is that what you're looking for?"

Keisha pulled away, distancing herself from Layla and regarding her with apprehension.

"Here at the Colony, we live by a saying," Layla continued. "*A poisoned life cannot be purified until it is fully understood. As an impure, I must acknowledge, accept, and despise the poison inside me so I can be free of it.*" She allowed a moment for that to sink in. "You can't be free from your poisoned life if you can't talk about it."

Keisha's eyes shifted to the wall. A look of concentration crinkled her brow. "They told me I could start over. I could become somebody else." Her fisted hands tapped a jittering beat on her thighs, as though she were trying to keep her anger under control. "They told me I could be free of everything I've done and be pure. That's what they said."

Isaac finally stepped up to the plate, leaning forward and resting his forearms on the table. Layla allowed him to reclaim the reins. She had to see if he would be able to control his interview, although so far, she wasn't impressed.

"The Colony isn't just a place where people can hide from their poisoned life," he said. "It's a gift offered to the few people who are worthy of it. If you're not willing to accept your impure life, you're not worthy of our gift that allows you to rise above your past and start again. Do you understand?"

Keisha's nod was barely perceptible.

"Purification is earned. It takes months of sacrifice and hard work, and you have to overcome some extremely challenging obstacles. Very few people at the Colony have the necessary fortitude to achieve purification."

"They told me they could erase my memories of my old life." She looked at Layla. "My poisoned life."

There. A little more promising; the recruit had accepted Colony jargon. That was the first step.

"Tell us about your poisoned life," Isaac said.

"What does it matter?" Keisha snapped, still directed at Layla.

Layla caught Isaac's helpless glance. All this antagonism was baffling. Isaac needed to pull this mess together.

"You wanted to know why I'm here?" the woman continued. "I've done terrible things. I don't want to do them anymore. I want to forget everything and have a new life. That's why I'm here." Her body shuddered, still from the rush of adrenaline.

Layla searched for a sign of remorse: an apology, a silent prayer, a hung head, tears. But she didn't see anything except bitter hatred, seemingly targeted at her. She fought an impatient sigh. Over thousands of intake interviews, she'd seen the Keisha story a hundred times: angry, emotional young women who felt betrayed by a world that owed them something. Outwardly they were grown-ups, but in terms of maturity, they were nowhere near adulthood. Sometimes Layla saw opportunity in all that angst, but more often she saw selfishness and a liability to the mission of the Colony.

They needed to make this quick so they could get on to more promising candidates, but Isaac seemed bent on digging deeper. "It's safe here. Nothing you say will ever leave this room."

Silence. Layla counted slowly to five and slid her chair back. "I think we're done here," she said to Isaac. She addressed Keisha. "I'm sorry. I don't believe you're capable of purity."

Keisha flew up and lunged. Layla stumbled backward and hit the wall with a thud. Keisha's long fingers wrapped around Layla's throat, but the black painted nails didn't yet sink into her flesh. It was an empty threat; a show of intimidation, nothing else. She'd seen worse.

"Sister Layla, is it?" the woman bellowed. "How did you get such a virtuous title? Did you sell your soul to an imaginary god?"

Layla's eyes darted to Isaac, who cowered next to the table, wringing his hands, either too insecure to intervene or unsure how. That was probably best. A panicked Isaac would surely aggravate this woman to real violence. Everyone had a breaking point.

"I'll tell you what I'm capable of," Keisha snarled. "I could cut that baby right out of your belly with a butter knife and not even flinch if I accidentally slipped and sliced its head right off."

The door flew open, and Michael and a security guard grabbed each of Keisha's bulging biceps and pulled her back.

Keisha didn't resist, but she leaned forward so that her face hovered inches from Layla's. "I'm a monster, and I need to die."

"Let's go," the guard said as he spun Keisha away from Layla. He offered a polite nod to Layla. "Ma'am." His gaze lingered on her belly, and his thick eyebrows drew together as if he was worried about the fetus.

Their grip on Keisha wasn't strong enough because she easily shook them off. But the moment was gone. She listlessly headed toward the door and without a glance back, she left.

Isaac pressed his lips tightly together. She'd known Isaac long enough to practically read his mind: *You didn't give her enough time. You didn't give her a chance.* But she'd done the right thing. Cut out a baby with a butter knife? A monster, indeed.

She straightened her tent-shaped white linen tunic, a maternity rendition of the Colony uniform. "Let's go, Isaac. We have a lot of intakes today. Call in the next one."

But Isaac's usual complaisance was gone. "Listen, you know I'm your biggest fan, Lay. But sometimes you're a little too quick to judge. I've never seen you explode like that on a recruit, and she was just about to open up. You set her off. They've traveled a long way in the heat to get here, and they're tired—"

She held her hand out in front of her. "No. First, I'm in charge. Full stop. Second, I've seen hundreds, maybe thousands of recruits. I can sniff out the bad from the good within the first two minutes. You haven't been doing this long enough to have such good judgment."

She leaned over and rested her hands on the table, suddenly weak from the confrontation with Keisha. "But you've been here long enough to realize that what we bring in from the poisoned world is what we become inside our walls." She pointed a finger at the door. "That was not Colony material, at least not in my purification program. This isn't a refuge, and we're not in the business of saving individual lives. The work of the Colony is the only priority. Period."

Isaac scowled for a moment and moved his gaze to the door. "I don't belong here. This isn't the right assignment for me."

Thank god he said it so she wouldn't have to. His heart of gold was an impediment to his ability to be objective. He'd need to find another role at the Colony, but that wasn't her problem, and she had a long day ahead of her.

"Report back to Mia. She'll find you a new assignment." She leaned over the conference table and pressed a button. "Michael, bring in the next candidate."

He stiffened. They'd been close for years, and she knew he saw her callousness as a sign of betrayal. *Our little Princess of Pain,* he and Jonah used to call her back when they were inductees. She repressed a sigh as nostalgia washed through her. But this was business. It wasn't personal.

"You're excused."

His expression hardened as though she were suddenly a stranger. "Thank you, Sister Layla, I'm at your will."

She ignored his sarcastic remark and watched him let himself out, then picked up the next folder and readied herself to go it alone.

2

"You're not paying attention to me." Layla smeared a thick layer of butter across her roll and took a bite, savoring the grease that coated her mouth. Most pregnant women craved pickles and ice cream; her baby seemed to want murdered animals. She shuddered as the image of a slaughterhouse flashed in her mind. Butter was the closest thing to meat she allowed herself.

The dining hall was nearly empty at one o'clock except for the physician's loft, which overlooked the main seating area. It was reserved for the doctors, and even James refrained from dining there with them. *They've given up a life of prestige and wealth to join the Colony, and this is the least we can do for them*, he'd explained.

"I hear you loud and clear, beautiful girl." James probably intended his smile to appear warm and genuine, but she read it as patronizing. With him as both leader of the Colony and her life partner, they walked a fine line between their personal and professional relationships. She knew he loved her, but professionally she'd somehow become an unappreciated, disgruntled middle manager in his eyes.

"The quality of this week's intakes wasn't like it used to be. You should've seen the woman I interviewed this morning." She could still feel the weight of that hateful stare. "We have more addicts than ever. Michael said it's practically impossible to find clean recruits."

"That's life in the poisoned world, Lay," he said through a mouthful of bread.

She winced at his offhand attitude. Sure, things had been bad out there for a long time, but it was nothing to be flippant about. Crime was up, as was drug abuse and suicide. The poisoned world had become perilously toxic. But that didn't mean there weren't good young people who needed a clean break and someone to take a chance on them. *You have to find the hidden gems, just like you were, Layla*, her friend Mia had told her when she'd first started.

He put his hand over hers, and she yanked it away.

"I could research pockets in the States and Canada where drug abuse incidence is lower," she said, "if I had internet access. You know—"

"Oh, that's what this is about." His smile faded and he flopped back with an eye roll.

"I've been appointed with an enormous responsibility. My program is the largest on this campus. It's doubled in size since I started." She could hear her voice rising to a whine. She paused to take a calming breath, but the baby was pressing against her diaphragm and she couldn't fill her lungs. She arched her back and gave him a gentle nudge with her hand. Three more weeks … three more weeks.

"Exactly. You're doing an excellent job. Opening another external line to the poisoned world is too risky. Each line significantly increases—"

"—our risk of being hacked. I know that, James. You've said it a hundred times. But what about the risk of HIV and hep C that comes with more drug abusers? You insist Eugenesis is not in the business of curing diseases, so why aren't we more careful about who we bring in? Not to mention the increased time and effort it takes to clean them up before they can even join the inductees. Some of them have been in the meth clinic for weeks."

Her favorite Mediterranean couscous salad appeared in front of her, but she had no desire to eat it. She wasn't sure if it was the frustrating conversation with James or her changing sense of taste due to her pregnancy that turned her off, but she shoved the plate away.

James threw her a dismissive wave. "There's a place for everyone on this campus. If they aren't well enough for your program, they'll be placed in a different one."

She was only vaguely aware of the other experimental units on the campus. James refused to discuss them. Like everyone else, she was on a need-to-know basis. The access restrictions imposed by the Eugenesis council were ridiculously excessive, if you asked her—downright paranoid. But that was a fight for another day.

James picked up his cheeseburger and squeezed the bun gently. Grease dripped from the meat and onto his plate. Normally, that would've completely grossed her out, but she found herself staring at the small pool forming on his plate beneath the underdone patty, oily and slightly pink. She could detect the malodorous, gamy scent of grass-fed beef, but instead of repulsing her, it made her mouth water. She had the urge to lick his plate.

She forced herself to look away. "Mia gets outside access. How is her work more relevant than mine?" Mia was a GS-5, and Layla was only a GS-4. Sure, Mia had been there a lot longer, but Layla was running out of arguments.

"Mia's work requires her to have external communications. Come on. You know we all have to make sacrifices here."

"Sacrifice? What have you ever sacrificed, James?"

His smarmy smile returned; he was going to dodge the question. He held up a french fry as if it were a peace offering. "You are brilliant and beautiful and perfect as the leader of the purification program. The inductees practically worship you. All your new ideas and changes have done wonders for the program."

She wasn't interested in making peace or being mollified. She stood and slid her chair under the table with enough force to make it screech against the ceramic tile and turn the heads of the physicians on the upstairs balcony. She scowled at them. "I have to get back to the intake room."

"Layla, don't leave mad. Come on, tell me what kind of research you want, and I'll get it for you."

"You're missing the whole point," she called over her shoulder as she stomped away.

"Have a great afternoon, beautiful girl," he yelled after her. "See you tonight!"

She grunted with exasperation as the dining hall door slammed shut behind her. A hot breeze swept between the buildings and her long hair whipped across her face, stinging her eyes. The medical research building, which loomed high above any other on campus, was directly across from the dining hall, connected via an enclosed bridge on the second floor. The design had turned the space between the buildings into a pesky wind tunnel.

She growled. She was obviously too emotionally charged to go straight back to the recruiting center. She needed to unwind.

She crossed the walkway to the medical center, which had a small gym on the first floor. Despite Dr. Farid's warning to take it easy, she had no intention of giving up the muscle mass she'd built over the last couple of years. She still jogged on the treadmill, albeit significantly more slowly, and she still pumped weights. She'd gone into this pregnancy with Dr. Farid's mandatory seventeen percent body fat, and she planned to be back down to thirteen within three months of giving birth.

She gathered a few dumbbells and straddled the bench. Most people used the fancy weight machines, but Jonah had taught her the greater benefit of free weights. *Those machines might build bulk, but they do nothing for your stabilizers. You're only getting half the workout, which I know isn't good enough for our Princess of Pain.* It occurred to her that she hadn't seen Jonah in the gym for a long time. Weeks, maybe. She made a mental note to check up on him—not that mental notes worked these days. If she didn't have it written in her planner or better yet, on her arm, it was unlikely to ever make it to her forebrain again.

She did three sets of rows, chest presses, biceps, and triceps before she called it quits, just enough to cool her head without requiring a shower and change of clothes. She gave herself a quick rinse in the locker room sink and headed back toward the recruiting center.

The intake room, where she spent two days a week interviewing prospective recruits, wasn't much more than a sensible lobby serving as the gateway to the recruiting center. Beyond that, through another set of gates, lay the induction and purification facilities on a campus that included housing, dining, laundry, exercise facilities, and an infirmary. Her favorite building was the ritual center—Torturetown, as some of the newer inductees had called it a while back. Thankfully, the nickname hadn't stuck. It took newbies only a few days to realize the solemnity and import of the pain rituals. They were nothing to be disrespectful about.

"Good afternoon, Sister Layla. With pain comes peace." Three inductees cleared the path to allow her to pass by, as they always did. Their genuine smiles warmed her heart and reminded her how fortunate she was to be here.

"With gratitude comes the Father's love. How's your day so far?"

"Wonderful."

"Keep up the good work." She gave each a quick hug and continued down the path past the purge clinic.

She paused in front of the double doors and checked her watch. She had a few extra minutes. She badged inside and sauntered down the hallway, glancing through the one-way mirrors into the sterile white purge rooms. Two were empty. One contained a solo inductee lying prostrate across a hard marble bench. His linen pants and shirt were dazzling white, freshly laundered, indicating he'd come early to mentally prepare for his cleanse. She watched him for several minutes, but he didn't so much as flinch from the discomfort of his position. He was in the zone, no doubt anticipating with great pleasure what was to come. Her neck tingled as though she were experiencing his moment vicariously.

The door opened and Brother Zane entered, carrying the bullwhip. Although she couldn't hear his introduction, she whispered the words along with him. "Remember to focus on your breathing, in and out to the count of four. The Father loves you very much and wants you to be cleansed of the poison that consumed you during your life as an impure."

Her eyes widened as Brother Zane lifted the whip over his head. It truly was magical. Her hand mindlessly circled her belly as the leather strap lashed the inductee's back. It didn't tear through the linen or draw blood; the first two lashes were intended to be softer, allowing the inductee an opportunity to request a halt. The ritual was fully voluntary, even once it had begun, but it was reserved for only the strongest of mind, body, and spirit. If inductees hadn't yet found that strength, they wouldn't be granted the honor of the cleanse.

Brother Zane finished all ten lashes and settled on the floor next to the inductee. He pressed a cool damp cloth to the young man's face and offered soothing words—how proud he was, how proud the Father was, and how much closer the young man was to purification—as shuddering sobs racked the inductee's depleted body.

Layla couldn't help being a little jealous. Her cleanse had been so long ago that she barely remembered the exhilaration. But at that moment, just reliving his suffering was enough to fuel her for the rest of the workday. She smiled at her reflection in the glass. Witnessing his progression to the next step on his purification path felt like an omen of her own success. The winds of change were coming, and she would finally get the credibility and respect she long deserved.

3

L ayla paced the small intake room to get the blood flowing in her legs. Eleven intakes in a day were far too many for a single interviewer, especially one carrying an eight-month fetus. She pulled the folder on Vanessa Sykes from her stack and readied herself for another tough call. The whole day had been one disappointing recruit after another. She felt edgy, still irate at James and still troubled about Isaac walking out with that bitter comment.

She eased herself through some yoga stretches while she skimmed the details of Vanessa's recruitment. Vanessa had grown up in the Midwest back in the States, moved around a lot, dropped out of high school because of mean girls, and ended up in a bad section of Milwaukee, where she found a "family" of drug dealers and addicts who were more than willing to give her the friendship she craved. It was a common tale.

The door opened and Michael entered with the woman. "Sister Layla, this is Vanessa."

Michael was the perfect image of a recruiter, clean-cut and confident with a warm, inviting face. In the field, he would wrap a blanket around a desperate young prostitute or a wild-eyed addict as if they were his own family. Maybe the recruiting team would be a better calling for Isaac, too. She'd have to talk to Mia about it later.

Layla's first look into Vanessa's face startled her. Beyond the noticeably purplish-black eye and slightly healed split lip, the wrinkles in the corners of her eyes and deep lines on her forehead suggested she was older than the Colony typically recruited. Layla couldn't help glancing down at the file to check her age. Indeed, she was thirty-one. This was a new issue she'd have to talk with James about. They had an unspoken rule to limit recruits to twenty-five years old tops, but maybe the guideline needed to be made explicit.

She extended her hand, falling into her usual intake greeting. "Vanessa, I'm so thrilled to meet you. And thank you so much for enduring the long trip to visit our center."

The woman's eyes were wide with terror, so Layla got up to pour two cups of strawberry-infused ice water. She usually waited several minutes into the discussion to offer water, until she had a good idea of the recruit's temperament. The cup was hard plastic, not glass, but still heavy enough to do some damage if thrown across the table. Nonetheless, Layla believed that this level of service built rapport.

She set one cup in front herself and one in front of Vanessa, slightly to the side. Vanessa didn't speak or move toward the cup.

"I hope Brother Michael and his team made your trip comfortable."

The woman still didn't speak, and Layla found her stare to be unsettling.

"Vanessa?"

She waited several seconds before turning to Michael. "Is she still high?"

She knew she wasn't. She had plenty of experience with recruits who were still coming down from the shoulder phase of a meth hit, the hours after the initial rush. Silent staring wasn't typical behavior. Even if Vanessa didn't want to speak, her eyes would've been darting all over the room and she'd likely have already been out of the chair. She certainly wasn't showing any signs of tweaking.

Michael frowned. "No, I don't think—"

"Allison," Vanessa breathed.

"Sorry?"

"You're Allison. Allison Stevens." Vanessa's eyes grew wider.

"No, my name is Layla"—she corrected herself—"er … Sister Layla. I'm in charge of intakes here at the Colony. And you've expressed an interest in joining us, isn't that right?"

"I saw you all over the news. You were on TV—your picture, I mean. You were … You killed a police officer." She whispered the last sentence as if she were afraid someone might overhear them.

Layla forced a chuckle. "You must have me confused with someone else. I've already told you my name." She was losing control of this interview, and she struggled to regain the upper hand. "Let's talk about you, not me. Tell me a little about yourself. Where do you live?" She fell back to simple, unchallenging questions.

"Don't you recognize me?" Vanessa asked, her gaze still eerily set on Layla's face. "We grew up together, in Madison. We were friends." She put a hand over her chest. "Vanessa. Don't you remember me?"

Layla rose and took a reflexive step backward. There was something deeply worrisome about the conviction in the woman's voice.

Vanessa stood as well. "We were best friends. I used to stay at your house." Her voice seemed to be pleading as she searched Layla's face.

A muscle under Layla's eye began to twitch. Why was this crazy woman's misunderstanding upsetting her so much? She wouldn't allow this to continue.

"This intake is over," she said to Michael, as calmly as she could.

He shrugged questioningly, but she turned on her heels and stalked to the door.

"Come on, Vanessa," he said behind her, "I'm sorry. You aren't quite the right fit for this program."

"Okay, Butch," Vanessa called after Layla in a sarcastic tone. "I guess you really are the bitch everyone said you became after your dad died."

Layla froze, her badge up to the scanner to open the door. Her father's voice rang in her head: *Hey, Butch! Come down 'ere!*

A wave of nausea moved through her, and she put a hand against the wall to steady herself. Her eyes darted to the video camera in the corner of the room. Had they heard that? With a trembling hand, she pressed her badge against the scanner and marched out.

But Vanessa's voice seemed to follow her out of the building. *Allison Stevens. You killed a police officer.*

4

"**B**reaking news! A UFO crashed out by Tonopah. Slater, you better go check it out."

Nick Slater tossed his keys and the bagel bag onto his desk and flopped into the chair, spinning around to face his computer. He set his coffee next to the keyboard and rolled the mouse over the pad to wake up the screen. "Already did, first thing this morning. Turns out it was just your mother. She stumbled drunk out of her double-wide and fell off the porch. Sent up enough dust to cover the sun for a week."

He didn't bother to look, but he knew Osborne would be giving him the finger. Given Osborne's size, it might have hit home a little too hard, but he didn't care. The guy was an asshat. Even worse, he was a lousy reporter.

Vivian paraded over wearing a miniskirt and a low-cut shirt that left nothing to the imagination. She was apparently trying to pull off the Erin Brockovich look, but he found it a little pathetic at her age.

Osborne made an obscene gesture behind her, and Nick rolled his eyes and went back to his email.

Vivian popped her gum twice. "Hey, Nick."

He despised gum. Especially noisy gum. "Yeah."

"Boss Man wants to see you in the fishbowl." She popped her gum three times in rapid succession.

Shit, that had happened a little sooner than he expected, and awfully early in the workday. The chief was a bully 24/7, but he was a downright raving lunatic before noon.

"What's he want?" His eyes shot up to the fishbowl. The raving lunatic was pacing like a caged animal, waving his arms in frustration. Nick felt sorry for the poor bastard on the other end of the speakerphone.

Vivian popped her gum and tossed her head in the direction of the fishbowl. "Better get going."

He exhaled a long, slow breath and shuffled toward the chief's garish glass office, which sat on an elevated platform in the center of the expansive reporting floor, the better to separate his lordship from the minions. He hesitated at the bottom of the eight steps for a moment for the benefit of his group.

To be honest, he was a little surprised that the Harris piece merited a fishbowl show. He'd buried the story at the bottom of Investigations, certain it wouldn't attract the chief's attention. Or maybe this wasn't about the Harris piece at all. Maybe he was about to get a promotion. Sure, that was possible.

He glanced back at his group. As usual, they'd all turned their chairs to face the fishbowl, coffee and doughnuts at the ready for the big show. Osborne held up his iPhone and gave him a cheerful thumbs-up.

The glass door swung open. "Get in here."

Probably not the promotion.

The chief stomped back to his desk and spun his fifty-five-inch screen back so that Nick could see it. "Tell me that sometime late Sunday night, someone hacked into your computer and ran this goddamn story with your goddamn byline. Because I sure as hell know that any reporter who works in my shop would never be so imbecilic as to post a story that I hadn't approved."

Imbecilic—nice one. "Listen—"

"And tell me how an investigative journalist thinks that running a folo four years after the story is of any interest to readers in the Greater

Phoenix area."

"It was really—"

"And then explain to me why the hell you work for a paper that delivers actual news when your investigative interests are obviously better suited for a tabloid."

Nick tightened his jaw to repress a scowl. This wasn't the first time the bastard had accused him of conspiracy chasing. In fact, he immediately discredited any story that scrutinized big money or questioned big power. "There are hundreds of government scandals uncovered by brilliant reporters every day. You have no reason to believe—"

"Your obsession with that Stevens girl is affecting my ratings."

That wasn't true at all. Every paper was a sinking ship these days. No one read the paper anymore. They were too busy tweeting about the best ways to kill the virus or watching PewDiePie play video games.

"That girl killed a police officer and probably killed Austin Harris," Nick said. "She's the linchpin of the entire story. I have no doubt that now she'll be scared up from wherever she's hiding, and we'll finally get the truth."

He was so stunned when the chief didn't cut him off midsentence that for a moment he thought the lunatic might be considering that he was right.

But the man leaned over his desk and rested on his knuckles. "I know you're the one who's been writing the virus series in that damn conspiracy blog."

Shit. He hadn't been expecting that. He played dumb. "What?"

"Pen name Aeger Caedis. Every reporter has a writing style. You think I wouldn't recognize yours?"

Nick shrugged. He didn't have any proof. "I don't know what you're talking about."

He picked up a notebook. "'Did the lyssavirus really come from China?' by Aeger Caedis, an article about the mysterious missing patient zero." He tossed the notebook across the desk so Nick could see that he'd recorded every one of his virus articles. "Millions of dollars have gone into tracing the early deaths, and thousands of scientists agree they started in China—yet you say that because no one has found patient zero that it must be a huge government conspiracy."

"I never said it's a government conspiracy. I said it's interesting that they didn't trace it back that far. It's like they gave up ten feet from the finish line. Who are they protecting?"

The chief flopped back into his chair. "You're a goddamn disappointment."

Nick flinched and immediately hated himself for it. Those words stung, even as a grown man, but he didn't want the chief to know it.

The chief turned his monitor back to its original position. "I'm reassigning you to local news."

Oh god, no. That was not an acceptable outcome. "You're sending me to beat? Come on. You know I don't belong with those guys. That's not even journalism. It's NPR, for chrissake."

"Get out of my office."

"Listen, you're making a mistake."

"Out of my office!" He swung his arm at the door with the dramatic flair of an umpire calling a strike. Oh, the fun of being a prick with a live audience. Then he settled into his chair and went back to work as if nothing had happened.

Nick stood paralyzed as adrenaline coursed through his veins. He was by far the best investigative reporter the paper had ever had, even at his age. No one chased the facts like he did. No one had his persuasive charm, which was necessary to get to the truth. And sure as shit no one had his work ethic.

This was purely personal.

He looked down at Osborne, who pretended to be falling off his chair laughing.

Fuck it. No better time than the present.

Nick's legs finally moved, and he slammed both palms onto the chief's desk, delighting in watching the man shrink back. "Who are you really working for? Who bought you that fancy house in Fountain Hills?

Because it sure as hell wasn't this paper. You buried the Malloy case, and then you buried the real story behind the virus. Someone paid you off."

Come on, psycho, say the magic words. You know you want to.

He pushed harder. "No one bothered to find out who made the warning video or where he got that restaurant picture. I'm the only one who investigated the story, found dozens of holes, but you couldn't shut me down fast enough. Hundreds of thousands of deaths, yet no one pursued how it spread so fast. Not a single paper in the country. You don't think that's strange? Of course not, because whoever paid you off paid off every other paper."

The chief's mouth twitched, but still, he didn't swing the ax.

Nick gave him one last shove. "You're not just a prick, you're a pathetic sellout. And that's why Mom walked out on you."

Nick wanted to laugh at how crimson red the man's face turned. He hadn't seen that neck vein pop out like that since the night Nick stole his Porsche and took his friends on a joyride. Must've been fourteen or fifteen.

"Fired." Spit flew from the chief's clenched teeth. "You're fired. Get. The fuck. Out."

Nick straightened, trying to appear stoic, but he felt the slightest upturn of his lip. The chief grabbed the first thing within reach, a stapler, and threw it right at his head. He ducked, and the stapler hit the edge of the whiteboard instead of the window. Damn. It would have made his day to see the fishbowl shatter into a million pieces.

But his mission was accomplished.

He pivoted and held up both middle fingers for the audience below, relishing the shocked look on Osborne's fat little face.

He looked back over his shoulder. The chief—now simply Dad—was still red-faced, seething. White foam had collected in the corners of his mouth, and his breath came fast. For a minute, Nick wondered if he was on the verge of a heart attack, but he fell back into his chair, growling obscenities under his breath.

As Nick stepped over the threshold, both birds still flying, he couldn't remember the last time he felt that dignified. He'd regret it later, probably, but for now, he felt like a god.

5

Nick surveyed the other patrons as he took a seat at the end of the bar. He hoped it would be empty this time of day. It wasn't, though he shouldn't have been surprised. The world had grown so depressing and gloomy that drowning one's sorrows over a pint, even at ten in the morning, had become a national sport, ranking second only to major league opioid abuse.

A man four seats down eyed him. Nick nodded politely, trying to remember the guy's name: Curt or Dirk or something. The man stood, dropped a bill on the table, and called out to the bartender. "See ya, Darcy!"

He growled at Nick on his way out. "Glits are not welcome here."

"I'm not a glit," Nick called after him. "I live on Forty-First Street." It wasn't just an insult to be associated with the glitterati, it was dangerous. Violence was the result when glits came out from behind their fancy protective walls into the dregs. Bloodshed. *Covered in red glitter*, as the crime scenes were often described.

Darcy set a pint of Guinness on a coaster in front of him. "It's the suit. You can't dress like that around here. And why aren't you at work, anyway?"

He wished he hadn't made his aunt Darcy his first stop after storming out of the building. He didn't regret his separation from employment. Not yet anyway. In truth, the paper had only impeded his important mission. His research had been scrutinized, his words neutered until they'd lost all meaning. He'd been immobilized, like an unloved, neglected dog tethered to a fence. But now, as a free agent, he could investigate his way. The story was out there, and he was damn well going to find it and tell it. There was only one small problem. His bank account. He needed Darcy's help.

He wrapped his hands around his glass and nodded at the TV screen to stall. "What's going on?" A hospital was surrounded by fire trucks and police cars, lights flashing.

"The virus. Thirty-seven more dead in a hospital in Missouri, of all places. No idea how it got inside."

"Are they sure it's the virus?"

"Yep. The eye spasms."

He shook his head and squinted at the screen. The virus, once called by its true name, the lyssavirus, before it had been clipped presumably to save characters on Twitter, had plagued every country on earth. Even now, after a year and a half, it hadn't been fully eradicated. He could still hear the voice on the YouTube video "A Desperate Warning to the World" delivering a speech that every human on the planet today could recite by heart.

Today is October fourteenth, 2022. It is with great despair that I report a virus has been released from the Gansu Province in China and will soon enough spread across the globe. It is unlike anything the world has seen before. I have had firsthand experience with this virus. I've seen what it's capable of, and I am sending this message as a warning to stay out of public places. Stay off the streets. Quarantine in your home with your loved ones.

I'm begging you.

The anguish in the man's voice had been enough to send chills down anyone's spine, and yet no one had believed it, not until the bodies started piling up. By the time the world's military forces had gotten off their asses, it was too late. The virus was relentless. It sparked panic, fear, and distrust so contagious that the run on gun stores outpaced the run on toilet paper.

Shoot first, ask questions later became the mantra. Every grocery store was surrounded by a SWAT team. Parks emptied, schools shut down, and the cities became eerily silent, as if an alien spaceship had dropped down and abducted all human life.

The economy should have recovered, but fear kept people inside even after stores and restaurants reopened. No one felt protected, and everyone was trigger-happy. Walls went up around wealthy glitterati neighborhoods, leaving everyone else to suffer in poverty and fear, the dregs of society living in the dregs of what once was the most powerful country in the world.

He looked up from his reverie to see his aunt studying him. "Oh, no. Don't tell me he fired you."

"In the powerful words of George Orwell"—he mimed a long drag on a cigarette and spoke with an English accent—" 'The further society drifts from the truth, the more it will hate those who speak it.' "

Darcy smirked. She was one tough lady. She'd been one of the fifty-three women and four men laid off from state social services. She'd worked there twenty-five years, longer than any of the male counterparts over which she had seniority, but no one had bothered protesting the gender inequality. It was simply one more troubling sign of the times. With her meager savings and a little help from Nick, she'd scooped this dank, windowless bar in Central City out of bankruptcy. *If I can't help these people, I can at least ease their suffering* had been her rationale. Here in the dregs, people needed that.

"Was it the article?" she asked.

"It was just the last straw. Nothing's ever been good enough for that asshole."

He decided not to mention the sellout insult. Darcy had never liked Nick's father. *What kind of dad makes his son call him sir?* he'd overheard her asking Uncle Jay when he was just a kid. Now she refused to talk about him or Nick's mother, who'd packed a suitcase and walked out the door when Nick was only ten years old, never to be heard from again.

Her expression dulled as she picked up Curt or Dirk's glass and wiped the bar.

"Listen, Darce, I'm not letting it go. We'll find 'em. The article was just posted, and right now someone, somewhere, is feeling very scared. If they believe the cops are snooping around the Vitapura site, they'll come out of their hiding place." *She will*, he wanted to add. Allison Stevens. But that was just his gut feeling.

Her lower lip trembled. "After your uncle died, I never thought I'd find another soulmate, but I did. I couldn't do anything about losing Jay. But dammit, Pete was stolen from me. Stolen. And I need to make it right. They have to pay for what they did."

It wasn't the first time she'd said these words, but Nick nodded empathetically. He'd doubted her story when she'd first come to him, distraught—devastated, actually. In his experience, when a victim was that grief-stricken, sometimes they invented stories as a coping mechanism to deal with their loss. *Pete Malloy and Danny Garcia didn't go to a meth lab in Tempe. They went to the Vitapura Wellness Center. Scientists were torturing kids there. They implanted ports in their spines, Nick. Just imagine that. And they were injecting them with illegal genetic drugs. Pete knew everything, and that's why they killed him.*

Nick had tried to console her, but she didn't want his hugs or his Scotch. She'd looked at him with fire in her eyes and stabbed a finger at him. *Find them, Nicky. You're a reporter. Go do your fucking job.* It was the only time he ever heard her use profanity. He'd studied her quivering face for several moments, unconvinced, but agreed to look into it. Only then did she collapse into sobs.

But his battle for a police investigation into Vitapura had been futile, resulting in nothing but a formal complaint against him. He hadn't dug up a shred of physical proof. It wasn't until the center closed six months later that he'd been able to sneak inside, and only then had he become convinced Darcy had been right all along.

Once he began poking around, the silent war began. He'd driven out to Black Canyon City, explored the deserted Vitapura site, and returned home to find his apartment had been tossed. He'd purchased a surveillance device and found his credit card had been canceled. It infuriated him that they knew who he was, but he didn't know who they were.

And he had no doubt that they'd come after him again, but he wasn't about to put that scare into Darcy.

He picked up a dusty deck of cards on top of an even dustier Pictionary board game box. No one played games anymore. "I'll cheer you up."

She held up a hand. "I've seen 'em all, Mr. Copperfield."

"What about the one where I swallow the card? Come on, that's genius."

"Yep."

He faked a dejected look and dropped the cards back onto the board game graveyard, sending up a cloud of dust, and finished his beer in one long gulp. He dropped a five on the bar. There was a time when he could've dropped a twenty, but these days he needed every penny just to keep a roof over his head.

And that thought brought him to the moment he'd been dreading.

"I'm gonna have to close out my investment account at the bank of Darcy's bar."

He could tell just by the way she slouched over the sink that she was disappointed by his request. It wasn't that she still needed his start-up money. She'd already recouped it and even paid him a little interest, but as long as it was in her possession, she knew Nick wasn't living hand to mouth. Sadly, he was.

In a more cheerful tone, he added, "And then I'm heading home to check the tapes."

She wordlessly plodded to the back office and returned with an envelope, which she slid across the bar. Forty-three hundred dollars, his entire net worth. He'd once been worth fifty times that amount. The stock market had been performing so well, it was just dumb to keep cash in low-yield savings accounts. When the crash hit, it came hard and fast, sweeping through the US, Western Europe, and Asia in a matter of days. The damage was analogous to the stock market crash of 1929 and left the world in ruins.

Darcy rested her elbows on the bar and gazed at him with tired eyes. She'd aged so much in the past two years; the twinkle that once lit up her face was gone. "Take care of yourself first, Nicky. I don't know what I'd do if I lost you, too."

"I will, Darce. Promise."

Outside in the unforgiving heat, he slipped off his jacket to air out the damp armpits of his white dress shirt. As his eyes adjusted to the bright morning sunlight, he caught sight of the unmarked white van parked a block down the road on the opposite side of the street. Was that the same one he noted when he left the *Sun* this morning? A van like that had no reason to be in this part of town, and it wasn't lost on him that the driver would have a perfect view of Darcy's bar.

The van pulled off the curb and made a U-turn. The glare off the windshield prevented him from getting a good look at the driver, and he dropped his eyes searching for a license plate number. The plates had been removed.

"Chicken shit bastard," he mumbled. "I'll find you. If it's the last thing I do in this life, I'll expose you to the world."

6

ayla pulled her hair into a tight bun on top of her head and reached into the makeup case for some mascara. Steadying her hand with her pinky finger against her cheek, she expertly pulled the mascara brush through her lashes. It was as if she'd been doing it her entire life, although she could only remember applying mascara over the past few months. *Muscle memory stays with you even after significant memory loss*, Dr. Jeremy had explained back when she was an inductee. That was before she'd understood that the Colony had used a genetic drug to erase her memories to give her a fresh start and a new purpose in life.

Still, it explained why she could pull on hose without poking a fingernail through the flimsy material and why she could walk in three-inch pumps without wobbling. The brain, with its many mysterious functions, was truly remarkable. But she didn't like getting dressed up or wearing makeup. She'd take the Colony's traditional white linens over this fancy uniform any day, but image was critical for new inductees.

The rebranding had been her idea. Leaders needed to present a more professional first impression to recruits and inductees so that newcomers, or what they referred to as Stage Ones, could see that the Colony offered a better alternative to their current situations. To someone down on their luck, the welcoming face of someone who actually spoke to them with respect and kindness was a rare and powerful thing. It made for a much more successful transition.

She appraised herself in the mirror, applied a little lip gloss, and pulled on the white jacket matching her gleaming faux leather maternity skirt. The buttons had no chance of clasping over her belly. Thank goodness her shirt hid the stretch panel. She sighed at her corpulent reflection.

James's voice came from the back of the room. "You look beautiful."

"Thanks." She puffed her cheeks and grinned at his reflection in the mirror as he wrapped his long, muscular arms around her. Even though she was still a bit sore at him for yesterday, his embrace made her remember how special she was. James loved her, and she loved him.

"Only presenters are allowed in the dressing room," she said. "Are you planning to deliver a cameo appearance? These are Stage Ones, your favorites."

He chuckled, and his eyes sparkled with adoration. "Next to you? No way, I'd look like a clumsy oaf."

She snickered at the goofy, old-fashioned expression. There was something to be said for hanging out with twentysomethings—they kept her young at heart—but she was thirtysomething, a decade younger than James. In the eyes of the inductees, Brother James was more fatherly than brotherly, although that didn't make him any less important in their eyes.

As she turned to face him, her eye caught a suitcase next to the door. "Where are you going?"

"The States. We're looking at a possible new facility in Iowa."

James had been spending a lot of time traveling to evaluate and establish new sites. It was a good sign that Eugenesis was growing, and since James was so senior in the organization and most knowledgeable about Colony operations, he was the only one the council trusted for this important task. Even though she was used to long stretches without him, she still missed his companionship.

"Just a few days," he said, "and you'll be so busy you won't even notice I'm gone."

That part was certainly true. Layla's days had gotten longer and longer.

Between recruiting and the purification program, she was spread thin.

Marissa swept into the room and sidled up to Layla to examine her makeup. "Showtime. It's a good one today, eleven hundred or so. Justin has the room practically vibrating with excitement, which is amazing since it's after lunch." She scowled. "Ew, you're shiny."

James stepped aside as Marissa swooped in on Layla's forehead with a fluffy brush of loose powder. "See you in a couple of days, beautiful girl."

"Bye, handsome, I can't wait," Marissa replied with a wave.

Layla giggled. Marissa's witty verve made her outshine everyone around her, a confidence that followed her from her poisoned life, no doubt, something Layla would never have.

Layla's makeup artistry evidently left something to be desired, because Marissa snatched the bag away and fished until she found a pencil. "A lot of questions have been coming in about social media connections with the poisoned world. Maybe you could address that?"

"Gotcha," Layla said through pinched lips as Marissa drew on lip liner.

"Oh, and there's been a bit of panic about the wolves and coyotes. Can you do a quick reassurance that we're all safe in here?"

"Sure thing."

"We have a full agenda today, so keep it short and punchy. Up-up, time to go." Marissa clipped on a wireless headset mic and fixed Layla's hair one last time.

Layla was usually tense when lecturing an audience this size, but she relaxed as they entered the wings and she heard the yelling and excitement. Stage Ones were the toughest crowd; they tended to be skeptical and suspicious of the Colony's motivations and its cult-like traditions. It was so much easier to impress them after they'd been warmed up by a pro, and she was profoundly grateful for her PR team.

"Ready." She smiled and stepped onto the stage.

She squinted into the bright stage lights, smiling broadly and waving, even though she couldn't see a single face. God, she'd come a long way. She could remember sitting in the audience for these keynote talks like it had been yesterday. James had conducted them back then, back in the days when she'd been so shy she couldn't even make eye contact as she stuttered a barely audible *Hi, Brother James.*

She held out her arms, palms up. "Welcome to the most exclusive club on Earth!"

The Colony slogan had been another of her brilliant ideas. If they were to convince people to join them, they had to put a stake in the ground: Either this was the most exclusive club on Earth, or they were just some fanatical desert cult. Go big or go home.

The applause went on too long, so Layla gestured for them to quiet down and sit. She hadn't planned her speech for today, but she was good on her feet once she got over the initial stage fright.

"With pain comes peace." Her voice reverberated through the expectant auditorium. "Thank you for being here. Thank you for dedicating yourselves to the process of purification." She paused for another round of applause but cut it off quickly. She had a lot of ground to cover, and Marissa would be giving her the throat-slitting gesture soon enough.

She waddled as gracefully as she could around the stage, speaking dreamily to the floor. "As I stepped out here today, I was flooded with the memory of the day I was sitting out there, just like you. But it wasn't in this grand lecture hall. It wasn't even on this beautiful site here in Mexico. It was in a small dark room in a desert town back in the States, among maybe twenty or thirty inductees. I listened to the vision of the Colony directly from Brother James."

This got a single "Woo!" The crowd laughed.

"Oh, good! I'll let him know he has a second fan."

This got a bigger laugh. By now, most inductees would've seen them holding hands around the campus, and they might have assumed she was having James's baby, not one that had been created in a lab and implanted in her uterus.

"Brother James told us that we would work harder and suffer more than we ever had before," she continued. "He told us that pain would be a welcome experience, something we'd learn to desire, not avoid, and it would open our minds to bigger and better experiences. Many were skeptical of this, and many couldn't learn to accept pain as a positive experience. Those inductees left us."

As expected, several people booed. One of the many mindset changes the Colony cultivated was a sense of superiority: us versus them, the pure versus the impure. Inductees were encouraged to disdain those not selected to be pure. It helped them abandon their poisoned life.

"That part is still true. Some of you will not find a home here. Purification will not be your path. And you know what? That's okay. Our facility has grown not only in numbers but in purpose."

She took a moment to catch her breath, as the little guy pushed her lungs into her throat. "Most of you have arrived here from a disadvantaged situation. So many of you are victims of poverty, broken homes, drug pushers. You were stuck in a world filled with poison, a place where opportunity and wealth are only available to a select few, where doors are not opened without the right connections."

She was surprised by the silence. No indignation about the injustice of it all. She'd have to remember those lines for her next group of Stage Ones.

"But here you'll come to understand that your personal growth is entirely up to you. Everyone here—and I mean everyone—has an identical chance to achieve the highest designations in the Colony. And while you're growing mentally, physically, emotionally, and spiritually, you'll also be contributing to the vision and mission of the Colony: to save the human race."

This line got thunderous applause, and she took the opportunity to summon her support crew. Her stomach felt crampy, and she needed to sit down. She circled her index finger at Marissa, who always seemed to read her mind, and Marissa dashed away.

"A recruit recently asked me an excellent question the other day. 'Sister Layla,' he said, 'Why is our presence here secret if the work we're doing is so important? Is it illegal?'"

A stagehand scurried over, set down a stool, and handed her a bottle of water. Perfect. She leaned back on the stool, taking the pressure off her lower abdomen.

"I explained to him that laws are set by the local governments, and every government has its own problems to deal with and presidents with egos and personal agendas. But as you'll come to learn, our exclusive club isn't affected by local governments. The organization that funds and leads this colony, and the many other colonies, is a global alliance operating outside the limitations of any country. Our global alliance has one single objective for one of the most important global initiatives that exists today. That puts us above the law."

That was all they needed to understand. It would give them a sense of security, but it would also underscore the Colony's influence. They were part of an extremely powerful organization. Once they were fully indoctrinated, the alliance superpower concept would fade to a vague idea. As their weakened minds and bodies struggled to hold on to reality, they'd more readily embrace the long-standing spiritual figurehead of the Colony, the Father. The strategy had worked for years, and no one planned to change it.

"We employ the best and brightest scientists, who've given up their lives in the poisoned world to fully dedicate themselves to the purification of the human race, just as you have. Our work here is so crucial that we will always be protected behind these walls, protected from the poisoned world in all ways. I know the howling wolves out there sound threatening, but you have nothing to be afraid of. Our walls and steel gates cannot be penetrated."

She raised a fist, eliciting a cheer. God, she loved her job sometimes. "And I know some of you worry that this is all too good to be true, too good to last. That someone will take it down. But this I can promise you: The global power behind this organization will keep you safe and happy, enabling you to fully dedicate yourself to your path toward perfection and purification."

This was a good spot for a dramatic pause. She took a long drink of ice-cold water.

You're Allison Stevens. You killed a cop.

A droplet of water landed on her chin as her lips popped free of the bottle. Shaken, she looked over at Marissa.

Marissa mouthed *social media thing.*

Right.

"And what does it mean to fully dedicate yourself? It means when you come inside our walls and accept our challenge to embark on the process of purification, you leave the poisoned world outside. That's a huge commitment, I know. Many of you have left friends and family. But they're not on your path. They're not struggling and suffering with the daily schedule you endure. They don't understand, and they don't have what it takes. They don't have a fire inside them."

"But you do." She stabbed a finger at the blinding light. "When you chose this, you chose the exclusive club. You chose a new family, a new circle of friends, and a better world. You chose to release your poisoned life."

A chant broke out. "Release your poisoned life! Release your poisoned life!"

She had no doubt that Justin started it, but within seconds the auditorium was pulsing. "Release your poisoned life!"

She silenced them again. "Here, we're creating a better world, for us and our children and their children. So why do we keep it a secret? Because everything outside our walls is impure, poison—no, toxic. Our club is exclusive, and we don't want just anyone banging down our doors, now, do we?"

She could have continued, but she felt this was a perfect high point for her to exit. Mic drop, as Justin would say. She waved and blew some kisses as the crowd clapped and stomped.

Just before she stepped backstage she heard a single snap, as if someone had thumped her on the back of her head. She whirled around and took a few steps back toward the center. The stage was empty. But that thump—it made her blood boil, and the audience's applause ground on her nerves like fingernails on a chalkboard. Unbelievably, a howl of fury was building in her throat.

Stabbing pain in her groin ripped her breath away. She folded over, nearly falling to the ground, eyes pinching shut.

Screams from the audience made her lift her head. Marissa and two men were surging from the wings, panic on their faces. She looked down again.

Her dazzling white skirt was turning stark red.

7

"The baby is fine."

Layla rolled over in her hospital bed as Dr. Farid entered her room.

"The heart rate is normal, and there are no signs of fetal distress." The doctor smiled at her. "As for you, you're also fine. Placenta previa is not uncommon, and it will most likely resolve. As long as we monitor it closely, you'll be able to carry full term."

Layla seemed to dissolve into the bed. She hadn't realized how tense she was. The fetus she carried was the single most significant advancement that had occurred in the field of genetics, the first pure human baby of the F1 generation, genetically edited to possess qualities that would better serve the human race. Sadly, it was her second attempt to deliver a prototype, but she no longer mourned the stillborn baby she'd carried last year. That had been an important step toward this scientific breakthrough, and it was an honor like none other to be chosen for such a purpose. She was like Eve in the Christian Bible's Garden of Eden.

Dr. Farid jotted something down in her chart. "You'll be on bed rest for the rest of your pregnancy."

Layla's relief turned to dismay. "No, no…" She closed her eyes. The timing couldn't be worse. There were incoming recruits on top of everything she'd packed into this month, knowing she'd be out for delivery and time with the baby before returning to work.

"What's most important, that child or your obsessive work ethic?" Dr. Farid raised her eyebrows. "I'll keep you here in the infirmary overnight, and tomorrow we'll get you set up in the comfort of your own house. I'm sure you have plenty of reading to catch up on." She gave Layla a squeeze on the shoulder and left her alone.

She'd have to call Mia first thing. And who would cover the intakes? What about coddling the inductees? And the staff meetings...

We grew up together in Madison.

"Leave me alone!" She shut her eyes tightly, as if it might squeeze the voice right out of her head. She wished she could erase that awkward ten minutes of Vanessa Sykes from her mind. She'd made a conscious decision to release her poisoned life before her purification. She knew she had a past—obviously, everyone had a past—but it simply didn't matter anymore. Her past didn't define her; her future did. Her purpose within the Colony walls was all that mattered, so she'd eagerly and willingly shoved what few memories of her poisoned life she had into her unconscious mind and moved on.

Until yesterday. Why was this plaguing her now?

I saw you on the news. You killed a police officer.

That just couldn't be true. She wasn't capable of killing anyone. But Vanessa Sykes hadn't been lying about knowing her—her nickname, her father's death. There was no doubt about that.

She pressed the button to lower her headrest and rolled onto her side.

"With pain comes perfection. With perfection comes purification. This is the Father's will for me. As a pure, I am responsible for the purification of the Colony and the propagation of purity into the world. This is the Father's will for me."

The chant was an old one from her earliest days at the Colony, but it was still her favorite. She'd learned it the first day of her purification, and she fondly remembered the overwhelming sense of peace and happiness of that day, the warm embrace of the pures who supported her and welcomed her into their family.

It was also the first time she'd met the Father, the spirit and brains behind the Colony and Eugenesis. The moment had been magical, like a child catching Santa Claus sliding down the chimney, and she'd enshrined the encounter for months, until the inevitable day she learned her Santa was just a man wearing a suit. It had taken months to recover from her sense of loss. The magic was gone, but her purpose and devotion were stronger than ever. The Father's vision for the Colony and its contribution to the human race was nothing short of genius.

This was where she belonged. There was nothing for her in the poisoned world.

She rolled to her other side, searching for a position that would make the active fetus stop stretching and bruising her insides. The little devil wanted to do aerobics every time she wanted to sleep. Maybe he'd be athletic. A runner, like her. She grimaced and rolled out of bed. More likely, he'd be a boxer.

She paced the small room, hoping the movement would lull him into a relaxed state. She idly opened the cupboards and drawers, inspecting the contents. Maybe someone had left a book behind. No luck. She unhooked her chart, which hung at the foot of her bed, and resumed pacing as she tried to decipher Dr. Farid's chicken-scratch handwriting.

A label in the patient information section caught her attention: *Carrier Strain: Sensus 253/380.*

Dr. Farid hadn't been the physician in charge of the implantation of the fetus. Dr. De Luca, an older physician with a full white beard and an Italian accent, was the physician in charge, a world-renowned fertility expert. He'd never mentioned the word sensus, as far as she could remember. *The baby will be pure, Layla. Just like you, only better. Physically and mentally superior to all of us.*

What was a sensus?

Her phone vibrated, and she waddled back to her bed to dig it from the covers. She sighed with relief. "James. Did you hear?"

"Oh, baby, I'm so sorry. I feel terrible for not being there with you tonight. Are you okay? Are you in pain?"

For some strange reason, his soothing voice made her feel fragile. She hated the infirmary, and she desperately wished he was here holding her hand and running his fingers through her hair, the way he had the last time she'd been in the infirmary. The day she'd lost the first fetus.

Her chin quivered as she tried to hold back tears. "No, I'm okay," she said in her little girl voice. "Are you in Iowa yet?" Maybe he'd come back for her.

"No. There was a problem with my flight, and I had to do a connection in Houston."

"Oh, what, they didn't have a first-class seat for you?" She smiled at her wit. It was something Marissa might have said.

"Worse. They didn't have any booze on the plane."

She chuckled. James didn't even drink. His favorite party joke, which she'd heard a hundred times, was *Why should I drink alcohol when I can be this much of a dork without it?*

"You gonna be okay until I get back, beautiful girl?"

She was about to ask if there was any way he could cut his trip short when the fetus gave her a sharp kick in the ribs. She bent at the hips. "Argh, I can't get to the end of this pregnancy fast enough." Her gaze landed back on her chart. "James, what is a sensus strain? It says that on my chart. Carrier strain sensus two-fifty—"

"Oh, looks like my flight is boarding. I love you, Lay. Hang in there. I'll be back as soon as I can."

She scowled at the phone as the line silenced. Did he seriously just hang up on her? He'd never done that before.

She felt more comfortable in her bent-over position, so she carefully knelt on the ground and did some push-ups. *Never waste an opportunity.* Jonah had whispered those words of wisdom during a meditation circle back when they were working together with new inductees. As the inductees knelt on their bruised, tender shins, sweating and chanting to release the pain, he would walk behind them, pressing down on their shoulders for a little extra challenge, holding a deep squat. *Pain for them, pain for me.*

Satisfied, she returned to bed and picked up the chant again until she finally drifted into a restless nap, dreaming of death and crime and the horrible destruction and devastation outside of her safe, strong Colony walls.

8

"**A**nother drink, sir?"

James dropped his phone into his suit jacket pocket. Bullet dodged, but he made a mental note to reprimand Dr. Farid. Allowing Layla to read her chart … how could she be so careless? Dr. Farid had been explicitly briefed on what Layla should and shouldn't know about her pregnancy.

He refolded his newspaper to another page and smiled up at the first-class lounge attendant. "Please."

"My apologies, sir, we've run out of Talisker. Would you like something else?"

"Yes, how about something from the Scotch Highlands?" James offered a friendly smile. He certainly could have just asked for a Glenmorangie, the only Highlands Scotch that the Houston airport stocked, but he liked to give people an opportunity to learn something. To better themselves. The world was bad enough without adding indolent stupidity to it.

He pulled his phone back out from his pocket to see who was buzzing him and accepted the call.

"Sir, my operatives have informed me that the reporter Nicholas Slater has been loitering around the Vitapura Wellness Center again."

James exhaled a long, slow breath. Despite the influence his team wielded on the local media, Slater couldn't be dissuaded from what he thought was the story of a lifetime. He was like a pesky mosquito. They'd swat him away, he'd fly off for a few minutes, and then back he'd come.

"Shall we eliminate him?"

Oh, for god's sake. When you were a hammer, the whole world was a nail. James rolled his eyes. "We don't need that kind of exposure. Nick Slater is of no consequence to us. Give him enough of a scare to shut him up. Get the local authorities involved."

"Yes, sir."

James hung up the phone as the attendant set down a glass and hurried away. The fact that she hadn't waited around for a nod of approval meant she'd failed. A quick Google search on her ever-important phone would've given her the answer. He took a sip to confirm his grim surmise and wrinkled his nose. American single malt. Not even a Scotch whiskey.

It was the little things like this that reminded him why he was so dedicated to his work. The human race was truly deteriorating, not only in numbers, sadly, but in fitness—and not just physical fitness, although certainly obesity and lifestyle diseases were growing at an alarming rate, but intellectual fitness. No one exercised their minds anymore. They just shoveled in mental junk food all day long.

He tossed his newspaper aside and turned his attention to his upcoming meeting. Something had been nagging at him. This summit would provide an important update, and the teams were excited. The scientific rationale was clear and well-vetted across his staff, and the genetic analyses were conclusive. But even so, no one in the research or clinical program could explain to his satisfaction the broad phenotypic variation across the subjects. Until it was crystal clear, the program wouldn't be ready for prime time, and he knew the council members were anxious. They were looking for quick, early validation so they could move straight into feasibility testing.

Each of his eight sites would be represented by two delegates, a clinical leader and a site leader. The clinical leaders were not a risk. They'd been trained since medical school to keep their opinions and theses within the small group until the supportive data were available. They did not run around spewing hypotheticals.

The site leaders, however, would be more difficult to constrain. They were competitive, and each site wanted to be viewed as more productive, more advanced, and certainly more deserving of a larger slice of the budgetary pie. They were far more likely to exaggerate successes and downplay the side effects as unexpected outliers. Moral obligation wouldn't be enough to keep these leaders tight-lipped; he'd need to appeal to their self-interest. They'd need to believe that sidelining with members of the council, trying to bypass him, would be detrimental to their careers. He'd have to ensure they realized that they were all in this together. No one could be the lone hero.

The attendant returned, sliding his drink check across his lounge table. "Sir, your flight to Kauai is boarding."

His eyes flashed to the tattoo on her forearm. "*Unus pro omnibus, omnes pro uno.* Do you know what that means?" He reached into his jacket pocket for his wallet and held out a credit card.

"Huh-uh. I don't speak Spanish."

"It's Latin, just like the words inked on your arm."

It was clear from the blank look on her face that she didn't realize *carpe diem* was Latin.

"It means one for all, all for one."

Finally, a light went on behind her eyes. "Oh, yeah! Like the three musketeers!" He was momentarily impressed that she'd read the book, before she continued, "Yeah, we had to watch that movie in English class when I was in, like, eighth grade." She handed him a receipt and switched back into mindless robot mode. "Sir, have a great flight."

One for all and all for one. If he accomplished nothing else over the next two days, it would be that. No one could take their data and go rogue. The new model wasn't ready for field testing; it wasn't even ready for expanded Colony testing. He couldn't risk someone getting Stewart all worked up. Stewart Hammond was way too emotionally driven, with the patience of a toddler.

He tucked his wallet back into his jacket and studied the departures board, threw his leather satchel over his shoulder, and clutched his rolling carry-on. If he got so much as a sniff that anyone on his team was less than fully committed to the agreed-upon next steps, they'd be removed and replaced.

He redialed the last incoming number as he walked toward the gate.

"Sir."

"I'd like you to send an operative to Kauai. I may need your help in facilitating some personnel changes. Just a backup."

"Yes, sir, I'll have him on the next flight out."

Qui totum vult totum perdit. He who wants everything loses everything.

9

Nick leaned his Diamondback mountain bike against the wall, tossed his helmet onto the futon next to his open laptop, and flipped on the oscillating floor fan to cool down the million-degree apartment. It was hotter than a stripper on a searchlight, as Uncle Jay would say. He grabbed a tinfoil-covered piece of cardboard cut to the size of his single west-facing window, the poor man's blackout blinds, set it on the windowsill, and turned on the floor lamp.

The Harris case had been eating at him all day. He pulled a bottle of Cuervo from the minifridge and knocked back a shot without bothering with salt or lime. He sipped the second shot slowly, willing his mind to clear as he appraised his wall.

The floor-to-ceiling mind map was his masterpiece, an intricate spiderweb of three-by-five notecards, newspaper articles, and photos of government officials who'd been involved in the aftermath of the virus. The center of the web was a poster-size blowup of the still image that had accompanied the YouTube audio clip that became known as "A Desperate Warning to the World." The warning had gone out on every social media platform. It had played on every news station for weeks and been translated into every language. The unidentified source—Nick was certain it was a US government official, a whistleblower—spoke for less than two minutes: 272 words, the exact length of the Gettysburg Address.

Of course, no one remembered Lincoln's beloved words or his inspirational message anymore. The pipe dream of human equality had long since faded.

But Nick was far less interested in the speech than the image. While most people focused on the shocking carnage on the cement in front of the restaurant, Nick's eye had been drawn to a long crack down one of the pillars beneath the restaurant's slightly lopsided red awning. It had an uncanny similarity to the crack in the Liberty Bell.

Next to that photo was another, taken when the military swept through the small town of Jiuquan to clean up. It was featured all over the world with the headline "Ground Zero Is Virus-Free." The two photos appeared identical, except the Chinese military's image of the restaurant didn't show a crack in the pillar.

It could be a goddamn hair on the camera lens! the chief screamed when Nick showed him both images. But there were other small discrepancies, like the crooked canopy. To Nick, it looked like a cover-up. And sure, he was suspicious and untrusting; that's what made him a great investigative journalist. Until two days ago, anyway.

But why had no one else questioned the crack?

He poured one more shot of tequila and turned his attention to his more urgent obsession. Hanging from the opposite wall was a map of the Vitapura Wellness Center in Black Canyon City, hand-drawn and rendered on his computer and printed on a five-by-six-foot sheet of paper. Its underground maze of empty corridors and rooms beneath the employee housing section was nearly the size of the main facility, yet Vitapura had denied using the underground sections for anything other than storage. It didn't make any sense. The layout was too elaborately designed and constructed to be a storage facility. It had to have cost a fortune.

It didn't take a rocket scientist to realize they had to have been hiding something, yet no investigation ensued. There was no crime in building an underground compound or even lying about how it was used, but Nick had spent hours exploring the maze, looking for evidence of misconduct. The printout was covered in notes and findings, but maddeningly, nothing insightful.

He lifted his eyes to another image, a satellite view of the grounds. In red ink, he'd drawn a bull's-eye where Austin Harris's remains had been found. In blue, he'd marked the seven spots where he'd set up hidden cameras a few days ago, just before publishing the folo.

Four long days had passed since the article went live, and he was getting nervous. Maybe they had nothing more to hide. More likely, they had insider knowledge that the investigation wouldn't be reopened. But he planned to give it a full week before giving up.

He powered up the monitors on his desk and opened the camera viewer program. Seven squares appeared onscreen. He selected View Motion Detection and clicked past various jackrabbits and a single coyote.

And then he was delivered a gift from the gods.

His stomach flip-flopped as he watched an unmarked white van pull up to the locked service gate. The driver stepped out of the van, swinging a small duffle bag. Nick paused the video and zoomed in, trying to get a good look at the man's face. It was too grainy for any detail.

He copied and pasted the image into Photoshop and opened the noise reducer. The image cleared up enough to show a clean-cut Latino man, possibly Indian, wearing a collared shirt and black slacks. He looked too polished to be from the dregs.

Nick distractedly slapped the print button and continued the video.

The guy surveyed the area before creeping along the cement wall away from the camera until he was out of sight. Twenty-two minutes passed before he returned from the same direction. He circled to the shade on the passenger side, blocked from Nick's view, and remained there for four minutes and twenty seconds. Had he been waiting for someone? He must have given up, because he climbed back into the van and left the scene.

The van wasn't close enough to the Harris gravesite for him to have been paying respects. Nick scrolled back and zoomed in to inspect the van. Mercedes. Too posh for a cargo truck. In fact, by the looks of the super-high roof, it appeared to be a passenger van without windows. He zoomed more until he could make out the van's license plate. Bingo.

He picked up his phone and noticed a text from Darcy. *Anything from cameras yet?*

He replied, *Maybe. Call you later.* Then he scrolled through his contacts and dialed.

He didn't bother with small talk when Max answered. "Hey man, I need a favor."

"Slater. What's up?" Max had been his best source at Motor Vehicles for years, ever since they'd worked together to expose an elaborate criminal ring of luxury car thieves. That and the fact that Nick had introduced him to his future wife.

"Can you run a plate for me?"

"Shoot."

Nick read the license plate number.

"That's an exempt plate."

"What does that mean?"

"They're like diplomat plates. Any plate starting with DC means it's a federal vehicle, with plates issued out of Washington, DC. Specifics aren't given to state motor vehicle departments, but it does say it's registered by a company called EGNX."

"EGNX? That's it? Just the acronym?" Nick put the phone on speaker and grabbed his laptop. The only thing that came up for EGNX was an airport in the UK.

"Is there a name associated with it? Like the person who registered the vehicle?"

"Nah, that's it."

"Dammit." Despite all the connections he'd built over the years, he had no one in DC. "Hey, thanks a lot, man. We'll catch up soon. Say hi to the missus."

"Will do."

He hung up and stared at the white van frozen on his screen. "So, my great and worthy opponent, we finally meet after all these years. What were you doing out there, EGNX?"

There was only one way to find out.

He dropped his laptop into his backpack, grabbed his car keys off the table, and scooted out the door.

10

"Okay, so the next delivery of recruits will be on Sunday." Layla scrolled through her notes from the last recruiting team meeting, her tablet comfortably atop her round belly as she sat propped up by pillows in bed. "And it looks like they're coming from region four."

"Which is?" Mia sat cross-legged in the leather chair next to the bed, her laptop opened across her ankles. She never took her eyes off the screen as she scooped hummus onto the end of her carrot stick and shoved the whole thing in her mouth with a *crunch*. Somehow even when she ate like a pig, Mia was adorable.

Layla couldn't help being jealous of Mia's trim figure and flexibility. Mia was thirty-eight, one of the original founding members of the Colony with James, but she didn't look a day over twenty-five. Perhaps it was because she was pure. She'd been given the pain elixir, and she could feel nothing. *It's a blessing and a curse*, she'd once said, as she showed Layla the grotesquely scarred back of her calf. She'd accidentally rolled onto a smoldering log at an inductee campfire ritual and hadn't noticed until someone asked who was cooking meat.

Layla snapped back to the moment. "Region four is Florida and the southeastern states, so mostly prescription painkiller addicts—Oxy,

Fentanyl, Vicodin. Probably not many meth addicts. So look for the usual signs of withdrawal. You know: agitation, sweating, that kind of thing. If they aren't showing any signs, they might be too far gone."

The fetus was rammed up against her diaphragm again, and she reached for the handheld toggle switch next to her pillow. Thank god for the invention of the adjustable bed. Housekeeping had been kind enough to set up a hospital bed in the living room so she could have a bit more open space and natural light during her long bedbound days. This was only the second day, and already the hours were crawling. She had no idea how she was going to survive the rest of this pregnancy.

Mia flipped her long dreads behind her shoulder and continued typing frantically, two hummusy fingers quarantined above the keys.

"At this stage," Layla added, "we're only looking for remorse and hope. We won't look at submissive tendencies until later in the process."

"What about spiritual mindset?" Mia asked.

"That all goes to stage two. We push hard on psych testing in early induction so that we can fast-track the hi-pos early."

Mia raised her perfectly tweezed eyebrows. "Hi-pos?"

"The high-potentials. They're identified during the first few weeks and separated from the main induction group."

So much had changed since Layla had begun running the purification program, not only in terms of the numbers and quality of recruits but in how they were inducted and readied for purification. The antiquated induction process James and Mia had designed years ago was a shadow of the new factory-style system. Layla's production system churned out pures fast enough to keep pace with the voracious appetite of the research program. It was no wonder that Mia looked overwhelmed.

Layla idly rubbed her belly. Maybe she should ease up a bit. "Hey, listen, Mia, why don't you send Isaac back for another week? He's been involved long enough to get through the next round. Michael can help with the interviews."

"No, no, it's okay. I can handle it."

"Seriously. He's—"

"Hm-mm. Isaac's been reassigned."

Wow, that was fast. She hoped he wasn't stuck somewhere mundane like facilities management. Despite her criticism of his recruiting tactics, he was smart and deserved an important role. "That's great! Where is he?"

"He's, uh…" Mia looked at her lap. "He's been assigned to a GS-5 program."

Layla felt a flush crawl up her face. "A GS-5? What's the gig?"

"You know I can't say." Mia still didn't meet her gaze.

She forced a chuckle. "Duh, I know. It's fine. I shouldn't have asked. It's none of my business, anyway."

The response was overtuned, and Mia saw right through it. "Honey, your value and contribution to the Colony are not based on the rank of your assignment. The bottom line is that we were looking for a specific personality type for this particular role, and Isaac hit the mark."

Her sympathetic tone only made Layla angrier and more jealous. Layla's rank gave her quite a lot of status on campus, but GS-5 was a big step up. In the need-to-know hierarchy, Isaac now knew more than she did. He'd been promoted above her.

Her eyes swam with tears as an even more painful realization hit: James hadn't told her. He hadn't warned her to soften the blow when she found out, and that meant he didn't think she could handle it. It was yet another example of how he undermined her work.

"Hey, hey, don't do that. It's not personal." Mia swiped her thumb under Layla's eye to wipe a tear away.

"Yes, it is, and you know it." She'd confided in Mia about how James's overprotectiveness had grown to the point of holding her back within the organization.

Mia set her laptop on Layla's overbed table and lay next to her, her thin body comfortably perched on barely six inches of mattress. "Finish your pregnancy, and I promise I'll force a conversation about this. Okay?"

Layla was too embarrassed to look at her. She nodded and stared at the belt of her fluffy robe, stretched to its max around her belly. "It's just … I've worked so hard." She tried to control her vocal cords, but the words came out sounding choked.

"Lay, that fetus needs you. Forget about your GS right now. You're doing the most important job in the Colony. Not the pain program—"

"The purification program," Layla corrected with a sniffle. She'd been trying to change the old way of thinking since she'd taken on a leadership role. *It's not about the pain, you guys, it's about the purification. We're selling an evolved human state, not a sadistic torture cult.*

"Right, sorry. But my point is you're a carrier. You're carrying the future of the human race. That makes you a GS-10 in importance."

Layla repressed an eye-roll. Mia was only trying to help. She took a deep breath and exhaled to the count of four to release her anger. She wanted to have a good attitude for the fetus. He needed her.

Mia smiled. "That's better. Now, don't worry at all about recruiting. I'll make Michael help me, and I'll invoke the recruiting gods in a primitive prayer dance, and we'll emerge unharmed and victorious until the tribal chief returns to her position at the head of the village."

A soft knock at the door was followed by an even softer voice. "Hello? Sister Layla?"

"Come in, Harmony." Layla wiped her nose on her sleeve.

Harmony stepped inside with three large bags and startled at the sight of Mia. "Oh, I didn't—"

She stumbled over the door threshold and released the bags to catch herself. Plastic containers of food crashed to the ceramic floor, splattering what must have been tomato sauce all over the floor and walls.

Layla grimaced as Harmony cried out, "Oh my gosh. Oh my gosh. I'm so sorry. Oh, Sister Layla, I'm so sorry."

"I got this." Mia rolled from the bed in a graceful way that only she could pull off, calling out, "it's okay. No need to cry over spilled marinara." She disappeared into the kitchen leaving Layla alone.

Alone with Mia's open laptop, which happened to be displaying her email inbox.

Layla's eyes traveled down the screen of messages until they landed on a subject simply entitled, *Isaac Reassignment.* The email was from James.

"Where do you keep your supply of paper towels?" Mia called out.

Butterflies fluttered in her belly. "Uh, should be in the laundry room."

She heard the splashing of water in the sink and more whimpering from Harmony. Her gaze returned to the email. A GS-5 level? What could it be? Why would James and Mia choose Isaac over her? It was so unfair.

As if it had a mind of its own, her hand moved closer to touch the pad, paused a moment and extended an index finger, gently moving the cursor down the page.

She had to know. She deserved to know.

"Well, that wasn't so bad." Mia materialized in front of her.

She yanked her hand away from the keyboard and faked a muscle spasm to cover her wrongdoing.

"Oh god, cramp. Cramp in my calf." She grabbed her leg and groaned.

Mia grabbed her foot and flexed it, scrunching her face into a look of empathy, as if Mia had any idea what pregnancy was like, or painful cramps for that matter.

Layla fell backward and exhaled.

"I better get going before this place gets struck by lightning." Mia snapped her laptop closed and slid it into her bag.

Harmony collected Layla's still full water glass to unnecessarily refill it with fresh water. "Bye, Sister Mia. Again, thank you for your help." Harmony lowered her eyes to her feet. "With pain comes peace."

"With gratitude comes the Father's love," Mia responded appropriately. As custom dictated, she pulled Harmony into a quick hug. "Bye, Sister Layla," she called over her shoulder. "Be well."

Layla's gaze lingered on Mia's tote as she waltzed out the door.

Harmony cleared her throat. "Um, I brought you some prepackaged meals. You just need to put them in the microwave."

God, she'd been so close. The cursor had been hovering right over the email. All she had to do was click. Why hadn't she moved faster?

"You know," Harmony continued, "like if you get hungry."

"Yes, thank you." She picked up her phone and pretended to be reading her email to discourage additional pointless chitchat. What would

Mia have done if she'd caught her? Would she have told James? What would James have done?

"And I also made little baggies of fresh fruit and nuts. You can just take the whole baggie right into bed with you."

"How thoughtful."

Harmony gathered the clean clothes from the washer and set up the ironing board. Great. She'd have nicely pressed pj's to wrinkle in bed.

She did her best to ignore Harmony's puttering. She didn't want to appear ungrateful, but having a stranger fuss over her made her uncomfortable. Naturally, James had insisted. *Layla, I know you. You'll be up and down every five minutes if you don't have some help.* If she'd refused, he would've canceled his trip and rushed home, and she didn't want to be a burden.

"I put on a fresh toilet paper roll in the bathroom. There was only a little left, and I didn't want you to run out before I get back tomorrow."

Layla wanted to reassure Harmony that pregnancy hadn't impaired her dexterity to the point that she couldn't grasp a toilet paper holder and slide on a new roll, but as usual, she bit her tongue. "Thank you. Now, you've done more than enough. Go home and relax. You have an early morning. I'll see you tomorrow afternoon."

"Thank you, Sister Layla. May the Father watch over you."

"Bye, now." She held her smile until the door clicked shut.

She couldn't be irritated with the inductees. It was part of the process. She'd been in exactly that place before. Removing the inductee's strong sense of self and replacing it with a central figure that represented something collective was imperative. There was simply no other way to secure unwavering commitment and dedication to their vision.

But sometimes she just wanted to punch the Father in the face. Figuratively, of course.

11

Nick parked his open-top Jeep Wrangler fifty yards or so from the service gate and swung out to inspect the area. He circled the truck, kicking up dust as he scanned the deserted landscape at the base of the foothills. The Vitapura facility certainly was a tranquil place to unplug and unwind. He inspected the key reader at the gate. Nothing had changed. Next he set off along the wall in the direction the van driver had gone. Footprints weren't easy to track on this terrain, but he was able to identify the zig-zag print from the soles of the driver's boots at several points along the wall. It didn't appear he ventured out into the brush. Still, to be thorough, Nick extended his walk for fifteen minutes, inspecting the wall, the ground, even the sagebrush and cacti as far as twenty feet off the wall.

He returned to the gate empty-handed. No sign of any disturbance along the wall or the surrounding area. Maybe the guy had been looking for something and found it. Or hell, maybe he'd simply wandered off to take a shit while he waited for some rendezvous that never happened.

He plodded back to the Jeep and gazed down the long dirt service road. He wiped the sweat off the back of his neck and mindlessly scratched it. His muscles felt stiff, and he foolishly blamed them for his inability to understand what had happened here. If only they'd relax, release the blood flow to his sluggish brain, a lightbulb would flash on, and he'd finally understand what he was missing.

You're a goddamned disappointment.

The words weighed on him. They always had.

In his father's eyes, success meant following the rules. Write the mainstream stories. Don't step out on a limb. And never believe you have a story just because your gut says you do. Instincts are not facts. That's not reporting. That's chasing a conspiracy theory.

He paced the driveway, shaking his arms and rolling his head. What was he missing? A guy in a white van. Eleven minutes of walking along the wall. His shirt, which had dried after his bike ride, was again soaked with sweat. His arms and legs were covered in a thin layer of dust that itched. He badly wanted a shower and a Guinness.

But he'd sooner spend the night out there than leave empty-handed. This was his story, and that van parked in front of Vitapura's back entrance gate was the first sign of those sewer rats he'd seen in a long time. Damned if he was going to let them scurry on by.

The still, lifeless air made the area as desolate as a graveyard in a ghost town. There was no sign that this once lively, luxurious spa had employed hundreds and catered to as many guests. Now it was a mound of dusty buildings forty-five minutes down a bumpy dirt road from the hick town of Black Canyon City, the nearest place to get a cup of coffee or buy a pack of smokes.

He jolted as if the thought literally struck him, and he jogged back to the gate. Stepping lightly, he frantically surveyed the dirt near what would have been the passenger side of the van. The driver hadn't been stood up; he'd been relaxing in the shade of the van with a cigarette before the long ride back. Smoking wasn't allowed in most company passenger vehicles.

He dropped to his hands and knees, inspecting the area inch by inch. He almost gave up when his eye caught the cigarette butt, farther from the tire marks than he expected and dangerously close to the dry tumbleweeds. He dashed back to the Jeep and grabbed a plastic grocery bag from the center console.

"Oh yeah, baby. Come to daddy, you pretty little DNA specimen." He tenderly pinched the butt, dropped it into the bag, and held it up with satisfaction. Look at that: progress.

With more optimism than he had in a long time, he threw the Jeep into gear and peeled out in a cloud of dust.

He made it barely half a mile before he heard the explosion.

He hit the brakes too hard and lost control of the car, fishtailing for a couple of moments before running off the road. The Jeep hit a saguaro cactus and stopped abruptly, stalling the engine.

Panting, Nick cranked his neck around.

A black cloud of smoke mushroomed into the air, right over Vitapura.

12

our more crackling explosions echoed around him. Nick slammed the Jeep into reverse and hit the accelerator, escaping the spa as fast as he could.

So that's what the bastard had done. He'd planted explosives scheduled to detonate long after he was gone from the scene. Based on the secondary explosions, he must've planted them near the generator room where he could do the most damage.

All the energy seemed to drain from Nick. All his hard work, the time he'd spent exploring that spa, the money he'd blown in surveillance gear, all of it was now spiraling up in black smoke. Obviously, the article had spooked them into action—but a spa inferno? What the hell were they trying to hide?

He'd have to think about it later, because right now he needed a plan. He'd be driving straight into a pack of police and fire trucks in a matter of minutes.

One hand on the wheel, he groped under the passenger's seat until he found the topo trail map of the Black Canyon City area. Except for the acreage still owned by Vitapura, this entire section of land belonged to the Bureau of Land Management, who'd opened it up to off-road vehicles to attract tourism. All-terrain vehicle shops and touring centers had sprung up, and wider trails were developed to accommodate four-wheelers, many of them sprouting from the back doors of the shops along the freeway.

Nick needed to find one before the incoming fire trucks found him.

He slowed enough to keep one eye on the map. The best option was a flat quarter-mile stretch through vegetation that connected with the treacherous Old Black Canyon Highway. It was technically rated difficult, although erosion after an uncharacteristically wet winter had probably upgraded that to severe. He slowed down to a crawl at the power lines and rolled off the dirt road. Cactus and rocks weren't a problem for the Jeep's high clearance and thirty-seven-inch tires; the problem would be the sandpits. He wouldn't have the momentum to get through them, and that'd be the end of the line.

He leaned out to get a better look at the terrain and cringed at the vibration of the rocks and cacti shredding the undercarriage. He downshifted to first, hit a boulder, and stalled out. In the stillness before he restarted the engine, he heard the first sirens.

"Shit." He yanked the car into reverse and steered around the rock into a gulch. His Jeep, his precious motherfucking Jeep—this was gonna fuck up his gas tank or rip off a muffler, but he had to get to the foothills to find cover.

At the Old Black Canyon Highway, he cranked the wheel to bump up onto the road. *Highway* was a gross overstatement; it was more of a dry riverbed, rocky and undulating, with steep banks on either side. He crawled at a turtle's pace, white-knuckling the steering wheel, fixated on the road to keep the tires from sliding into the deep ruts created by water runoff. The breeze had carried the smoke from the explosion across the valley, and his eyes burned and teared, but he couldn't spare a free hand to rub them. After an eternity, the trail flattened, and he could see trucks up ahead barreling along the freeway—the beautiful blacktop surface known as I-17.

"Booyah!" he bellowed, pumping a fist in the air.

He slid the Jeep into fourth and raced down the last leg of dirt road, bursting into the rear parking lot of the permanently closed Canyon

Sports All-Terrain Vehicle Tours.

He couldn't afford to be spotted here, but he needed a moment. He whipped to a stop, pulled out his phone, and checked the time. Four-thirty. He could make it.

He sent a quick text. *I need you, baby.*

***

Nyla Madden, forensic analyst at the Phoenix Police Department Crime Laboratory—and Nick's dynamo ex-girlfriend, who'd always been too good for him—was pacing the waiting room when Nick stepped through the door.

"So how's the little one?" He couldn't remember her daughter's name, but maybe she wouldn't notice.

She narrowed her eyes and yanked him down the hall by the sleeve of his shirt. "You know I could get into serious trouble over this, don't you?" She shoved him inside the lab as if he were resisting arrest and kicked the door closed behind them.

"Whoa, watch the manhandling. I'm not the bad guy."

"You're a widely known reporter, and I need this job. You know as well as I do that DNA analysis requires a warrant. Let's get this over with."

"Only if I was planning to do something with the data, which I'm not. I'm only looking for a lead." He handed her the bag containing the cigarette.

She flopped onto a rolling stool and snapped on latex gloves. Using tweezers and scissors, she snipped the cigarette butt into three parts and dropped them into fluid-filled tubes. She positioned the tubes onto a rack inside what Nick would've thought was a printer but whose label identified it as a BioQuant Precision ID Whole Genome Panel. DNA analysis had come a long way since high school genetics, when he'd used a vortex mixer and centrifuge.

Nyla peered nervously out the window as she peeled off the latex gloves. She thrust out a hand and waggled her fingers. "Give me the print."

He pulled the folded printout of the image of the van's driver from his pocket. She smoothed it over a scanner and scooted her stool forward to watch the facial recognition software scroll through images. Nick peered over her shoulder.

No matches. His heart sank.

"Well, he's not a felon," she said. "Our funding was cut last year, and now we're only able to keep felony records."

She rolled back to the PCR analysis machine, tapped a couple of buttons, and returned to her computer. She opened another program and drummed her fingers while she waited.

"What the hell?" Nyla gaped at the screen. "He's been scrubbed."

"What? What do you mean?"

He bounded around the desk to look for himself: *Sequence complete, Error 0339 TS/SCI.*

"He's with a top-secret organization." The color drained from her face. She scurried to the door and craned her neck up and down the hallway.

SCI—the acronym hit him.

"Sensitive Compartmentalized Information," he murmured. "Jesus." Like Area 51.

She hustled to her computer, tapped the escape button, and selected Delete Record. Then she took him by the arm and dragged him to the door.

He swung around. "Listen, Nyla—"

"Whatever you're getting into here, you better be a whole lot more careful than this. Whoever smoked that cigarette is far more powerful than you or me." She rolled onto her tiptoes to give him a peck on the cheek. "And don't involve me again. I have a family to consider."

She closed the door before he could say thanks.

He couldn't help scanning the parking lot as he hurried back to the Jeep. Some top-secret organization? Government? All these years, he'd figured he was looking for some underground group of scientists with no ethics, like a band of villains from a Marvel movie, or a bunch of young

MIT dropouts, or—

"Jordan Jennings." He swung himself into the driver's seat. What had become of Jordan Jennings? He snickered at the memory of the guy: super-brainiac geneticist, nerdy as Bill Nye the Science Guy. Maybe he should look—

His phone rang. Darcy. He started the engine. As soon as he pulled onto the interstate, Darcy's name flashed on the call screen again.

He hit the speakerphone. "Hey, I just got on the freeway, let me—"

"Don't come back." Darcy's voice had a sense of urgency he hadn't heard in a long time.

"What?"

"You're all over the news, Nicky. Vitapura. They have pictures of your Jeep driving away from the explosion. There's a manhunt."

Shit. He glanced at the phone, grateful he maintained the account under Uncle Jay's name. "Meet me at the locker."

He disconnected and pulled into the parking lot of a vacant indoor Go-Kart center, bumping over the large cracks from years of heat and neglect, and parked. He hopped out and set his phone gently on the pavement under the wheel of the front left tire. Dammit, he felt like he was putting down a beloved pet. He pursed his lips as he slid back behind the wheel and rolled over the phone, flinching at the sharp crunch.

The breeze picked up, rolling an empty beer can and a tumbleweed in front of the idling Jeep. He crossed his arms over the steering wheel and lay his forehead against them.

The bad guys—EGNX, now that he had a name for them—had been chasing him away since he'd first taken an interest in the case. They didn't put much of a scare into him in the early days; he was only a nuisance, touting a conspiracy no one of any consequence would believe. He'd received a handful of subtle warnings, including a harassing visit by the local yokels and a restraining order that he ignored.

If he hadn't been so goddamn obsessed and stubborn, he might've realized how much power they really had. He might've quit years ago when the warnings were still gentle. A statewide manhunt was a whole new level. Either they wanted to kill him in that explosion, or they wanted to put him behind bars, where his unfortunate demise would undoubtedly go unquestioned.

He was in over his head, plain and simple. No, he was on the ocean floor with an empty dive tank and sharks circling.

He pulled in a ragged breath and surveyed the area. Every direction seemed like the wrong one. Every road felt like he'd be driving straight off a cliff. It was like his world was compressing, the air around him being vacuum-sucked away, leaving him gasping.

He squeezed his eyes shut. What was he without the story? An unemployed dregs piece of shit. That's what.

He gripped the wheel as his nerve coalesced again. Quitting wasn't his M.O. And dying wasn't in the cards for him. Not yet, anyway.

13

2:14 a.m. Layla's watch glowed like an earthbound star under the night sky as she leaned against the back porch railing, inhaling the cool desert air. The full moon cast shadows against the rocky canyon walls behind her cabin, where the terrain made it impossible to continue the thirty-foot cement walls, the hallmark of the Colony, that made her feel safe and secure. The canyon was treacherous enough that no human could climb up or down. Or so they'd told her.

Distant howls seemed to drift on the moonlight itself. Could wolves and coyotes climb the canyon walls? Perhaps there were other areas along the perimeter where the wall didn't exist. Maybe they weren't as safe as she thought. A chill ran up her spine, and she backed into the cabin, locking the door behind her.

Would Allison Stevens be scared of wolves in the distance?

Her poisoned life was haunting her. She crawled back into bed, but she still didn't feel ready to sleep. She flipped onto her side, the only comfortable position she could find these days, which faced her toward the console table with James's home computer. She had her own laptop, of course, as well as the latest model tablet and a phone, all charging next to the bed. The Colony was filled with computers and devices colonists used to message their Colony friends and stay connected to the goings-on of the poisoned world. It wasn't conducive to morale to force too much separation from the world. But the information flowed one direction, into the Colony, and all content was monitored and filtered by Eugenesis.

Layla's GS-4 level, which now felt more insulting than edifying, meant she didn't get access to the world outside the Colony.

But James did.

On James's computer, one could, hypothetically, look up the name of a particular citizen and potentially discover details about said citizen. Of course, no one would do such a thing, least of all her. Reconnecting with one's poisoned life was forbidden. She didn't even know what the punishment was because she'd never seen it happen. It was impossible. The cultural indoctrination was deep. *Poison* was a powerful word, surgically selected to make colonists want to excise old urges. But even if that hadn't been so, there was simply no technical way to send communications outside the walls.

Unless someone had access to a computer like James's.

We grew up together in Madison.

She rolled over. No, she wouldn't do this. She couldn't do it. There were cameras everywhere. Everyone was watched at all times.

Even herself and James? In the privacy of their cabin?

She pushed up and looked around the room. James had assured her there were no hidden cameras, no recording devices.

No, it was a dumb idea. Even if no one was watching, she wouldn't be able to get into his computer. She'd need a password to override facial recognition, and she didn't know it.

And more importantly, it was forbidden.

She lay back down, but her overactive, cabin-fevered brain obsessed over the idea. When she became pure, she'd been dosed with the intelligence elixir, which was supposed to enable her to learn faster than impures. She hadn't felt a noticeable change, but she sure did love puzzles. Could she crack James's password?

In that breathless silence unique to two a.m., she rolled out of bed and powered on his computer. Most people chose passwords based on something personally significant: an anniversary or the middle name of a child. But other than his work, nothing was important to James except her and the fetus inside her. She covered the facial recognition scanner and waited for the read error followed by the password prompt. She tried several combinations of Layla with various numbers. Nothing.

Frustrated, she shuffled to the kitchen and poured herself a glass of water. She leaned back against the counter, eyeing the cursor in the password box blinking brightly at her across the dark room. Taunting her.

Why was James such a mystery?

Didn't you do anything fun besides stalking me in the poisoned world? She'd always been interested in his life before the Colony, but he was oddly tight-lipped about it.

Nope, he'd replied proudly. *I followed you everywhere you went, hiding in the shadows in my overcoat and sunglasses.*

That's super creepy. She was flattered, even though she knew he was lying. But he had loved her, even then…

Then!

She fumbled her glass, spilling water all over herself.

She'd been a student, right? A graduate student. That would have been what, maybe 2010? '11?

She set the glass in the sink and returned to the blinking cursor. It only took three tries before the password was accepted.

Allison2012.

The system portal opened before her, and she stepped back as if she expected an alarm to engage or the screen to self-destruct. Neither happened. Instead, the logo EUGENESIS spread across the screen, directly above a browser search box.

The fetus moved slightly, sending a ripple across her torso, reminding her that she was supposed to be lying down in bed. She left the computer browser open and lay back down on her side, her eyes locked on the blinking cursor.

It wasn't fair that she didn't have access. Mia had access, and now probably even Isaac had access. She was at least as deserving as Isaac—

no, she was more deserving. This shutout was just an assertion of dominance from James. He was stifling her growth so she'd be dependent on him. It was unjust.

And so what if she typed "Allison Stevens" in the box? Would she be breaking the rules just by doing a small search? Being inquisitive about her poisoned life wasn't the same as reconnecting with it. *I don't even know when my birthday is!* It was her fallback argument whenever the topic came up. And James had his evasive fallback reply: *Your life is here now, Layla. What does it matter? Don't ask me who you were or why you came here. All it will do is upset you and distract you from your work. I promise you're in a better place now than you ever were.*

She could tell he meant it. And until now, she'd been content with the answer. But then Vanessa Sykes had breezed into the intake room and reignited her curiosity with details that had completely possessed her thoughts.

Guess you really are the bitch everyone said you became.

Was she a really bad person? Had she killed a police officer?

She had to know. If she'd killed someone, James shouldn't have kept that from her.

She crawled out of bed again and sat down at the desk chair, regarding her fingers as if from a distance as they typed "Allison Stevens" into the search window. She sat back and stared with amazement as the results loaded onto the screen in front of her.

She scrolled through the results until she saw an image. She clicked. No surprise—it was herself looking back. She looked different: shorter hair, paler skin, but it was certainly her. Allison Stevens, the Layla of the poisoned world.

The image was included in a "Be on the Lookout" release from the Phoenix police department: "Allison Stevens, age 29, person of interest in the murder of DEA Agent Vincent Wang."

Oh god. She recoiled from the computer screen. She *had* killed a police officer.

She should have shut down the computer right then. Looking into her poisoned life was bound to upset her, just as James had said. But instead, she found herself reaching for the mouse to scroll down. Opening Pandora's box, was that the expression?

She landed on an obituary. "Madison mourns the loss of patient rights activist who took his own life by means of assisted suicide." Her dad. She could remember brief moments from his funeral. "He is survived by his loving wife, Rachel Leigh Cassidy, and daughter Allison Cassidy Stevens."

Layla clicked on the image. Even black-and-white and grainy when she enlarged it, she could see the trust on the face of the young girl looking up at a woman who held her hand. Her mother, Rachel Leigh Cassidy— her real mother. She traced a finger around her mother's face. What had she been like? Was she still out there somewhere?

A message flashed onto the screen, and she flew backward. Her breath hitched. Only a notification. James's flight from LIH to IAH has been delayed.

She stared at the message. IAH wasn't the airport James usually flew into. She clicked on the message. The aircraft was arriving late in Kauai. Hawaii?

He'd lied. Why would tell her he was going to Iowa? What was in Hawaii?

She typed "Kauai" into a new browser window, which pulled up an image of a man and woman lounging in a tropical heaven, sipping champagne: "Kauai, the most romantic place on earth."

Her stomach roiled. Was he with a woman? Someone beautiful and thin? Layla stared at the gorgeous woman holding the glass. Her perfectly flat stomach; her long, tanned legs. She pictured James sitting next to that woman, calling her his beautiful girl and meaning it, because she was so much more beautiful than—

Three loud knocks on her cabin door startled her. "Sister Layla? I'm sorry to disturb you. This is Eric from security."

14

O h dear god. They discovered her.

Layla flew from the chair and did the only thing she could think of: She turned off the power supply to the computer.

"Sister Layla?" the security guard called. "I don't mean to intrude. Brother James wanted us to check up on you. Is everything okay? I'm letting myself in."

She heard the click of the lock on her cabin door and dropped into bed.

The door opened in a whoosh, and the desert breeze swept a peculiar sewer stench right into the cabin, along with a tall, skinny security guard with eyebrows so thick they came together like one long caterpillar. She recognized him but couldn't place from where.

She pressed her palm to her nose to block the smell. "What's the problem?"

"I noticed your light was on so late." He swung his eyes around the room. "Are you feeling okay?"

"I'm fine. I just couldn't sleep."

He walked to the sliding glass door and looked out onto the patio. What did he want?

After a long moment, he took several steps back toward her. His caterpillar unibrow shortened with suspicion. "Are you certain everything in the house is secure?"

She nodded. Was this a test? Had she set off an alarm of some kind?

He kept his eyes on her as he unhooked his radio from his belt. "The cabin appears secure. Sister Layla is safely inside."

He set the radio on James's desk and took a seat at the foot of her bed, watching her intently.

Panic brewed inside her like a hurricane forming over the ocean, churning, gathering strength. A tremor spread through her body until she was visibly shaking. She pulled her blanket higher, clutching the edge with a death grip.

"Ma'am?" He lifted his hand to scratch the back of his head before leaning forward, bracing himself on the bed just inches from her leg. His breath smelled of garlic and alcohol, but also something truly rancid that reminded her of the pungent smell of James's cold cuts after they'd gone bad.

She slid one hand to her throat as she was overtaken by the sensation that something here was different. It was as if she could hear the hurricane in her body, a rumbling in her chest, followed by a crackling and buzzing in her head like a downed power line.

She rolled out of bed and regarded it with wide eyes, certain she'd been shocked. Maybe the electrical system that reclined the bed?

"Are you okay?"

Her eyes landed on the name embroidered onto the right breast pocket of his jacket: E. Ortiz, EGNX Security.

That's when her head exploded. Jabbing pain between her eyes, as if someone had stabbed her in the forehead, made her suck in air. Her muscles stiffened, causing her body to jerk with each attempt at movement. But before she could panic, the pain dissipated, and a tingling warmth washed through her. The room turned red and cloudy, and she squinted to peer at the darkening figure near her bed through tunnel vision.

And—she had to be imagining it—his caterpillar unibrow was

morphing into slimy, squirming maggots. They crawled down his face, disappearing into the corners of his eyes, squirming up his nostrils and into his open mouth.

He is the plague.

A lifetime of anger cascaded into that single moment. With an inhuman, guttural cry she'd never heard before, she lunged. Her right hand seized him by the throat and rammed him against the wall.

"You." Saliva flew from her lips, and her fingertips curled until her nails dug into the soft flesh of his neck. "Poison." It was a growl, like an animal.

The guard stood motionless, his arms splayed against the wall as though he was glued there. He stared back with wide eyes, his mouth open in a silent scream, frozen in sheer terror. She could smell the maggots feeding on his rotting flesh—but instead of sickening her, they fueled her.

"You aren't one of us." Blood burbled up between her fingers and she squeezed harder, digging deeper into the sinewy tissue. She wanted a tighter grip. She had an overwhelming urge to wrap her fist around his trachea and yank it from his throat. A chill of pleasure ran up her spine. The acrid smell of blood, the viscous texture—

like pancake syrup

—overpowered the stench of rot, and she wanted more. So much more.

The rotting flesh on his face was detaching from the bone. With her left hand, she shoved her thumb into his drooping eye socket to get a good grip on his cheek and yanked. It pulled off like slow-boiled chicken breast meat from the bone.

He is poison. He is the plague.

"Sister Layla? Are you okay?"

The face in front of her wavered. The maggots were gone.

She blinked several times, trying to clear her head. Pain shot down her rigid spine into her legs. Her hands were fisted so tightly she could barely straighten her fingers. Blood covered her palms, punctured by her fingernails—her blood, not his.

At once, her muscles relaxed and her knees buckled. She caught herself on the edge of James's desk, knocking over the pen holder. The pens hit the wood floor with a crash that for some reason sounded like the shrill cry of a wounded bird. The noise was torturous, and her hands flew up to cover her ears.

The guard knelt on one knee to pick up the pens. "It's okay, ma'am. I didn't want to alarm you, but I thought you should know…"

She gaped at the back of his shirt. There was movement underneath it, as if he were flexing some unnatural muscle group.

"…wolves or coyotes on the property."

Not muscles. Maggots. His torso seemed fluid as they boiled up beneath his shirt, squirming to get free.

"…probably after our livestock, but just so you're aware…"

He is poison. He is the plague.

Before the maggots could break away, she grabbed the iron off the ironing board and swung it downward with all her might. The satisfying crunch of his skull delighted her.

But then he got to his feet, blood dripping from his caved-in head. "Here you go. You seem a little disoriented. Why don't you have a seat?" He reached out with a gangrenous black hand.

She fell back onto the bed. Another crackling sensation in her skull and the guard flickered from monstrous to normal.

"Ma'am? Have I upset you?"

She leaned forward. She could still feel the handle of the iron in her grip, but there it was on the ironing board, right where Harmony had left it earlier. What the hell was going on? Terrified, she returned her gaze to the guard who now hovered over her. He reached up to scratch the back of his neck again, this time peeling off layers of skin before moving toward the door.

The hammering between her ears was beginning to slow, but adrenaline was still blasting through her veins. She trembled on the edge of the bed, mouth open, staring vacantly.

His voice seemed to come from far away. "I'm glad everything is okay.

You give us a call if you need anything."

Her front door slammed shut behind him, creating a seismic aftershock she was sure shook the whole house. She exhaled. How long had she held her breath? The smell of death lingered in the stifling hot cabin. The sickening stench of poison. Plague. Sweat poured into her eyes. She rolled out of bed onto shaky legs. She needed air.

She flung the front door open and staggered into the cool night.

15

Nick stumbled over to the poker table with a sloshing whiskey in one hand and a handful of chips in the other. It was barely noon, far too early to be drinking for anyone but a complete lush. He collapsed into the only available seat at the poker table.

"Name's Nick. Whatch'all playin'?" He slammed his whiskey onto the felt-covered table, splashing booze onto the pile of chips of the player to the right. "Oops, sorry 'bout that."

He awkwardly flung his left hand over the rail and slowly opened a tightly clenched fist to drop four purple five-hundred-dollar chips onto the table with a snort and a grunt.

"Jesus," the guy to his left muttered.

"'M in!" Nick threw a chip into the pile.

With a sigh, the dealer reached into the pile, removed the chip, and set it back down in front of Nick. "Sir, we're in the middle of a hand. You'll need to wait until the next hand."

"Oops, sorry 'bout that," he repeated. He tilted his chair back on two legs and eyeballed the casino. Cool place. Nice bar, with a damn good liquor selection. Lots of people. Lots of security cameras. He blinked a couple of times and shook his head.

"Showdown," the dealer called.

Nick leaned back a bit too far and lost his balance. He grabbed for the chair on his right. The front chair legs slammed back down, hurling him chest first into the rail.

"What a jackass," he heard from somewhere at the table.

"Hey maaan, yo. Whassa game?" Nick asked the guy to his left.

"What the fuck you think? Hold'em."

"Riiiight. 'M in!" He declared, loud enough to turn heads from the other tables. He tossed his chip into the pile.

The dealer again removed his chip and changed it for five black hundred-dollar chips. He leaned over the table and looked Nick in the eyes. "Sir, are you sure you're sober enough to play?"

"Wha? Yeah. Hell yeah I can play, riiight?" He slapped the guy to his right with the back of his hand. "Yeah, I can play."

The dealer tossed two cards face down in front of every player.

"Ah, shit," Nick said, looking at his hole cards. "What the fuuu…?"

"Bet is a hundred." The dealer looked at him.

Nick looked around the table.

"Sir. I need a black chip."

"Sorry." Nick tossed the chip, and it rolled across the table. He giggled.

The dealer dropped the flop—five of hearts, king of spades, seven of spades—and Nick vacantly watched the bet go around the table. When it came to him, he shouted, "'M in!" and tossed a purple into the pile.

"Sir, are you asking for change, or raising the bet to five hundred?" The dealer's voice was significantly sharper.

"Raise it!" Nick pointed a finger at the ceiling.

Half the table folded.

At the turn card, Nick threw out another purple, out of sequence. The dealer moved to protest, but the player in sunglasses seated at the dealer button smirked and said, "Let it go."

The rest of the players folded. Only Nick and Sunglasses remained.

"Ah, shit." Nick picked up his hole cards, one in each hand, and eyed them, back and forth, back and forth.

"Sir, keep your cards on the table." The dealer was seething now.

"Riiight."

"Showdown." The dealer revealed the river card.

Nick leaned over the table to scrutinize the final card: king of hearts. He tossed a purple.

"Purple hearts!" He pointed to the chip and then the card. "Geddit?" His head bobbed proudly.

Sunglasses did not smile at his joke. Instead, he saw Nick's five hundred and raised him a thousand.

"Ah, shit … Ah, man," Nick whined as he looked at his remaining chips, a purple and four blacks. "Shit." He groped in his pocket. "Wai …wai … I goddit. I goddit." He pulled a stack of bills from his wallet and began meticulously counting. "Twenny … fourdy … sisty…" He slammed a hundred on the table. "I goddit." He grinned. "Call."

Sunglasses flipped his hole cards. Nick leaned over the rail to see: ace of spades, seven of clubs. Two pair.

"Respect." He sat back down and raised his eyebrows in Sunglasses' direction. "I wouldn't have played those rags even if you did get lucky and pull a pair out of 'em. Ballsy move." He flipped his cards. "Fives full of kings." A full house.

Sunglasses flew out of his chair, tore his shades from his face, and gaped at Nick's cards.

Nick pulled a handkerchief from his pocket, picked up his whiskey glass, and wiped the spilled booze from the leather rail. "Thanks for the game, fellas. What was it again? Hold'em?" He laughed at his joke. "No hard feelings, right?" He nodded at the dealer. "Color me up, will ya?"

Sunglasses looked ready to explode. "You son of a bitch."

Nick knew better than to engage. Nothing made a man want to take a swing like being hustled. Add insult to injury, and you were just asking for a trip to the hospital. Not that he hadn't won fair and square; a pair in the hole was a nice start. But three of a kind on the flop? That was a winning hand by itself, damn good luck. The kings were just icing on the cake.

He picked up his chips and made his way toward the cashier but was intercepted by two suits. "Sir, may we have a word with you?"

Nick glanced up at the camera in the corner. "You bet." He shoved his chips into his pants pocket.

"Right this way."

He trailed the management team, bracing himself for the riot act, and cast a furtive glance back at Sunglasses, who appeared to be gathering a group.

The suits ushered him into a closet-sized office with no windows. A wave of fear washed through him. He hadn't been to Vegas in a long time; perhaps the eighty-sixing procedure had become a bit more physical in recent years. Ever since the virus, aggression had significantly increased.

The leader positioned himself directly in front of Nick, well inside his physical comfort zone. "Sir, we take cheating very seriously in our casino."

Nick glanced down at the man's nametag, which read MANAGER ON DUTY. The man had a dopey Gomer Pyle way about him. By the insecurity in his voice, Nick guessed he'd probably been trained for situations like this but hadn't had to deal with one on his own watch.

His fear melted away. "I didn't cheat." He made a show of looking at all the furniture for surveillance devices.

"Do you have a form of ID on you?"

"Yes, I do. I'm an adult, after all." He didn't move to get his wallet.

"May I see it?" Gomer took a small step backward, now seeming uncomfortable with his initial assertiveness.

Nick rolled his eyes. This wasn't going to be any challenge at all. Might as well cut to the chase. "No. Nor will I sign a document giving you the legal right to arrest me if I return. I've given you plenty of good camera shots to post on your Facebook page. You can spin your wheels to make sure I never gamble in this town again, but let's be honest. No one's managing a black book anymore. It's every shop for itself."

He leaned back against the metal desk, bracing himself with his palms, pressing his fingertips hard enough to leave good print impressions.

"So let's cut a deal. The house rake for a shitty joint like this is, what, five percent? Tell you what. I'll hand over half my winning chips, you cash me out for the other half. That's more than you'll make all day. You have one of your goons give me an escort to my car so that Sunglasses and his fuckwit friends don't break my face, and you can have the moral high ground. I'll take my business elsewhere. No need for an ugly scene, no blood to clean up. Whaddaya say?"

Nick's eyes darted from one glowering face to the other as the seconds ticked by. A lot of seconds. This was the warehouse district of Las Vegas. They were sketchy at best, and down here they probably didn't even have a gambling license.

Finally, Gomer Pyle shifted his glower to his partner. "Get Mr. Slater some cash."

Nick kept his face impassive, but he was impressed. He knew they'd eventually identify him, and he gave them a head start by dropping his first name at the table, but still. This was much sooner than expected.

"And so we're clear, Mr. Slater," the man was continuing, "we're a close-knit group out here. I'll spread your name around. You might be able to hustle the big houses, but I wouldn't return to this neighborhood if I were you."

The big houses? Who was he kidding? Vegas was shattered, just a bunch of enormous unstaffed hotels with cruddy brown half-filled swimming pools and prostitutes who'd give you blow job for a buck. But he shrugged and dropped his gaze, hoping his body language read *Ah, shucks, you got me.*

Someone appeared with his cash; Gomer was making good on the deal. Nick allowed the goon to grab him by the arm and haul him to his Jeep, although he couldn't resist a wink and a smirk as he passed by Sunglasses and his buddies.

As soon as he was certain no one was following him, he pulled over on one of the twisting back roads of the warehouse district and dialed Darcy on his burner phone.

"Okay, all set with the strategic misdirection. I've been seen and recorded here in Vegas. My identity will make the rounds, and Arizona state police will bury the warrant."

"They'll put out a bolo in Nevada."

He could hear the worry in her voice, but he forced himself to snicker. "No way. They don't have the resources for extradition. They won't chase a warrant across state lines. If the cops come around, tell them I took off. Otherwise, I'll check in when I can."

"Listen, Nicky…"

"Hey, don't worry. We knew this day would come. I have everything I need. I'll be back in a few weeks. Just gonna lie low until the case lands in the cooler."

He left it at that, but he wasn't sure if and when he'd be back. No one had been hurt in the explosion, presumably; the Vitapura campus had been completely abandoned. But if the EGNX people were serious about finding him, with all their power and money and influence, they could put the FBI on his tail.

He turned the Jeep down the sleazy part of Fremont Street and dropped his speed to fifteen miles per hour as he eyed the eternal lineup of used car lots. He pulled into Barter Brother's Used Cars, partly because they hadn't bothered to rebrand with the euphemism *preowned*, as all the others had, and partly because he could've sworn that was Danny DeVito himself standing out front, waving him in.

He didn't need a great deal or a fair trade. He was looking for a shady cash-based business transaction, the kind where they'd throw in a set of old plates registered to the mechanic's eighty-five-year-old grandma.

Because despite what he told Darcy, Nick had no intention of lying low. Gotta strike while the iron's hot, as Uncle Jay would've said.

16

Layla woke shivering and pulled her comforter over her head. Her phone dinged with a text message, and she squinted with one eye to read it.

James: *I'm 15 min out. Want me to bring you some lunch?*

Something smelled. She put a hand over her nose.

Ugh.

She jerked her hand away, opened her eyes, and threw the blanket off to inspect her hand. Dirt. And ... was that blood?

She gasped. Her memory of last night was nothing but flashes in her mind: E. Ortiz, EGNX Security. The guard. He'd been inside her house. There'd been blood—*was* blood. An attack.

What had she done?

The poison. The plague.

Oh god.

She rolled out of bed, slightly dizzy, and her feet came down on something crunchy. She lifted the legs of her pj's. Her feet were orange with dried caked clay mud, the kind found well beyond the main walkways. Her heart felt like it stopped beating and she closed her eyes, searching for a glimmer of memory. Had she walked in her sleep?

A cool breeze lifted her hair. The front door was standing wide open.

After a tentative glance outside, she closed the door and tiptoed to the bathroom. Her reflection in the mirror brought another flash of memory.

The maggots. Feeding on his rotting flesh.

It had to be some sort of hallucination, probably brought on by the scare the guard had given her barging into the house so late at night. She'd seen drug addicts hallucinate, panicking as they described whatever horrible things they thought they were seeing. And the sleepwalking was probably related, too. That's all it was.

Her phone flashed another text. *You up, sleepyhead?*

She tore the bedsheets off the bed and tossed them, along with her pajamas, into the washing machine. She just stepped into the shower when she heard James call out, "I'm home!"

***

James had set up her place at the dining table with a meatless cheeseburger, french fries, and a green salad.

"I saw you eyeing my cheeseburger the other day," he said with a smirk.

It was a nice gesture, but Layla had no appetite. She picked at her salad greens. All she could think about was the beautiful woman on the Kauai website, the most romantic place on earth. "How was Iowa?"

"Terrific. I'm thinking the site could serve as a stage one recruiting center. Since we're getting most of our recruits from the US anyway, there's no sense bringing them all the way down here if there's a chance they'll be a better fit for the British Columbia colony, right?"

She wanted to stand up and slam her hands on the table. *Who is she, James?* But she nodded mindlessly, unable to bring herself to confront him.

"Lay?"

She jerked and looked at him.

"So would you want to?"

She didn't know what he was referring to. "Uh, yeah."

"Great, I was hoping you'd agree. Farm work can be quite rewarding."

She squinted at him. "Huh?"

"Ha! I knew you weren't listening. I'll assume it's your pregnancy, not my lack of charm." He winked. "I need to jump in the shower. Big day ahead. Not all of us get to lie around and daydream all day." He kissed her forehead and tottered off to the bathroom, humming his favorite Beatles song as if nothing had happened. As if everything was normal.

How long had he been lying to her?

A knock on the door startled her. She froze, though she wasn't sure why. James apparently couldn't hear the knock over his *na-na*'s from "Hey Jude."

She waited a full minute before tiptoeing to the door and peeping through the spy hole. The porch was empty. She eased open the door and picked up a yellow folder that lay on the doorstep with a handwritten sticky note.

"Brother James, you left this in the car this morning. Your driver, Will."

She sank onto the sofa and set the folder on the coffee table in front of her. She'd never looked through James's work. His role in the organization meant he needed to keep secrets. *I can't be with you if I can't trust you, Layla, and I very much want to be with you.* They'd established strict boundaries early in their relationship, and she'd always respected his privacy.

Well, that was before the lying. That was before he broke her trust.

She opened the folder and pulled out a small stack of papers. The top page was a meeting agenda in James's familiar format.

Global Carrier Meeting, Kauai, Hawaii, USA

Chair: James Elliott, Mexico (attending)

Co-chair: Stewart Hammond (not attending)

She sighed with relief. It was a meeting, not a woman. But her brow wrinkled as she read on.

Agenda

8:30–10:00 Sensus recruiting update—site leaders

There it was again. That word: sensus.

China: 980 successful implantations, 773 sensus births, 79 praefuro

Canada: 610 successful implantations, 604 sensus births, 54 praefuro

Mexico: 380 successful implantations, 212 sensus births, 26 praefuro

The list went on: UK, Japan, Philippines, Argentina, New Zealand. She stared at the agenda for a full minute before her mind was able to piece together what she was reading. Her medical chart flashed in her mind: *Carrier Strain: Sensus 253/380.* That was her. She was number 253.

Her mouth went dry.

She wasn't the first carrier of the pure generation. She wasn't Eve in the Colony's Garden of Eden. She was just one subject in a pool of hundreds. James had lied to her all this time, leading her on and making her feel special.

The shower turned off. She skimmed the rest of the agenda.

10:00–12:00 Sensus placement program—Madeline Barnett

12:00–1:30 Lunch

1:30–3:00 Praefuro Case Reviews—Alessandro De Luca

1. Criteria for isolation in salvage

2. Risk mitigation—

The bathroom door opened, and James's heavy footsteps thudded into the bedroom. Layla slid the papers back into the folder, gently opened the front door, and set the folder on the doorstep where she found it.

A cloud covered the sun, and the bright cabin darkened. Or maybe it was in her head. At that moment, she had only enough energy to crawl back to bed and under the covers. A tightness had formed in her chest, and her eyes burned with angry tears.

She'd given everything to James. All she'd wanted in exchange was honesty and equal footing. But it was all bullshit. All those times James had placated her with his soothing voice and endless offers to get her whatever she needed had only been his way of keeping her from finding out the truth about everything—her past, her pregnancy, and all the other secrets the Colony seemed to be keeping from her.

And how had she responded? With childish whining and indignation: *But it's not fair!*

"See you tonight, beautiful girl." James kissed the back of her head.

She didn't offer a reply, and he didn't wait for one. The front door closed behind him, sealing her in with her sacrifice—and god, she'd sacrificed so much. Her days were endless, yet she'd carried a full workload while carrying two fetuses to term. She didn't know anyone who could match her stamina or work ethic. And this is what she got for it: lies from the person she trusted most, a lousy GS-4 rank, and two long years of pregnancy. It was amazing she still had her sanity after everything—

You're Allison Stevens.

She howled, pulled the pillow from beneath her, and covered her head until she could hardly breathe. Allison Stevens. Her poisoned self. Had she been this pathetic when she was Allison Stevens? Had she been this weak and powerless?

She stretched open from her fetal position, threw her legs over the bed, and rose fully erect, inhaling deeply, palming her tears away. Just the change of position made her feel stronger.

Allison Stevens had killed a cop. She must have been ruthless.

Allison Stevens had been a fugitive. She'd dodged the police, escaped the long arm of the law, and ran away to the Colony. She was dauntless.

Allison Stevens would be disgusted by the spineless jellyfish she'd become.

Her feelings of betrayal turned to defiance like the flip of a light switch. No longer would she live in James's world of lies, and no longer would she suffocate under his protective wing.

She wanted to see the other sensus carriers herself. She wanted to know what had been so important that James had to keep it from her.

She stomped over to James's computer and flopped into the chair with a thud. The screen blinked on. A moment later, a red prompt flashed: FACIAL RECOGNITION ERROR. PLEASE ENTER PASSWORD.

She stabbed at the keyboard.

INVALID LOGIN ATTEMPT.

17

Layla typed in the password a second time, slower.

INVALID LOGIN ATTEMPT.

She backed away, staring at the screen. And that's when she noticed the paper coffee cup. James's coffee. He'd been on the computer this morning.

Her mind flashed with the memory of the guard knocking at her door. She leaned over the desk to inspect the power strip. Hadn't she flipped it off in a panic when the guard came in? Yet the screen had blinked on when she touched the keyboard a moment ago. James had turned on the power strip. She glanced nervously over her shoulder, as if she expected him to be standing right behind her. If he suspected she'd used his computer, surely he would've said something. He should've been furious. But he'd shown no sign of anger. In fact, he'd been downright cheery.

She rubbed her itchy palms together. Now what?

She rummaged through James's desk drawer until she found a campus map. She'd just have to find the carrier program herself.

The Mexico colony was significantly larger than the Arizona colony had been before they'd migrated across the border. This one was as big as a college campus, built in five clusters forming a pentagon, with three to five miles between clusters, each with its own security access gate. A central security building at the hub was positioned to quickly send guards anywhere they were needed.

Naturally, Layla wasn't privy to the purpose or activities of the other clusters, but she knew that one of them would be where they conducted basic scientific research and another would have to be where they kept the other carriers. Where would James hide them? Somewhere far from her purification center, no doubt, probably near the medical facility so the doctors would be close by. If the other carriers were carrying F1 fetuses like her, Dr. De Luca was the logical choice as the physician in charge. It made perfect sense; he was the fertility expert. It was just as logical that his office would be somewhere near the carriers.

She opened her laptop and searched the directory. Dr. Alessandro De Luca, Building R. She grabbed the campus map again and ran her finger over each building until she found R. It was in a cluster on the north side.

Her stomach flip-flopped as she picked up her phone and dialed. "Hey, Mia. Is Michael on campus, by any chance?"

"Nope, he's in the field. He's delivering a group tomorrow. What's up? You okay?"

She pounded a fist against her forehead. "Yeah, I'm okay. I was just hoping he'd drive me to the rose garden so I could get some air. It's okay, I'll sit on the porch."

"Okay. Later, gator."

She tossed the phone onto the bed and put the map back in the drawer, taking a moment to make sure James's desk looked untouched, and scooched back into bed with her laptop on her belly, the directory search still open.

She keyed in the name Eric Ortiz, the EGNX security guard who paid her an unwelcome visit last night, and stared at his ID picture. God, the horror had seemed so real, the maggots oozing from his face, nestling back inside his rotting head. She could still smell the decomposing flesh, the poison, and feel the churning force that fueled her bizarre driving need to purge him from the Colony.

The fetus shifted and stretched, and crushing pain shot through the back of her head, radiating around her head to her temples. The room appeared impossibly bright, and she squeezed her eyes tightly. She closed the laptop and slid under the covers, but try as she might to drift off to sleep, the events of the last twelve hours spun through her mind like a desert tornado. Breaking into James's computer. Opening Pandora's box. The strange visit from Eric Ortiz. The mud on her feet and clothes. The lie about Iowa. The password change.

The maggots.

The poison. The plague.

The enormous full moon, and the wolves howling in the distance.

And finally, sleep.

The pack of wolves moves in toward the guard, curled on the floor of the ravine. He's injured, but even if he could stand, he wouldn't be able to outrun the pack. He stares, paralyzed with fear, begging God to save him, but his time is up.

The pack strikes as one, their fangs sinking into the flesh of his arms and legs, his bones snapping like twigs under the pressure. The beasts pull in opposite directions until the muscle tissue tears into meaty chunks, which they swallow whole. They growl and snap at each other, fighting to get their jaws into the fleshy abdominal cavity.

Layla stands in the wash, her feet caked with orange clay, enraptured by the attack. Blood mats their thick fur, and she almost wants to reach out to touch it, to feel the warm stickiness. Her attention turns back to the guard, now just a bloody carcass surrounded by piles of shredded clothing. The alpha wolf bites down on the exposed rib cage and thrashes his head, separating the upper torso from the lower half of the body. He drags it twenty feet down the ravine, his own special meal.

But then the wolves are gone. It's Layla herself who hovers protectively over the torso. A low growl escapes her, and the other women and men, the thin, weak omega members of her pack, obediently return to pick at the lower remains like a happy family over a Thanksgiving Day turkey.

The rumble of Layla's stomach woke her. Harmony's soft humming and the sound of her puttering filled the living room. Layla wanted to choke her into silence. She squeezed her eyes and tried to fall back into the dream. Her stomach rumbled again.

She threw the covers off. "Harmony!"

"Oh, you're awake. Hi, Sister Layla. I hope I wasn't—"

"I'm starving."

Harmony did a double-take at Layla's abrasive tone. "Oh. Okay. Um, would you like some hummus and pita bread? Or I can make you some avocado toast."

God, that shrill, annoying voice. "I want a steak." Her mouth watered at the thought.

Harmony took a couple of steps closer to Layla. "Sorry?"

"A steak." A juicy, rare steak. Barely warm in the middle, dripping with blood.

"But you don't eat meat."

The girl's insufferable sheepishness was enraging. "For god's sake, Harmony, stop being a whiny little bitch and go find me a fucking steak."

Harmony made a mewing sound and shuffled to the door.

"And some pancake syrup," Layla mumbled as she pulled the covers over her head. She swallowed the saliva that was practically dripping from her mouth and closed her eyes to return to the wolves.

18

Nick packed up his tools and leaned back to admire the gun vault installation behind the passenger seat of his newly purchased 1994 Chevy pickup. Accessibility was awkward, but sure as hell no one would suspect it was back there. He surveyed the parking lot of Henderson's Ace Hardware to make sure he was still alone, then filled it with what remained of his stash, eight thousand dollars in hundreds and fifties. Carrying cash was risky in the dregs. Not only was crime at an all-time peak, but law enforcement wasn't known for ethical behavior these days. He'd heard plenty of stories about large sums of cash confiscated under the pretext of "suspected theft" that were never seen again.

But leaving a credit card trail would be the quickest way to get dragged back to Arizona. Go directly to jail. Do not pass Go.

He set off for the hour-long drive east from Henderson to Lake Mead. The lake was spectacular in the spring, and Lake Mead had developed quite a trendy bar scene. Back in the old days, he wouldn't have been able to find a tavern that wasn't already five deep from the bar. But now, even in the early afternoon when vacationers had finished water skiing or fishing, most establishments were practically empty. Recreational areas like this one had taken as much of a hit as the Strip back in Vegas. Most folks these days couldn't afford a car, and even if they had one, they couldn't afford to fill the tank with gas. It would be the perfect place for him to hunker down for a few days and do some research.

Just as he'd suspected, the lake scene was as dead as a lump of lead. He pulled into the empty parking lot of a random dive bar. He needed a cold beer and a quiet place to come up with a strategy. Now, with EGNX and the authorities on the hunt for him, he'd have to operate stealthier than he had in a long time. And never stop looking over his shoulder.

Despite the new complications, the fire in his belly hadn't burned this hot since his discovery of Vitapura's underground maze. He was on the cusp of getting the story. He was sure of it. If he weren't getting close, they wouldn't be so hot on his tail.

He inhaled with a grin and allowed himself just a moment to imagine the astonished look on his father's face when the old man saw the story break on cable news, the talking head bubbling, "and bringing you this shocking story is acclaimed investigative journalist, Nick Slater."

He forced himself out of his pickup before the Pulitzer Prize fantasy surfaced. A bell chimed when he strode through the front door. The bar had an old-time saloon motif, and he took a seat at a stool at the end of the bar, next to a fake antique Wanted Dead or Alive poster of three shady-looking men holding shotguns. Cheesy. The bartender, wearing a tasseled faux leather vest and a cowboy hat, gave him the once-over before setting her phone on the register, exchanging it for a flashlight, and sauntering over to him. She flipped on the flashlight and moved it between his eyes, then leaned back against the counter as if that frenzy of activity had exhausted her. "Yeah?"

He might have passed her virus test, but she still frowned at him. Probably because he hadn't shaved in three days and his last shower had been an armpit and groin rinse in an Ace Hardware bathroom sink.

"Heineken." He could be equally uncongenial.

Most inner-city bars had installed retinal scanners at every entrance to check for nystagmus, the only early physical indicator of the virus. If an eye spasm was detected, not only would a blaring alarm create mass hysteria and a human stampede out the back door, but the National Guard would be alerted and on the scene within minutes.

Smaller bars in rural areas couldn't afford the expensive scanners. If they wanted customers, they'd have to take their chances with the ol' flashlight test.

She popped the bottle cap and set in front of him. No coaster, no glass, and certainly no customer service.

A headline on the television caught his attention: "Science Research Center Converted to Homeless Housing." The reporter, whose voice was muted, was standing in front of the well-known genetics research center in Massachusetts, the Broad Institute.

For the second time that week, the name Jordan Jennings popped into Nick's head. Jordan, who'd worked at the Broad, was a respected geneticist known for his early work in CRISPR-Cas9 gene editing. He'd consulted for Agent Peter Malloy at the Phoenix DEA on the case that had ultimately led to Malloy's suspicious death, bringing Darcy to Nick's door for help. Jordan was some sort of child genius but definitely on the autism spectrum, as Nick recalled, the kind of guy who could talk about science for hours on end but couldn't get through twenty seconds of small talk without clammy hands and awkward tittering.

He pulled out his Surface Pro, connected to his personal Wi-Fi, and searched "Jordan Jennings Broad Institute." The Broad Institute was now permanently closed, but it appeared Dr. Jennings had been hard at work. Much of what turned up was scientific articles he'd authored, but the most recent result was presentation listing for a professional conference, UCLA Biogenetics Symposium 2023. He'd given a talk, "Can Gene Editing Take Down the Next Virus?" Interesting.

He opened the Malloy folder and looked up Jordan's last known phone number.

A woman answered.

"Hi there. My name's Nick Slater, looking for Jordan Jennings. Is this still his line?"

"Nope."

"Do you know—"

She disconnected.

Charming. "Nice talking to you."

He lifted his gaze as a loud drunken group of five stumbled in through the front door. Glits, by the looks of the Gucci handbags flaunted by the two blondes who bellied right up to the bar. Nick rolled his eyes and sighed. Just his luck he'd pick the one bar in town the day drunks favored. He pulled his beer closer and angled his computer away.

The shutdown of the Broad Institute wasn't particularly puzzling. The National Institutes of Health had assumed responsibility for most major drug development once research funding had dried up. What puzzled Nick was that the NIH seemed to have defunded all its genetic research. It could be possible that other countries had taken the lead in genetic research, but he had no way of finding out, thanks to the national censorship. GEOBLOCKING PROTECTS OUR INTELLECTUAL PROPERTY! the billboards still read. That had been the end of global news reporting and the beginning of the rapid decline of the first amendment. It still infuriated him.

He opened his notes and started at the top.

Allison Stevens, still missing in action. Stevens had been associated with Agent Vincent Wang after her prints were found on the knife that took Wang's life. Wang had been working with Malloy and Garcia on the LXR case, and he'd clearly been onto something the night he was stabbed behind the wheel of his car during a stakeout of Stevens's apartment. He must've known she was involved.

Nick was certain that Stevens was somehow connected with the LXR genetic drugs, the case that Aunt Darcy's boyfriend Pete Malloy had become obsessed with, but he didn't have hard evidence or a source, despite throwing a wide net. He'd interviewed everyone he could think of: friends, relatives, business associates. The only thing he'd learned about Stevens was that she was an alcoholic with a weak constitution and mental health issues and she'd been sleeping with Harris, her boss.

Which is why when Harris's body turned up near the Vitapura Wellness Center in Black Canyon City, Arizona, Nick had expected

Stevens to reemerge, dead or alive.

"Hey, man." One of the five rowdy customers—some douchebag wearing a Hawaiian print T-shirt under a sports jacket, no joke—nodded over at Nick. "Where'd you get that fancy computer? Steal it?"

The other four laughed.

Nick gave the douchebag a friendly wave and a snicker. *Yeah, brah, joke's on me.* He'd had enough trouble for the week.

His whole case hinged upon finding Allison Stevens, and now that Vitapura was gone, he had no idea where to go next. Perhaps he should consider revisiting other interviewees from his early investigation and push them a little harder about what they knew about Stevens. For someone with a weak constitution, she sure was good at hiding.

All at once, the group burst out laughing, and Nick glanced up from his screen. They gawked at him, waiting.

"I said, you're the first dreg piece of shit I've seen around here. You must be lost, missed your turn onto the Strip."

That was his cue. He closed his laptop and dropped it into his backpack. He certainly couldn't risk losing his computer to a group of glit bullies. It was all he had left if he was going to continue chasing this story. He slid a buck across the bar and moved toward the door.

The douchebag stepped in front of him. "I asked you a question."

No, technically he hadn't; he'd made a declarative insinuation. But Nick didn't say so.

The guy mimed sign language and spoke in a hollow-sounding voice. "Are you lost, mister?"

Another round of giggles as his two buddies moved in, creating a tight group around him and blocking his path to the door. The Gucci sisters regarded the situation with looks of boredom from the edge of the bar, which implied this kind of scene was probably something that happened frequently. The latest form of violence wasn't about race or sexual orientation; it was about financial status.

Nick took a step back and held his palms up. "Hey, sorry, fellas. My bad. Didn't realize this was an exclusive bar. Let me buy y'all a round.

Whaddaya say?"

He called over to Suzie Sunshine. "Ma'am? I'd like to buy a round for my friends here." He pulled out his wallet and laid a hundred on the bar.

It was enough to stun them momentarily, and he wasn't sure the bribe was going to work. Then the douchebag's face spread into an evil grin. "Hear that, Vicky? Our friend here's buying us a round. Grab that Johnnie Blue from the top shelf. I'll have a double. Fact, make that five doubles." He held his beady eyes on Nick as he spoke.

Prick. Nick pulled out two more large bills from his wallet and slowly laid them on the bar. "You have excellent taste, sir. Not surprised, given your outstanding taste in suit designers." Nick sidled up to the guy and gently lifted his lapel to inspect the inside lining.

"The fuck?" The man backed away, slapping his hand.

"J.Crew, right? That's some expensive shit." He gave a knowing nod.

The douchebag glanced over at the women to see if they'd heard the compliment.

Nick used the half-second to push his way through them. "He's a keeper," he called out to the women. "Great to meet y'all, but I gotta run. Enjoy those drinks!"

He hustled out the door. Unbelievable. Twice in one day, he was running from thugs. He headed back toward Henderson, irritated that Lake Mead was now blown for him. Maybe the douchebag was right. The best place for a dregs piece of shit was back in the dregs.

He finally pulled into the parking lot of a city park. Homeless men, women, and children huddled in what little shade they had outside a sea of tents and cardboard houses in what once might've been a nice ball field. He pulled over and slipped the wallet out of his jacket pocket.

"Victor Beaumont." He read off the driver's license. "That's the name of asshat douchebag if ever I did hear one."

Smooth, Nicky, he heard his uncle say in his head. *Excellent misdirection with jacket lapel.*

"Aw, shucks. He was drunk. Easy mark."

Okay, maybe his Uncle Jay wasn't exactly a role model for moral excellence, but Nick had loved him. His own father's moral compass had been rigidly pointed at true north. The man had never so much as run a red light, but he'd also never once told his son that he loved him. The chief hadn't come to his high school graduation, where as class valedictorian, Nick had delivered a speech to four thousand students and parents. Uncle Jay had been there, though, sitting next to Aunt Darcy on the front row, screaming like a wild banshee: *That's my nephew!* The chief didn't believe in handouts. *You want something, Nick, you work for it.* It was Uncle Jay who'd tossed Nick the key to an old beat-up Volkswagen Jetta. *A college kid needs to have a car. How else are you going to pick up beer for your dorm parties?*

Heat crawled up Nick's neck. He wasn't sure why he was still pissed about the fishbowl scene at the *Sun.* He'd hated working for that asshole and was relieved to be done with him. Never should've taken the job in the first place. If Jay had been around at that desperate moment of a bad life choice, he would've mimed tying a noose around his neck and hanging himself, or maybe projectile vomiting until he lay spent over a toilet.

He opened Victor Beaumont's billfold, removed three crisp Benjis from the stack, and put them in his own wallet. He lifted the rest over his head and released the bills into the wind. They drifted upward for a moment and then softly rained down on the ballpark. He grinned as the subdued microcosm below came to life, kids first, then adults hopping up from their cardboard beds to clutch the bills as they fluttered within reach. Whoever said money didn't fall from the sky?

He kept the wallet, though. Victor's hair was shorter than his and a bit lighter, but otherwise, they looked alike enough that this could pass for a fake ID. Might come in handy.

Nick looked down at his vibrating phone. Unlisted number. He accepted the call but didn't speak.

"Yeah, hi. Uh, is this, uh, Nick Slater? The reporter?"

A corner of Nick's mouth turned up as he recognized the voice. "Dr. Jennings. It's good to hear your voice, man."

"Yeah, sorry for that blow-off when you called earlier. It's complicated."

"What's complicated?"

"They're looking for me."

Uh-oh. That was a bad sign. Jordan had been so paranoid after the death of the DEA cops that he hadn't even wanted to answer a handful of questions. *Whatever's going on, I don't want to end up with a bullet in my head like those guys.* It had taken quite a bit of coercion to get him to talk, but even then, he'd felt Jordan was holding back. But that was a long time ago. Perhaps his anxiety was more mental than situational.

"Who's looking for you?"

"The recruiters. If they discover the work I've been doing, I can promise you, I'll no longer be a free agent."

"What are you talking about? Who's recruiting you?"

"Listen, I have something to show you. I know I sound a little manic, but I have some new data. Some really fucked-up data. It's the story of the century."

Music to any journalist's ears—but Nick wasn't working on a story about scientific data. He just wanted to find EGNX.

"Who's after you?" he repeated.

"Can't talk. If you want to know more, meet me in LA tomorrow afternoon, two p.m. in Union Station. I'll be at the bagel shop next to Starbucks. Don't say a word to anyone, and make sure you're not followed or traced."

"Wait, just tell me—"

But Jordan was gone.

Nick scowled at his phone. LA?

He propped his laptop open on the dashboard and read the notes from his interview with Jordan. Jordan had been working with the Phoenix DEA to identify the genetic composition of a drug found in the possession of one of the victims, LXR102016, a genetic modification of a pain gene—the Frankengene, Jordan had called it. *This thing has been so CRISPRed up it no longer looks like anything in normal human DNA. And it's got the highest uptake I've ever seen.*

Nick hadn't understood everything Jordan had told him then. The kid spewed out science babble like a second language, and not one Nick spoke. At the time, he hadn't been interested in the science; he'd only been looking for clues into what happened to the DEA cops. This time, he scoured the transcribed page.

"It's an illegal biohacking ring. They're using kids like pincushions. Giving them inhuman genetic drugs to make them fearless. Make them feel no pain. It's like a modern-day biotech practice of eugenics."

Eugenics.

EGNX.

Shit. No way. He stared at the word until his vision blurred. It was dumb. Nothing but a case of pareidolia, seeing a pattern that wasn't really there.

Or was it instinct, that characteristic his father had believed was nothing but a distraction to good investigative journalism?

That was all the push he needed. He turned his phone off and stashed it in the metal lockbox under the passenger seat. From his backpack, he unwrapped a second burner phone and activated it.

He opened a map page in Google. Drive time to LA was five hours.

19

L ayla climbed into Michael's minivan, whipping her head around to throw him a dazzling smile.

"You're a lifesaver. Normally, Will takes me over to my appointments, but he wasn't around this afternoon."

"Will, the executive driver? I didn't realize you had that much corporate clout."

She slapped him good-naturedly. Once she reached her third trimester, Michael had been kind enough to taxi her from building to building in her small part of the campus, but he'd never taken her out of the purification center. She didn't want him asking questions.

"Is everything going okay with the pregnancy?" She could see genuine concern on his face as he pulled onto the empty dirt road.

"Yeah, it's just a routine checkup." They drove in silence for a minute. "Michael, do you remember that recruit I walked out on last Monday? I believe her name was Vanessa Sykes?"

He snorted. "How could I forget? She was furious. I convinced her it was your pregnancy hormones talking."

She smiled and rolled her eyes. The crazy pregnant lady. "Did she say anything else about how she thought she knew me? That was so unsettling."

"Nah. She just said she hopes you rot in hell."

Layla winced. "Ouch."

"Yeah." He laughed. "Seriously, though, I can't imagine doing your job. Having to weed through some of these folks we bring in."

She nodded.

They turned right onto another road, and Layla was reminded how big the campus was. Who had insisted the clusters be so far from one another? What were they trying to protect?

"You know we don't have a choice, right?" Michael's tone sounded apologetic. "We're trained to bring anyone who wants to get on the bus, even if we haven't actively recruited them, because if we don't, they'll take their resentment to the public. We can't afford the exposure."

She studied him. "Is that so?"

He softened his voice and smiled warmly. "'If your heart is pure and you're willing to release your poisoned life, you're welcome to join us. Please help yourself to a sandwich and some fruit, and take a seat wherever you like.'"

How embarrassing. Despite the fact that she was in charge of recruiting, she had no idea how the field recruiters actually worked. It was another example of the silo culture James enforced. There was no communication at all between the recruit supply chain and induction and on into purification. She added this to the many grievances she planned to take up with James at some point.

They were approaching the gate. "Well, I'm sorry about that thing with Ms. Sykes," Layla said. "I feel terrible about it. I hope she landed in another good program. I've thought about apologizing to her personally."

He didn't take the bait. Michael was a devoted member of the Colony, a true by-the-book rules follower. He knew as well as she did that assignments outside her purification program were confidential.

Michael held out his badge at the gate so the guard could scan it and leaned back as the guard dipped forward to inspect the car through Michael's window. Layla was ready with her story, but he only gave her a respectful nod and said, "Good luck with your pregnancy, ma'am. Thank you for your service."

Interesting.

"Here y'are." Michael pulled up in front of a replica of the infirmary in her cluster. Down the walkway was a second-floor bridge to another building, likely a dining hall exactly like the one she ate lunch in every day. It was eerie.

"Thanks, Michael."

"Do you want me to wait?"

"No, no. I'll get someone there to take me or I'll call you to come back. He'll be doing some tests, and—well, I'll spare you the gory details."

"Whew. Thanks for that." He left her standing in front of the door.

Instead of walking into the building, she turned toward the dining hall. She wasn't interested in the infirmary. She was looking for a housing unit of sorts. If there had indeed been a hundred eighty implantations, as she read on James's meeting agenda, they'd have to have some facility big enough to house many women. There would have to be a nursery with nurse-mothers, wouldn't there?

The dining hall was quiet at that hour between lunch and dinner. She took a seat, careful to stay out of view of the upper physician's loft in case Dr. De Luca was having an afternoon espresso, and pulled out the campus map. This cluster had eight buildings. Two of the buildings were long and narrow. Could be dorm-style residence halls. But they could also be research labs. A square building sat catty-corner to what she thought were the dorms. Possibly the nursery? Then there was the dining hall, the infirmary, and three L-shaped buildings. She'd start at the two rectangles. She wasn't sure she'd have access—

"Sister Layla?"

She yelped and fumbled her map.

"I'm so sorry! I didn't mean to startle you." A young brunette flopped onto the chair opposite her. "You probably don't remember me. I'm Caitlyn Riggs—oops, I mean Caitlyn." She closed her eyes and whispered. "I despise my poisoned life."

Layla repressed a grin of pride.

"You did my intake a year and a half ago? I achieved purification last year. You facilitated my ceremony."

Layla didn't remember. She'd facilitated a ceremony every week until recently, and every one of them was a blur. "Of course! How are you?"

"Great. I just received my second implantation."

Layla glanced down at Caitlyn's flat stomach.

"Oh, well, I'm not showing yet. Three months. Are you a carrier, too?"

A hot blush crawled up her face. One of her own intakes was a carrier, one who'd already delivered a pure child. The girl looked to be barely twenty, and she knew more about the program than Layla did.

"Yes." She smiled graciously. "I wanted to contribute to the vision of the Colony. It was a difficult decision, given my workload, but I felt it was important while I'm still young enough to carry a child." It was sanctimonious bullshit, but she couldn't resist.

"God, you're amazing," Caitlyn breathed.

And that's when the idea hit her. "I was supposed to have a tour of the facility so I could provide a status report to the council, but it looks like my tour guide has had to cancel. I don't suppose you might have some time this afternoon to show me around the campus?" Even if Caitlyn didn't, she wouldn't say no to a Colony leader. Respect for the hierarchy was the Colony's greatest strength.

"Oh!" Caitlyn squealed and clapped her hands. "I'd be honored."

Layla grinned. "I only have one request. We need to keep this tour on the down-low. No introductions or attention. I want to see the true carrier environment, just everyday life. Deal?"

Caitlyn positively blossomed under the implication of trust. "Deal."

Layla followed Caitlyn down the stone path toward the residences, past a meditation group of six young women in various stages of pregnancy. They looked like teenagers. Layla felt so old. So tired. So behind.

"...recently repaved this path," Caitlyn was saying. "One woman tripped and fell right onto her stomach. She was six months. Thank god the baby was fine, but you should have seen the panic among the medical personnel. She was practically a celebrity."

"I'll bet." Given the reaction of the front gate guard, carriers seemed to be revered as heroes here. "What's the current carrier count here at the moment? Do you know?"

Caitlyn looked to the heavens as she tried to mentally calculate. "I'm gonna say like sixty? During my first gestation, we had eighty or so. But the last few months, a whole bunch have been displaced."

"Interesting." Layla nodded a bit too emphatically as she recovered from the mental shock of that number. Eighty carriers. That was an awfully big secret for James to keep from her. Did he think she'd never find out?

They arrived at the first residence hall building, and Caitlyn keyed them in the front door. A female security guard—the first one Layla had seen at the Colony—sat at a desk, and Layla felt a rush of panic.

The guard looked up from her computer screen and gave them a wave. "Morning, ladies."

They scooted to the right and down a hall.

"What do you mean," Layla asked casually, "that they were displaced?"

"They didn't pass the psychosocial testing sequence. It's this new thing they're doing." Caitlyn opened a door and stepped aside. "Here's my room."

It was nothing like the inductee housing in the purification program, which was little more than a box with a twin bed and a toilet. This was a luxury suite in comparison. A state-of-the-art kitchenette with all the amenities waited comfortably behind an overstuffed chair with a throw blanket folded over the arm. Along the opposite wall stretched a queen-size bed, a dresser, and—

"Wow, is that a Jacuzzi?" She instantly regretted her surprised tone.

"Yeah, but the water only goes to ninety-eight degrees."

Layla herself didn't have a Jacuzzi in her cabin. She stepped back into the hall to mask her envy, her mouth set in a hard line. "It looks like the program is treating you well. That's great to see."

Caitlyn's face fell. "Oh, I didn't mean … I'm not complaining about the water. I—"

Layla waited patiently while Caitlyn formed a proper apology.

"Sister Layla, believe me, I am so grateful every day to be here. All of us are. Our calling is the most important within the Colony—the whole world, really. Please forgive my insolence." She dropped her gaze to the floor.

Layla allowed a moment to pass. "Of course. Now, you were telling me about the displaced carriers?" She continued down the hallway toward a back entrance.

"Oh, yeah. Well, we have these tests we gotta do every day. Personality tests, like inkblots and stuff like that. And intelligence tests. And once a week, we do the psychosocial tests. They're the worst."

"Why?"

"They attach all these electrodes to us to monitor our vitals, and then we have to just sit in a room alone with a stranger and have this completely awkward conversation, like 'What's your favorite food?' or 'Did you ever have a pet?' Then we talk for a couple of minutes, and depending on our vitals, we either pass or fail. Sometimes they'll bring in someone else, and we gotta do the whole conversation part again. I just try to be as friendly as possible, but who knows what they're looking for."

Personality assessments and intelligence tests were conducted in her program, as well, but this psychosocial test was new to her.

"This one time, I was alone with this hateful woman. I asked her what her favorite food was, and you know she said?"

"What?"

"Babies. Can you believe that? She said, 'Babies. Have you ever tried them? I like them with ketchup.' I know she was just trying to be mean or scare me or something, but that's totally rude, don't you think?"

Layla could feel her eyebrows draw together. In her experience at the Colony, nothing was spontaneous. That hateful answer was intentional. What could they have been hoping to evoke from this young woman?

"I had to take deep breaths because I was scared I'd failed," Caitlyn said. "I think they want us to be calm and not get angry or upset."

They passed a small yoga studio, where a dozen or so girls rolled back on an exercise body ball.

"If they do fail, where do the displaced carriers go?" Layla slowed her pace to peer at the contented faces of the women. What a life.

"Um, I don't know."

Salvage. Don't fuck up, Catie, or you'll end up in salvage.

Layla's head spun back around. "What did you say?" Profanity was forbidden in the presence of a Colony leader.

Caitlyn looked at her feet. "I said, I don't know where they go."

Layla gaped at her. Had Caitlyn said *salvage*? Had she imagined it?

Caitlyn scooted ahead, continuing the tour. "Um, this is our testing center. There are a bunch of different rooms with different equipment and stuff. It's closed today because we only do testing on Mondays and Thursdays."

"Is it unlocked? Can we walk through?"

"Yeah. It's pretty boring, though. The waiting room is all we can see. The testing rooms are locked. Only the technicians can open them." Caitlyn badged them inside. "The rooms have no windows, only a mirror that's way too high up to even see your reflection in. I don't know why they did that. Maybe it makes the room feel larger or something."

The outer door opened into an unimpressive waiting area with oversize chairs and a water cooler. Both opposite corners opened to a long sunny hallway. One side was covered in windows to the outside of the building. The other side was lined with doors evenly spaced about six feet apart. That made sense: a central observation room with viewing into each of the testing rooms made the job easy for one or two observers. Her eyes drifted to the high ceiling. Not a full two stories, but certainly one and a half.

"Where's the staircase?" Layla didn't realize she'd asked the question aloud until Caitlyn answered.

"Oh, there isn't a second floor. It's just these rooms."

Layla kept walking until she reached a door marked MEDICAL PERSONNEL ONLY. Her badge certainly wouldn't open this door, but James's supervisor key code would, and she'd seen him use it enough times to have memorized the number long ago. Being the boss's girl had its perks.

She had just reached out to press the numbers when she heard Caitlyn behind her.

"Oh hello, Dr. De Luca."

20

Nick parked the pickup in the El Pueblo parking lot, threw his backpack over one shoulder, and hurried down North Alameda Street. God, he hated LA. He couldn't fathom why all these people chose to live in this grimy, overpopulated city, when the desert southwest, with its wide-open space and big sky, was just a few hours away. Like most inner cities, the streets of LA were clothed in trash. Even wealthy cities had been crushed by the economic depression, and there simply weren't enough resources for regular garbage collection. Garbage cans overflowed, and the wind dragged paper cups, plastic bottles, and Styrofoam containers down the unkempt cobblestone sidewalks and gutters.

Union Bagel Shop was barely wider than the door he stepped through to enter. He wiped the sweat off his forehead with the back of his wrist and appraised the customers. Even though it had been a few years since he'd seen Jordan Jennings, he was certain he couldn't miss the guy: rail-thin and slouchy, like someone who always felt self-conscious about his height, and that mop of hair, which Nick was sure had never seen a pair of scissors or even a comb.

But not one of seven customers at the small tables resembled Jordan Jennings.

"May I help you?" asked an Indian girl from behind the counter. She looked to be fifteen or sixteen, and he didn't have the heart to say he was just waiting for someone.

"Yeah, I'll … uh…" He lifted his eyes to the menu above her, as if expecting it to offer something that every other bagel shop in the world didn't. That guy better not have stood him up, because he had no way to call him back to chew him out.

An older man stepped up next to the girl—her father, maybe, who spoke with a strong accent. "Sir, we have fresh batch of bagels, just from oven. Come this way. Very delicious." He opened the waist-high swinging door and motioned Nick inside. "Fresh bagels, come take your choice."

"It's okay, I'm just waiting—"

The man caught his wrist. "Please, sir."

Confused, Nick followed him through the kitchen and out a back door that led into a drab cement hallway. The man spoke quietly, even though they were alone. "Dr. Jennings is waiting for you. His lab is at the end of the hall, down one flight of stairs."

He wanted to roll his eyes. Was the drama necessary? The stairwell was grungy, with filthy aluminum stairs and a handrail he refused to touch, and when he reached the bottom of the stairs, he expected to enter a basement parking garage. But as he flung open the door, he nearly swallowed his teeth. He'd stepped into another world.

The wide low-ceilinged room, maybe the size of an indoor tennis court, was brightly lit by fluorescent lights. Three long black countertops in the center of the room held machines and robotic equipment—Nick could only assume they were genetic research instruments—lined up end to end. The room smelled like bleach and fast food.

"Hey, man, thanks for coming." Jordan Jennings sidled up carrying a large soda cup from McDonald's. He didn't offer a handshake, but Nick wasn't surprised.

Nick nodded toward the room. "What is this place?"

"This is my lab." Jordan's long dreads bobbed up and down proudly. "Guess you could say we've gone underground, huh?" He laughed at his joke. "Come on, this way. Meet my friends."

Nick followed him into what looked like a college dorm common area, with two beat-up sofas, two unmatched recliners, a coffee table covered in McDonald's bags, and of course a foosball table.

A man and a woman sat waiting.

Jordan gestured to the woman, who looked to be in her late twenties. A long pink scar stretched from her eye to her upper lip. "This is Jenna Wolfe. She's a dog walker by day and in charge of our animal studies by night."

"Hey," she said with a nod.

"Gang fight?" Nick asked as he sank into one of the recliners. He immediately regretted the crass joke.

But Jenna didn't seem even slightly offended or embarrassed. She sat forward, with her elbows on her knees, as if inviting him to have a closer look. "I was mauled by a chimpanzee."

Jesus.

"And this is Abder, computer analyst and hacker extraordinaire. His dad owns the bagel shop and much of what remains of LA."

Abder reached over the coffee table for a firm handshake. "He doesn't just love me for my money. That's what he tells me, anyway."

"So why all this secrecy?" Nick asked. "Why are y'all hiding out?"

"Because if they knew what we're working on, we'd all be dead." Jenna's duchess of doom demeanor was a bit much for Nick.

"Who?"

Jordan made a few swipes on his phone and held it up. "We call them the company, as in 'We've got company.'"

"Or like every conspiracy movie you've ever seen," Abder added.

Nick looked at his watch and moved to the edge of his chair. "Listen, Jordan, I was hoping you had something on the Malloy-Garcia case."

"Huh? The what?"

"You don't remember? Peter Malloy's victims with the spinal ports? The LXR drug?"

Jordan frowned and shoved his phone into Nick's chest. "Brah, look at the picture."

Nick's shoulders drooped. He'd just driven an awfully long way for some new insight into his story. He was tired and hungry. The last thing he needed was a new conspiracy theory. But he took the phone.

The image was an outdoor restaurant filled with people. Jordan leaned back on the arm of the recliner and pointed. "These two here"—a man and a woman wearing business attire sat at a table, deep in conversation—"and these two"—two men. "They hired us to cure the virus. And then they tried to recruit us to join the team."

"To cure *the* virus? The lyssavirus?" Nick felt his mouth go dry, as his eyes flew up to Jordan's face.

"Get this," Jordan said. "About a year and a half ago, when Abder and I were at the Broad, we were approached by some guy who said he was from the NIH to run an analysis on a DNA sample. They were looking for point mutations—specifically, any insertions or deletions that seemed abnormal. We didn't ask questions. You know, a job's a job, and the NIH is a US government-funded research organization."

Nick shook his head. "But that was way before the virus—"

"Wait for it," Jenna said. "He hasn't gotten to the punchline yet."

"So anyway," Jordan continued, "I gave the gig to Abder, and Abder ran the analyses and reported back to his contact at the NIH. Done." He scrolled through his phone again. "Check it out. Time goes by, say five, six months. It was right after we came out of quarantine. I was still in Boston at the Broad, but I flew out to deliver this talk at UCLA. I had this theory that our prime editing platform could kill the virus. Prime editing is all the shit now. You remember how CRISPR worked, right? Don't get me wrong, CRISPR is genius, but what it's best at is snipping, and if your guide RNA doesn't get the scissors to the right spot, the wrong gene could be edited. CRISPR's been known to make huge mistakes like that. But even if it gets to the right spot, you still have to provide the new DNA piece and cross your fingers that it gets installed correctly." He shook his head. "So many ways it can fuck up."

The last time Nick had talked to Jordan, he couldn't stop talking about how CRISPR would change the world. Now he thought it was crap?

Jordan's finger stopped scrolling, and he tossed the phone onto the couch beside him and leaned forward, draping himself over the coffee table. He grabbed two straws from the rubble of plastic cups and laid them in a parallel line, then slotted french fries between them to create what Nick had to assume was a DNA ladder.

"But prime works differently. Instead of chopping out this whole chunk of gene, it just nicks one strand."

Abder handed him a pair of scissors and mumbled to Jenna, "At least he didn't use my basketball shoelaces this time."

Jordan snipped one of the straws. "So one strand is cut like this and the pegRNA, the little helper smart car, comes rolling in and delivers a new DNA segment to attach to the strand, like this." Jordan pulled a ChapStick from his pocket and attached it to the end of the cut piece of straw. "This new bit, the ChapStick, is accepted into the DNA strand, and this old section of straw that's flailing off to the side is removed by the cell machinery. But now you can see that the ChapStick doesn't match the straw on the other side of the ladder. This mismatch has to be resolved, so we send a different RNA smart car to snip the other side." Jordan cut the straw opposite the ChapStick. "And that's it. The cell machinery is triggered to repair the broken strand, and it does that by perfectly matching up with the edited strand." He looked up expectantly at Abder.

"Sorry, man." Abder shrugged.

"I gotcha." Jenna reached into her purse and produced a small tube of Vaseline lip balm. "Best I can do."

Jordan lined up the ChapStick and the Vaseline tube and joined them using a french fry. "And that gives us a perfectly edited DNA strand. No mistakes." He beamed at his kindergarten science diagram.

As much as Nick hated science babble, Jordan did have a way of dumbing it down for the slow-witted likes of himself.

Jordan picked up his phone and continued scrolling through photos. "Anyway, so in my talk, I explained how my programmed gene edits would target the genome of the virus and stop the destruction. The process might've taken several doses over weeks. Problem was, I couldn't get a sample of the virus to run tests with, the cleanup by the government was too thorough."

Nick nodded. After the virus had been released, satellite imagery and drones were used to identify hot spots where the virus had gone on its rampage, killing hundreds at first, then thousands a day. Nations deployed their militaries to the sites in such force, setting up barriers monitored by soldiers with full armor, machine guns, and flame throwers, that by the time the troops cleared out, there wasn't so much as a blade of grass still alive.

"Most genetic research sites had already closed up shop in the wake of the economic collapse, so no one was even asking if the problem could be solved by science. Even though I had a great theory, I couldn't prove—oh, here it is. Yeah."

Jordan held up his phone. It showed a woman in business attire leaning an elbow on a bar table. Based on the angle of the shot, it looked like the picture came from a body cam.

"Not sure I see where this is going," Nick said. "Who's this?"

"She told me she works for a top-secret government organization, and she pulled out a vial of what she said was the viral DNA. She wanted me to test my prime editing theory."

Nick perked up. "Did you do it?"

"Hells yeah, I did. But here's the punch line. I gave it to Abder first to analyze the genetic code, and guess what? Abder recognized it. He has an eye for genetic structure. He pulled the analysis from that original NIH contract, the one from months before, and sure enough, it was nearly identical."

Nick leaned in, his elbows on his now trembling knees. His voice had dropped to barely above a whisper. "Are you telling me the US government had the lyssavirus before it was released? They knew about it?"

"I don't know if they knew what it was, but they definitely had it."

"I knew it!" Nick exclaimed, with a loud clap of his hands. Finally, some real, tangible evidence.

"Tell you what it wasn't, though. It wasn't a lyssavirus." Jordan tied his mop of hair into a man bun and secured it with a rubber band from his wrist, a sign that Jordan was getting serious. "We still don't know what it is. Maybe they don't either."

The gravity of what Jordan was suggesting didn't escape him. If they didn't know what they were dealing with, how would they ever be able to eradicate it?

"So what happened next?" Nick asked.

"We dragged our feet, or at least that's what we wanted them to think. They'd check in, and we'd tell them we were working on it, we were having trouble with uptake, that kind of thing. But we were just trying to buy time, because we wanted to run our own animal studies."

Nick glanced at the duchess of doom, who took a drag off an e-cigarette.

"A couple of weeks go by. Then one morning I walk into work and there are all these guys in suits going through my lab. Government types. My boss comes up to me and says, 'Pack up your office, we're closing.'" Jordan's expression darkened. "There weren't just white collars there, either—cops or maybe military, I'm not sure, carrying loaded rifles like they were holding up the place. They took everything, I mean everything: vials, reagents, flasks… And they took my lab notebook."

"Jesus. Who were they?"

He shrugged. "No one ever told me. I'm not sure my boss even knew. That was the end of the Broad and my lab."

Nick gestured to the lab next door. "I'm guessing that's not the end of your story, though."

Jordan smirked. "A paranoid nutjob like me? A guy who wears a body cam pretty much every day? No freakin' way would I put all my virus in one basket. And my lab notebook—well, my *real* lab notebook"—Jordan reached into his jacket pocket and pulled out a black composition notebook, battered and folded in the middle—"never leaves my person."

Government men with armed military backup. Nick's mind flashed to his apartment. Every thought, every hunch he'd ever had about the origin of the virus was written on a card and hung on his living room wall. The unsettling realization made him reach back to make sure his laptop was still in the bag.

"So what happened after they closed you down? Did they get what they needed?" Nick's mind was already racing through his next steps. He'd have to get names from the NIH. Could Nyla run a forensic analysis to identify the original viral DNA? Maybe he could ID the woman who'd given Jordan the vial. So many leads, so little time.

"They got two vials of my prime-edited CNS stem cells, so yeah."

"But what they didn't get was our animal data, which I had at my lab in Ashland." A wisp of smoke drifted from Jenna's mouth. "And that's unfortunate for them because what we've been seeing is pretty disturbing."

"Something new?"

She glanced at Jordan, who shrugged weakly. Abder was shaking his head, his expression positively bleak.

"Something different? Something even worse?"

Her tone was flat as she pushed herself out of the sofa. "Brace yourself. This is monkey business on a whole new dimension."

21

Layla spun around to see Dr. De Luca and a younger assistant marching toward them.

She was caught.

Dr. De Luca's eyes burned into hers before he shifted his attention to Caitlyn. "Ladies, can I help you with something?"

Caitlyn fumbled for an apology. "Oh, goodness, I'm sorry, I know the testing center is closed, but Sister Layla just wanted to see it, and—"

"Is that so? Layla, *cucciola*, you should have called me. I would've been happy to show you our facilities."

Layla's thoughts raced for an excuse, but none came.

The doctor tilted his head, waiting for a reply, his forced smile not masking his scowl.

Screw him. She glared right back. "Well, that's kind of you to offer, but I didn't want to trouble you. You're obviously quite busy with such an expansive program. And Caitlyn's been a terrific tour guide." She put an arm around Caitlyn's shoulder. "Who knew so much work had gone into the carrier program?"

They locked eyes. Layla could feel Caitlyn looking back and forth between them, breathlessly anticipating who would break first.

"Indeed. Now, you're supposed to be on bed rest, yes?" His eyes never wavered as he addressed Caitlyn. "Cucciola, please escort Layla back to the infirmary. Get a driver to take her home."

"Of course," Caitlyn murmured.

Layla broke the deadlock and marched out of the testing center. This would certainly get back to James, but she didn't care. It was time for a confrontation. She glanced over her shoulder to make sure Dr. De Luca wasn't watching before heading back up the path away from the infirmary. She had no intention of leaving until she learned everything there was to learn.

"Uh, Sister Layla?" Caitlyn was scurrying behind her. "The infirmary is this way."

"No, the nursery."

"Sorry?" Caitlyn skipped to catch up.

"The nursery. Where do the babies go after they're born?"

"Oh. We don't see them when they're born. The doctors take them straight away."

Layla halted. "What?"

"They go to their forever homes."

Forever homes. They were taken out of the Colony? Hers, too? They would whisk her baby away to some stranger in the poisoned world? No, this wasn't what she'd expected, at all. Would she not get some time with him? To hold him and count all his tiny fingers and toes?

"Sister Layla? Are you okay?"

Oh god. Had they lied about her first delivery? Perhaps the baby had been born alive. Healthy. And just … swept away…

Well, where is he? Can I hold him yet?

I'm sorry, Lay, James had replied, his eyes downcast.

She'd known something was wrong because James never dropped his gaze. He believed in direct eye contact in all communications, good or bad.

Why not? What are they doing to him? Is something wrong?

He didn't make it. I'm sorry.

In the moment before grief overwhelmed her, she'd gaped at him, trying to read the emotion on his face. It hadn't been anguish or loss; she'd known that even then. Only now did she realize what that look was: guilt. Guilt for lying to her face, for knowing she'd feel like a failure for months. He'd always known she wouldn't get the see the baby. He'd just been too gutless to tell her. And he would no doubt pull the same move this time, allowing her to wallow in sorrow for months, knowing it had been her last chance.

She had to get back. She would march straight into James's office and confront him. How could he do this to her? How could he lie to her about something as important as the death of her baby?

Caitlyn's face materialized in front of Layla's, steeped in concern. "Do you need me to get medical? I can run over—"

"No!"

Caitlyn flinched as if she'd slapped her.

"I mean no, I'm fine. I'm sorry. I just realized how late it is. I promised Brother James I'd have this council presentation ready tonight."

"Oh, I'm so sorry for keeping you. Let me walk to the infirmary, as Dr. De Luca—"

"No need. I have a driver. But thank you, uh, Caitlyn. Really, so generous of you to take the time to show me around."

Layla hustled back toward the cafeteria. As hard as she tried to hold in her feelings, her face twisted, and angry tears welled in her eyes. She palmed them away and dialed Michael.

In a voice much too cheerful, she said, "Hey! I'm done. Any chance I can get a lift back home?"

As she waited for him, she tried to clear her head. Her brain felt stuck, like a vinyl record on an old-time record player, repeating the same lyric over and over with a sickening screech in between. Everything she believed was a great big lie. All this time, she'd stupidly thought she was the only carrier. Why would a Colony as big and powerful as this implant a single carrier? How could she have been so naive?

But somehow everything she saw and learned today paled in comparison to what James had done. The man she loved, the one person she trusted implicitly had lied to her about their very own baby.

The van pulled up and she climbed into the passenger seat, turning toward the window so Michael couldn't see her red blotchy face.

"I heard you needed a ride." It wasn't Michael's laid-back California voice.

She whipped around. The narrow face and eyebrow bar were unmistakable.

Eric Ortiz, EGNX Security.

22

"When that top-secret government official handed me that vial of whole blood, it was like Christmas morning," Jordan said over his shoulder as he led Nick down the hall. He held the door open for Nick, Jenna, and Abder.

Nick whistled. He counted eight computers, each with three raised monitors.

"We crunch a lot of data." Jenna crossed the room and parked in front of a computer beneath a poster that read SAVE THE RAINFOREST above a picture of a monkey swinging from a tree. Ironic.

"So back to the sample." Jordan pulled a chair from one of the nearby computers and gestured for Nick to sit. "We ran a whole blood sequencing panel to find genetic mutations without naturally occurring polymorphs."

"Meaning we were looking for anything that didn't seem human." Abder perched on the edge of a desk.

"Jesus. That's possible? Humans with nonhuman genes?"

"You wouldn't believe what's possible nowadays with genetic engineering," Abder said.

"Wordski." Jordan's dreads bounced as he swung around and opened an Excel file. A long list of gene names filled the screen, and he slid the cursor to one section. "These here in orange, these are the target genes, the genetic mutations we had to rebuild. They're all related to neural activity."

There must have been fifteen or so genes, all with names Nick had never heard of. "So did it work? Were you able to fix the mutations?"

"Technically, yeah, but that was only in the lab. *In vitro.* Our next step was to create an injectable to test in animal models." Jordan sucked in the remaining Coke from his cup. "We started with mice, but the uptake was poor. Even though we share ninety percent of our DNA with mice, brain cells are a bit different, so we moved into primates."

A screech from across the room made Nick swerve around. Jenna's monitor showed a cage filled with monkeys.

"Over here," she called.

Nick crossed the room to look over her shoulder.

"This is the cynomolgus monkey model," Jenna said. "We were lucky enough to get them cheap from a pharmaceutical company that used them for drug testing."

On the monitor, ten or twelve monkeys were swinging across a caged jungle so elaborate it could've been the movie set for *Tarzan.*

"First, we transfused them with the mutated viral DNA and isolated them for a week. Then we gave them IV infusions of our cocktail of prime-edited genes. Sure enough, the viral genes were repaired, and the cynos' behavior normalized."

"But here's where it gets weird," Jordan said.

She nodded. "Watch this." She clicked to video playback of a smaller cage. "These are our three subjects. At this point, they'd been together in this cage for a week. Pretty boring. No interaction. No grooming, no gesturing. They hardly even exercised."

She fast-forwarded the recording and stopped. All three monkeys lay on the floor of the cage. They looked dead.

"Sleeping?" Nick asked hopefully.

"That's not how primates sleep," Jenna said.

The video continued with no movement from the animals. A minute later, he saw Jenna arriving in front of the cage door, carrying a bucket. She dropped it to the floor with a crash. The monkeys didn't move.

"Fuck!" Her voice echoed in the large room. "Jordan! Hurry!"

She fumbled with a key, swung the cage door open, and hurried inside. As soon as she dropped to her knees to examine the bodies, all three monkeys sprang to their feet. There was a flurry of activity as she sat back on her heels, obviously stunned.

In less than fifteen seconds, the monkeys were outside the cage, after slamming the door and locking her inside.

Jenna paused the video and pointed to two of the monkeys. "You probably missed it, but while these two were distracting me, Zen—over here—unclipped my tranquilizer gun and pulled it from the holster. I didn't even notice, not until…"

She started the video again. Jenna got up and moved toward the door. The big monkey she called Zen held up the gun and pointed it at her. The other two monkeys took up places on either side of him.

"Jesus Christ!" It was just like an episode of *Planet of the Apes*.

A door slammed off camera, and all three monkeys turned toward the sound. Jordan's mop of hair flashed past the camera and out of sight again.

"Don't scare them! Don't scare them!" Jenna shouted. "They might charge if—"

Zen gently laid the tranquilizer gun on the floor, and all three monkeys sat down in unison.

A ball of uneasiness and confusion settled like a kettlebell in Nick's gut.

Jenna looked back at him. "You can't see it in the video, but when Jordan came into the hallway, they all gave a play face, which looks like a human smile. It's a show of submission."

On the video, Jordan slowly opened the cage door. They didn't need luring or coaxing. They knuckled their way back inside and swung up to the highest plank.

Jordan spoke up. "No one knows primate behavior like Jenna. She's been working with them for fifteen years. We've analyzed all the tapes up until this incident, and we're dumbfounded. Somehow, these cynos managed to plan and coordinate a—a prank, and as far as we can tell, they never overtly communicated with each other. No gestures, no facial expressions, no sounds."

Nick wondered if he was being set up. "Are you suggesting they used some sort of telepathy?"

He expected an emphatic no, but not one of them answered. He found that unsettling for a group of scientists.

"I don't get it," he said. "If they wanted to escape, why didn't they go? Why didn't they try?"

"I don't believe they wanted to escape," Jenna said.

"Then what?"

"I believe they were giving us a message."

"Like 'We're smarter than you think'?"

She shook her head impatiently. "It's not the trick I keep thinking about. It's the dart gun. Zen knew it was a weapon, and he could've shot me, but he didn't. He was showing me that he had the upper hand."

"Over you?" It really was *Planet of the Apes*.

"Maybe I'm crazy, but I think it was an expression of dominance," she said. "Superiority."

"But not using primate symbolism," Jordan added. "Using human symbolism."

While Nick's mind was racing to figure out how this could possibly fit with a cure for the virus, Jenna was clicking out of the video and standing up.

"Some time has passed since that incident," she said. "I go inside the cage to feed them and clean up. I talk to them, like usual. They watch me carefully, but there haven't been any other tricks. No threats or aggression. But a week ago, we made a new observation. Come on."

They left the computer lab and walked down a hallway that brought them to a long observation window. Inside, two monkeys sat along the back wall, their heads down and eyes closed, apparently napping. A third monkey on a raised platform swung down to the floor as soon as the humans arrived. The others climbed to their feet and looked up.

"Give them a wave," Jenna said.

Nick did as he was told. All three of them waved back. God, it was strange.

"Do something else."

Nick did the first thing that came to his mind, the famous arm gestures of the Village People's "YMCA."

All three monkeys mimicked him.

"Holy Houdini, Batman." He couldn't help smiling. It was remarkable.

"In college, I worked with chimps using sign language," Jenna said. "It took months to teach them a simple gesture. But watch this."

She held up one hand, her fingers moving quickly through the American Sign Language alphabet. As soon as she stopped, the monkeys imitated her—all twenty-six letters.

"So what are you concluding?" Nick asked in a hushed voice. Maybe the monkeys could hear him. Maybe they could read his mind. "That they're more intelligent than humans?"

"I wish that were all." Jenna's voice lowered. "The thing is, this is a one-way polycarbonate observational window. The other side is mirrored."

23

Layla gaped at Eric Ortiz, unable to speak.

He turned back and appraised her. "Glad I could be of service. You shouldn't be walking quite so much."

He pulled out of the driveway and toward the long desert road.

She clutched her bag tightly on her lap and stared at the dashboard. Where was Michael? Why was this man answering Michael's phone? She was too afraid to ask.

"You know, I'll bet you're feeling tired and heavy, so far along in your pregnancy." His voice was low. Dreamy. "But I for one think a woman is never sexier than when she's pregnant. You have that glow. Everything about you is full of life."

The hair on the nape of her neck bristled.

"Are you planning to breastfeed?"

She could feel him staring at her chest.

He chuckled softly. "Oh, I'm sorry, that's probably none of my business."

Another minute passed.

"I just have to ask. I can't help it. Can I put my hand on your belly? Feel the baby?"

"No!" She finally snapped out of her terrified silence. She grabbed her bag tighter and faced him.

Michael startled. "Why are you yelling?"

Pain stabbed her in the middle of the forehead. Confused, she groped for the door handle.

"Stop!" Michael swung the car to the side of the road and hit the brakes, just as she flung the door open and stumbled out of the van. "Layla!"

He hopped out from behind the wheel and ran around the car.

"Stay away!" She scooped up a rock.

He put his hands up and stopped a safe distance away.

The thundering ache between her eyes made her drop the rock and press her palms to her eyes. She bent over, worried she might vomit.

It's Michael. It's not the guard. It's just Michael.

A minute later, she felt his arm around her. "Hey, what's up with you? Do you want me to take you to the infirmary?"

"N-no. I'm okay. It's … I have these migraines lately. I just … I'm so sorry."

He helped her back into the van and jogged around to the driver's side. "Are you sure you don't want to see the doctor? I'm worried about you."

She was still trembling, but she managed to steady her voice. "No, no. She knows about the headaches. It's just pregnancy business as usual. Her recommendation is to sleep it off. I'll go straight to bed."

They drove in silence. Layla's head still throbbed, and she considered trying some meditative chanting, but the thought—no, the feeling, the physical sensation—of Eric Ortiz sitting right next to her, driving the van, was too vivid. She could still smell him.

What was it about that guy that upset her so much?

Thankfully, Harmony was gone by the time she arrived home. Layla crawled under the blanket, raised the back of the bed, and opened her laptop. She clicked on the bookmark she saved: Eric Ortiz, EGNX Security.

She'd stared at his image so many times and for so long that it was burned into her brain. The tiny scar on his long forehead, just over his furry eye bar. The lump on the bridge of his nose, a little left of center. He'd probably broken it at some point. His mouth was pressed in a hard line, as the Colony required ID pictures without a smile, but she could still remember his teeth. Long front teeth that matched his long face, yellower than the mouthful of squirming white maggots crawling over his lips.

Can I feel the baby?

Sure. In a minute.

And the stench. The rot that came from his insides when he leaned in to speak to her.

You're barefoot. I should walk you back and help you clean up.

His voice whipped through her head like a sandstorm, clear as day, then wiped away in a haze of dust.

She stared at the face on the screen another minute, willing it to mutate into the dead, decaying face she could still so clearly envision. She needed to see it. To make it real. But he remained maggot free, his skin still attached to his face. His wide-eyed surprised look was nothing more than the expression of someone not used to being photographed.

The pounding between her ears had softened to a pulse. She closed her laptop. This was all illogical. She was behaving like a mental patient.

She picked up her phone and dialed 911. Campus security.

"How can I direct your call?"

"May I speak with Eric Ortiz, please?"

She'd casually thank him for stopping by to check up on her. It was very considerate of him.

"One moment."

She picked at the scabs on her palms while she waited. *Her blood, not his.*

"I'm sorry, ma'am, Mr. Ortiz isn't answering his line. Can I give him a message?"

In the pit of her stomach, she'd known he wouldn't be there, yet the operator's words still shook her, the way James's words had shaken her after her C-section. *He didn't make it.* It was a feeling of impending doom.

"No, thank you. I'll try again another time."

She dropped the phone onto the bed next to her and rolled over. A sour taste filled her mouth, yet she couldn't seem to swallow. The fetus squirmed inside her, as it had been doing far more frequently lately, reminding her once again that its time was almost up. She lifted her shirt and studied her pale white belly as it stretched, forming grotesque, distorted shapes, testing the limits of her skin elasticity as if an alien monster were preparing to burst through. Was her skin strong enough to hold it in? Would the dark tendrils of veins that extended across her belly and down her sides rupture, filling her abdomen with blood?

She felt imprisoned by this creature that had invaded her body and hijacked her internal organs. She was nothing but a life support system for it, useless and worthless in her own right. Perhaps this was her destiny. She breathed deeply, submitting to her subservient rank. She was but a humble carrier, one of hundreds. A vessel for an evolved human.

And in that moment, her mind opened and the recollection of that night with Eric Ortiz flooded her like a tsunami. The splashes of memories, the fragments of their conversation that had haunted her for two days fell into place like dominos.

Her eyes flew open.

"Oh god, what have I done?" she whispered. She sank into her bed and curled into a ball.

The earth will be purified.

It was all over. They would be coming for her soon, and when they discovered what a monster she was, they'd force her outside the Colony walls, where her lungs would fill with poisonous air. The poison would travel through her arteries, through her extremities, and back to her heart, which would instantly turn black and stop beating. And then the wolves would shred her corpse, just as they had shredded Eric Ortiz in her dream. It had been a dream, right?

Layla's belly tightened as a dull ache spread from the front of her lower abdomen to her back. She stretched her legs, taking some pressure off her diaphragm, and took in a slow, deep breath. This wasn't the first false contraction she'd had, but it seemed so aptly timed that she wondered if the fetus was trying to deliver a message: *You are my host, and I need you safe and sound.*

She rubbed her hand over the hard lump that jutted from her side—a foot, maybe. "The work of the Colony is the only priority, isn't that right?" The foot bump disappeared. "We have an important mission to fulfill."

And right now, her only priority was to make the problem disappear.

24

Nick took a seat next to Jordan as he clicked through his computer for the file.

"They must've tracked my phone," Jordan said, "because they found me here in LA when I was hiding out at the university. I got a cryptic text asking me to meet them at this restaurant."

He opened a video file. The camera work was a bit shaky, but Nick watched as lanky Jordan sat down at an outdoor table with the man and woman he'd pointed out earlier. The traffic noise and sounds of downtown LA obscured any chance of hearing the conversation between Jordan and the recruiters.

"Jenna took the video," Jordan said. "I figured if they were top-secret government people, they'd pat me down for a mic or something, so I didn't wear my body cam."

Nick had always prided himself on his interviewing skills. He was patient; he took time to build rapport, to allow the subject or source a moment to get comfortable. But not this time. Right now, he just wanted to shake the story out of Jordan. "What did they say?"

"They gave me a really hard sell. It was insulting. They tried to convince me that if I ever wanted to work in the field of genetics again, I needed to hear them out."

"And?"

"And I was like no way, forget it. That's not how I work."

Nick pointed to the video. In it, Jordan hopped up, pushed in his chair, and moved toward the exit. "That's all? Where'd you go next?"

"Nowhere, it turns out."

Two men at another table sprang up to intercept him. After a verbal exchange and lots of frustrated body language, Jordan returned to the table with the recruiters.

Nick wrung his hands like a junkie waiting for a fix. "And?"

"The dudes were actually very polite. They asked me to please continue the discussion, to hear 'em out, so I went back."

"Well, who do they work for?"

Jordan shrugged. "They stuck with the top-secret story, but they softened their pitch and tried to bribe me with a fully equipped lab and everything I needed, including the virus. Human subjects."

Nick recoiled. He couldn't imagine voluntarily being anywhere in the vicinity of the virus.

"I was tempted, not gonna lie, but in the end I told them I was getting out of genetics research. Wanted to open my own DNA analysis shop and call it Jordan Genes. Get it? Like the designer jeans?"

Nick was distracted by movement on the screen. "What's that? What's she doing?"

"She wrote a phone number on a piece of paper. Too top-secret for business cards."

"Wait. Back that up, like five seconds."

Abder leaned in and took over.

Nick watched closely as the woman slid a sleek leather folio from her bag. The glint of metallic lettering in one corner of the cover flashed in the noon sun. "Did you notice what was printed on her folio?"

Jordan shrugged. "Her initials?"

"Hang on." Abder paused the video and zoomed in until the folio filled the screen. He opened Photoshop, dragged the image over, and opened the sharpen tool.

"They're all computer wizzes in India," Jordan said with a wink.

"I'm not Indian, asshole, I'm Egyptian." Abder brushed his cursor over the letters.

Nick's heartbeat picked up as the blurry letters became clear.

EGNX. The same goddamned organization responsible for the LXR drugs. Responsible for the death of Peter Malloy. Framing him for blowing up Vitapura. Now responsible for the virus. Small motherfucking world.

Nick spun around. "We need to find those recruiters."

25

The afternoon sun was low on the horizon as Layla turned the corner to start the steep walk up the hill to the security building, her armpits already damp. She jolted when she heard Mia's voice.

"Layla? Where on earth are you going?" Mia jogged to catch up with her. "I was just coming over to challenge you to a game of cribbage."

Damn it. "I was just going for a walk."

"Okay. Well then, I'll walk with you. You shouldn't be moving around so much."

Layla whirled around to face her friend. She and Mia had been as close as sisters ever since her purification. They'd never once argued. She knew every one of Mia's secrets and vice versa. They'd always supported each other.

"I'd rather be alone," Layla said, trying to mask the edge in her voice. "I have a lot on my mind."

"That's what friends are for. Come on. Let's walk this way so you don't have to climb the hill."

"No, Mia, really. I just want to be alone."

Mia pursed her lips. "Is it James? Are you in a fight?"

"No—"

"Is it about the GS-4 thing? Listen, if it's bothering you that much, I can talk to him. You're probably going crazy at home. The bitterness can build up when you're all by yourself, and…"

Mia's voice seemed to swell with each word until Layla heard the snap inside her head, followed by the eruption of fierce heat from inside her gut.

"Get the fuck out of my way and leave me alone!" Her hands flew up on their own accord and shoved.

Mia stumbled and landed on her backside, sending up a puff of dust. She blinked rapidly up at Layla, her mouth falling open. Layla didn't move to help or offer an apology. She simply went on her way up the hill, toward the security building.

The long walk gave her time to come down from her fit of anger and feel remorseful for pushing Mia to the ground. She'd call later and apologize. But right now, she needed to focus on her story.

A blast of blessedly cool air hit her as she passed through the revolving doors. She approached the security reception desk, a somber look on her face.

"Oh, hello! What can I do for you, Sister Layla?"

"I'm afraid we have a situation on my campus. I need to have a word with Mr. Aroyo."

Several minutes later, an imposing figure in the uniform of what looked like a military general strode through the double doors into the reception area, approaching without so much as a smile. She'd never met the man, and James had described him as formidable but fair. She was certain he knew who she was, but he didn't bother with a proper introduction. He scowled at her, as if she were interrupting his important work.

She couldn't lose her nerve now. She lifted her chin. "I have a situation, and I need to review the security camera files of my inductee housing and the surrounding area for the last seven days."

"I'm afraid that's not possible. Security files are confidential." He pivoted.

"The situation may involve inappropriate behavior from one of your guards toward several young women."

He halted and scanned the open reception area. Without looking back, he barked, "This way."

Perfect. The Colony had a zero-tolerance policy for any behavior deemed disrespectful. It included physical aggression, bullying, and of course, sexual harassment.

He led her down a hall to the corner office and closed the door behind her. He leaned back against his desk and crossed his arms over his chest. "What kind of inappropriate behavior?"

He didn't offer her a seat, but she took one anyway. She leaned back and touched her fingertips together, a relaxed and confident posture she'd seen James assume a million times.

"That's what I'm trying to figure out. Until I have evidence supporting the accusations I've been hearing from some of my young female inductees, I'd rather not formally press charges."

"Evidence of…?"

"Because if what I'm hearing is true, it will not reflect well on the security organization chosen to protect us from the poisoned world," she continued, "nor on the Colony as a whole. For the time being, I've asked those involved to kindly keep quiet until my investigation is complete. My hope is that this situation can be resolved quickly and quietly. But first I need the facts."

Her voice remained steady, and for once she felt in control. Capable.

He was clearly taking this more seriously now. "We don't have a procedure for civilians to review video footage. Eugenesis has strict regulations concerning privacy."

She pushed herself out of the chair. "I assume that means you're unwilling to accommodate my request. In that case, I'll have to move forward with a formal complaint. Once that happens, I imagine dozens of additional complaints from other young women will emerge—you know how quickly rumors spread around here—and we'll have a full-blown #MeToo movement on our hands. The council will not be happy to know that you refused to cooperate so we could keep this under the radar. They don't like to be burdened with administrative problems."

She hesitated long enough for him to respond. He might call her bluff; James would never let an issue like this climb all the way to the council. But perhaps he didn't know James like she did.

His jaw tightened. "Well then, the files are in the control room. Knock yourself out."

***

Layla leaned back in her chair and took in the expansive wall of videos in front of her: forty monitors in an eight-by-five rectangle, each switching views every ten seconds or so. A thick-set surveillance guard sat at a workstation next to her, a bag of potato chips open next to his keyboard. He'd been kind enough to show her the computer folders containing the last seven days of videos, organized by date, time, and camera number but gave her no additional guidance on how to find the specific views she was looking for.

She rolled her chair back to get a better look at the entire wall of screens. The views and angles appeared random, but it only took her a couple of minutes to recognize the pattern. Each view change appeared to be a different cluster of the campus.

She waited for the view to cycle around to her cluster. Her eyes moved from screen to screen, back and forth, up and down, as her brain began categorizing the views: outdoor versus indoor shots, views with a sun glare, cameras pointed at a path, views of building entrances. She pushed her chair back a little further, her eyes bouncing around the monitors. Another cycle back to her campus. It was like building a puzzle. Her mind was clear, her vision laser-focused.

The surveillance guard's chair groaned as he shifted position, and she could feel him watching her intently, but she didn't care. She was on the verge of finishing the puzzle. Her eyes darted to each screen as she followed the mental path. Monitors eight, thirteen, twenty-two, three, thirty-seven, twenty-nine, six. That was her walk from her house to the recruiting center and into her intake room. She ran a path from the infirmary to the purge room and back to the cafeteria.

"Ha!"

"What on earth are you doing?"

She turned to the guard, eyes wide, grinning. She'd mapped the entire cluster through the lenses of forty cameras in a matter of minutes. How? She had no idea. She dropped the grin and shrugged. "Just getting the lay of the land." She was sorry she'd aroused his curiosity. She needed to work privately. She kept her eyes on the monitors until he swiveled away from her and powered on his tablet.

Time to go to work. She opened the folder from Saturday, hours 00:00–04:00, Camera 8, and fast-forwarded until two figures emerged from the dusk, one in white. A pregnant ghost.

Mr. Ortiz! One moment!

Layla watched him turn back toward her. There was no audio, but his voice rang out in her head.

Sister Layla, you're barefoot. I should walk you back and help you clean up.

No, I'm fine, she replied. *You mentioned wolves making their way onto the campus. I believe I know how they're getting inside. Can I show you? I'd like to know what you think.*

The two figures, herself and Eric Ortiz, moved off-screen.

Layla tilted her head just enough to ensure her office mate wasn't looking over her shoulder. With the mouse, she right clicked the video and selected Send to Trash. Then she opened the trash folder and selected Delete Permanently.

She glanced sideways again and opened the folder for camera 12. She scrolled through until the same two figures appeared, moving away from campus.

Are you planning to breastfeed? he asked. *You know it's the most important thing a woman can do for her baby.*

Mmm, maybe. Here. It's right over here.

Again, the two figures moved off the screen, and again, she deleted the video. Beyond that point, they'd walked out of the range of the cameras. There was nothing more to delete. She closed her eyes and lay back against the chair, warmth washing through her as she replayed the rest of the scene in her mind.

The light of the full moon lit the path, but Layla knew the way well enough even without the moonlight. This was one of her favorites walks with James. But this walk was different. She had only one reason to be out here.

He is poison. He is the plague. He will be purged. The earth will be purified.

The sharp gravel felt like shards of glass beneath her feet, but she carried on without so much as a tentative step until veering off onto a hard dirt trail. The divots of soft, sticky mud there cooled her inflamed soles. It was cold that night, colder than most nights, and she fought to keep her teeth from chattering.

"I just have to ask—I can't help it," Ortiz said. "Can I put my hand on your belly? Feel the baby?"

"Sure, in a minute. We're almost there."

They reached the canyon cliff. It was one of her favorite places on the whole campus. She and James called it their bench. They'd spent countless hours here, their feet dangling over the edge, talking about their future. This was where they'd first kissed. Where they'd fallen in love.

She gazed out over the shadowy canyon. So majestic. Magical.

She took a step down onto a flat rock with a slight overhang. "The wolves—or maybe they're coyotes, I'm not sure—are down in the canyon. They can climb up right here, I think."

Ortiz remained behind her, perhaps afraid to stand too close to the ledge.

Despite the cool air, a tinge of salty sweat came to her on the gentle breeze. It was slight in comparison to the overlying reek of the poison, but she delighted at his struggle as he grappled with his instinctive fear of standing on a dark cliff and his paraphilic attraction to her pregnancy.

The fetus stirred.

"The baby, he's moving," she breathed. "Would you like to feel?"

That was enough. He stepped onto the ledge beside her. She took his hand and placed it on her belly. The fetus responded with a vigorous kick.

He exhaled in a heavy sigh.

"Poison," she whispered.

"What?" His eyes were clouded, dreamy, his entire focus melting into that warm palm on her belly.

"You are the plague." With her free right hand, she gave him a hearty shove.

He made no sound as he tumbled, and she didn't hear him hit the sandy bottom of the ravine. The night was silent except for the melodic, liberating howl of the wolves in the distance.

She rubbed her belly as the fetus shifted, dropping lower in her abdomen, now content.

"The earth will be purified." Tears filled her eyes. She'd never felt so deeply devoted to the vision of the Colony. "As a pure, I am responsible for the purification of the Colony and the propagation of purity into the world. This is the Father's will for me."

She opened her eyes to the sound of potato chips crunching.

The guard was leaning back with one hand rustling in the chips bag. His tablet rested against his computer monitor, the image of a sword between two halves of a watermelon splashed across it. His eyes flashed to her for just a second before returning to his game.

"Oof, I must've drifted off while I was trying to put all the pieces together," she said, pushing her hair back and offering a lazy smile. "You know, I suspect those girls were just looking for attention. I'm glad I didn't sound the alarm."

He nodded and shoveled a handful of crumbs into his mouth.

"I'll just let myself out, then. Enjoy your game—that one's a classic."

As she pushed her chair under the desk, her eyes landed on a black man on one of the screens. He wore a lab coat, but his unruly Afro and big round glasses were unmistakable: Isaac. He carried a small bag—dinner, maybe?—and badged himself into the heavy-looking door of an unmarked gray brick building.

The view changed, and she cursed under her breath. She sat back down heavily and fiddled with the strap of her sandal as she waited for the cycle to come around again. Why was he in a lab coat now? He had no medical training whatsoever. What could he be doing that required a GS-5 rank?

The screen switched back to Isaac's building. Her eyes darted from one monitor to the next. She traced the path to the door; it led to a dirt road. A wide-angle screen from across the road showed a handful of picnic tables and off to the right, just a hint in the corner of the screen, was the entrance to a sports field. The ball field lay between the purification cluster and the science cluster, which is where James headed off to every morning. Her eyes bounced between the screens until she located the building, small and set away from the rest of the campus.

Mr. Potato Chips had returned to slicing fruit on his tablet with a greasy fingertip.

"Excuse me, do you know what this building is?" Layla pointed to the anonymous cinder block building just before it flashed away to the next view.

"Mm?" He glanced briefly at the monitor and then tapped New Game on his tablet. "That's salvage."

Layla heaved herself out of the chair to cover her discomfiture. Despite her relationship with James and her importance to the Colony, she'd only heard that name once before.

Don't fuck up, Catie, or you'll end up in salvage.

26

I t had been a long day. James gazed down from his sixth-floor corner office at the sea of scientists and subjects flooding out of the research center to return to their residences. He was strict about shift end, insisting on a security sweep to ensure no one remained in the building after six p.m. His overachieving research and medical teams couldn't be trusted to leave on time.

Work-life balance is a central value here at the Colony. Burnout results in a higher likelihood of illness, higher emotional stress, and lower productivity.

His Lights Out program had not been warmly embraced. Many physicians preferred to work at night when it was a little quieter, and most had never in their professional lives been constrained by set work hours. But James had been relentless, even authorizing security to physically remove staff members from the building if they resisted. It had taken a couple of months, but the culture had shifted and he'd eventually received feedback that staffers were pleased with the new way of life. They were using the fitness facilities, eating better, and getting eight hours of sleep.

And as they slept, his second shift, the reversion team, toiled away at trying to solve what seemed to be an impossible scientific problem.

He glanced at the clock. Ten minutes to six. He sifted through the folders on his desk, pulled out the one labeled NIH-Jennings and dropped it into a drawer, and spread the others across his desk. Site updates, mostly—case counts, carrier profiles, and observational data, the kind of things Stewart would be looking for if he happened to replay their short meeting and zoom in on James's desk. Managing Stewart's relentless suspiciousness and overactive mind was a significant part of James's job. He made a final sweep of his office, then flipped through his notes. Stewart didn't have the patience for science babble, which is why he refused to receive updates directly from the medical team. *If they can explain it to you in a way that you can explain it to me, then I can trust your recommendations.*

James was fortunate; Stewart did trust his recommendations, wholeheartedly. So far, anyway.

He stretched his neck and settled behind his desk.

At six o'clock, prompt as usual, he engaged the video conferencing screen, and a full-sized Stewart Hammond appeared barely five feet in front of him, as if he were seated on the other side of the desk. There was nothing cutting-edge about the technology—it had been around for decades—but James didn't like it. That close, Stewart could see any drop of nervous sweat, any twitch, any other physical sign that something wasn't right.

James grinned. "You look a little rough this morning. Big night of Scotch with the boys?"

"Christ, you can't believe how these guys drink. All night long. And what am I gonna do? I can't excuse myself and leave. That'd be rude. And the whole cultural thing about keeping your guests' glasses full? All true."

James knew it well. He'd handled the negotiations with China to launch the Chinese carrier program; Stewart was only in Beijing to celebrate its early success. James was all too happy to allow Stewart to take the credit. He had more important things to do.

"Any issues out there?"

"They fought for more autonomy, just like you said they would. They want to develop their own protocols, and they don't want Eugenesis oversight. But I think I've been able to rein them in."

The China colony had been one of the more difficult ones to establish, but it was by far the most important. Due to the high population, the Chinese authorities turned a blind eye to even the most aggressive recruiting efforts. Recruits, especially young females, could be bought cheaply from their families, and the sacrifice was viewed as honorable.

"So how did the carrier summit go?" Stewart asked.

Small talk was over. James rocked back in his chair and casually crossed his legs. "Quite well. Our recruiting efforts have really picked up lately. We've managed to shorten the induction program overall, and we've established a fast-track path that can get a recruit ready for implantation within weeks if she's physically healthy and enculturates quickly. We're finding our best recruits in the poverty-stricken areas, although that's also where we find the most disease and drug abuse."

Stewart nodded soberly, but James could see the joy burbling underneath. The carrier program had been Stewart's dream from the beginning, even though it had gotten off to a rocky start.

"We'll need to ramp up the adoption program," James continued. "I talked with Madeline already. She's expanding her reach to influencers in Eastern Europe and Russia. Getting the offspring into those countries is a bit more difficult. We'll need government support."

He was stalling. Stewart had a hard stop to their call in thirty minutes. He hoped they'd be cut off before he had to talk about the praefuro strain. "Also, we're looking into an observation method so that we don't have to rely on self-reporting from the placement families. One idea is to send an au pair—"

"And what about the praefuro strain? Did they figure it out?"

Damn. He resisted glancing at the clock. How much time did he have to eat up? "Well, not entirely. We know that the mutation is caused by an additional insertion point, and we've already identified MAOA as one of those points, but it's not enough to explain why the praefuro mutation occurs in only a fraction of the carriers, nor does it explain the variation in phenotype response. There must be more going on than we understand. There are about twenty thousand different genes expressed in the brain, so it's like looking for a needle in a haystack. I have our best geneticists on it, but the technology just isn't there yet."

"How can we have the best geneticists in the world and the most advanced technology, and not have these answers?"

It was a rhetorical question, and James didn't answer. But the truth was they didn't have the best geneticists in the world. Not yet.

He changed the subject to one that would carry him out on a positive note. "But we've made some progress understanding the phenotype itself. We believe the rage syndrome is due to fetal microchimerism."

"Oh, no." Stewart flopped back in disgust. "You're not going geek on me, are you?"

"Nah, it's a simple concept."

"That's why you're my man."

James grinned. "During pregnancy—all pregnancies, actually, not just our carriers—the fetus sheds stem cells that pass through the placenta and are taken up in the mother's bloodstream. The fetal cells are carried all over the body, including to the brain, where some of them turn into fully developed neurons and are integrated into the mother's brain. What's interesting about our situation is that these stem cells, which contain the modified DNA, appear to be replacing the carrier's normal functioning cells, which then results in this rage syndrome."

Stewart whistled. "Christ, that's right out of a horror movie. Babies that hijack the brains of their mothers."

James laughed. "Well, let's not describe it that way to the council. A better analogy is cancer metastasis. Cells from the primary cancer tumor break away and travel through the blood or lymph system to create new tumors on other organs. This process works the same way."

Stewart nodded his approval. He liked analogies. He endlessly communicated with governments and world leaders, many of whom didn't speak English and required a translator. A metaphor that all people understood was a huge bridge across a language gap.

"But if you don't fully understand the genetics," Stewart asked, "how can you figure out which furos have the rage syndrome?"

James despised Stewart's nickname for the carriers of the praefuro strain, but he overlooked it as usual. "Exactly the problem. But we have some ideas of what behaviors to look for, and as soon as we see early signs—appetite changes, hostility, confusion—"

"So a typical pregnancy." Stewart rocked forward and chuckled.

James grinned at the joke for the sake of his boss, but in reality, what they were dealing with was no laughing matter. "We run some tests and isolate them."

"And the offspring?"

James went back to his notes. "We've observed their behavior to be surprisingly homogeneous. We haven't seen anything noteworthy besides the heightened awareness and the neurologic anomalies. Lack of crying, lack of emotion, no imitation of facial expressions. Many of the signs of autism, except they have excellent visual tracking and high engagement in their surroundings, including exceptional eye contact. In that way, they're similar to the sensus offspring. For now, we're keeping the praefuro offspring with their carriers in the den. There's a bond there that we're not yet ready to disturb. We need more time to observe and gather data."

He finally raised his eyes to find Stewart leaning in, as if over his desk. Even though the video screen was five full feet away, it still felt as though his personal space was being violated.

He sat back.

"How much more time?" Stewart asked.

It wasn't a question so much as a reminder that his patience was running out. Stewart had been all too clear about packaging the praefuro as a military model. Full characterization of the strain, including predictability, was necessary before negotiations could begin, and Stewart wanted it wrapped in a pretty pink bow yesterday. When you had as much money and influence as Stewart Hammond, you weren't accustomed to having to wait for anything.

James sat up straight and answered with conviction. "Two, three months. At least." He expected to know if the praefuro strain was viable a lot sooner than that, but he needed the buffer.

Stewart's jaw tightened, as expected, and James was ready. He waited until Stewart opened his mouth to speak and cut him off. "A misrepresentation of what we're dealing with here could damage our credibility. We have no room for error. And meanwhile, the other strains in development are already gathering a lot of interest at the top levels. We don't want to lose the trust of our buyers." If there was one thing James understood about Stewart, it was how much the man valued his reputation.

Stewart's facial muscles softened a bit. "Absolutely. I would never suggest we cut corners on a product as important as this. Keep up the good work." He checked his wrist. "I've got a plane to catch. Take care."

The video went dark.

Navigating meetings with Stewart was becoming more and more challenging, but if James stepped down from providing the updates, Stewart would go around him, and that would be a death sentence to his unauthorized reversion program. Still, he wasn't sure how much longer he could keep Stewart at bay.

He looked up at a knock on his door.

It opened just wide enough for a head to fit through. "I have the analysis you asked for. The security guard, Ortiz."

James nodded, and his lead research manager set the report on the desk. He could read the answer on the woman's drawn face, but he asked anyway. "So?"

"Nothing. No genetic mutations, no illness, no diseases."

He studied her for a moment, hoping for a *but we did find something else.* No such luck. He dropped his head into his hands and rubbed his temples. It didn't make sense. "You're a hundred percent sure? There's not even the slightest chance you might've missed something?"

Naturally, his top geneticist answered as any good scientist would. "With the genetic analysis technology we have today, which is to my knowledge the most accurate system on the planet, I can tell you with confidence that the subject had no genetic or health abnormalities whatsoever."

He let his breath out. "Thank you for running it. Twice. Sorry to be so skeptical."

"Not a problem. Any time." She looked at her watch. "The reversion team is coming in now. I better get back down there."

James gave her a wave. "Yeah, of course. Remind them how grateful I am that they're willing to work the night shift. I know that's not easy. Hopefully, we'll get it right soon." He wanted to say something to push her harder, to force her and her lab to work faster, smarter. He wouldn't be able to keep his reversion program a secret for much longer.

"You bet." She pulled the door closed behind her.

James looked down at the single paper in front of him. He didn't know what he was reading, just a whole bunch of acronyms and numbers, but he fully trusted his top-notch research team.

What he didn't trust was everything else: Stewart's judgment. Eugenesis' oversight. And most of all, he did not now, nor would he ever, trust the praefuro model.

His eyes shot to the single framed picture on his desk, the ceremony uniting him and his beautiful girl, never more beautiful than the day she'd gazed into his eyes and said, *I'm forever yours in purity and perfection.*

"You made a mistake, my beautiful girl, you made a huge mistake. Tell me why you did it, Lay. Help me understand." He pursed his lips and growled at the inscrutable analysis in front of him. "And what about you, you cockroach? What are you hiding? What did you do to my girl?"

The paper didn't answer him either, so he unlocked the bottom drawer of his desk and dropped it next to a handheld radio with a Scotch-taped label reading ORTIZ, a Ziplock bag of short black hairs, and a specimen container of dried orange clay from the path behind their cabin that had somehow turned up on the front doormat.

Layla was in trouble. Serious trouble.

He drifted distractedly to the big window. On most days, he stood at that window and admired the elegance—the purity—of the perfect sphere as it sank behind the horizon, igniting the desert sky with brilliant reds and oranges. Tonight, however, dark, ominous clouds had barreled in, a warning that storms were imminent.

27

Nick had been surveying the Boulevard Bistro from the coffee bar across the street for over an hour, as the Monday morning crowd began to thin. Jenna was certain she'd seen the recruiters conducting other interviews in the outdoor dining area on multiple occasions.

It's not like I'm stalking the place, she said defensively. *It's on my dog walk route. I go by it at lunchtime pretty much every day.* And she insisted they weren't casual lunches. *The recruits always have that uncomfortable posture people get when they're being questioned. You know, arms shoved between their knees, deer-in-the-headlights look.*

Nick barely slept last night. The enormity of EGNX had his brain churning. An unknown organization with top-secret government designation, who he'd alleged was responsible for illegal genetic experimentation on human subjects, was also connected to—maybe even implicated in—the development and release of the virus.

The suspicious deaths of two cops and the disappearance of a biotech CEO and his lover now seemed like a story for a high school yearbook.

He swallowed the last of his lukewarm coffee and crossed the street to the bistro. It was a long shot, but it was an obvious starting point that wouldn't raise unnecessary suspicion.

An overly charismatic host sashayed over as soon as he stepped through the door. "Hey, there! Breakfast today?"

"No, thank you." He pulled out his wallet and presented a badge that read ICE COUNTER TERRORIST UNIT, complete with an image of himself under a different identity. It was in fact a real badge, not that the host would've known the difference. He'd procured it while investigating a US Customs Port of Entry, suspected of being a thoroughfare for drug traffickers. One smokin'-hot tip had led him to a whistleblower, and he'd been given a full ICE uniform, badge included, to help expose a massive bribery scam. "I'm hoping you might have some information about some people who frequent this restaurant."

The host's confident smile disappeared. "Oh, uh, maybe I should get my manager."

"Thank you very much."

Nick flipped his wallet closed and looked around the restaurant.

The host returned in a matter of seconds with his boss, a short, stout man wearing a three-piece suit. "Can I help you, sir?"

He flipped his wallet open again and allowed the manager to inspect his badge while he unlocked his phone and opened Jordan's photo of the man and woman recruiters. "I'm looking for information about a couple of customers."

The manager pulled a pair of reading glasses from his vest pocket. The curious host leaned over his shoulder to study the picture.

"Have they been in here recently?" Nick asked.

"Yes, yes, I have seen them sometimes." He spoke with a thick accent Nick was certain was exaggerated for effect. "But I do not know who they are. They come, they have delicious lunch, they go." He shrugged and removed his glasses.

"Do they pay with a credit card?" Nick narrowed his eyes, hoping to project a slight distrust in the manager's response—to light a fire under his ass, as Uncle Jay would say.

"We take only cash." He gestured with both arms toward the door, where Nick could only assume hung a sign that made that clear.

"What about these two?" He zoomed in on the two men Jordan had also pointed out.

The manager pulled on his glasses again and peered. "Yes, also regular customers."

"How regular? Once a week? More?"

The man shook his head and shrugged again. Useless.

Nick turned to the host, who had the expression of a kid with the right answer for the teacher. *Pick me, pick me!* "What about you? Do you recognize them?"

The host glanced at his boss and waited for a nod. "I didn't recognize the first couple. But the two men, they come pretty often. I'm pretty sure they work at the Wilshire Grand."

"And how do you know that?"

"They asked me once if I wanted to meet them at the Sky Bar after my shift. It's this super-nice bar at the top of the building, but it's exclusive to the building tenants, so it's sort of an honor to get an invite. It was a while ago."

"Was the invitation social, or something else?"

"At first I thought it was, um, social. I was going to go, but then they started asking weird questions, like about my happiness. I got the feeling they might be religious, so I flaked out. So"—he lowered his voice—"are they like terrorists or something?"

Nick kept a neutral expression. "I appreciate your time. Thank you."

He stepped outside before they could ask him for a business card and headed down the street toward the Wilshire Grand with a little more optimism. The Wilshire Grand was one of the largest and most iconic skyscrapers in the city. At one time, every tourist paused in front of its imposing, earthquake-proof glass walls. But today the sidewalks were empty except for the tenant employees, who pushed through the revolving doors on their way to the office without looking up.

Nick surveyed the security desk from the sidewalk. There appeared to be no ID scanner. Incoming employees merely flashed their badges to the lackadaisical security guard as they pushed through the turnstile and kept moving to the elevator bank.

He entered the building and sauntered over to the wall directory. His first impulse was to look for EGNX or something like it, but the seasoned professional in him knew it wouldn't be so easy. And go figure—no EGNX. Most of the listings appeared to be law firms and consultant agencies. He surreptitiously took a photo of the entire directory. He'd have to look up each one.

He browsed the directory one more time before approaching the scowling black security guard. He glanced at the man's badge and offered a hand. "Ernie. It's my first day today. I don't have a badge yet."

Ernie ignored his outstretched hand. "Name and ID."

"Victor Beaumont." He handed over Victor's driver's license.

Ernie's eyes darted between Nick's face and the driver's license for several moments and returned to his computer screen. Nick leaned over the desk to steal a glance.

"You're not in the directory." Ernie shifted the screen out of view and frowned.

"Probably because it's my first day."

"Which firm?"

"McMillian and Sons."

"Don't see you." He leaned back in his chair, exhaling a long breath that reeked of halitosis. The conversation was over.

Nick threw his arms out to the side. "What the fuck? Is this a racist thing? What, you don't like white guys?" He swerved around to yell at an innocent bystander. "Yo, you believe this guy? He doesn't like white guys! What's that about, huh? What's that?"

Nick would've bet a fifty that Ernie would wave him in to avoid a scene, but Ernie didn't blink an eye. Nick couldn't help admiring the guy.

He glowered and opened the camera on his phone. "What's your name and badge number? I'm going to have you reported."

Ernie held up his badge with icy dispassion, and Nick snapped a photo. He grinned. Abder would have one printed for him by this afternoon.

He stepped into the lobby and texted the image to Abder, then held the phone to his ear. "Yeah, hi. This is Victor Beaumont, new staffer. Yeah, I'm trying to get into the building but—what's that? Are you kidding? Ah, okay. Yeah, see you next week then. Sorry about that. I thought it was today."

He shrugged a *sorry* to Ernie and left the building.

***

It was after twelve when Nick strolled into the Union Bagel Shop and plucked a warm raisin bagel from the rack in the back of the store. He met the team downstairs in what Jordan preferred to call the frat room. *I never got to join a fraternity. I was too young. So this is my very, very sad frat house.* Jenna and Jordan sat around the coffee table in front of paper plates piled with chicken wings and tater tots.

Abder jumped up and promptly steered Nick over to a blank wall. "Stand against it and don't smile." He took several pictures and left, grumbling about how Nick would look more Wilshire quality if he got a decent haircut.

Nick plunked the loaded shopping bag he was carrying onto the floor next to the sofa. "I have a lead on two of the recruiters. What I really need now is a research assistant."

Jenna leaned back from her plate, holding up sticky fingers. "I'm on it. What do you need?"

Nick waved his phone with the Wilshire directory of tenants. "Find the bad guys."

"Ooh, a mystery!" She licked her fingers and finished off by using most of a stack of paper napkins and took his phone with her out of the room.

Abder appeared not a minute later with Nick's finished Wilshire Grand badge. "Hope you didn't piss the guard off too bad, because he'll remember you, and this isn't high quality." He bent down and poked at the boxes in Nick's shopping bag. "Yo, what's all this?"

"Fifteen hundred dollars' worth of surveillance devices."

"This shit is dope. And I thought I was a geek." Abder held up a box the size of a pack of cigarettes. "What's this one do?"

"It's a signal amplifier. Listen, I'll do a full show and tell later, but right now I need you to log on to your computer so we can set up the GSM devices."

"You got it." Abder scooted toward the door, rubbing his hands together. "This is so cool. We're like spies. You must be one hell of an investigative reporter."

Nick felt his face flush, not from anger but more from a sense of self-loathing. "Let me be clear. This is not investigative journalism. This is surveillance abuse, and it's illegal. It is not cool. It's criminal."

Abder and Jordan raised an eyebrow at each other.

"The people on the other side of this are operating above the law, unconstrained," Nick continued. "But you and me? We could be arrested or killed in a second. So let's not get a James Bond complex that makes us believe we're the heroes who'll come out unscathed at the end of the movie."

Abder sobered. "Yeah. Sorry, man."

Stay frosty Oscar Mike—another Uncle Jay-ism. Stay cool on the move. Jay was a stickler about not getting too cocksure. Nick had never been truly ashamed of his crooked past, and maybe that was because he'd idolized his uncle. And Abder wasn't entirely incorrect that a lot of the skills Uncle Jay had taught him, like hustling and pickpocketing, did in fact contribute to his investigative reporting success, especially undercover.

But exposing bad guys was risky business. If you wanted to find the sewer rats, sometimes you had to crawl around the sewers—but if you didn't keep your wits about you, the sewers would swallow you right up.

Jenna strutted into the room beaming. "Next time, give me something with some challenge."

Nick fought to repress a grin. He was warming up to the duchess of doom.

28

"What's with your appetite lately?" James asked as he finished his avocado toast.

Layla sat across from him at the table. She hadn't touched her toast; what used to be her favorite snack now repulsed her, that weirdly creamy texture smeared on dry cardboard. Yuck.

"I'm just not hungry. I'll eat it in an hour." It was a lie, as most verbal exchanges with James had become.

It was afternoon on Monday, and James still hadn't left for his office. He barely left her side all day yesterday, inquiring what she was doing on her computer and insisting on going with her when she went out for a walk. *What if something happens with the baby? Or what if you fall?* It was laughably transparent, but he hadn't so much as hinted about her field trip to the carrier facility. Maybe Dr. De Luca hadn't mentioned it after all.

Or maybe James knew all about it and simply didn't want to admit he'd been lying.

"What are you up to this afternoon?" he prattled. "Bonbons and Nancy Drew?"

She wasn't ready to confront him, not until she dug up everything he thought he'd buried. Not until she found out what was being kept secret in salvage, why carriers were sent there for failing a psychosocial test.

"Mmm." Layla pulled out her phone and swiped into her calendar. "I have some intake profiles to review from Mia. She's struggling out there on the front line. I'm not sure I trust her judgment." Another lie. Mia had an excellent eye for Colony material. But Mia's recent suggestion that the intake process should involve a wider multiphase evaluation was an insult to the work Layla had put into the current process. What audacity.

It was obvious that James wouldn't leave if she didn't push him out the door, and she was starting to feel the early signs of a headache.

"All this bedrest time could have been much more useful if I had access to the internet. Instead of sitting here watching Mia flounder around trying to figure what's going on with some of these recruits, I could research their backgrounds, learn something about their communities, or even find better recruits."

James stiffened.

"Oh, but my work isn't important enough to you. So I'll just sit here and revisit each and every intake profile, manually. Thanks. I love spending the last days of my pregnancy doing grunt work."

She glared at him for a minute, scooped up her laptop, and stalked into the bedroom.

James despised arguments. In his world away from her, they didn't exist. No one ever argued with the boss. But in their relationship, he was undeniably conflict averse. He'd either give in or put space between them. And this was one long-standing issue he wouldn't back down from.

She barely opened her email when she heard the front door click shut. She peeked out the window and watched James crawl into the backseat of the executive town car. Mission accomplished. She grabbed her phone and dialed. "Coast is clear."

Harmony arrived in minutes. Layla met her at the door, seized the brown paper bag, and hurried to the kitchen. The pounding in her head was threatening a full-blown migraine, and she couldn't afford to sleep the afternoon away.

She groped for a fork and knife, then tossed them aside and picked up the pork chop with her hands like a barbarian. She bit into it, closing her eyes, savoring the first bite. It wasn't the taste that she relished; it was the texture. The sinewy feel of animal connective tissue, and the way her teeth tore through the muscle fibers. She couldn't help envisioning the carcass just after slaughter, freshly skinned and hanging from the butcher's hook.

She took another bite.

She could feel Harmony's stare burning into her. She didn't need to open her eyes to know the girl would be backed up against the door, trembling. Yesterday, she cowered in one corner of the living room while Layla inhaled her third cheeseburger of the morning. *It's just pregnancy hormones*, Layla had mumbled with a full mouth as she tossed the bun into the trash can.

She kept her eyes closed as she took another bite. She imagined the butcher wielding a large buck knife, peeling back the skin, exposing the red flesh she now gleefully chewed. So delicious. Warmth washed over her, and her headache dissolved.

She finally felt satiated enough to open her eyes and offer some comfort to her delivery girl. "I'm sorry, I don't mean to seem ungrateful. It's just a wild craving. I can't explain it."

"Um, it's okay," Harmony whimpered.

Layla sucked the bone, chewing the end like a dog. She knew it was uncouth, but she couldn't help herself.

"Do you need me to bring you another?"

She wanted to say yes—two more, even—but she resisted. She'd put on another three pounds over the last week.

"Um, okay, well … um. Do you want me to stay and do some work around the house?" It was a polite offer, but her tone was begging to be set free.

And anyway, Layla had a big day ahead. Salvage was a long walk from her cabin, and once she arrived, she'd have to figure out a way to get inside. And once inside … well, then what? Would Isaac be there? What would she say to him?

"You don't have to stay." She rinsed her hands under the kitchen sink and shook off the extra droplets. "But you have to promise to keep these deliveries just between the two of us." She winked.

"Okay. Well, text me if you need anything, and I'll come right away." She was out the door before Layla could say goodbye.

Layla pulled on her running shoes, tied her hair into a low ponytail, and rushed out the door.

***

"Isaac." Layla moved out from beneath the security camera as the door opened.

"Uh, hi. I got your text." Isaac pulled the door closed behind himself before approaching her. He shoved his hands into his lab coat pocket and hunched his shoulders. "What are you doing here?"

She pretended to look hurt. "Aw, is that how you greet an old friend?" He'd see right through her ingratiating charm, but he'd shrug it off. Isaac couldn't hold a grudge.

True to form, he offered a lopsided grin and squeezed her shoulder. "How's the pregnancy? You surviving?"

"I can't wait to see the day when I no longer waddle."

He chuckled and asked again. "What brings you all the way out here?"

She rolled her eyes. "Mia sent me over to do a walk-through. I'm conducting an analysis of the carrier program, and she suggested I ask you to give me a tour. I understand this is where the displaced carriers finish out their pregnancy?" Shit, she hadn't meant to sound so unsure. "Anyway, she thought it'd be good for me to check it out."

His eyebrows drew together. "Mia? She told you to come here?"

"This is salvage, right? Your new gig? Congratulations, by the way. It's a great opportunity for you. GS-5, that's really something." She was babbling, and she clamped her jaw down to stop.

He nodded slowly, but it turned into a head shake. "I ... don't think so. Mia would never refer to this program as salvage. She despises that word."

She locked up, searching for a way out. "Okay, yeah… You're right.

But Isaac, please—I need to see it. James and Mia have been lying to me all this time about my pregnancy. I just want to know what's going on. Please."

He turned toward the building.

She grabbed his arm. "Look, I know I was a bitch to you in recruiting, and I don't deserve your friendship. But I've given my life to this Colony. I've carried two fetuses to full term, and through it all, they've hidden the truth from me."

He was looking down at her as if she were a fly on his sleeve.

"Now I know, and I have to understand what's been going on. I want to see what's so important that I had to be shielded from it."

He glanced again at her fingers clutching his arm. "You should talk to James."

"You know as well as I do that he won't be honest with me. Isaac… You know it."

She could see him battling his better judgment, and she wished she could let him off the hook, but there was no way she was going to walk away. If he didn't let her in, she was prepared to snatch his badge from his coat and force her way inside.

He relented. "Okay. I'll take you inside, but I need to explain something first. It'll help you understand what you see."

He led her to a bench and helped her down. "Do you remember our training class? The trainees who were called for purification with us? We met that first day in the garden, the old garden."

"Yeah." Layla was overwhelmed with nostalgia. Jonah, Sofia, Nicole, and the two of them. They'd hugged and jumped around, so excited to be chosen, as Mia had introduced them to their new phase of life. God, it'd been so long since she'd seen her old friends.

"Our class was added to an experimental cohort. The five of us were assigned to test an experimental drug called LXR-999. Did you know?"

"The intelligence elixir and the sleep elixir." Her purification gifts. They'd all gotten gifts.

"Right. But you were removed from the cohort. James selected you to be a carrier, so you weren't dosed with 999. You weren't dosed with anything. The carriers were a special class. They'd never take that kind of risk with a carrier."

"No, I was." She could hear the doubt in her voice. "I got IV injections every day for weeks."

"That's just what they told us. You, Jonah, and I were the control group. They never actually gave us those drugs. They gave us a placebo. They needed to compare the group that got the real drug with the group that only thought they got the drug. That's how the study was designed."

Layla squinted at him as she tried to process what he said. "So my elixir wasn't real?"

"Yeah. I thought it just didn't take with me. I tried to fake it for a while, but…" He chuckled. "Well, you can't fake intelligence."

Another lie from James, another secret he'd kept. *You have to give it time, Layla. Some people require more doses.*

"What about the sleep elixir?"

"Did you ever feel refreshed after a couple of hours of sleep?"

She dragged herself out of bed every morning after five hours of sleep, and most of the time she felt like she was half dead.

"Sofia and Nicole were dosed with 999. They got the active drug. And there were two other cohorts after ours that also received 999." He looked down at his hands, wringing in his lap.

"What is it? Did something happen?"

He rubbed both hands on his pant legs and took a deep breath, still talking to the ground. "Nine subjects in total were dosed with 999. They finally stopped dosing after the first subject, Nicole, started having strange side effects." He looked down again. "But by then it was too late. The damage had already been done. To all of them."

Trepidation crawled up the back of her neck. "What happened?"

"The drug was meant to improve brain function by increasing the speed at which synapses fired. It targeted genes responsible for regulating neural circuits. But there was an off-target effect. The drug edited a different gene, a gene downstream of the serotonin 5H-T-2A cell receptor pathway…"

He was jabbering. How had he learned all this in such a short time?

"Isaac." She hated to interrupt. He was obviously upset. "I don't… I don't understand what you're saying."

He looked up at her. "Sorry. It's just… The brain is complicated. Some genes have multiple functions and can be activated from different receptors on the cell." He shook his head and tried again. "They didn't mean to do it. The science was solid and well-intended, Layla. Don't blame anyone."

Layla looked past him at the door he so deliberately closed when he exited. "What is going on in there? I need to know."

He pursed his lips. "You'll just have to see it for yourself."

29

Nick waited outside the Wilshire Grand for the right moment. It was after two o'clock, and to his relief, watchdog Ernie wasn't on his throne. But he still needed some cover. He paced in front of the building. After what felt like forever, a trio of women stumbled to the front door of the building, laughing at their conversation. By the looks of them, they were returning from a boozy celebratory lunch. He trailed them inside.

Just as they waved through security, he called out. "Hey, Linda! Wait up!"

They all turned toward him as he jogged through security, waving his badge at the fill-in.

"Hey, Linda." He picked the least wobbly of the three women and flashed a seductive smile. He held up his badge. "Victor. Don't you remember me?"

"No."

The two other ladies moved in protectively around his target and eyed him, glowering, with their hands on their hips.

"Linda, right?" he asked confidently.

She held up her badge. Gloria.

"Oh, shit, sorry about that. How embarrassing. I mean, it was just one night. And it was dark in the club."

The elevator chimed and they stepped in, facing him in perfect Charlie's Angels formation, prepared to take him down if he dared trespass further.

"You sure you didn't give me a fake name that night?" he called, as the doors closed between them.

He snorted at the stunt and stepped into the next elevator.

The elevator opened on the twelfth floor, and he strode down the hall with purpose until he made a complete lap around the perfectly square layout. He'd studied the blueprints on Abder's computer. It was a common cellular floorplan with twelve individual glass-walled offices, six interior offices, and six window offices along each of four corridors, plus four spacious conference rooms on each corner. He slipped into the stairwell and walked down one flight, careful to keep his head down and his face out of view of the cameras.

The lobby directory indicated three companies on the eleventh floor, including Big World Enterprises, the only company, according to Jenna, whose web presence consisted of nothing beyond a suspicious landing page. He made the same lap on this floor, this time with his phone to his ear as if engaged in conversation.

At the southeast corner conference room, he spotted the female recruiter. She was unmistakable, her hair tightly pulled back into a severe bun over ears too big for her head, leaning back against the conference table and talking with two men in identical black pants, white shirts, and light blue ties. They looked like a couple of young missionaries.

Nick turned into the next stairwell and climbed half a flight, barely interrupting his pace to shove an elbow through the protective glass over the fire alarm and pull the lever. The piercing shriek of the alarm echoed in the stairwell as he kept moving to the twelfth floor.

Pissed-off staffers were filtering out of offices and conference rooms. They tromped disinterestedly into the stairwell.

"Isn't this like the fourth time?" someone complained as they passed.

Perfect. He swiveled around and joined the marching herd, exiting again on the eleventh floor. Thanks to city fire codes, electronic doors in commercial buildings auto-unlocked in the event of a fire, to give firefighters easy access into the offices. He checked that the conference room was empty and slipped inside.

He turned in a complete circle to take inventory, then moved to the corner and yanked a surge protector power strip from under the window. He replaced it with one from his bag. Very unlikely to be detected—who noticed a power strip? He did the same with the mouse that controlled the conference room projector, also unlikely to send up any red flags. Finally, he knelt and replaced an iPhone charger dangling from the wall. Winner. A charger was likely to be taken along by whoever—

"Hey, man. What the hell you doin'?"

Nick's eyes shot up.

"Don't you hear the goddamn alarm?" the security guard asked.

Nick held up the charger and let it fall into his bag. "Remember the one a few weeks ago? One of those asshole firemen stole my charger and my Kindle. You believe that shit? I'm not falling for that again." He stalked to the door and joined the guard to head down the hallway.

The guard waved an angry index finger. "Those guys put their lives on the line every day. What's the big deal if they swipe a thing or two? You rich kids can afford it." He held the stairwell door open to let Nick walk ahead of him and glanced at the badge clipped to his shirt. "Victor Beaumont. Like the old-time actor?"

Nick beamed. "Yep, just like him."

Once out on the street, he wormed his way through the mingling crowd. A single fire truck had arrived, and two men sauntered over to the main entrance without the slightest sense of urgency.

"Frankly, I'm happy for a little fresh air," one woman was telling her friend. "My office is way too stuffy."

You're welcome. Nick shuffled away. Damn, it felt good to be back.

He sent a text to Abder—*Game on*—then turned onto Grand Avenue to find a cab. The blare of a car horn startled him, and as he swung around to make sure he wasn't the offending pedestrian, he recognized the missionary twinners from the conference room. They were headed east on Fifth Street.

"What are you boys up to?" he asked himself in his best Theo Kojak voice.

He darted across the street just as the light changed. Keeping a safe distance, he followed them out of the Financial District toward the poverty-stricken Skid Row.

30

The placard above the door read POST-CARE RECOVERY, but as Isaac explained it to Layla, the original name, salvage, was meant to portray the damaged test subjects inside as precious cargo recovered from a shipwreck, ready for restoration. Unfortunately, as time passed and the precious cargo that had been abandoned there was not restored, the name took on a more derogatory connotation.

Mia had insisted that Isaac never speak the word.

"'Because they aren't scrap salvage,'" he said. "Those were her exact words. I didn't even know what it meant."

Layla followed Isaac through two sets of doors, like entering a prison, and as soon as she stepped into the corridor, she realized that's exactly what it was. These weren't the clean, comfortable observation rooms of the infirmaries and testing centers. These were cells with cement floors, cinderblock walls, minimal furniture, and steel bars to protect the rest of the Colony from what someone in a powerful position considered to be salvage.

Salvage. Layla knew what it meant, all right. She'd done intakes with recruits who'd grown up in junkyard vehicles—cars, buses, anything with a roof. The thought that a human might be described that way filled her with outrage.

Isaac stopped in front of a cell. The walls were covered floor to ceiling in disturbing drawings scribbled with crayons, faces with the eyes scratched out and wild-haired monsters with long pointed teeth and claws. Random words and sayings were scrawled between them: *They're hee-ere* and *When can I die?*

"This is Nicole." He spoke softly, perhaps hoping the occupant wouldn't hear him.

The woman who lay on the cot facing the wall was rail thin. Her once long, bushy hair had been buzzed in a military haircut.

Layla clutched the bars. This couldn't be *her* Nicole, with a round, freckled face just perfect for her pudgy little frame. Her Nicole, who danced about like a little kid who needed to pee, so desperate to pass on the latest juicy gossip: *Layla, oh my god! I have to tell you something!*

No way it could be the same woman.

"Nicole?"

The woman rolled over and put both palms on the floor, slithering off the bed onto her hands and knees, a lioness on the prowl. Her round face had grown so thin that Layla could see prominent cheekbones now, and her wide eyes appeared sunken, as though they'd been sucked into her skull.

"Laaaaaay-la," she breathed. "So nice to see you." She tilted her head completely sideways and stretched her lips into a grotesque smile, exposing her gums. She had no teeth.

Layla stopped breathing.

Hand over hand, Nicole pulled herself up to standing, her face just inches from the bars. Still with her head tilted in that unnatural way. She held up her hands so Layla could see that her fingernails had been removed, then put both index fingers into the corners of her mouth and stretched, pulling her lips so tight that Layla winced, expecting them to tear. It reminded her of that cat. The one from *Alice in Wonderland*, that terrifying Cheshire cat.

Layla drew back.

Nicole released her red, stretched lips and laughed, the piercing,

maniacal cackle of a witch. "Teeth and fingernails and hair are poison."
Then she dropped back onto her hands and knees, cranked her neck
around, followed by her body, and slunk back to her cot. She curled back
into the fetal position facing the wall, her arms wrapping around her head.
"Isaac, get that fucking cunt away from me. Those hideous teeth! And
hair. It's the most disgusting thing I've ever seen." She went into a
retching fit that sounded unfeigned.

"Oh my god," Layla breathed.

Isaac pulled Layla away. His voice was low. "I'm sorry. She's ... well,
she's not usually so mean." He stepped quickly in front of Layla and
peeked into the next cell, then shook his head as if he were embarrassed.
"You might want to look away."

"Okay." She looked to the right, directly into the ghostly stare of a
woman she didn't recognize. A long stream of drool hung from her gaping
mouth.

From across the corridor she heard grunting, like a pig. *Don't look. Don't
look.* But her curiosity got the better of her, and she glanced back toward
the animalistic noise.

"Oh, god."

Stark naked, leaning over and gripping the bars with one hand, the
cell's occupant was masturbating feverishly with the other. He howled and
climaxed just before she turned away, his ejaculate splattering the floor of
the corridor. His eyes were fixed on her, his mouth open in a freakish
blend of surprise and euphoria.

Layla's hands flew to her eyes so fast they made a smacking sound.

Isaac grabbed her by the arm and dragged her to the end of the hall. "I
know, I know. It seems scary and, well, bad. But the doctors are working
on repairing the damage. They've had several treatments, and believe it or
not, they're getting better. That's what they tell me, anyway."

"What happened?" she whispered. "Why are they like that?"

"Their serotonin levels are off the charts. It's like a bad acid trip they
can never come down from."

Finally, a language Layla could speak. She'd seen acid trippers come through the recruiting center. Most of the time, she rejected them. The risk of hallucinogen persisting perception disorder was too high, especially for long-term abusers. She couldn't risk a disturbance in her Colony caused by a flashback that might last hours or even days. But the tripping behavior she witnessed in the recruiting center was nothing like what she just saw.

Isaac seemed to read her mind. "From what I understand, the altered perception and the synesthesia they experienced initially has created a new reality in their minds. Even though they're cognizant and can remember past events, they've forgotten what normalcy is. It's like they're living in a dream world every day. They have dramatic mood swings, but some days are better than others. Yesterday I played an entire game of Go Fish with Nicole." He smiled at the memory. "She thought we were on a boat with fishing rods, and for the rest of the day, she kept asking when I'd bring her fish dinner."

All this time, and Layla hadn't bothered to look up her old friend. She'd buried herself in her work and her happy life with James. Nicole had given up her life in the poisoned world. She'd worked just as hard as Layla had, suffered every day for the gift of purification. And hers was to live in a prison cell as a freak. The Colony—*her* Colony—was responsible for this.

"How long has she been like that?" she finally asked.

His silence was answer enough. *Since the beginning.*

"And Sofia?"

"She didn't make it." He didn't look at her as he led her to a staircase. "She took her life. It was a year or so ago, they told me."

"How?" she whispered. She didn't know why she asked.

"She pulled all her hair out. Stuffed it down her throat until she died of asphyxiation."

Layla felt the muscles of her face tighten with fury. She wanted to scream. She wanted to hit someone. *Saving the human race isn't a marathon. It's a sprint, and it doesn't come without sacrifice.* Somehow, in all the time she had nodded in agreement with that mantra, she never thought about who was in that lot or what they would sacrifice.

"You came here to see the praefuro," he said. "They're downstairs. Follow me."

She didn't want to go. Her gut told her to turn around and walk away before it was too late. But from somewhere deep inside, a different mantra bubbled up from her poisoned life.

And the truth shall set you free.

31

Nick slid into the shadow of an overfilled dumpster as the twinners entered a church. Maybe they really were missionaries of some sort. Hadn't the host at the bistro said something about a religious pitch? But not even a minute passed before they stepped back through the ornate arched wooden doors and continued on to Crocker Street.

Nick had seen pictures and news stories of the homeless camps on Skid Row. He'd once written a feature on the homeless crisis across the nation, including images from all the major cities. But what he was looking at now was like nothing he'd seen before. Police barriers blocked the entrance to Crocker Street in both directions, with graffiti-covered signs that read NO MOTORIZED VEHICLES BEYOND THIS POINT. Not even half a block beyond the barriers, a long string of portable toilets lined both sides of the road. Jesus, there must've been a hundred. The stench was unbearable, and he wondered when the last vacuum tanker had come through. All that could be seen beyond the toilets was a sea of tents, sleeping bags, blankets, and cardboard boxes. The entire street had become a homeless camp. That was the city's response to the growing problem: a closed road and a hundred unattended portable toilets.

Nick had thought himself worldly. He was a journalist. He was in touch with the people; he was one of the people, in fact. He sat at Darcy's bar for a Guinness and indulged the grumbling patrons—*I only made thirty bucks today. How's a man supposed to feed a twelve-year-old boy on thirty bucks?*—before falling into his rickety twin-size bed in his studio apartment. He thought he understood the suffering that plagued the country.

But this was beyond anything he'd ever imagined.

He covered his nose and mouth with his arm and trotted past the toilets. No wonder the stench was so bad; most people had given up on the johns and done their business in between them.

The camps were eerily quiet. Most adults were asleep, weary from the hot afternoon temperatures, lying on top of threadbare blankets, but the children were awake, playing quietly with whatever they had. Toy trucks with only two wheels. A one-armed Barbie doll with no clothes. They stopped playing as he tiptoed past, their vacant stares following him as he choked at their emotionless faces, sallow from illness and malnutrition. Would they ever know a life better than this?

A door slammed. The twinners had entered a second church. He leaned against the corner of a brick building to wait and instantly regretted it.

"Dammit," he muttered, peeling his sweat-drenched shirt away from his skin.

"Mm-hmm," came from beneath him.

He hadn't realized his feet were inches away from an old man sitting cross-legged against the wall. The man wore a tattered LA Angels T-shirt and sweats with holes in the knees, and he squinted up at Nick with a toothless grin across his shriveled, weathered face. He reminded Nick of someone you'd see on a *National Geographic* cover: "Oldest Man on Earth Happy to Be Alive at 163 Years Old" or something just as inane.

"This is the west wall right here," the old coot said. "Get hot enough to melt yer skin right off. Most people move along this time o' day, but not ol' Red. I been here fifty years. Tough as leather by now."

"Fifty years. That's a mighty long time." Long enough to see everything on this block.

The old man didn't answer.

"You here when the Angels won the World Series? What was that, '98? '99?"

"Hell yeah, I was. That'd be '02, yessir." His head bobbed. "Took dose Giants for a ride, yes they did. Best o' seven. Yep." His gummy grin spread ear to ear again, and he waved a hand. "Ain't no need to butter me up with small talk. You followin' dose fellers, ain't ya?"

Nick did a double-take. The old man was sharp.

"Yeah, dey come round ever' now and again, bringin' folks some bagels. Downright Christian of 'em."

"You get that bagel from them today?"

"This? Nah. Had this one for a couple days now." He pulled off a piece and pushed it between his gums and his inner cheek like a fat chaw of chewing tobacco.

"What are they doing down here? Just goodwill?"

The twinners emerged from the church and continued down Crocker. Nick itched to follow, but something told him ol' Red had more to say.

"Ain't nobody do nothing for just goodwill," the old man said with a chuckle. "Nah, they come roun' to get the young'uns. Took ol' Reese's li'l girl a few weeks ago. Reese didn't wanna give her up at da beginning, but he got no way to keep her safe." His face darkened. "They came back and hauled 'er away. Better life for da girl, I figure."

"Is that so?" Nick's stomach fluttered, and he struggled to keep his voice calm. "Any idea where they took her?"

"Nah. Best I just mind my own bidness." The bagel chaw was too big, and saliva threatened to spill over Red's lips. He slurped it back.

"What about your buddy Reese? Does he stay around here?"

"Seen him workin' over at the kitchen on Fourth sometimes."

Nick had a dozen more questions, but he didn't want to overwhelm the man with frantic interrogation. He lowered himself to a squat, which somehow attracted a dozen gnats. He swatted them away from his face but held the awkward position. "How many others they take, besides Reese's girl?"

Red pressed his gums together and frowned, making his face look squished.

Nick shifted his gaze back toward the church. He'd pushed too far, and now he needed to walk it back a few steps. He swatted the gnats again.

"Dem are drain flies," Red said, ignoring the swarm around himself. "Some people call 'em moth flies. Come up from the sewers after the rain. Most folks think they're a damn nuisance, but they don't bother me none."

"Seems like you're a pretty easygoing fella. My uncle said that's the secret to a good life. Don't sweat the small stuff."

A full minute passed before Red spoke again. "A bus come out, oh, ever' couple weeks to pick up the kids, haul 'em off after the sun go down. I seen 'em a few times at the mission. They take, oh, ten 'er fifteen at a time. Been going on for a couple years now."

Jesus Christ, this was human trafficking. A shudder washed over Nick despite the sweat drenching his hair, face, and shirt. "Anything written on the side of the bus? A name?"

Red shrugged. "Too dark to tell."

Nick's legs were numb by the time he decided the man had nothing else to tell him. He pushed himself up the scorching hot wall.

"It's been great talking with you, Red." Nick pulled a fifty from his wallet.

The man held up his hand. "No, no, you keep that for yourself, sonny. I gots all I need right here."

The man had nothing but a pile of ratty blankets, a three-day-old, half-eaten bagel, and his dignity. The old-timer grinned up at Nick for the third time, and Nick couldn't help grinning back at him.

Nick took his time strolling over to the soup kitchen on East Fourth Street. A large sign on the stoop read NO VOUCHER, NO MEAL. NO EXCEPTIONS. He pulled open the squeaky door and slid inside.

The dining area was empty, which wasn't surprising given the stifling heat inside. One long row of three folding tables took up most of the narrow space. He glanced up at a bulletin board covered with black-and-white photocopies of missing persons: Jill Renister, 22 years old, last seen July 14, 2021. Aidan Broughton, 24 years old, missing since March 2020. God, there must've been hundreds. And all in their twenties.

"Dinner's not till five." A short, wiry sixty-something black man remarked as he walked by carrying an urn of coffee. He set the urn down and eyed Nick suspiciously. "Whatcha need?"

"I'm looking for my colleagues, couple of guys around my age. They come by here today?"

"Nope. Don't know anything about that." His eyes darted away and he moved quickly past Nick.

Nick followed him to the kitchen. "Are you Reese? I'm not a cop. Just looking for my friends."

No answer. He walked through a set of swinging doors. The sign above it read KITCHEN STAFF ONLY. KEEP OUT.

Nick reached for his wallet and pulled out the fifty that Red had refused, but when he lifted his eyes, he was staring straight into the barrel of a revolver.

"Whoa, whoa, whoa!" He backed up into a prep table that clattered as it slammed against the wall.

"Put your wallet back in your pocket and get the hell out of my kitchen."

"Listen, I'm just—"

"I do not like cleaning blood off this old cement floor. It tends to get stuck in the cracks." The dude's tone was so sober, Nick had to believe he'd done it before.

"Okay, okay. I'm going." He tucked his wallet away and backed out through the swinging doors.

That's how it was in the dregs. Good citizens, even someone who'd spent a lifetime devoted to charity, could no longer rely on help from law enforcement. People had taken to defending themselves. Gun sales had never been higher. It was like the old Wild West. Even though Nick had posed zero threat, whatever arrangement that man had with the twinners needed to be protected. No bribe, no discussion.

But Jesus. Nick shrugged his sweaty shirt away from his skin. That was enough for one day. He retraced his route back to Fifth Street and was holding his breath past the toilets when his phone buzzed in his pocket.

Abder: *We've got a lead. Get back asap.*

32

The lower level of the salvage building was dimly lit and much cooler, and for a moment Layla felt as though she were back in the purge room again. She bumped into Isaac as he paused at the bottom of the stairs.

He spoke in a low, calm voice, as if they were entering a nursery of sleeping toddlers. "There are lights on the floor indicating where you should walk. It allows you to keep a safe distance from the praefuro cells. They're unpredictable. They can act sweet, but in most cases, it's a way to lure you closer."

"What happens if you get too close?" Layla asked at a normal volume.

Isaac switched on the soft floor lights, which provoked a flurry of rustling along the corridor. "We keep it on the dark side. It's calming."

"But what happens if you get too close?" she repeated.

"They have a voracious appetite for raw meat, and they'll take it in whatever form they can get it."

Layla blanched.

"Hey there, Lucinda," he called. "How's it going?"

"I'm six months pregnant in prison, how do you think it's going?" the woman answered. "Who's the newb?"

Layla stayed glued to Isaac.

"This is Sister Layla."

The woman got up from a small desk and walked toward the steel bars. How long was the woman's reach? Could she grab Layla?

"Sister Layla?" A voice came from behind them. "Is it really you?"

Layla spun around to see another woman, with a smaller baby bump, rushing to the bars. She gasped and stumbled backward, clanging into Lucinda's cell.

"Keep moving," Isaac said, a note of urgency in his soft voice.

She tried to regain her balance, but Lucinda's hand curled around her wrist and drew Layla's entire arm between the steel bars. Her second hand grasped Layla's long ponytail.

"Isaac!" Layla swung her free arm madly, searching for Isaac. Out of one eye, she saw Lucinda's wide, hungry eyes. Her lips were wet with saliva.

Oh, god. No, please.

Seemingly without reason, Lucinda's grip relaxed, releasing Layla's hair and her wrist. Isaac slid an arm around Layla and pulled her out of Lucinda's reach.

"Oh god," he breathed, "I'm so sorry. I was trying…"

His voice faded away, a faint whisper from somewhere so distant she had no hope of following. Layla felt a moment of pressure around her head, a thickness as if she'd submerged herself in the bathtub or a pool of mud.

Forgive me, Layla.

She could hear Lucinda's apology loud and clear, but the woman's lips weren't moving. Layla was staring right at them. She peeled Isaac's arm from her, barely registering his faraway protests.

She's with us. The words surrounded her, filling her head like music through earbuds. Her eyes darted to Isaac, who seemed to be yelling at her, screaming her name. But it was as if someone hit the mute button.

Instead, she heard a calm, oddly affable *Welcome, Layla.*

She slowly moved down the corridor as each woman greeted her, their voices vibrating between her ears but not passing through the medium of air. They were speaking directly to her mind.

The greeting from the last cell was cold. Sarcastic. *Welcome to salvage, the junkyard for humans, where you're only kept around for the sake of your offspring. Better hope yours hangs on for a while.*

"No." Her voice reverberated, bouncing off the walls and back at her loudly enough to break the strange spell she'd fallen under.

"—calling security. I don't want to, but you have to leave now. Right now. You've already caused a disruption, and they don't like disruption. I swear to god—"

"I'm going." She shoved Isaac out of the way and trundled back toward the staircase. "I should never have come here. I don't belong here."

Laughter issued from the cells behind her. Her chest felt tight, and she prayed she wouldn't have a heart attack before she got out.

What had they done to her? How did they get inside her mind?

She glanced backward as she gripped the handrail, pulling her heavy body up the narrow staircase, certain that a hand would grab her and pull her back down like a bloodthirsty demon from hell.

She's one of us.

No. It wasn't true. She was Sister Layla, leader of the purification program. She was pure. A carrier of a perfect evolved fetus. She wasn't salvage.

Isaac spun her by the arm at the top of the stairs, but she yanked free.

She would run back to her cabin as fast as her thick legs could move. She would erase this evil, twisted place from her mind, never think of it again.

Her voice quivered. "I'm sorry. It's my fault. I have to get out. I have to go." She knew she was rambling. Tears burned her eyes. "I'm not a monster. I'm not one of them. I'm not."

She shoved the door open and staggered into the afternoon sun, sucking wind as if she'd just surfaced from the ocean. The hot desert heat burned her lungs, but it had never felt so good.

Her wobbly legs managed to carry her to the softball field, where the dugouts created a bit of shade on the grass near third base. She lowered herself to her hands and knees until her panting subsided and her body stopped trembling. But instead of continuing the long walk to her cabin, she rolled onto her side and curled up. She just needed a few minutes of sleep.

When she opened her eyes, night had fallen, and her heavy lids closed again.

33

"**C**an you play it again, but slowed down a little?" Nick leaned over Abder, mopping the sweat from the back of his neck with a stack of McDonald's napkins. From Nick's surveillance device planted at the Wilshire, Abder had picked up a single voice, a woman talking on a phone with the cadence of an auctioneer. Nick couldn't be sure if it was his recruiter.

"What's the problem?" Her irritation came through clearly, even on the recording. "That's not the way I operate. I have a schedule to keep." There was a long pause of twenty-two seconds before she spoke again. "No, the fifteenth. Tonight is Esther Noho. Double run with Michael and Sage. I want a full load, under thirty, PHP fifteen or better, HIV okay, no addicts."

Abder stopped the recording.

"That's it?" Nick asked incredulously.

"Hung up without so much as a 'thanks for calling.' Rude."

Nick looked down at the keywords he'd scribbled. *Under thirty*. Thirty passengers? Thirty years old? "Have you run a search yet for Esther Noho?"

Jenna breezed in and flopped onto the sofa. "Jordan's passed out in his lab. Pulled another all-nighter."

Abder was unfazed. Must have been a common occurrence. He continued. "Yeah, no listing under that name in greater LA or even on Facebook. I thought maybe she's listed under her husband's name, so I tried a few other searches."

"What is it?" Jenna asked.

"Esther Noho. What do you think? Asian?"

"That's probably not a last name, my little glittabee."

"I live in an underground lab with a paranoid genius and a salty jungle lover. I think I'm pretty far from a glit."

Nick saw Jenna tense for a comeback, and he held up his hands. They didn't have time for a family fight. "What is it then?"

"Noho's North Hollywood. Short form. You know, like, that's a thing we do in SoCal."

"Isn't Hollywood a nice area?"

"They've been trying to clean it up for years, but it's a dump." She pulled her e-cigarette from its charger, changed the pod, and ripped it.

Nick watched the vapor swirl around her head as she slowly exhaled. "I did some fieldwork this afternoon," he said, waving the smoke from his face. "I think we might be looking at a human trafficking situation. I think they're taking kids off the street."

She perked up. "For genetic testing?"

He was still trying to put together the pieces. "Hey Abder, can you pull up a map of North Hollywood? Look for a mission or church or something."

Abder got there in a couple of clicks. "Nada."

Red's voice echoed in Nick's memory. *Reese didn't want to give her up in the beginning, but they came and hauled her away.*

"Skid Row," he said. "That's where they're sending buses. I think they're looking for young, presumably homeless, people in downtown LA. So let's assume they have more than one collection spot. The woman said 'PHP fifteen.' What's that?"

Abder and Jenna shrugged.

"Then, 'HIV okay, no addicts.' That's pretty clear."

"Who they'll take?" Jenna asked.

"Exactly. If they're picking up similar kids in Skid Row, what's the Skid Row of North Hollywood?"

"Street Lives Matter." Jenna stabbed a finger at Abder's screen, a silent command to look it up. "Remember? Wasn't it Esther something?" She turned to Nick. "There was this huge news story like a couple of years ago, right before the virus. This billion-dollar grant came from some rich bitch for the development of a huge homeless camp. It had full bathrooms, showers, and everything, and trash management, and even electrical outlets. Kind of like a nice campground."

"Here in LA?" he asked.

She nodded. "The only stipulation was that it had to be walled in, so there was all this controversy about creating something that looked like a concentration camp. Thing is, the homeless people wanted it. They were dying for better sanitation. It was the wealthy people who were trying to protect their human rights. It was absurd."

Abder muttered something about glits that Nick didn't quite catch.

"Anyway," Jenna continued, "they finally agreed to build it with a tall fence instead of a wall. Not that the fence ever made a difference. People moved not only into the camp but outside of it as well, all around the perimeter, so they could use those fabulous bathrooms."

Abder pulled it up on his computer. "Esther Feldon."

"That's it." The odds of two Esthers associated with a homeless camp in LA were just too low. How many Esthers could there be in 2024? "I need to get to that Noho pickup. How long will it take me to get there? Gotta make it before the sun sets."

Abder jumped up. "I'll drive you."

"Great. And I'll need to stop at a secondhand store on the way." He was about to audition for the role of a lifetime. Gotta dress the part.

34

"**W**inner." Nick lowered his binoculars. The first two letters of the license plate of the plain white Mercedes bus parked a block from the camp's main entrance were DC, just like the van that had been in front of the Vitapura Wellness Center. He scanned the area. No sign of the driver, and by the looks of it, no passengers either.

"What are you going to say?" Abder whispered, even though they were a quarter mile away.

"I'm still working on that."

He'd considered attaching a magnetic GPS tracking device but rejected that idea. Even if he were able to follow the bus without being discovered, he'd still have to get into wherever it ended up. If the place was anything like Area 51, it would have not only a sophisticated anti-jamming security system he'd be unable to bypass but armed guards around the perimeter.

No, the easiest way to infiltrate an organization was to be invited inside. Getting that invitation was the tricky part.

How were the victims selected? Were they forced onto the bus like prisoners? Would they be drugged? Would the driver have a passenger roster?

"Maybe you could just sneak on," Abder said. "You know, like when the driver is distracted. That happened to my sister one time. She got onto a Greyhound bus. These two guys were fighting in the parking lot and the driver got out to break it up, and she just walked on. She made it all the way to San Francisco for free."

Abder's nervous babbling was not helping.

"I'm just going to have to wing it." Nick snapped the binoculars shut and tucked them into his backpack. "Take good care of my things, will ya? I'll be back for 'em real soon." It was the same promise he'd made to Darcy, but he'd been a lot more optimistic back then.

"Okay." Abder had the look of a kid on his first day of kindergarten.

"And don't mess with my surveillance stuff." Nick gave the poor guy a wink.

He walked along the perimeter of the fence, stopping at every person to ask for loose change. It was a strange thing to do, asking homeless people for money, but somehow he'd managed to collect a dollar and twelve cents by the time he got within twenty yards of the bus.

He took a seat at a picnic table opposite a kid smoking a cigarette like his life depended on it. "Hey man, can I bum a smoke?"

The kid gave Nick the once-over, then tossed him the pack and a lighter. "Bet."

"Thanks a lot." Nick hadn't smoked for ten years, and his hand shook as he flicked the lighter. He inhaled gently to keep from coughing and set the pack and the lighter on the table.

The door of the bar across the street swung open, and a rowdy group of bikers burst into the parking lot with beers in plastic cups. The kid didn't move to collect his smokes. He seemed mesmerized by the bikers. He also didn't seem all that interested in conversation, so Nick kept to himself. He hated to admit he was enjoying the cigarette. Across the empty parking lot, the bus was still dark. Where was the driver? Why would they have parked the bus here so early? He'd assumed it would pull up like a Greyhound, load up, and go.

The kid spoke, jolting him out of his thoughts. "Lowkey, I still can't walk into a bar. I don't know how all these people do it, like the virus never even happened."

The kid seemed too young to be so paranoid. He returned his gaze to Nick. "You here for the Colony?"

"The what?"

The kid nodded at the bus. "You going?"

Nick shrugged. "I don't know. Where is it, anyway?"

The kid swung his legs over the bench to face him. "It's out in the desert somewhere, like some science research center. They do experiments and shit like that. If you get invited, you get a chance for, like, special medicines you can't get anywhere else."

"No shit." He took another puff to hide the shock on his face. They were actually telling people about the medical experimentation? How was it possible this place hadn't been exposed? Where the hell was the media? The cops? The FBI?

"Yeah." The kid reached out a hand. "Eddie."

Nick shook it. "N—Vic. Victor Beaumont." Jesus, he'd almost nearly blown it. "So what'd you have to do to get a bus ticket?"

Eddie lit another cigarette. "I learned about it from a nurse at City Health Services. She said she'd recommend me if I wanted. She showed me this picture and—bro, I'm not shittin' you—it was like heaven, like some high-class resort, with great big walls she said keeps the virus out. That was all I needed to hear. I signed up right away."

"Sounds great. Think they'll take me if I ask? Gotta be better than this shithole, right?"

"Facts, bro. Got nothin' to lose."

"When do you go?" Nick didn't want to remove his cell phone from its hiding place in his left boot, scuffed Timberlands two sizes too big, but it had to be after nine.

Sirens wound up in the distance, and Eddie jerked in the direction of the lights. Nick wondered if the kid was running from something other than the virus.

"I'm gonna go see what's going on," Nick said.

He eased back toward the camp, out of the well-lit picnic area. Three black-and-whites had pulled in and were surrounding the parked bus. The sirens had silenced, but the red and blue lights continued to flash. Could it be a bust?

A minute later, a second van rolled into the parking lot. In the strobe of the flashing lights, Nick could barely make out LOS ANGELES COUNTY PRISONER TRANSPORT on the side. The passenger door opened, and a brawny guy wearing a cowboy hat, khakis, and boots took his time climbing out of the van. He held a clipboard in one hand and surveyed the area before swaggering to the rear door.

A dozen or so people filtered out of the back.

"Holy fuck," Nick whispered.

By this time, Eddie had drifted across the parking lot, joined by some six others who presumably ventured over from the camp.

"Gather round, my friends," the man in the cowboy hat called in an unexpectedly high-pitched drawl that reminded Nick of the captain from *Cool Hand Luke* ("What we've got here is failure to communicate"). "Let's get in a single-file line."

He couldn't hear what the captain said after that, but it was clear what was happening. One by one, he cross-checked the passengers' IDs against his roster.

Eddie fell to the back of the line and gestured animatedly at Nick to come. Nick shook his head. If they'd put out an APB on him back in Phoenix, one of these cops might recognize him. And if that shitbrain Victor Beaumont had reported his wallet stolen, that would be another red flag.

Eddie waved again.

He had stupidly assumed EGNX was quietly stealing people off the street—*Come on, get on the bus, little girl, I have candy*—but this was a full-blown police-endorsed operation. Once again, he massively underestimated his opponent. He had to abort. This wasn't the right time for him to get onto the bus. He needed time to come up with a better plan, procure a proper fake ID and some slick body surveillance devices.

He looked up at the line again. "Shit."

Now at the front of the line, Eddie was pointing to Nick. The captain's cowboy hat rotated toward him and the man gave him the once-over, then put one hand on his weapon and strode toward Nick.

He could've run. Even in his oversize Timberlands, he could've outrun a man in shitkickers. Hell, he probably wouldn't even bother chasing him. But goddamn Uncle Jay jumped into his head: *You gotta learn how to overcome your monkey brain*—Jay's expression for the brain stem. *Your monkey brain will tell you to flee the scene, fight or flight. But you know who doesn't look guilty? The curious guy walking* toward *the scene.*

"What's your business here tonight?" the captain asked.

"No business, just seeing what all the commotion's about."

"You have some ID?"

Nick pulled out his wallet and handed over Victor's driver's license.

The captain glanced between Nick's face and the ID several times. "'Scuse me a moment." He raised two fingers and gestured to one of the patrol officers.

Damn. He hadn't expected to be passing this ID to a cop. A bouncer or bus driver would barely have given it a cursory glance, but cops were trained to notice the details. He breathed through his nose to keep calm.

"Can I get some backup? I got a ten sixty-six."

Nick didn't know police codes, even after all these years of dodging local authorities. He assumed it had something to do with fraud or theft, because the patrol officer cuffed him and walked him to a patrol car.

Time for a Hail Mary. "Why am I being arrested? What the fuck did I do? I was just hangin' out. Ain't no crime in that."

The officer shoved him into the back seat without a word.

He reevaluated the situation while he waited for someone to return to the car. He'd be identified the moment they booked and fingerprinted him or gave him the ol' cheek swab. Once his identity was out, they'd connect the dots and figure out exactly what he'd been doing at the pickup site. They'd also see there was a warrant out on him for arson by explosion.

His only hope was to get a break on wrongful arrest. He twisted his hands to loosen the cuffs against his wrists. Keeping his body as relaxed as possible and his eye on the cops, he slowly and painfully worked his right hand free from the cuff.

It wasn't his first rodeo. *Make fists and pull away just a little, like you're pissed off, right when they cuff you. The cuff will lock around the fat meaty part of your hand, then open and close your hands until they get good and sweaty.*

He fish·:d his phone from his boot and hit the audio record button. He cradled the phone between his knees and shoved both arms behind him, just as the driver door opened.

The captain fell into the car, wedging himself between the seat back and the steering wheel and glaring at Nick through the cage from the rearview mirror. He didn't speak for a good thirty seconds. "I see a lot of scumbags during my workday. A lot. This cesspool of a city is overflowin' with scum. So when I catch a scumbag crossing the border, coming into my state, into my city, it makes me wanna tie 'em to my trailer hitch and drag 'em back to where they came from."

Ouch. Nice visual.

"Unfortunately, that option isn't available to me anymore." He inhaled loudly through his nose. Must've learned that in anger management class. "I could take you down to my station and book you. Drunk and disorderly, assault. And this time, your lawyer daddy can't buy off the prosecutor."

Lawyer daddy. Victor's father, protecting his good-for-nothing son. That sure did explain the thuggery.

"But I don't think he would even if he could," the captain continued. "I'll betcha he already realized what a piece of shit you are and stopped throwing money at you to get you off his porch. That's why you're hiding out in my town with a three-inch thick rap sheet, isn't that right?"

He could play this off. "I'm not drunk or disorderly, and I haven't assaulted anyone."

"That's not what my report will read."

"Let me guess: Unless I want to buy a coupla tickets to the policeman's ball?"

The captain's silence was answer enough. And if Nick hadn't left every last dollar he had back at Jordan's lab, he would've handed it over, with pleasure. *Come on, Nick, work it out.* He was the son of an attorney. And an arrogant douchebag.

He scooted forward on the seat and held the man's stare. "You're detaining me for no reason whatsoever, and you haven't read me my rights. I realize the world has changed, but the basics of our constitution are still in place. Furthermore, despite what you think, my father will be more than happy to fly out on his private jet to sit at my table in the courtroom. He eats dirty cops for lunch."

He was walking a fine line between antagonizing the man enough to say something stupid and enraging him to the point that he would shoot Nick in the back of the head.

The captain pulled his firearm from the holster and laid it on the dashboard. "Forty-five hundred people die of violent crimes in this city every year, especially in this kind of neighborhood. I don't take kindly to threats."

Bingo. He kept his shoulders as rigid as possible and slid his right hand to his lap. He dropped his head as if thinking, while his thumb raced over his phone screen. He raised his eyes back to the rearview mirror. "And I don't take kindly to a shakedown. My dad taught me that a good negotiator looks for smart trade-offs." He lifted the phone so that the captain could hear the *whoosh* and see a message being sent with an attachment. "Our little conversation here may not be admissible in court, but this is exactly the kind of thing the liberal media eats up these days. Police intimidation. Harassment. I'm willing to bet you don't want that kind of negative publicity, not after being hit so hard with the virus."

The captain snatched up his gun.

It wasn't until that moment that the solution came to him. A goddamned stroke of much needed good luck. "You can put a bullet in my head if you want, create a whole cover-up problem for yourself and your men. But I have a much simpler solution. Put me on that bus with all those other people. My friend over there said it's a pretty nice place. I wouldn't mind seeing it for myself."

Nick could tell by the man's grin that he knew it was a one-way ticket to hell. "Wanna get on the bus, do ya?"

He shrugged. "Nothin' else to do around here."

He stopped talking. A good negotiator lets the other guy think he's won.

The captain didn't respond. He stepped out of the car, said a couple of words to the officer, and moseyed back to the prisoner transport van.

The door flew open just as Nick tucked his phone back into his boot. "Let's go."

With each step across the parking lot, Nick expected to be shot in the back, but he was still standing by the time they reached the bus.

The officer removed the dangling cuff and held out a hand. "I'll need your phone."

Nick's shoulders dropped. He reluctantly removed it from his left boot and handed it over, then climbed onto the bus.

Had he really done it? Was he officially undercover, on his way to EGNX? A fluttery sensation swept through his gut.

He was welcomed by the friendliest smile he'd ever seen. "Hey there. My name's Michael, and I'll be your chauffeur. Please help yourself to a sandwich and some fruit, and take a seat wherever you like."

Nick eyed the twenty or so faces staring at him. God, they looked so young. He eased down the aisle feeling like the field trip dad and took the seat next to Eddie.

Eddie greeted him like they'd been best friends for years. "Sick. You made it!" He fist-bumped Nick's limp hand.

The door closed, and the bus started moving. Buzzing with nervous excitement, Eddie launched into a story that seemed as if it would never end. Nick was too tense to pretend to be friendly. He was itching to unlace his right boot and retrieve the spare burner phone he'd stashed there. He wanted to power it on, to be ready for anything.

"...walk into this, like, group therapy thing, and the guy who's leading it is rippin' a dab pen. I'm like, bruh, what? Then—I'm not shitting you— he passes it around the circle, but I know I gotta get on the bus tonight.

Didn't know if they'd make us do a piss test…"

Nick tried to get his bearings as Michael followed the flashing lights of their police escort. Were they headed south? Maybe east?

When they reached the city limits, the police lights fell away and the bus's windows went black. A video screen behind the driver lit up, and the passengers hushed as a radiant face filled the video screen. The woman's hair was pulled back tightly, and she wore soft makeup.

Nick leaned forward and squinted to get a clearer look. He couldn't believe his eyes.

"Welcome to the most exclusive club on Earth," she said with a warm smile.

Allison Stevens.

35

G od, I'm so hungry.

Where am I? Which direction is the damn cafeteria? A cool breeze blows my hair off my neck, and I shiver. I shouldn't be outside in the dark without a coat. It must be forty degrees.

The fetus in my belly kicks hard as if reminding me that we're starving to death.

I listen to the crunch of gravel as I leave the stone path and follow the fragrant scent of spices wafting through the air, whetting my appetite even more. I still don't see the cafeteria, and I'm not even sure I'm headed the right direction. I should turn back, but I'm practically mad with hunger.

I arrive at the source of the scent, and I understand: I'm at the fields. All our vegetables, fruit, and herbs are grown here. I pass by lush rosemary bushes nearly as tall as me. It makes me laugh every time I see them. We couldn't use this much rosemary in a lifetime. I move between potatoes and carrots, past squash. Every planted row is labeled with signs on thin wooden sticks, lit with solar lights to be visible even in the winter months when darkness falls before the dinner rush. Might need to send a lackey out for more rosemary in case of a last-minute run on roasted potatoes. God forbid we run out of rosemary potatoes.

I move through the rows quickly now, as if my very survival depended on finding immediate sustenance. I cross a wide dirt road, unwrap the chain holding the wooden gate closed, and walk toward a barn, the smell of manure and urine getting more *pungent with each step. Giddiness tickles my insides. It reminds me of the way I felt when I'd glimpse James before we were together. Brother James, I used to call him, looking up at him all doe-eyed and dopey.*

I was a pathetic little thing.

I swipe a string of drool from my mouth with the back of my hand and open the stall door. Four lambs manage to run past me, but I yank the door closed before the last little guy gets out.

I drop down onto the prickly straw and sing gently. "Layla had a little lamb, little lamb, little lamb."

I wrap my arms around his neck. He's so soft; I just want to squeeze. But he bleats in my ear, and I startle. My stomach rumbles. Or maybe it's the fetus moving again, I'm not sure.

I hug Little Lamb and feel his fast pulse. It starts to slow but becomes louder. And louder. And—

Layla jerked awake. Someone was knocking on a door, calling her. People outside. Men.

"Go away," she mumbled. Her voice was hoarse.

But she heard the click of the latch as they let themselves in. God, could she ever get an evening of privacy? She squeezed her eyes tightly against an onslaught of flashlights.

"Christ almighty," said a stranger from above her.

"What the hell?" The crunch of footsteps across the straw floor of the stall was like nails on a chalkboard.

She didn't open her eyes. She threw an arm over the fluffy woolen neck of her lamb. "Leave us alone." She was already drifting back to sleep.

Retching sounds penetrated her haze like acid rain.

Then, from somewhere above her, the click of a radio. "Sir, we've found her in livestock, along with a slaughtered animal. She appears to have eaten most of it."

36

Layla was too exhausted to resist as she was lifted onto a gurney. Her head lolled to the side as guards secured her arms and legs with restraining straps and wheeled her out. The cool breeze outside the barn woke her up, and she opened her eyes to a circle of shoulders and backs surrounding the gurney as they rushed her toward a set of headlights.

Her stomach contracted. Its contents rose in her chest with such force that she arched against her constraints as she heaved. She didn't even have enough warning to turn her head. Viscous chunks of meat and stringy, bloody animal fur landed on her lap. She barely got a breath before she vomited again, this time with more fluid that ran down her legs and pooled on the gurney.

Three security guards spun away from her, burying their faces in the crook of their arms.

The sour smell of bile blew in her face, and she vomited a third time.

Layla had a little lamb.

She heard again the snap of his tiny neck as he crumpled to the ground. She'd leaned over him and laid her head on his warm, fluffy body. She'd inhaled his scent and pressed her lips into his wool, feeling his slowing pulse against them. Then she'd opened her mouth wide and bit down.

"Oh my god." She choked. Coughed and sputtered. The memory flashed anew, and she heaved again, but her stomach was now empty.

"Oh my god," she repeated as tears fell from her eyes. Her nose dripped onto her lips, and she pulled against her restraints so she could wipe it. "Let me go."

But they kept walking.

She finally pulled enough air into her lungs to cry out. "Let me out of here!"

But no one spoke during the entire drive to the infirmary.

Her gurney was met with a full medical team the moment they rolled her across the threshold and swept her down the hall and into a private room.

"James. Please, someone call James." She needed to hear his comforting voice even more than an explanation of what was happening to her.

She watched in silence as a nurse unbuckled her wrists and began removing her clothing using a pair of large scissors. Another nurse filled a tub with warm water and soap and began scrubbing Layla's bloodstained hands, arms, and face. Layla watched the soapy water grow dusky, becoming a dark, sullen pink.

And then Dr. De Luca was there, gazing down with pouted lips and his usual disdainful coldness, but the first voice she heard belonged to James.

He stepped in front of Dr. De Luca and immediately recoiled, covering his mouth and nose with his arm. "Jesus, what did you do?"

She wasn't sure if he expected her to answer. No matter, because no words would form in her mind anyway. The look of profound revulsion on his face was nothing she'd ever seen before.

"Clean her up and send her to salvage."

Salvage. Oh, god, she was one of them. One of those monsters.

James turned to leave, but she grabbed his sleeve. "Wait, James, please!"

He yanked his arm from her grip and smoothed the sleeve of his expensive navy blue suit. "You're a killer, Layla. You can no longer be trusted in this Colony. Or by me."

37

J ames steeled himself to Layla's cries as he stalked out of the room and down the hall toward the stairs. But it wasn't until he was safely inside the stairwell that he paused to think.

"Fuck!" He slammed his palm against the cool cement wall. "Of all the shitty timing."

He buried his head in his hands and squeezed fistfuls of hair. This screwed up everything. If he didn't distance himself from Layla, convince Stewart that the development of the praefuro model was the single priority, Stewart would get suspicious. Start doubting his motivations. Start nosing around the research center until he sniffed out the reversion program.

And that was not a risk he could take.

And he had about thirty seconds to come up with a plan. He had to put her away. Away from him and away from doing more damage to the Colony. But goddammit, salvage wasn't the answer.

He'd have to throw his trump card: the security guard.

He pulled out his phone.

The head of security picked up immediately. "Yes, sir."

"I'd like a full in-person report on your investigation into the death of Eric Ortiz."

"Of course. Should I come to your office at, say, nine o'clock tomorrow?"

"No, I need it immediately. I'll come to you." He looked at his watch. It was after nine p.m. It had been an awfully long night for the security team already, and he could tell by the silence on the other end that a meeting now would be quite an inconvenience. "The Ortiz matter has made it onto the radar of the Eugenesis leadership team, as a matter of Colony safety and security in light of what—" He couldn't say Layla's name. "In light of tonight's incident. In fact, I might ask Stewart Hammond to come along."

"Sir?"

James rarely involved Stewart in site issues, and frankly, most of the operations leaders found Stewart to be eccentric and unpredictable.

"Thank you in advance for accommodating us on such short notice and so late in the evening. We'll look forward to your honest, straightforward assessment." He spoke slowly to make his point clear, dropped his phone in his shirt pocket, and continued up the stairs to the observation room.

Stewart was leaning against the glass with both hands, watching Layla's room below. When the door closed behind James, he turned with a drawn expression that James had seen him fake more than once before. "I'm so sorry, James. I know you cared for Layla."

James strolled over to the coffee machine to avoid the observation window and slammed an empty coffee cup onto the fill tray. "You know I hand chose her. She had all the qualities of the perfect carrier. Never did I think she'd end up a rager."

"I know. I remember."

He picked up the carton of milk and pointed it at Stewart. "I built her from nothing. As Allison Stevens, she was a pitiful wretch of a girl, always falling to pieces. But as Layla, she blossomed into a perfect, obedient experimental subject." He shook his head. "All that work, and it was all a waste."

"Not a waste at all. We'll have the offspring. She'll be the goose who laid the golden egg. Her contribution to Eugenesis is extraordinary. You should be extremely proud of your efforts in developing her, even if her time has been cut shorter than you'd planned."

James sipped his coffee, keeping his gaze on the back wall.

Stewart laid a hand on his back. "Come on, it's been a long night. Let's go back to the office, and I'll pour you a drink. I brought back a fantastic bottle of Baijiu from China. I was going to give it to you as a gift for surviving this long week, but tonight's as good a time as any. Whaddaya say?"

James stretched his neck to both sides. "Thanks. I'll take you up on that in about an hour. Right now, I need to swing by security. They've been running an investigation into a missing guard whose body was found at the bottom of a nearby ravine. They suspected it was an accident, but they now believe it was foul play, and the investigation has taken a turn toward Layla as the assailant."

Stewart's brow furrowed. "Is that right?"

"I didn't believe it at first, but now, after what's happened tonight— well, I need to hear what he has to say." He stepped out and called over his shoulder. "You wanna meet at the cigar bar later?"

Stewart's voice stiffened. "Mind if I join you for that discussion with security?"

James shrugged. "Be my guest. It'll be helpful to have a second set of ears. We can discuss what we think over that bottle."

He winked.

***

Amadi Aroyo had been James's hire to head up the security team. Nigerian-born but raised in Guatemala, Aroyo was well over six and a half feet tall with an imposing appearance and an unshakable expression of stone. Yet he didn't rule with an iron fist. He was thoughtful and judicious, which James thought was a good fit for the Colony.

Stewart took a seat at the conference table but James remained standing, his hands clasped behind his back. It allowed him to put some distance between himself and Stewart.

"As you requested, I asked my team to check up on Sister Layla on Thursday evening," Aroyo said. "Mr. Ortiz volunteered to stop by your shared cabin after his shift ended and ensure the cabin was secure. He radioed back affirming that was the case. Since his next shift wasn't until Sunday morning, he wasn't identified as missing until he didn't show up for his shift. I sent a team to his room and asked them to check the campus boundary walls for signs of a breach. Only then, late yesterday, were his remains discovered at the bottom of the ravine."

"So you didn't ask Layla about the guard?" Stewart asked, his brow furrowed. "Why wouldn't you have started there?"

Aroyo glanced nervously at James, who nodded. "Brother James preferred we didn't upset Sister Layla during her difficult pregnancy."

James shrugged. "As I told you, I had no reason to suspect Layla had anything to do with the missing guard. I wasn't about to saddle her with such a shocking accusation."

Aroyo continued. "The mistake I made was allowing Sister Layla to access our backup files in the surveillance control room. She'd woven a story about a potential harassment issue and said she wanted to verify the claims. Given her relationship with you, sir, I allowed her to look at the tapes. Of course, that occurred Saturday evening, before we realized Mr. Ortiz was missing. I had no reason to be suspicious."

The deletion of the tapes had been an unexpected and regrettable setback. Video footage of Layla leaving the cabin with Eric Ortiz would have been proof of a rational state of mind. James had considered secretly restoring the deleted files with his own copies, but that would've left a digital trail leading right back to him.

"You didn't accompany her inside the surveillance control room?" Stewart's tone was accusatory, and James wished he'd stay quiet. If Aroyo felt under fire, he might hold back important information that Stewart needed to hear.

But Aroyo didn't seem bothered by the tone. "No, sir. She was in the room with one of my staff for about twenty minutes and left without filing a harassment claim."

James leaned against the edge of Aroyo's desk.

"In the absence of the security footage, we questioned the residents of the neighboring units," Aroyo said. "A young woman spotted two people leaving your cabin and walking down the path toward the ravine. It was dark, and she wasn't able to identify Sister Layla, but she described a woman with long hair walking with a wide gait, as pregnant women often do."

James already knew the answer, but he asked for Stewart's benefit. "Did the witness note any aggression? Rage behavior? Fighting, clawing, biting?"

"No, sir. She said she thought perhaps you and Sister Layla were out for a late walk, maybe to relieve some pregnancy discomfort."

It was so late, and James felt his muscles tensing with impatience. He wanted to blurt out the right answer, the one that he was painstakingly nudging Stewart toward, but he bit his tongue. This had to be Stewart's idea.

"Once we had this eyewitness account," Aroyo continued, "we attempted to contact Sister Layla at home. We found the cabin empty. We alerted Dr. Elliott and began a campus-wide search. She was found in the barn."

James turned to Stewart. "What do you make of it?"

"It sounds calculated. She pushes him over a cliff—"

He lifted a finger. "That's assumed. We still have no proof of that."

"—and then she deletes the tapes. She's trying to hide it."

James could see the wheels turning in Stewart's mind. He just had to be patient.

Stewart addressed Aroyo. "Curious. The guard—did he have any known diseases?"

Aroyo shrugged. "Not that I'm aware of. He'd been here a long time, since we opened our doors at this site, so he'd have received medical clearance back then."

James jumped in, trying to keep his voice steady. "Two years ago, we didn't have the analysis panel we have today. Maybe we missed something. But it's a moot point. Attacking livestock is a brain stem response, an act of rage."

Come on, Stewart. Argue with me.

"No, James," Stewart said, "she didn't attack the livestock. She was hungry. She needed to eat meat, and that's characteristic of both ragers and predators."

"What are you saying?" James asked, as if he didn't follow.

"A rage attack would've involved destruction to the gate enclosures and panicked animals. That would've been heard by the farmers, but there was none of that. She simply helped herself to some dinner, so to speak."

"Hmm." It wasn't difficult to appear tormented.

"Didn't you say she was a vegetarian?"

He nodded. *Almost there.*

"She was starving for meat, and the way she fulfilled her need was a calculated move." Stewart rose abruptly, his eyes filling with stars. "She's a predator. She's not a rager."

James took a seat, a subtle sign of deference, and allowed Stewart to take over.

Stewart swung around to Aroyo. "Call 'em up. I'm overriding James's order. She will not be sent to salvage. I want her moved to the den."

James scraped a fingernail along the edge of the guest chair. "Are you sure this is the right answer? I don't know. We can't afford a mistake."

"That's the difference between us," Stewart said. "You're a brilliant implementer, and that's why you're in charge of operations, but I'm the one with the intuition. You know the process. I know people."

James nodded as Stewart stabbed a finger at Aroyo's phone. "Make the call. We have another predator right here in Mexico. What a day. Let's go get that drink, Jimboy. Now it's a celebration."

James repressed a sigh of relief. It wasn't the perfect solution, but it would buy him some time and keep Stewart out of his business for a while longer. And these days, every minute mattered.

38

L ayla didn't know why the ambulance had suddenly switched directions and brought her to the room she now occupied. James had instructed the medical staff to send her to salvage. She heard it loud and clear, even though he covered his face in overwhelming disgust and cowered from the woman he promised to love and cherish for the rest of his life.

But this wasn't salvage. Perhaps Isaac didn't have her room ready just yet. Maybe, given her incredibly important leadership role in the Colony, James had insisted that she get a larger corner cell, with cherrywood prison bars instead of ugly steel. Or maybe the surgeon wasn't available to remove her teeth and fingernails.

She inspected her fingernails. Two were broken, and she filed the sharp edges against the light blue cement wall she lay facing.

The interior wall color for general housing had been her idea. *We have enough white around here. We're not trying to stupefy our people into a state of purification by lack of visual stimulus. Now, do you like Sapphire Ice or Cloudless Sky better?* The longer she looked at the Cloudless Sky wall in front of her, the more she wanted to throw something at it. Something bold and staining, like a glass of red wine.

Or a bucket of warm sticky blood.

She rolled onto her other side and took inventory of the room. Just as she expected, it held a desk with a built-in device charger, a two-shelf bookcase without books, and a five-drawer bureau, all white and all with wheels so that they could be moved to the resident's taste—also her design. She'd studied furniture catalogs for hours before selecting this particular brand and style.

It had felt so important at the time. Everything she did, every decision she'd made, had seemed so critical to operations. Only now did she realize how trivial it all had been, pointless busywork that James had overhyped as engineering genius. *There's just no way I could've come up with that idea, Lay. We're so lucky to have you.*

She wanted to puke.

Of course, she just spent an entire night puking, and her throat burned as a reminder. Even after nothing remained inside her to expel, they pumped her stomach through gastric lavage. *We can't risk food poisoning with the baby so close to term*, Dr. De Luca said. It was barbaric.

But then, wasn't what she'd done even more barbaric?

An overhead light illuminated the room, followed by the sound of a voice over an intercom. "Hello, Layla. How are you feeling this morning?"

She looked up to see Dr. De Luca peering down through a plexiglass observation window that ran the length of the small room. She didn't answer, partly because her throat hurt and partly because she was certain that Dr. De Luca was not her friend, despite his cheery Italian accent and endearing pet names that always sounded so heartfelt. *Cucciola! Bella!*

No pet names today, though. Just a frown. "I thought you might appreciate to hear what has happened to you, how you have come to be here. Yes?"

She didn't sit up, nor did she turn away. She wanted to hear him tell the truth for once, if she could even trust him to do that.

"Why don't you come? Sit at the desk so we can have a mature conversation."

His condescending tone enraged her. She chewed her lip.

"Perhaps another time, then." He got up to leave.

"No." She practically coughed the word as she pushed herself up and staggered to the desk, still so weak from yesterday's events. She fell into the chair.

Just weeks ago, she never would have allowed Dr. De Luca to talk to her like that. She was a Colony leader, and he was a Colony employee. And while the employees were well respected, they were not of the same stature as the Colony leaders. They were not pure.

But she could see that the tables had turned.

"There, now. That's better, yes?"

His arrogant smirk made her want to punch the window. Instead, she locked her jaw to avoid a scowl and clasped her hands over her belly like a student waiting for a lesson.

He straightened up and shifted to a colder clinical tone, erasing the melodic charm of his accent. "The fetus you're carrying has a genetic variation of the original strain, a gene defect. It is an unintended consequence of the genetic design we created for this strain. It's rare. A new discovery, yes? We are still trying to understand it."

Layla watched his body language carefully. He was a pompous ass and seemed to revel in it, but she didn't detect that he was lying or hiding something. She let him continue.

"Your original strain, the sensus strain, has shown to be promising, and we've had nearly three thousand successful births across our sites. The variant, which we call praefuro, occurs in about one in ten sensus gestations. It's new to us, and since we don't fully know its capabilities yet, we need to maintain close observation of the carriers. That's why you are here."

"Is it ... dangerous?"

"We cannot answer that yet."

Layla's hands, which were resting on her pregnant belly, fell to her sides. The nape of her neck prickled with fear. Was she carrying some kind of monster? Was it turning *her* into a monster?

A killer?

"I want it out of me," she whispered before her voice shot up to nearly a shout. "I want it out of me. Take it out."

Dr. De Luca leaned in toward the glass. "That is not an option."

She jumped out of her chair and pounded a hand on the barrier. "Please don't do this to me. I don't want it. Please make it go away."

He remained impassive.

"I'll carry another baby. Another strain. Please."

"Eugenesis is aware of the praefuro strain," he said. "They have a deep interest in the offspring."

That was just sick. Twisted. This was never part of the plan. "Why on earth would they want something like this?"

He didn't bother to answer her question. He pushed himself out of the chair and slid his clipboard under his arm. "We would like you to meet some of the other carriers. They are like you, carriers of the praefuro variant. Talk to them, cucciola. You will notice a bond will form." He pressed his lips together in another disingenuous smile. "You will feel welcome. *Famiglia.*"

A mechanical hum behind her made her spin to watch the wall opposite the observation window slide open onto an expansive great room with large wooden beams and wood-paneled walls. Somewhat ridiculously, it looked like a log cabin. The focal point of the room, a colorful play area occupied by six or eight children toddling about, took up about half the space. Lounging in a nearly perfect circle of sofas, recliners, and rocking chairs around it were a dozen or so pregnant women. One mother cuddled an infant tied to her stomach with a baby wrap. Beyond the mothers in a far corner, a few others sat in a small dining area. Classical music unspooled soothingly from speakers.

Layla took it all in with a sense of foreboding. "Why aren't they in salvage with the others?"

His smile faded. "Yes, I remember your *escursioni* around the campus. For someone who is supposed to be on bed rest, you have been a busy bee—*ficcanaso*, we say in Italy."

She didn't care about his little Italian lesson. She waited for an answer.

"Not all praefuro are alike," he said. "We will do some additional testing. Some observation, yes? It's a unique opportunity. You should feel gratitude."

"Gratitude? Are you serious?"

But he turned his back on her, and the observation room went dark.

She drifted toward the opening despite her bad mood. The great room was so different from the other facilities. So cozy and inviting.

Warmth washed through her as she stepped over the threshold. This place was delightful, simply magical. The tranquility of the whole scene. The ethereal aura that seemed to emanate from the mothers themselves in their circle. She felt drawn into the room.

But as she approached the circle, the edges of her thoughts became fuzzy. Her heartbeat slowed—really?—so much she felt light-headed, as though she might faint.

A whiff of something heavenly snapped her back to the moment. Someone was serving meat—hot, rich, juicy. Her stomach rumbled, and one of the mothers looked up and smiled placidly. Layla turned away from the circle. Maybe she'd visit with the carriers later. Right now, she needed to eat.

To *feed*.

39

Nick's eyes popped open as soon as the bus slowed at what he assumed was a security gate, but the rest of the passengers didn't begin groaning and stretching until the blackout glass windows reverted to transparent.

He hadn't slept. While a symphony of snoring had echoed through the cabin in full surround sound, he was drowning in a sea of story fragments, unable to fuse them together into a plausible hypothesis. EGNX murdered Agent Peter Malloy for discovering their secret of conducting illegal drug experiments. Austin Harris and Allison Stevens were involved. Harris wound up dead; Stevens disappeared, only to reemerge as the EGNX welcome committee, under the alias of Sister Layla. Her warm, engaging recorded speech hardly jived with all those accounts of emotional instability and depression.

Over the four years that he'd stumbled around searching for answers, EGNX had grown so much in size and power, they only barely concealed their identity. They took kids right off the streets with a police escort and slipped through border control with nothing but a wave from the driver.

They had known about the virus before it was released, then they had stolen Jordan's cure. What were they doing with it?

His answers would come from behind the daunting wrought-iron gate that the bus just passed through. He shivered, nudging Eddie into a snort.

Eddie raised his seat upright and looked out. "Whoa! This place is fire." His exclamation was enough to get the rest of the bus sitting up.

Nick might have been more impressed if he hadn't already been familiar with the Vitapura Wellness Center. This place looked exactly like he'd expected, only bigger. They might've named it Vitapura Grande. Desert palms wrapped with white lights and decorative plant urns lined the walkway to a Spanish-style adobe building that blended into the sprawling, rust-colored desert. Once again, EGNX had clearly spared no expense.

The bus exhaled to a stop, and people moved to stand up.

"Welcome to the Colony, my friends," Michael called from the front. "This is the end of the line for me. Once you exit the bus, you'll be greeted by our team of welcome agents and intake assistants who'll introduce you to the Colony, explain the next few days, and get you situated in your temporary residence. Restrooms are just inside for you to freshen up, and make sure you pick up a mango smoothie before the walking tour. I'm not exaggerating when I tell you you've never had anything so delicious."

"I can't believe I'm here," Eddie said.

"Me neither," Nick answered as he stepped into the aisle. And he meant it.

The aridity of the desert air was stifling even to Nick, who'd grown up in Phoenix. They had to be somewhere in central Mexico—the Sonoran Desert, perhaps, or Chihuahua, given the seventeen-hour drive, including the slow-down-and-wave through a border control station. They were nowhere near the coast, that was certain. Mountainous terrain rose to both the east and the west, effectively hiding their location from the cities while providing a steady water supply from rivers. Palm trees weren't actually that easy to sustain in the desert.

Nick followed the group to a patio with mist sprayers, like you'd see at a fancy outdoor restaurant back in the old days. He smiled. They really had rolled out the red carpet for their unsuspecting victims. Part of him wanted to blow his cover and warn all these kids that it was a trap.

Couldn't they see it was too good to be true?

Eddie handed him an ice-cold mason jar with a handle and a straw. "Bro, this shit slaps. This is my second one."

Nick gratefully accepted the smoothie and prepared to slake his thirst, but his appetite vanished as a woman all in white stepped onto the patio with two armed security guards.

"Welcome to the most exclusive club on Earth! My name is Alianna. I'm a junior recruiter here at the Colony, and I'll be taking you on a walking tour through the induction campus. But first things first. I hope everyone's had a chance to use the facilities. We'll be leaving in just a couple of minutes."

As he moved toward the bathroom, Nick couldn't help counting the security cameras hanging from each of the pillars holding up the decorative trellis. Eight that he could see. That was a lot of coverage in such a small space. What were they looking for?

By the time he returned from the bathroom, Eddie managed to put away three smoothies, and his face glowed with happiness.

Alianna waved her arm to get the attention of the group. "I'm going to repeat what you already heard from your recruiter because it's important that everyone realizes the conditions on which you've been invited to join us."

She drew nearer as the group's small talk petered away. "First, you're interviewing for a position at the Colony. Although our recruiters have been trained to identify the types of candidates we're looking for, you're not guaranteed a slot in our induction program until you've been fully evaluated. Over the next three days, you'll be given a set of psychological and intelligence tests, you'll visit our infirmary for a physical, and we'll need to take blood for a full DNA sequence test."

Nick wondered if the DNA test would include a forensic identification. Given what he'd seen so far, it was likely.

"At the end of the three-day recruitment period, you will either be deemed ineligible for the program or you'll be invited to sign a five-year contract. The contract is not negotiable."

She paused a moment to let that sink in.

"If the Colony decides you aren't a good fit or if you decide that the program is not for you, you'll be scheduled for a return trip back to your pickup location, with a small financial settlement for your time and trouble. Any questions about this process?"

"Yo, how much money we get?" asked a bony girl with a head of ratty bleached-blond hair with four-inch dark red roots. It reminded Nick of a candle wick. She stood with her hands on her hips and attitude all over her face.

Alianna forced a smile. "Well, if I gave you five hundred dollars, would you get back on the bus and go back home?"

"Lowkey, yeah, prolly."

Alianna pulled out an envelope, fished out five bills, and strode over to the bony girl. "Thank you for your consideration. Go ahead right back through those doors, and our next shift driver will get you situated on the return bus." She handed her the bills.

"Pfft. Later, y'all." Candlewick gave a wave and sauntered back to the bus.

Nick's mouth fell open. That was it? They could come in, collect a stack of Benjis, and go back home? Impossible. How was that an effective recruiting program? How had the Colony flown under the radar all this time if people landed right back home after a round trip on a comfy bus with a belly full of mango smoothie and a pocket full of cash?

"Would anyone else like five hundred dollars to go home?"

Nick expected every hand of that group of zoomers to shoot up, but to his surprise, no one took the offer.

"Good," Alianna said with a smile. "That is the first test of your fitness for the Colony. If you don't actually want to be here, we don't want to have you. Our program evaluation process is extensive and costly. We don't want to waste your time, and we don't want you to waste ours."

She gave another benevolent smile. Nick shifted his weight; they were eating out of her hand now.

"Okay, follow me," she said. "We're going to start with the first of our four pillars of success, physical strength and fitness. We'll begin the tour at our state-of-the-art recreation and fitness center."

Unbelievable. Nick fell in with the group and followed Alianna. Apparently when you had all the money and power you need—

"Excuse me, sir."

Nick whipped around to see two guards moving in on either side.

"Our head of security would like a word with you."

He slowed, unsure of how to respond.

"This way, please."

Eddie pulled back from the tour to wait for him, a look of worry on his face. Nick gave him a nod and a thumbs-up before following the guards up a perfectly manicured cobblestone path to a drab square cement building, offset from and overlooking the rest of the expansive campus.

40

Mr. Amadi Aroyo, head of EGNX security, according to his door plate, was a big enough guy to pull off intimidating, but Nick wasn't getting a menacing vibe. The man slouched over his desk, leaning on his elbows as he reviewed the iPad in front of him. His posture, coupled with his scruffy unshaven face, gave him the look of a grizzly bear protecting his dinner but his voice had more of a dopey teddy bear tone.

A poster-sized map of the Colony behind Aroyo's desk caught Nick's attention. The campus was much bigger than he imagined, built in a wheel-and-spokes design with the security building at the hub and clusters of buildings along the perimeter forming a pentagon. Interesting. Clearly, the intention was to silo the various aspects of the Colony's illicit research activities.

He lowered his gaze when Aroyo cleared his throat.

"It's my understanding that you were a last-minute addition to the group that came in from Los Angeles. Is that right?" Aroyo held out Victor's identification between his long index and middle fingers.

"That's right." Nick returned the card to his wallet.

"And how did you become aware of the bus?"

"I was just chillin'. Some dude hanging around the camp mentioned it. I didn't have anything else going on, decided what the hell." Nick gave him a half shrug and lowered his gaze to avoid being perceived as defiant.

Aroyo crossed his arms and looked at Nick through narrowed eyes. "Is that so? And what was the son of a wealthy attorney doing hanging around a homeless camp?"

Okay, maybe the teddy bear wasn't as dopey as he looked.

"I wasn't hanging around the camp. I was hanging around the bar across the street. Looking to see if someone wanted to buy a mo—" He coughed. "A Harley-Davidson."

Nick was a master at selling improvisational lies, especially when he had to dig himself out of a hole, but Aroyo didn't appear to be buying. He sat back and crossed an ankle over his knee. His amused expression read *Go on, tell me more of this bullshit story.*

What would Victor the douchebag be doing at a bar?

Nick raised both hands. "Okay, okay, I wasn't trying to sell a hog. Truth is, I was looking for the prick that fucked my girlfriend."

That seemed to resonate. "I'm aware of your history of aggression. This is the reason I thought we should speak."

Nick nodded contritely.

"It's not our custom to invite or accept recruits who have a history of violence or crime. That makes you a poor fit for the Colony. We're a community of peacefulness and kindness. We're successful because we're very selective in who we bring into the community."

"That was the old me," Nick said. "I'm making a fresh start. Looking for a change."

"I don't believe people can change." Aroyo moved to a freestanding electronic device in the corner of the office. "But this decision is not up to me." He returned with a gadget that looked like a pen. "Your finger, please."

Nick tried to keep a poker face, but it was game over. The machine was bigger and fancier than the one at Nyla's office, but he recognized the name on the side, BioQuant. This device performed DNA sequencing for forensic identification. Once they saw the name Nicholas Slater and associated him with the nutjob who'd been stalking them for four years, he'd be worm food. Just like Austin Harris.

"Ow." He pressed his ring finger against his jeans to stop the blood, while a flurry of escape options exploded and fizzled out like fireworks in his brain. A bribe? No. A threat? No. Pleading? No. Running? Maybe. Fighting? Aroyo had six inches on him, at least. Hell no.

It took less than thirty seconds for the screen to flash DNA MATCH CONFIRMED, followed by Nick's picture displayed on the screen. Too-long hair flopped over one eye, and his unshaven face and unsmiling mouth made the photo seem more like a mug shot than a government ID photo.

But it wasn't a government ID photo. It was his Wilshire Grand badge picture, taken only three days ago. Beneath the picture, the name read VICTOR BEAUMONT.

Abder, you beautiful little Egyptian hacker genius. I love you, man.

Nick slammed his open mouth shut before Aroyo could catch him gaping at the result. He tucked his long floppy hair behind his ear.

Aroyo hit a buzzer on his desk and scowled at Nick. "As of this moment, you're on my radar. Understand that you'll be observed carefully over the next three days—and mark my words, if I see so much as a nostril flare, you'll be on the next bus out. Handcuffed. Am I clear?"

"Yes, sir." Nick nodded without a hint of the satisfaction he felt. He'd perfected the solemn promise expression by his twelfth birthday. "Thank you for the opportunity."

He offered a hand, but Aroyo didn't move to shake it. As he followed the mall cop escorts out of the boss's office, Aroyo called out.

"Oh, one more thing, Mr. Beaumont."

Nick froze.

"That mobile phone you're trying to hide in your boot won't work out here. We have no cell service or Wi-Fi connectivity outside the Colony. You can leave it at the recruiting center and collect it on your way out."

He was marched like a prisoner from the boss's office and down the hallway past the open door to the surveillance control room. Oh, what he'd give to have a look in there.

"Do you mind if I take this phone out of my shoe?" he asked as humbly as he could. "Now that the cat's out of the bag, it's been killing me."

He squatted down and fiddled with his bootlaces, turning his head ever slightly to check out the expansive wall of monitors. The views changed every few seconds, affirming his initial instinct that the entire campus was covered by CCTV. He also registered the camera surveillance team: one dude with his feet up on the desk, shamelessly playing games on an iPad. That meant the cameras were more for show than actual prevention, and that would surely be to his benefit.

As he rose, burner phone in hand, he spotted an unmistakable head on one of the monitors. The candlewick girl sat among a group of white-pajama-wearing buddies in a large cafeteria, comfortable as a fish in the sea. She'd been a plant.

He kept walking, but he felt his mouth twitch.

Game on, EGNX.

41

Layla waited until afternoon naptime cleared the great room of carriers and children before she slipped out of her room. She scanned the vast empty den and lifted her gaze to the loft. The building was quiet, giving her a window of opportunity to poke around. What was so special about these children and their carriers? Why did they get a country club life while the others got a prison cell?

She wandered between the sofas to the play area. The sofa pillows, smashed flat by pregnant carriers, smelled like body odor and bacon. She stepped through a two-foot yellow gate that opened into the play area. The floor was uncluttered and the area meticulously organized. All the toys were put away. Did the carriers clean up before they gathered the young ones for naptime, or did the children clean up after themselves?

Educational toys were abundant. Blocks, puzzles, and interlocking toys of assorted sizes and shapes were stacked on small shelves along the perimeter. Freestanding stationary play cubes, maybe three feet tall with tiny doors for opening and interacting, were spaced a few feet apart in the center of the room.

God, how old were the children? How long had the program been going on?

She eased herself into a tiny plastic chair facing one of the cubes and opened a small door. There was nothing behind it but a panel. She pressed her palm against it and felt a small vibration, as if there were a motor inside the cube. She put her hand on top of the cube. No vibration. It was a peculiar sensation, and she was about to touch it again when she heard a voice behind her.

"We're not supposed to be in the playroom," a woman said. She held the hand of a young boy with jet black hair, whose black eyes were locked on Layla.

Layla rose slowly, unnerved.

"The area is designated for the offspring."

The offspring. It was an unusual way to describe a human child.

The boy released his mother's hand, entered the play area, and began pulling Legos from a bin. She watched him organize them into piles. He wasn't organizing them by color or size. What was he doing? He didn't seem to notice her standing over him until she spoke.

"You missed one. A red one."

He froze like a statue, his back still turned to her. He remained frozen, like a robot that had been switched off, for a few seconds, then resumed his sorting without touching the red Lego.

Layla stepped out of the playroom, chilled to the bone.

The woman patted the sofa next to her. "I'm Susan."

She didn't sit. Her eyes flashed to her room, and she wished she hadn't left it.

"I was in your purification program early on, before I joined the carriers."

She sighed and studied Susan's face. The woman appeared lucid and friendly, but Layla was struggling to feel at ease. She tried for small talk. "How old is your, uh… How old is he?"

"He's seventeen months. He's the oldest of all the offspring." She tilted her head as she monitored his play, eyes sparkling with the pride of a mother.

Layla studied him, too. He didn't look like he was playing. He looked like he was working, intently reorganizing the blocks in piles, his hands operating simultaneously but independently. Ambidextrous. Multitasking.

A shiver ran up her spine, and she forced herself to look away, almost afraid she'd be hypnotized by his rhythmic movements.

"What's his name?"

Susan threw her a look as though she were crazy. "They don't have names. They don't like to be singled out as individuals. At least that's what I hear. Tasmin—she's the other carrier that's been here almost as long as me—she says the whole is greater than the sum of the parts. Maybe that's all the same thing. I don't really get it."

Layla subtly took another step toward her room. "What do you mean when you say that's what you hear? The doctors told you that?"

"No, silly, the offspring." Susan returned her attention to the boy. "You don't hear yours?"

As if on cue, the creature inside Layla's belly stretched. She looked down in time to see her belly change shape from round to rectangular and then back to round again. Every time it moved, a wave of apprehension rippled through her.

She sat down next to Susan, suddenly more fearful of the alien inside her than Susan and her black-eyed offspring. "Why are they so quiet?"

Susan shrugged. "A long time ago, in my poisoned life, I worked at this behavioral center. You know, one of those places where they teach kids who have mental disabilities?"

Layla nodded to keep the story moving.

"Yeah, so they had these kids there. Autistic, they called them. The teaching staff and doctors always said they were special, like they had gifts that were different from regular people. This one girl? She was like ten, and she could play the piano like a professional, but she couldn't read or write or do math or anything like that. And she didn't talk." Susan raised her eyebrows in the direction of the child. "The offspring are just like them, I figure, but they're smarter. Even more gifted."

Layla lay back against the sofa pillow to calm the snakes coiling in her stomach and risked another look at the toddler in the play area. *A gifted monster busily organizing blocks. What are you making, little freak?*

The boy stopped moving, and Layla's heart jumped into her throat. Had she spoken out loud? She wanted to turn to Susan to read her expression, but her eyes were fixed on the child statue.

The boy rose and walked toward them with oddly deliberate steps for a child his age.

Layla couldn't swallow the lump in her throat. Was he coming for her? Would he attack? Her muscles tightened, and she hunched slightly. He was just a child, but that stony face and those listless eyes, which never seemed to blink, made her feel as though she should brace for attack.

But as he neared her, her rigid muscles relaxed. Her heart rate slowed. He reached out for her hand, and she offered it.

He took her hand in both of his. Warmth flowed from his fingers to hers, moving up her arm and radiating throughout her body. Her mouth dropped open, and her breath came so slow and regular she might as well have been snoring.

Another child appeared from nowhere. He was smaller, not quite as coordinated as he crawled up onto the couch and wrapped his arms around her round belly.

Layla's eyes drooped. She was weightless, floating in blissful oblivion.

We are not the enemy.

The words appeared in her head, but they weren't hers. Nor had they come from the child. They had formed out of nothing. Her eyes closed entirely as the sensation of floating dissipated, but she didn't have the strength to open them again. Or the will. She wanted to sleep.

We are not the enemy. A whisper now.

Susan spoke in a voice that sounded far away. "Oh my god. I've never seen them do that before. Tas, look!"

She wanted to know what that meant, but the heaviness had completely overtaken her now, and she allowed herself to be swallowed by darkness.

***

By the time Dr. De Luca appeared in Layla's room, with that smug look on his face, she was livid.

"What happened to me in there?" She stabbed a finger at the living room. "That is not natural. Those kids are not kids." Her voice escalated with each word. "It's like they hypnotized me. Or drugged me. I lost two hours of my life."

Dr. De Luca sighed as if she'd already exhausted him. "We believe it's simply a hormonal rush, a flood of dopamine released based on proximity between the carriers and the offspring. Like the McClintock effect, yes?"

"No." She despised doctors who couldn't speak in lay terms to those not medically trained.

"It's menstrual synching," he replied. "Sometimes when women live together, their menstrual cycles will begin on the same day. What we've observed here appears to be a lot like that. The offspring secrete high levels of pheromones that have an intoxicating effect on the carriers."

One hand drifted to her mouth. This was like witchcraft.

"We monitor the synaptic transmissions that signal the release of dopamine across a wide proximal range of the offspring. It's a sliding scale, yes? The nearer the carrier is to the offspring, the faster the synaptic transmission. A physical contact event can make the dopamine levels rise so much that it mimics the reaction of a powerful opioid or a high dose of cocaine."

"But why? Why did those things crawl on me?" She felt violated. They weren't babies wanting the soothing physical bond of a parent. They had purposefully manipulated her. Impossibly, they knew what they were doing.

Dr. De Luca removed his glasses and gazed past her into the great room, his eyes twinkling. His voice was low. "This is a new behavior, indeed. We've never observed the offspring choosing to make physical contact, even with their own carriers. This is an extremely interesting development. Perhaps there's something about you, specifically, that seems to attract them. Truly extraordinary. We will observe the behavior over the next days, yes?"

Layla's mouth fell open. "You can't keep me here."

"I'm sorry?"

"I'm not safe." Her voice rose. "This place isn't safe. You need to take me out of here."

"This is a research facility. An observation unit. You stay until we've gathered the data we need."

She lunged at the window and slammed her palms against it. "You son of a bitch!"

Dr. De Luca looked her in the eyes, his voice so low she could barely detect his accent. "Do you feel this rage, Layla? Can you feel your blood boiling under your skin? This is what happens when you are separated from your kind. This is the first phase of withdrawal. It isn't healthy for you or the fetus. It's important that you bond with the carriers and the offspring. Go now. Go rejoin the circle."

Her voice dripped with the venom that now coursed through her veins, and she spoke through gritted teeth to control the volume of her voice. "I refuse to be bonded to those things. They're not … they're … they're unnatural."

His expression dulled with an exaggerated sigh. He pulled a small cloth from his pocket and cleaned his glasses as if they were talking about nothing more important than the weather. "There's no such thing as natural when we speak of the human race, cucciola. Not anymore. There's evolved and unevolved. A relic like me will one day be viewed with the same disdain as we might view a Neanderthal: an earlier form of our species, more animal than human."

Layla winced.

"You're a pioneer of this evolution, the first of the pure humans, isn't that right? What did you think that meant, if not evolved? Maybe you should think about how you define 'unnatural.' I'm not the one who needs to be on that side of the window, yes?"

"You!" She was practically screaming. "You did this to me! I didn't ask for this!"

He leaned in, now as enraged as she was. It was his turn to speak through gritted teeth. "Like everyone in Colony, you will do as you are told. That is the only purpose you serve. That is the only reason you are here."

Layla roared with fury and pounded her fists onto her desk.

She surged away from the window to the edge of her room. The offspring were working, as usual, but the carriers had halted their languid chatting to find out what all the commotion was about. As soon as she crossed the threshold, the carriers stood to face her. Even the offspring turned their attention to her. They were waiting for something, but what?

Dr. De Luca was right: Her blood felt like it was boiling under her skin. Her pulse picked up. Her breaths, forced through clenched teeth, made her sound like a hissing snake.

The freak with the black hair and black eyes trundled toward her. She slid one foot forward in a fighter's stance, arms bent, hands relaxed. The world went silent.

Layla felt a familiar thickness around her skull. Mud in her ears.

We are one. It was a man's voice, not a child's, and it was so loud she covered her ears. Like the voices of the women in salvage, the words were inside Layla, filling her entire head. *We are not them.*

She pushed her own voice into her head. *Don't come near me.*

The offspring froze. *We are at your will,* it replied in its adult voice.

She tried again. *You're a monster. You should never have been born.*

The boy's empty eyes seemed to fill with life, and he opened his mouth in a silent scream.

Susan rocketed off the sofa in a panic, snapping Layla out of the soundless vacuum surrounding her.

The piercing shriek that broke from the offspring was deafening. The other offspring joined him, unnaturally frozen in random positions, their mouths open as wide as those freakish, unblinking eyes, screaming and pausing only to take in a long breath to start again.

The oldest boy, Susan's boy, stopped screaming and lifted an arm to his face as if he were going to block a sneeze. He opened his mouth wider and, using his tiny front incisors, he bit down into the flesh of his arm hard enough to draw blood. His eyes never left Layla's face as he raised his head, blood dripping from his chin. He bit down a second time.

The next oldest child fisted his small hands and beat them against his face, again and again.

Susan screamed. "Make them stop! Please, help!"

Several security guards burst in and pulled their weapons, aiming at the screaming children.

Yes, shoot them. Layla's stomach fluttered.

But Dr. De Luca's voice came over the loudspeaker, drowning out the screaming children. "Not the children. Remove Layla immediately."

Layla turned in a wobbly revolution, uncertain whether to seek an alliance with Susan and the others or to retreat to her room.

"This is Layla's doing."

42

"Layla! Layla, I demand a response!"

Dr. De Luca's lanky body leaned over the small interview table at which Layla had been forcibly placed. Both his hands were fisted, and his face flushed a deep red. Two armed guards flanked the door and glared at her with stony intensity. The temperature in the room was rising by the second.

But something was intriguing about this dynamic. Something about his anger and aggression made Layla feel that the power in their relationship had changed. Somehow she'd gained the upper hand. She sat perfectly still in her chair, her hands folded gently over her lap, her facial muscles so relaxed that she looked simply angelic in her reflection in the one-way mirror.

The doctor, however, exploded into an adult temper tantrum, throwing his arms up in exasperation. His lips drew back in a snarl as he glared at her from behind glasses that had slipped down his nose from the sweat. She fought the urge to remind him that aggression was not a virtue the Colony tolerated; she was rather enjoying his uncivilized means of communication. He looked like an ape waving his arms, making himself look big and scary in a display of dominance. Funny how strong emotion devolved even the most sophisticated humans into dumb primates.

"Talk." Spit sprayed from between his clenched teeth.

His interrogation had degenerated steadily over the last twenty minutes, fraying under her unflappable composure and her refusal to give him the satisfaction of an answer. Finally, she decided to take him up on his explicit invitation.

"Fine," she replied so quietly he was forced to scuttle to the table and lean toward her. "I'd like a meeting with the council. I want to speak to Stewart and the others—those you insist are so interested in the praefuro offspring."

He slammed both hands on the table and circled it until he was behind her.

He leaned down next to her ear and said softly and slowly, "I ask you one last time. What did you communicate to the offspring to make them react like that?"

The fact was that Layla herself didn't fully comprehend what had happened. She'd never heard anything like their stereophonic shrieking, nor did she believe that a child of that age could be capable of hurting itself. It had been truly unnerving. Yet she didn't feel their outcries had been directed at her. No, they were reacting on her behalf, as an extension of herself, a metaphysical appendage, and their screams and self-harm were an expression of her own self-loathing in the only way a child could convey such an emotion. It was her fury that had unleashed their explosive behavior. She was the molten magma amassing deep in the earth, and they were the erupting volcanoes violently releasing the pressure.

She was communicating through them.

We are one.

In some strange way, it was liberating.

She could almost hear the tension in the doctor's large muscle groups screeching with frustration, priming for discharge like the action of a handgun being cycled behind her. Her own body stiffened as she braced for the imminent release.

It wasn't a hit or slap to the side of the head, as she expected. Instead, he threaded his fingers through her long hair and yanked her head backward.

The joints of her upper spine crackled in response, but she wouldn't give him the satisfaction of so much as a wince. She stared up at him, upside down, unintimidated. "Now who's the one with the rage problem?"

He shoved her head forward hard enough that her nose and forehead slammed against the table.

The guards made no effort to defuse the physical assault or protect her. She wasn't surprised. If she were still Sister Layla, they would've wrestled him to the ground and cuffed him. But now that she was Layla the killer, she no longer had any influence; she'd been stripped of all authority.

But she had her dignity—for now, anyway. More importantly, she had something that Dr. De Luca very much wanted, something he'd never find by replaying the security tapes, no matter how carefully he studied them. And while that didn't earn her the basic human rights that she was clearly being denied in this brutal interrogation, it was leverage.

Blood dripped from her nose and over her lips, but she made no effort to wipe it.

Dr. De Luca took his seat opposite her, seemingly having regained his composure.

She leered at him. "You don't know anything about us. You think your science can explain who we are, and you think you can predict how we'll behave. But you're very, very wrong."

She flew up so quickly that her chair toppled over behind her. Out of the corner of her eye, she saw the guards move in, but Dr. De Luca held up his hand.

"I could kill you right now." She leaned over the table and lowered her tone to a growl. "I could yank that black heart right from your chest and squeeze it until it was nothing but a flaccid pile of tissue. And then I could summon those demon children to feast on your dead body." She wasn't sure if it was the taste of her blood or the idea of killing the doctor that made her drool. She ran her tongue over her bottom lip. "That's the difference between your unevolved brain and mine. Your rage manifests as violence; mine, as slaughter."

She wiped her mouth with her thumb and sat back down, folding her arms across her chest.

Dr. De Luca's eyes bore into Layla as he slowly slid his clipboard and his voice recorder back in front of him. He pressed a button on the voice recorder and spoke, slowly and deliberately, as if an assistant would be transcribing his words.

"Praefuro subject 01980. Upon identification of praefuro symptoms, subject was evaluated by Dr. James Elliott and Mr. Stewart Hammond, and it was suggested, based on the observation of a calculated predation and kill, the subject might be presenting a phlegmatic phenotype of the praefuro mutation. The subject was moved from the infirmary to the phlegmatic group housing known as the den. However, given the recent event that caused a significant disruption in the phlegmatic unit, it has been determined by the medical team that subject 01980 is a threat to the community and a risk to the psychosocial bond that exists there. Therefore, it is the recommendation of the medical team that the subject be relocated to the choleric unit in the salvage building to ensure she does not undermine the success of the program or put herself, the fetus, or others in danger."

They stared at each other, poker-faced, for another long minute. Layla smelled something new billowing from the doctor: fear. But it wasn't fear of her. He was well protected in that small space. It was something else, something bigger.

Layla had thrown a monkey wrench into his program. She'd done something he hadn't seen before, and that didn't just make her unpredictable. It made his entire praefuro program unpredictable. Once the council figured out that despite his impressive multisyllabic labels and pages of subject observations, he didn't truly understand the praefuro, his reputation would be ruined, and he would no longer be essential.

"*Finito.* Is that the word, Alessandro? Huh, *bello*?"

At the wave of his hand, a guard on each side scooped her off the chair and roughly dragged her from the room.

She kept her stare on the doctor until the door closed between them.

43

Nick pulled on his navy blue linen tie pants and tunic, wiped the foggy bathroom mirror with his bath towel, and winked at his freshly shaved face and clean hair. He couldn't remember a more refreshing shower, and he badly needed a bourbon nightcap and a good night of sleep. But that wouldn't happen tonight. He had a story to find, and the best time to start looking was when everyone else slept.

Eddie, who during room assignments had grabbed him by the arm like they were picking teams for kickball, wasn't in the room when he exited the bathroom. Probably outside having a smoke. *I've been wanting to quit anyway*, Eddie had whispered when the infirmary intern told them to enjoy the next three days because, after that, it would be no smoking, no drugs, and no alcohol.

Nick slipped under the covers and wanted to giggle with joy. He hadn't slept on a real bed since before the virus, and he was certain he'd never experienced the miracle of a pillow-top mattress.

He rolled over and shuffled through the booklets stacked on the bedside table. *Addiction and Recovery in an Immersion Environment. Pain as a Positive Experience. Is the Colony a Cult? An Interview with James Elliott.*

He was opening the cult booklet just as Eddie came back inside. "Bro, you gotta stand outside and look at the sky. I've never seen stars like that.

Think I saw the frying pan thing."

Nick grinned. "It's called the Big Frying Pan. If we're still here tomorrow night, I'll show you how to find Polaris and the Little Frying Pan."

"Bet." Eddie lay back on his bed with his head on his hands. "This is the best day I can remember. I never want to leave."

Peculiar that a kid as young as Eddie would want to give up on life to live in the desert in a cult. In fact, Nick had made an interesting observation over the day: Most of the people who traveled on the bus with them didn't appear to be destitute. A few had emerged from the homeless camp, and he couldn't figure out why a dozen or so had been delivered by prisoner transport, since Aroyo over in security had made it clear that they didn't recruit criminals. Who was this racket's target audience?

He slid the booklet back on the nightstand. "Aren't you a little nervous about this place at all? We all wear the same clothes, we have to follow their strict rules. We have to commit to five years—*five years*. That doesn't scare you?"

"Nah, bro. You know what scares me? Everything outside those huge cement walls. It's a shitty world for a guy like me."

"But you're so young. You have a whole life ahead of you. It's all about having choices." Nick cringed at his own words. He sounded like his father.

"No choices for me. I have HIV."

Nick closed his eyes. Now he understood the paranoia.

"My partner died the first week the virus hit LA," Eddie said, "before anyone even knew what was happening. He was getting monthly IV treatments at AltaMed. The virus pretty much took out the whole unit. Timing's everything, right?"

"I'm sorry." The virus was scary enough for a healthy young adult, but someone with HIV had to hide from the virus. Hide from the world. Eddie sure as hell would never get a job in times like these, when every employer required a DNA test.

"Yeah, rip."

HIV okay, no addicts, the woman in LA had said, as if it was an ad for yard help. "What about your family?"

"*Pfft.* They're beat." Eddie rolled over and faced the wall.

He wished he hadn't started the conversation. Eddie was all of maybe twenty years old, he'd already lost a loved one, and his family turned on him, maybe for being gay or maybe for contracting HIV. Nick could only partly relate. He had lost a mother, though not to death or, god forbid, the virus. His father was beat, as Eddie would say. But he did have a family. His aunt and uncle didn't have much in this life and they didn't always play by the rules, but they had always opened their hearts and home to him.

He was about to go back to the cult booklet he started earlier when Eddie turned back to him.

"You know, all my life I used to do that prayer, the one kids do," Eddie said. "'Now I lay me down to sleep.' You know that one?"

"Yeah."

"I always thought it would protect me from monsters." He snickered. "Then one day, the prayer just changed. And guess what it changed to?"

Nick shrugged.

"'Today is October fourteenth, 2022.'" Eddie rolled back onto his back, intoning flatly toward the ceiling. "'It is with great despair that I report a virus has been released from the Gansu Province in China and will soon enough spread across the globe. It is unlike anything the world has seen before. I have had firsthand experience with this virus. I've seen what it's capable of, and I am sending this message as a warning to stay out of public places. Stay off the streets. Quarantine in your home with your loved ones. I'm begging you.'"

Nick whispered the "A Desperate Warning to the World" along with him. It was strange how that voice had affected so many people, how the words lived inside every mind as both a caution and a solace.

"Thanks, bro," Eddie said when they were finished. "Feels good to be here. I don't care how long it takes to get a cure for my HIV, 'cause at least the virus won't get me. Give me liberty or give me death, right? You know who said that?"

Nick mumbled, "Patrick Henry," but the image of ground zero, the Liberty Bell crack in the pillar, flashed into his head, and for the millionth time, his mind replayed his unanswered questions. Why was there a discrepancy between the two pictures? How did the crack get there? Could it have been a hair on the camera lens? Had he seen something that wasn't real because he wanted to?

He returned to the booklet. The inside cover featured a profile picture of James Elliott with a short bio: *James Elliott earned a PhD in sociocultural anthropology and was awarded an honorary degree in clinical psychology from Stanford University for his rehabilitative work with the fifty-eight college students who were mentally and sexually abused in the Wake of God religious cult in California. He's widely published under the pen name B. J. Elliott in cult behavior and cult societies. Dr. Elliott is the Chief Operating Officer of Eugenesis, Incorporated.*

Eugenesis. EGNX.

Nick studied the face of James Elliott. He looked to be in his forties, with brown wavy hair, blue eyes, and glasses, but he didn't have a professorial look, as his impressive credentials might lead one to assume. His eyes were gentle, and although he didn't smile for the camera, his facial features were warm. He looked a bit like a modern-day Jesus Christ, and Nick had to believe that was deliberate.

He flipped to a quotation from the man himself: "I had the extreme privilege of studying under the esteemed cult expert Rick Ross, who spent most of his life deprogramming cult followers. By his definition, the short answer to the question 'Is the Colony a cult?' is yes. Now, let me explain why I can say that with both honesty and pride, and why I submit that it is foundational both to our success and to the happiness of more than two hundred thousand members across all our colonies worldwide."

Two hundred thousand members—Holy Mary, mother of God. Nick's scalp prickled for the umpteenth time that day.

This entire experience was surreal. The good-natured welcome from the driver. The video of Allison Stevens, delivering a compelling introduction to being among those chosen to come to the Colony. The walking tour of the state-of-the-art residences, facilities, and medical center. The dining hall, nicer than most restaurants nowadays. Nick scrutinized everything he saw today as if he were searching for the killer in a whodunit movie. He never expected that recruits would be shown the torture chambers or three-headed genetically modified creatures, but they visited several credible doctors who talked openly about their genetic research: educators who emphasized the importance of human and societal evolution, mental health professionals trained in addiction, depression, and the psychological impact of the virus and the economic collapse, and physical therapists and trainers who'd dedicated their lives to the Colony's mission of bettering the human race. And he saw hundreds of seemingly happy and productive members of this strange society who didn't appear brainwashed, tortured, abused or neglected in any way.

Sure, it had only been one day, but he hadn't heard or seen one thing that gave him pause, other than the security guards that had been assigned to follow him because of his unpredictable temper. And now he was reading a full-on admission that this was indeed a cult society—all neatly packaged in a handy easy-to-read booklet in the rooms of the recruits.

The transparency was unsettling, to say the least.

"Bro, hit the light," Eddie said in a sleepy voice.

Nick switched off the light and stared upward into the pitch black. Where was the evil? What was he missing?

Where were the guys who murdered Peter Malloy?

There was one person who had his answers, one person who he knew had been there from the start. Allison Stevens. And come hell or high water, he would find her. He would find her and make her talk if he had to shake every word from her.

He waited another couple of minutes until Eddie's breathing grew into full-blown snores, quietly collected his Timberland boots from the closet, and crept out of his room.

The sky was lit up by the stars, but he still had to walk slowly on the dark path to avoid tripping over the stones. The cool fresh air revived him, and for just a moment, before he berated himself for being a fucking wacko, he thought he might enjoy living at the most exclusive club on Earth.

His mind wandered back to his momentary glimpse of the surveillance monitors. No doubt several of those monitors had captured him slipping from his apartment. He could only hope the night shift was asleep at the wheel.

44

I t had to be well after midnight, and the campus was dark and quiet except for one well-lit building elevated above the others, which must have been the security center. If Nick was going to find his story, discover what they're really doing with all these kids, and expose Allison Stevens and EGNX, he certainly wouldn't learn anything in Fairytale Land, where the recruits were housed.

The map in Aroyo's office had shown five sections to the campus. Nick couldn't tell how far apart each cluster of buildings was, but given the size of the valley and the proximity of the hills and mountains, it couldn't have been more than a couple of miles. He could jog that distance in twenty or thirty minutes.

He skulked along the outside of his dormitory, creeping from building to building, until he came upon the imposing cement walls that sequestered the Colony. This perimeter was taller than the one around the Vitapura facility in Arizona. Huh. Maybe that was to keep out the wolves he heard howling in the distance. It wasn't something he'd be able to scale, but he noted several areas where animals had dug underneath, including several wide enough for a human to wriggle through, as long as he could hack through the brush first. Good to know.

He turned along the wall. The lavish xeriscaping of the recruiting campus evaporated once he got off the main walkway, and he was left scrabbling through cactus and brush. Keeping the security center in sight to guide his progress, he scuffled along for a full fifty minutes before his journey was abruptly interrupted by a chain-link fence perpendicular to the wall, butted up so tightly that not even a coyote could have squeezed through. He followed it toward the campus interior, hoping for a weak spot in the chain links. Or better yet, a gate.

Under his boots, the hard-packed clay terrain had softened. He squatted and scooped a handful of sandy soil. Something was different here. He moved onto to his hands and knees, squinting in the darkness, and felt around, careful to avoid the prickly pear plants. The vegetation here was sparse, younger. He found the nearly perfect straight edge of older dried clay surface.

This area had been dug out and refilled, and fairly recently. From his crouch, he followed the sandy section, looking for another edge to no avail. He continued slogging through the sand, another twenty or thirty feet when the realization hit: He'd found a tunnel system—one part of it, anyway.

And if they had tunnels, they had something to hide.

The tunnel ran along the fence line, making it easy to follow until it turned sharply toward a cluster of buildings. He stepped onto neatly groomed grass in front of a six- or seven-story building and crept along the perimeter of the building until he could go no further. A cluster of juniper shrubs had been thoughtfully planted right next to the wall, and behind the shrubs, at the base of the building, a dim light glowed through the dense, scaly leaves.

Nick dropped onto his stomach and wormed his way under the branches until he reached an eight-inch screened vent. He peered inside.

His first thought was that he was looking into a World War II trauma center, with rows of occupied hospital beds neatly lined up. He exhaled and looked down at the sleeping face below the small window.

The woman's eyes snapped open and stared straight at him.

Nick jumped, bumping his head on the tree branch above him. He stifled a groan.

All down the row of beds below him, patients stirred and turned their heads toward his window. No one made a sound.

He slithered backward a couple of inches as two bodies sat upright, slowly rose from their beds, and approached the window. They moved stiffly and their hospital gowns were crumpled from sleep, but there was something else constraining their movements. He squinted to get a closer look. A long yellow tube passed from the back of their gowns over a hook on an IV rack. His eyes followed the yellow line to a unit on the wall, where it connected to a digital display. It looked like they were on a leash.

Oh, Jesus. It hit him then. They were attached at the base of the spine, just like Pete Malloy's victims. The spinal port.

The woman below Nick's vented window stopped abruptly. She reached back and unhooked her tube, which had snagged on the bedpost, and stepped closer until she stood directly under the vent, her leash pulled so taut, it should have ripped from her body. She craned her neck to look straight up at him. Her eyes were unfocused with dilated pupils, as if she were intoxicated, and the eerie smile that transformed her long ashen face was so unsettling that a whimper escaped his throat. He was transfixed by her glassy stare.

It seemed as though minutes passed before either of them breathed.

Her melodious voice was barely above a whisper. "Phoenix."

His breath hitched. How did she know? Did she recognize him?

"The pray pharaoh will rise like the Phoenix, with new life. A new purpose." She spoke so softly he wasn't sure he was hearing her correctly. "A pharaoh's mission cannot be fulfilled until it is fully acknowledged and embraced."

She lifted both hands toward him as if she were asking for a hug.

That was it. Nick scrambled back from beneath the juniper tree. His skin crawled, and he shuddered, stumbling through the gravel until he was back on the paved path. His muscles were so stiff, he could only tremble. Sweat dripped into his panting mouth as he gaped at the dim yellow light radiating from the vent. At any moment, the vent cover would fly off and that ashen-faced woman would come crawling through, a demon from a horror movie.

Finally, his breath slowed and his head cleared. The crickets turned on like a switch, chirping from every direction. The night temperature had to be thirty degrees colder, characteristic of springtime in the desert, and his damp linen pajamas against his body sent an icy chill right through his bones. It took another moment to get his bearings before he began strolling, glancing back over his shoulder every few seconds, then speed walking, and finally full-on sprinting back to the wall.

He found the evil.

45

J ames downed three glasses of Pellegrino, hoping the cool water would calm his overactive sweat glands, and appraised the council members waiting for the meeting to start. It had been a long morning of touring the China site, and his colleagues looked exhausted. Even after two days in Beijing, he hadn't fully adjusted to the time difference, and he was certain the rest of the council members were jet-lagged as well. He'd tried to get Stewart to schedule the meeting in the US, but he'd lost. *They're dying to host us. It's a cultural thing, James. You have to be more sensitive to that kind of thing.*

Stewart had also insisted on the facility tour. James had to admit the site was impressive. With the import of colonists from the Americas and Western Europe, it was now the largest and most diverse colony on the planet. He couldn't help being a little jealous.

The twenty Eugenesis council members were also enthusiastic about the growth of the China site and the progress of the carrier program. The sensus strain had so far proven remarkable. The children, all younger than four years, were exhibiting the anticipated characteristics: higher intelligence, lower aggression, more cohesiveness and harmony. They were the true success story.

The praefuro strain was a different story. While the council was aware of the praefuro carriers, as well as the dozens of subjects who had been transfused with the praefuro stem cells, he wasn't sure they fully understood just how dangerous the praefuro were. That was Stewart's doing. Stewart downplayed the outliers, waved a dismissive hand every time they observed something unexpected. His boss wanted to steamroll ahead at any cost, while he wanted to hit the brakes. Somehow, he'd have to convince the council that the praefuro program needed more time to understand the wide range of rage and aggressive behavior they were seeing, and he had to do it without provoking Stewart to question his motives.

He stood at the window, pretending to admire the ellipsoidal National Grand Theater while studying Stewart in the reflection. The man worked the room like a seasoned politician despite the lack of social lubricants. There was a time when Stewart had made alcohol available at all council meetings—*The drunker they are, the more agreeable they are*—but the council must've wised up, because they recently requested that meetings be dry.

Stewart tapped his glass with a pen to get everyone's attention. "Shall we get started? The sooner we finish our business, the sooner we can hit the bar."

It got a snicker from the room, but the remark was a bad sign. Stewart was in one of his less-work-more-play moods, in which he was likely to cut off healthy discussion in order to move faster through the agenda. James took his seat at the end of the long boardroom table, opposite Stewart. 1:04 p.m. Back in Mexico, it was after midnight. If he were home, he would be lying in an empty bed, hugging Layla's pillow to inhale the scent of her face cream. An invisible claw gripped his heart and squeezed.

"I'd like to start by thanking Mr. Li Jian and his team for sharing his beautiful city with us." Stewart nodded to the Chinese council representative, one of a half dozen who managed the China site. "Today we want to provide an update and decide our next steps for a program that's near and dear to me, the praefuro program. James?" He sat down, his mouth curved in a wry smile.

James found Stewart's expression to be unsettling. Was he just excited or was he hiding something?

He picked up the slide advancer. "Thank you for being here today. It's the first time in a while that I recall seeing all twenty of us here in person. And today's discussion couldn't be more critical to the overall program. We've talked a lot about the praefuro program and some of the challenges we've faced with this strain. But today I want to take you back to the beginning. I want to remind you of our initial observations and how the program evolved because I think that will help all of us decide our next steps."

He felt Stewart glaring at him as he clicked to the first slide. This history lesson was not part of the original plan.

Gasps filled the room at the bloody scene, an infirmary room with a staff member crumpled on the floor and a pregnant woman looming over him. "This is Case Study One. Lucinda was implanted with a sensus strain embryo, which as you know is a genetic model featuring enhanced intelligence. She was in her third trimester, under medical observation for minor cramping, when she viciously attacked a food service worker who was delivering a meal. The worker had just set down her tray when she grabbed the butter knife and pounced, stabbing him several times. Once the knife got too slippery to hold, she tossed it aside and proceeded to shred him using her teeth and fingernails, continuing long after he stopped moving and breathing."

Hugo Lopez, from La Colonia near Madrid, crossed himself. It was a strange thing for a Eugenesis council member to do. How could a God-fearing Catholic participate in the blasphemy of playing God themselves?

"When interviewed later, the carrier claimed she had an overwhelming urge to kill and simply couldn't help herself. When we showed her a video of the attack, she vomited. But even then, she claimed—despite the gruesomeness—that she'd done the right thing. 'He was poison,' she said."

The next slide showed Lucinda in an interview room.

"We isolated Lucinda and ran genetic analyses of both the fetus and the carrier. We found a genetic mutation, a variant of the original sensus strain, which we named *praefuro*, the Latin word for storm or rage. The mutation resulted from a mistake; CRISPR, the gene editing tool, had edited the wrong gene. It had targeted and modified a gene called MAOA, which is associated with aggression."

Stewart was already giving him the move-it-along gesture, but James ignored him. The council wasn't here to drink. They were here to learn and understand, then weigh in on the path forward.

"Identifying the praefuro mutation was a good first step, but the strange attack remained a mystery. We exposed the carrier to a variety of other colonists—males, females, younger, older, Black, White, and so on—but she didn't react. Since we were unable to learn anything more, we transferred the carrier to salvage because her behavior was unpredictable."

He clicked again to an organized lineup of animal carcasses. "Our second case was a subject named Hui-chin. Hui-chin was found eating live rabbits and mice and storing their remains in her room. She claimed she craved meat. She was tested and the same genetic mutation was found, but when we asked her if she ever felt like killing a human, she said no."

The next slide, two corpses with dark purple rings around their necks, elicited another ripple of reaction around the table. "A month later, Hui-chin was admitted to the medical center for migraine pain, where she slaughtered two patients who were receiving IV treatments for hepatitis B. Her methodology was entirely different. She didn't attack in an uncontrollable rage, as Lucinda had. She patiently waited outside the treatment room, making small talk with the nurses until she was alone, and then casually strangled both of them with IV tubing pulled from a drawer. When a nurse ran into the room, she immediately relinquished her hold on the tubing and apologized."

Stewart was now thumbing his phone under the table. Good. The more distracted Stewart was, the better.

"When we questioned Hui-chin, she said the two patients were zombies and she could smell their decomposing flesh. We ran more tests and finally hypothesized that the phenotype we were seeing, expressed via these attacks, was being triggered by the presence of disease. Specifically a proliferative disease."

All eyes but Stewart's were on James. Pictures had a way of getting attention that plain old storytelling didn't. Time to slide in the finishing detail. "It was determined that the food service worker attacked by the first subject, Lucinda, had previously been diagnosed with a genetic cancer."

"Wait, cancer? That's not a—would that be considered a proliferative disease?" asked Jack Downs, a trillionaire oil tycoon. Jack's lack of medical background was an asset; he tended to ask clarifying questions that helped everyone at the table.

Jonathan Chambers, the council physician, answered first. "Yes. We consider any disease to be proliferative if the abnormal cells grow so rapidly that the healthy immune system can't destroy them. Cancers are a good example. We're also seeing the phenotype relative to viruses like HIV and HCV."

"Exactly." James nodded. "The discovery of the praefuro presents an ethical dilemma that comes with significant consequences."

Stewart looked up from his phone and stiffened. He didn't like it when James allowed the council to consider the ethics of what Eugenesis was doing. But they both knew better than to strong-arm these wealthy, influential people. The council members were ethical professionals with clarity of conscience and enough power to pull the plug on Eugenesis' work if they didn't like where it was headed. It was better to bring them along willingly than drag them to the next level.

"On the one hand," James continued, "we could say that every human is equally deserving of a happy life with reproductive potential, regardless of their genetics or health. That's the socially accepted norm in most of the world. However, because humanity's profound medical advancements have extended the lives of those with proliferative diseases, their unfavorable genetic traits have propagated into the generations to follow. Our population continues to rise, but our species is weakening. Disease rates are climbing. We're getting sicker. Through technology, we've all but halted natural selection—and the evolution of the human race."

There was no contesting this fact. They'd all seen the data.

"On the other hand, every species since the beginning of life on earth has competed for its survival. Humans are no different. Natural selection posits that the fittest will live to procreate and the unfit will die out. This is necessary for evolutionary success. Depending on where you sit on this issue—whether you believe in protecting every human being at any cost or advancing our stalled evolutionary process—is how much of an opportunity you might see in the exploitation of the praefuro model."

Stewart sat up straight and surveyed the others at the table before fixing his narrowed eyes on James. His expression clearly read, *watch it.*

James got to the point. "As Stewart so eloquently told us years ago, 'Improving the human race means driving favorable genes into the world.' We can all agree that the sentiment aligns with our strategy. Our broad distribution of the sensus strain offspring is our very successful first step." He looked from face to face, gathering momentum from their attentiveness. "But we find ourselves now faced with the reciprocal opportunity, eradicating unfavorable genes from the gene pool. This is the other side of the coin, the parallel strategy for improving the fitness of the human species."

The concept of negative eugenics wasn't new to the council, but Stewart had painted a different picture all those years ago, harshly criticizing the vision of Adolf Hitler of being profoundly misdirected. Yet, here they all were, creating their own definition of *unfit* to justify their actions and realize their vision.

But the council had to remember that the praefuro were killers. Killers of disease, sure, but also killers of human beings. Someone's mother, someone's spouse. He wanted to say those words aloud, but if he did, Stewart would see clearly which side of the ethical dilemma he'd chosen.

"So, I'll ask the council again, are you in favor of continued development of the praefuro model?"

Not one person in the room spoke up against the idea. Every head nodded except the impassive Li Jian's. James hoped he wasn't speaking too fast for him to follow.

Seeing the flock of bobbing heads, Stewart relaxed back into his chair and returned to his phone.

The council's reaction left him feeling utterly deflated, and he fought the impulse to slump over the table. He had hoped the immorality of killing people might be enough to slow the whole program down. Discord among the council would require time to settle. Weeks probably. And those precious weeks would get him closer to his reversion therapy.

"Very good, then." Moving on to Plan B.

"Our next discussion and decision is around the implementation of the strategy. The reason I described the two cases, Lucinda and Hui-chin, is to demonstrate the unpredictability of the rage effect."

Stewart's eyes shot back up. James was moving into uncharted territory, and Stewart hadn't approved this level of transparency. He specifically didn't want concrete data presented to the council.

"At the moment, we're seeing that carriers with the mutant gene aren't expressing the rage behavior in the same way," James said. "Lucinda's vicious brain stem rage attack represents the choleric extreme. Or in lay terms, Lucinda is a rager. Hui-chin's more thoughtful, calculated attack is the phlegmatic extreme. She's known as a predator. If only it were that simple." He clicked the slide advancer and pulled up a scatterplot. "This is the current state of our praefuro carriers, including early data on those who've undergone praefuro cord tissue transplants. What we learn from this plot is that time and aggression are inversely correlated. If a praefuro has a slower predatory phase before the kill, they tend to have a less aggressive attack. The opposite is also true. The more driven they are to kill quickly, the more brutal the slaughter. This is consistent across gender, race, and age."

He pointed his laser at the middle of the scatter plot, the area with the most dots. "But our praefuro don't fall perfectly into two camps, the ragers and the predators, as you've been told in the past. Most fall in the middle, between the two. It's a sliding scale. So ethically and practically, where do we draw the line? Which praefuro carriers do we believe are safe to send into the world to fulfill their mission and propagate? The top ten percent of the more thoughtful, less aggressive predators? The top half?"

"Why are we even having this discussion?" General Harding, a retired five-star general from the US Army, was by far the most influential person in the room, and most votes tended to follow his view on any topic. "Who said anything about sending them out into the world? How do we know that even the best of them will destroy our true gene pool enemies? We don't even know the whole list of diseases."

Exactly! James wanted to hug him.

"I agree." Jack Downs leaned in on his elbows, his face drawn with deep concern. "I think it's far too early to be asking this question, James."

Stewart flinched, and James felt his own confidence returning. Jack's funding of the program was essential. If Jack pulled out, the program would slow significantly.

James pretended to be surprised by the dissension. "Well, folks, like any experimental program, we need to start collecting real-world data. Simulations can only get us so far."

Those had been Stewart's exact words, and James felt a wave of satisfaction as they elicited a roar of indignation from the entire room. He was winning. The council would vote down the early dissemination of the praefuro.

"You're setting up the program to fail by pushing it out so fast."

"We don't even know all the questions, let alone the answers."

"You yourself just said they're unpredictable. How do we know they won't kill innocent people? Babies?"

"Can't babies can have proliferative diseases, too?"

"And what about tracking and measuring? That's not even been—"

"All of them."

Despite the softness of his voice, all eyes swung to Li Jian. It was the first time James had heard him speak in the group; to be frank, he was surprised the man spoke English. During the few interactions he had with the Chinese team, he had significant trouble communicating with Li Jian.

"Pardon me?" James asked.

"Your question, Dr. Elliott. You asked which praefuro subjects we should send out into the world."

The hair on the back of James's neck prickled as he waited helplessly for the man to repeat his inscrutable recommendation.

"We send all of them."

46

The entire council regarded Li Jian with incredulity. James studied Stewart, who didn't appear shocked at all by Li Jian's suggestion. James could've sworn the corners of Stewart's mouth briefly quirked up.

"With all due respect," barked Jack Downs, "what the hell are you talking about?"

Li Jian pushed his chair out and only partially stood to address the room. "The problems you are thinking about will be self-correcting. An unfavorable phenotype will not survive and therefore will not proliferate over generations." He gave a slight bow to James and sat back down.

No one spoke as they processed what he was saying.

"Perhaps you could elaborate on that for our colleagues," Stewart finally said.

Li Jian assumed the same half-standing position. "We must release all the praefuro. All. The praefuro who are not fit by societal standards will not be allowed to continue in the society. They will be jailed or killed, therefore ending their genetic lineage. Those who meet societal standards will thrive and reproduce." Again, he nodded at James and took his seat.

All at once, the other council members unleashed their outrage on top of each other. James let it roll as he tried to grasp what was happening.

He'd been crystal clear at the praefuro meeting earlier that month: There would be no sideline discussions about the praefuro model and its development. He needed to control the dialogue. Now it seemed the Chinese team had ignored his instruction and engaged Stewart in private conversations. He wasn't entirely surprised. The Chinese government had been unapologetic about their disinterest in working with a global team, and there had certainly been long-standing trust issues between China and the other world powers.

But this didn't seem like China's idea. He felt that Li Jian had just delivered a rehearsed dissension. Stewart was dipping Li Jian's toe into the water to test it. The smug look on Stewart's face was all the proof he needed.

James couldn't let the council be swayed. He knocked on the table. "Okay, okay, let's take it down a notch. This is a council meeting, not reality television." Not that Stewart would know the difference. "As the council, we'll decide with a cohesive vision under what circumstances the praefuro field test will begin."

Heads nodded around the table; that did the trick. Now he could steer them around any rash moves. "I'd like to propose we establish a team to develop a staged field test protocol that will ensure the safety of both the general public and the praefuro subjects. And we'll need a risk mitigation plan. I'll take that as an action item, and we can reconvene on the topic next quarter. Stewart?"

They couldn't afford putting it to vote. James knew what the count would be, and he didn't want to single out Li Jian and where China's loyalties laid. That was a discussion to be had with Stewart—in private.

Stewart plastered a smile on his face. "We're in luck. I happen to have late-breaking footage from our early praefuro simulations that I'm sure you'll find impressive—compelling enough to convince even James that it's safe to accelerate the program to a sensible field release. I don't see why we should allow slow administrative decision-making to impede our progress."

James felt the hot flush. Stewart threw a fucking wild card.

Goddammit.

"What kind of data?" General Harding asked.

Stewart beamed. "I've invited Eva Ridel, a brilliant choreographer from Paris who's been instrumental in sharpening our instruments, so to speak, to give us a virtual tour and allow you to see just how sharp we've become."

The room beamed at his clever word choice, but James was focused on stifling a verbal attack on Stewart. That snake.

If Stewart had planned to impress the council with simulation footage, that meant he'd have already sifted through hours of scenes and hand-picked his favorites. He'd show them only their finest praefuro and the seamless kills, and that sure as hell wouldn't be a representative sample. Learning how to stalk and eliminate a target took months of practice and training. They were far from that. Stewart would give them the false impression that it was all intuition, that the praefuro gene transplant could instantly transform an ordinary Joe into a fierce terminator.

A loud buzz over the door indicated it was opening, and Eva pranced into the room. James contained an eye-roll.

The next hour would be one of Stewart's Disneyland treats, a wild ride through his latest amusement park, the Gallery. The wow-factor would quell any objections from the council members, and he'll convince them that the Gallery is a robust Phase 1 study of the praefuro in the field. It'll be just like Stewart's virtual tour of the den, his cozy ski-lodge-style quarantine for his favorite pets, the phlegmatic praefuro—the predators. The council hadn't seemed at all concerned about the eerie drug-like state in which those poor women lived day after day. Shit, they wouldn't have minded a few weeks stay themselves.

The den. By now Layla would have been well assimilated in that den.

That familiar claw seized hold of his insides again as he imagined his beautiful girl sprawled across on the couch like a morphine addict.

"…and this group here who just entered the Gallery, these are the praefuro. Notice how intent they are on identifying their targets. They can smell…"

In a way, he hoped she'd succumbed to the bond, because maybe then she'd forget what he'd said that night she was found in the paddock, soaked in blood. Maybe she'd forget how he betrayed her, heartlessly walking away in the single most devastating moment of the only life she could remember, at the moment she needed him more than ever.

"This here is Keisha, she's one of our best. Even with all the chaos and noise around her, she's laser focused. Now look. She's locked onto her prey. And ... here she goes, in for the kill. Watch closely."

Maybe if his beautiful girl slept away the days in an opioid haze, she wouldn't be cognizant enough to despise him, to shut him from her heart before he could snatch a free moment away from Stewart and come home to explain.

Applause pulled James's gaze from his lap, but his vision swam.

He'd need a lot more than a moment, though. He'd need months to repair the damage he'd inflicted and earn her trust again. He discreetly swept a tear from his eye as the council remained mesmerized by Eva and her dog-and-pony show featuring Stewart's newest party trick.

He glanced at his phone to check the time. In a few hours, he'd be boarding his flight back to Mexico. He just wanted to go home. To be closer to Layla.

47

Nick followed the group out of the dining hall but slowed down as they made their way to the lecture hall for the day three afternoon agenda. The campus buzzed with people, robed in their white linen uniforms, moving from one building to the next. How many people lived here? What did they do all day?

"I'm going to back to the room to hit the john. My digestive system's been on overdrive since I got here."

"Weird flex, but okay." Eddie jogged to catch up to Deseret and Deirdre, or as Nick called them, the Salty Dees, because they clearly didn't like him.

Okay, boomer, they'd say with an eye-roll every time he spoke. *I'm not a boomer,* he'd reply, *I'm a millennial. But that's a four-syllable word, and I wouldn't expect you to know what it means.* It hadn't escaped Nick that no one else his age had come on the bus. Victor Beaumont's ID said he was twenty-nine years old; the second oldest person there said she was twenty-four. The Salty Dees couldn't have been more than eighteen.

They're using kids like pincushions. Every victim identified in Peter Malloy's investigation had been in their twenties, according to Darcy and Jordan. Based on this alone, Nick assumed he wouldn't be invited to stay after the three-day assessment. He usually had weeks to immerse himself in an undercover investigation, but now he had mere hours before the decisions would be made and the bus would be reloaded for the return trip.

He needed to find out more about that underground hospital. He wanted pictures. He needed to get inside to look at documents. But thanks to Victor's reputation as a douchebag, Warden Aroyo's watchdogs weren't letting him out of their sight. If he could get back into the security building, he might be able to poke around. Even a few minutes of being lectured by Aroyo would give him another look at the campus map. And with the slightest distraction or misdirection, he could swipe the dude's iPad.

Time to throw a curveball. "Yo, mall cops! I'm going back to my motel room to take a shit. Y'all coming along to watch?"

Eddie and the Dees looked back over their shoulders to see what was going on.

"Your self-esteem must be in the gutter to have taken a job following recruits around all day," Nick continued. "How do you look at yourself in the mirror every morning?"

Eddie backtracked toward him, his brows knitted as if Nick had gone off the rails. "Bro, step off." *What the fuck?* he mouthed.

The security guards still didn't react. No change in facial expression, no physical stiffening.

Nick pushed harder. "You could always put a bullet in your head to stop the agony of your useless existence—at least you could if those were real guns. What are they, like Airsoft?" He groped for the gun clipped to the nearest guard's belt.

Law enforcement personnel were trained to take immediate action if a civilian tried to disarm them, but these mall cops could see that Nick was a jackass and not a real threat. They'd probably wrestle him to the ground and cuff him—and among all the chaos, he'd swipe a badge from one of them. A security badge that could no doubt open any door.

But he was wrong.

The mall cop's arm shot down in a martial arts sort of block. The ensuing flurry of spins and steps happened so fast Nick couldn't process what had transpired.

He was in a chokehold. There was a knife, hard against his trachea.

"Fuck, bro, what the fuck?" Eddie was dancing around as if his feet were on fire.

The second security guard stepped casually over to Eddie and the rest of the small group that had gathered. "I'm sorry you had to witness this. Sometimes we get a troublemaker coming through, but we have the situation under control. Please carry on with your day. Again, my apologies."

"Dumbass sped," one of the Dees said to the other.

Nick had no clue what a sped was, but as he stood paralyzed by the knife at his throat, he was quite sure she was right.

The ninja cop released him and put away what looked like a five- or six-inch hunting knife. "Are you okay, sir? Did I break the skin?"

Still stunned by the guard's agility and even more by what sounded like genuine concern for his well-being, Nick reached up and brushed his fingertips against his throat. His fingers came away dry.

"Fine," he croaked.

"I'm afraid we're going to have to take you back to our security center. We've been instructed to bring you in if you showed any signs of aggression."

He nodded. That had been his goal in the first place, after all. But mental note: He wouldn't underestimate the Colony's mall cops again.

***

The interview room in the security center was barely large enough to seat one person on either side of the small rectangle table.

"I want to speak with James Elliott," Nick mewled. "I feel I've been treated unfairly and subjected to excessive force."

"I understand, sir," his escort replied. "I'll alert Mr. Aroyo, and someone will be with you shortly."

With that, Nick was left locked in the room. He scanned the corners and ran his hands under the tabletop. Nothing. No cameras, no listening devices. Only a one-way mirror, to which he eventually began talking, then berating, then attempting to smash with a chair, and finally beseeching.

Because it was twenty-six hours and twenty-three minutes before the interview room door opened again.

48

L ayla could tell Isaac was worried about her. She hadn't eaten anything in two days. It wasn't an act of rebellion, and it wasn't a depressive episode.

Quite simply, she wanted to starve the fetus.

It was irrational. The demon growing inside her would probably chew right through the amniotic sac and feed on her from the inside out, like the larva of a tarantula hawk. Still, she liked the feeling of control that denying it food gave her, the thrill of her stranglehold on the beast.

Isaac was sitting with his back against the bars of her cell, sighing heavily and repeatedly. Next to him on the floor was a tray of something that looked and smelled absolutely delicious. Undercooked meat. Her stomach rumbled. It wasn't healthy for humans to eat undercooked meat, and certainly for not a pregnant woman. Isaac had surely bribed someone in the kitchen to prepare it that way.

He sighed again, and Layla glanced up from her iPad. "It's not safe for you to be so close to my cell. I could eat you."

"Fine, if it means you'll finally eat *something*."

She rolled her eyes and went back to her iPad. Unlike the choleric praefuro—the ragers, as they preferred to be called—she had no interest in eating people, and she knew Isaac knew that. They both realized the only reason she was there was that Dr. De Luca didn't like her attitude. She wasn't the first to be punished by that arrogant egomaniac.

She scrolled idly through the apps. There were plenty of games to play, books to read, and even some world news to read, but every avenue of communication with anyone outside her cell had been blocked. She opened a word search game.

"He'll cure you," Isaac said.

"De Luca? Unlikely."

"James. James will cure you. He's been working on it."

Lucinda yelled out from her cell down the hall. "Sure he has, been working on it for months. And I ain't seen so much as a bottle of NyQuil to help us at least sleep away our shitty existence."

"I'll put in another request," Isaac called mildly.

"Sure you will."

He leaned his head back against the bars and lowered his voice. "It's called reversion therapy. I don't know exactly how it works, but it's supposed to reverse the mutation back to the wild type. It's just that the low doses haven't worked yet, and he's being cautious about escalating to the high dose. He hasn't found a subject he's willing to take that kind of risk on, and it's taking longer to test in monkeys, but—"

"Shut up!" Layla surged to her feet and loomed over Isaac, who scooted away with wide eyes. "Let me explain something to you, Isaac, because you seem to be as delusional as all those crazies upstairs. Eugenesis is a greedy, heartless organization that doesn't give a shit about you or me or anyone. We're all enslaved here to be exploited and manipulated and ... and hijacked so that they can become richer and more powerful." She drove two thumbs into her round belly. "And the only thing they want at this moment is this genetic monstrosity. Why? Who knows? But I'll tell you one thing. No one is going to cure any of us. In their minds, every last one of us is scrap salvage."

The fetus kicked her in the ribs. She punched it back.

The words of that crazy bitch—Keisha, wasn't it?—popped into her head. *I could cut that baby right out of your belly with a butter knife and not even flinch if I accidentally slipped and sliced its head right off.*

Layla gritted her teeth. *Where are you now, crazy bitch? I could use your help. Make sure you don't miss the jugular.*

"But James is doing something else—"

"Don't ever speak that name to me again," she hissed. "James is a selfish bastard, just like the rest of them. He doesn't care about anyone but himself." Least of all her. All of his promises, worthless lies. All of his kisses and loving gazes, some narcissistic perversion.

She turned her back on Isaac and stared at the wall in front of her. After a minute or two, she heard him pick up her dinner tray and shuffle away.

Her body temperature rose as the fury gathered like a tornado, building momentum, spinning out of control. It was impossible to tell these days who was regulating her autonomic system, herself or the fetus, but at that moment she welcomed the feeling. *Rage.* Even the word excited her. The storm inside her seemed to be condensing and constricting. She had the sensation of it gathering energy, forming a fireball in her chest.

Instinctively, she squeezed her eyes and focused on the spot in the center of her forehead, her mind's eye, as her old therapist, Dr. Jeannette, used to tell her to do.

A dark pool closed over her head, and she submerged.

Hello, ladies. Her mind's voice sounded different than her physical voice. It had a devilish hiss to it, perhaps like the voice of the serpent who spoke to Eve in the Christian Bible.

The walls between her and the others seemed to dissipate like smoke, and she could see them rising from their beds and desks and coming toward her, gathering around.

It's time for Eugenesis to pay, she thought.

Yes, it's time, they answered, nodding.

The fireball inside Layla's chest threatened to expand again. Perhaps it would grow so big it would explode, burning her to a crisp. *Their work is not in the spirit of a better human race.*

No.

They lied to us.

Yes.

We have to stop them.

Yes.

Sweat beaded on her forehead as the fireball pulsed and swelled inside her. She wiped her brow with the back of her wrist. The corners of her mouth turned up as the idea wriggled free. *We'll burn it.*

Yes.

I need your help to get out of here.

They all sat down in a large circle that filled Layla's mind.

Lucinda's voice echoed in her head around the vacillating image of Lucinda pointing at the door at the opposite end of the stairwell. *That door is another stairwell, but there's also a hidden door under the stairs that goes into the underground tunnel system. It connects with the research center and the infirmary. Not many people know it exists.*

How did you discover it? Layla asked in her serpent voice.

It's how I arrived. Shae, the sarcastic woman from the end of the hall, sat cross-legged and barefoot with her fingers threaded between her toes.

Shae was knocked out in their world, Lucinda continued, *but in our world, she came down that hallway swearing like a drunken sailor.*

Shae snickered. *Good times.*

The fireball spun faster in Layla's chest as the idea crystallized. She hated to manipulate Isaac after everything she'd done to him. His compassion was such a noble quality. But it was also a weakness, and now she would have to use it against him.

She scanned the beautiful faces of the women who waited silently for her guidance. *I'm asking you to make a sacrifice.*

We are at your will.

Her physical body was still facing the wall when Isaac sauntered by later. But her mental self—her new, evolved self—stood erect, high above the others, as she told them what they needed to do.

49

S aving the human race doesn't come without sacrifice.

Sacrifice was a culturally embedded mindset built from the first moment that a recruit became an inductee and nurtured all through that individual's purification. The Colony's vision was bigger than any individual's, and Layla didn't know anyone at the Colony who, when asked to make a sacrifice, would refuse. Herself included.

It was a lesson she'd been taught from the first day she could remember. She had sacrificed for more than a year with daily canings, pain-induced meditative states, and inadequate sleep. The stress of induction had made her lose so much weight that she'd been at risk of organ damage. And after rebuilding a strong, physically fit body, she'd sacrificed again to carry a fetus that was supposed to be a pure and evolved new generation of the human race.

And as if all that hadn't been enough, here she sat, her mind sacrificed to a parasitic monster and her freedom to an even bigger monster, Eugenesis.

Eugenesis was soulless in its abuse of their culture of sacrifice. As an officer of Eugenesis, James was well aware of every sacrifice being made for their cause, and Layla knew how hard he struggled to hide the forms of evildoing buried within their outwardly utopian society.

Like death. She'd been suspicious about the disappearances for years, but she hadn't asked because she hadn't wanted to hear the dirty truth.

Like purification. Purification was merely a euphemism for the inculation of healthy, compliant experimental subjects. A recruit awarded the honor of becoming pure was simply someone who would willingly submit to infusions, transfusions, transplants, and in vitro implantations of genetically modified DNA.

Like the truth. Sometimes the process killed people. Worse, it turned them into salvage, sending them to a junkyard for humans where they were kept around for parts.

Oh yes, Eugenesis would pay for its transgressions. And as was the case with any vendetta, innocent people would have to be sacrificed along the way.

He's coming. Lucinda, whose cell was closest to the stairwell, could hear Isaac whistling as he approached the door. She moved to the front of her cell and gripped the bars tightly.

Layla and the others did the same. Her eyes couldn't see them, but her mind could, and her mouth twitched at the wonderment of it. She took a deep breath and braced herself. *Thank you for your sacrifice.*

And thank you for yours, she heard in return.

The door opened, and Isaac stopped whistling. Before he had a chance to ask what was going on, all fourteen women—everyone except Layla—slammed their faces into the metal bars.

Layla registered their pain. She felt the blood dripping off their chins, soaking their shirts and hair. She heard the crunch of their noses and cheekbones. Violent, unbearable surges racked her body. She screamed in agony and buried her head in her trembling hands.

Layla, be strong. Lucinda's voice gurgled.

Layla's mind's eye shifted to Lucinda, who pulled back from the bars and flung her head forward again, crushing her forehead, shattering her teeth.

Layla sputtered and coughed. Nerve pain from Lucinda's cracked teeth shot through her like electricity. She whimpered and fell to her knees.

Sacrifice.

It was impossible, she knew, but her face was swelling with fluid from the violent blows. She tasted blood filling her mouth and throat.

"Isaac!" she cried out.

Somewhere in the distance, she heard Isaac screaming, "Help, please! Someone, help!"

"Raise the bars. Isaac, you have to raise the bars!" She gagged and coughed, expecting to see blood spew from her mouth, but none did.

The security alarm began to shriek. She was running out of time.

"Isaac, raise the bars or they'll die. You're killing them."

She felt a crack in her neck, and fireworks exploded in her head. At the end of the corridor, her mind saw Shae collapse in a heap.

"Please please please please please…" Layla was sobbing now.

Even in the cacophony of wailing and shouts, she heard the click. The bars retracted smoothly into the ceiling.

The self-induced pummeling ceased, and Layla's pain slowed to a throb. She opened her eyes as a handful of women, her sisters in their world, swarmed from their cells toward Isaac.

Isaac pulled his dart gun and clenched it in both hands, swinging it wildly around him.

Layla grabbed her hair with her fists and screamed into her brain. *No! He is not the target. The stairwell.*

The bloody, disfigured women staggered past her like zombies, scrambling right by Isaac to the door he'd come through.

The sun! Oh, my god, there's sunshine, Layla heard as the corridor emptied.

She turned the opposite way, floating on a sea of adrenaline to the door at the other end of the hall. The door to the tunnel system—another secret the Colony had done its best to keep from her. She tried the handle. Locked. She squinted through her sweat-soaked hair to see the numbers on the keypad.

"Layla, stop or I'll shoot."

She looked calmly over one shoulder. Isaac was barely a few feet behind her, his gun aimed between her shoulder blades.

She turned back to the keypad. "Don't. Don't add one more to this house of horrors. Don't make me one of them."

The pinch between her shoulders told her he hadn't lowered the gun, but she knew he wouldn't shoot. Anyone else in the Colony would have— Mia, Michael, Harmony. Even James. They would've flattened her with a tranquilizer dart or even killed her outright, fetus and all, because she wasn't conforming to the infallible laws of the Colony. A sacrifice.

But not Isaac. Isaac would never pull the trigger.

She keyed in James's PIN, flung the door open, and without looking back at Isaac, stumbled into the cool, dark tunnel.

50

The underground tunnel was dimly lit by dirt-caked emergency lighting. Layla lugged her mammoth of a body over the concrete floor, but she felt as though she were walking through deep sand. Every step propelled her forward, but the end of the tunnel seemed to be moving away from her at the same pace. Her head throbbed. Her muscles were weak, partly from the psychic trauma of fourteen women's self-destruction, but also from not eating for two days. Now she wanted to kick herself for her stupidity.

She glanced behind herself to make sure she was alone, even though she was certain she would've heard the door open, and continued to swing her heavy tree-trunk legs forward, counting the steps.

Thirty-four. Thirty-five. Thirty-six.

She took eighty-three steps before the tunnel widened and she passed a lineup of eight gurneys against the wall. Eight? How much transport back and forth from salvage was necessary?

She paused to listen for a search party behind her—still quiet—and slipped through the first door she came upon, pulling it gently closed behind her. Her breath hitched the moment it clicked shut, echoing throughout the enormous space in which she now stood.

The ward had to be twice the size of her lecture hall for recruits.

Hundreds of beds lined the space, one after another. On every bed lay a body attached to a wall panel by a thick spinal IV tube, with thinner IVs in both arms. Despite the glare of the fluorescent lights, not one patient in the room appeared to be awake—or even alive. It was a marionette doll graveyard.

Layla's instincts told her to flee, to go back into the tunnel and find the staircase back to the main floor. But her body, light as a feather now, floated down the aisle between beds. The sleeping faces were obscured by the tape holding their endotracheal tubes in place. Automatic ventilators next to each patient mechanically breathed life into the otherwise lifeless bodies.

Whoosh. Thump, thump. Whoosh. Thump, thump.

They were all in medically induced comas; they must be receiving a genetic treatment, something that required long-term infusion. She'd seen patients who'd been through similar treatment in the past, but only a handful, a cohort of four or six. Never had she seen a roomful of hundreds.

Double doors beckoned on the far side of the ward. She accelerated that direction, but her gaze landed on a woman with a dark black eye.

Oh god. Vanessa Sykes.

She unhooked the clipboard from the foot of her bed: *Vanessa S. Treatment: EGNX 44–9092. Praefuro, Choleric.*

She gasped and dropped the clipboard. It crashed to the floor, echoing through the cavernous room. But she couldn't run or hide because she was immobilized by the horror of her revelation.

It was a factory. They were making—oh, god. They were making a colony of ragers.

A wave of pain shot from her lower back through her abdomen and groin with such force that she doubled over. She lowered herself to her hands and knees to take the pressure off her back, breathing deeply as she'd been taught by Dr. Farid. *Release the pain.* She closed her eyes and took another deep breath. *Release the pain.*

A crash from the other side of the room made her tense up again, and her abdomen contracted so violently she nearly screamed. Her hand flew to her mouth to keep from crying out.

Another slam—maybe a cart being shoved against a bed or wall.

"You've got to be fucking kidding me," someone bellowed.

James.

Layla didn't move.

Hasty footsteps. "Sir, my men have surrounded the infirmary and the research building. She won't get far. We'll have her in custody in a matter of minutes."

"You don't have minutes," James barked. "You have seconds. Seconds! Or you'll be fired so fucking fast your head will spin." His heels clacked loudly as he moved away.

Layla exhaled as quietly as she could.

James stopped dead in his tracks.

She could only see him from the knees down, through the legs of the gurney she was huddled behind.

He turned in a complete circle. "Layla?"

Oh god.

She scrunched her entire face and screamed in her head. *Help me!*

A second later, she heard rustling from the far side of the room, followed by a dreadful gurgling.

James's feet moved toward the muffled choke. "It's a seizure. Call medical. Hurry."

In the other corner, another body seized. This one she could see from her position. The patient jerked several times and then lay still.

And then another.

"What the fuck is happening?" The clip-clop of James's shoes traveled down the aisle.

The noise grew, as more and more patients went into distress. The double doors flew open, and a physician ran into the room, trailed by several nurses.

Still on her hands and knees, Layla crawled along the outer aisle, away from the noise and the knot of medical and security staff. She reached the double doors and glanced over her shoulder. James had flattened himself over a patient as the doctor tapped liquid from a needle.

Layla pushed up to her feet and slipped out the doors.

Thank you, she pushed into her mind. But no one answered back.

Outside in the infirmary corridor, three more nurses ran right past her, their hands filled with needles. She had to keep moving. Her breathing was shallow now, and she shuffled, hunched over with her hands wrapped under her belly as if to prevent the inevitable—now imminent, gauging by the intensity and frequency of her contractions—parturition.

Despite her physical condition, her mind was clear. Laser-focused.

We'll burn it.

Hospitals were filled with flammable materials. There were closet shelves stacked with hand sanitizer. Oxygen tanks were abundant. She just needed a source of ignition: a match, a space heater—ah, the kitchen. A fire in the kitchen would create a distraction, and from there, she could help it spread.

Would lives be sacrificed? Yes. Because saving the human race doesn't come without sacrifice.

She stepped into an elevator and selected the second floor. If this facility was similar to those on her campus, that's where she'd find the pedestrian walkway to the cafeteria.

The elevator dinged, and she took one step out before she saw two security guards hustling toward her.

"Stop!" yelled one, as the other grabbed his radio.

She eased back onto the elevator and tapped the fourth floor. Damn it. She'd have to move quickly. She groaned and bent over, grabbing the handrail, as another contraction gripped her. She wasn't ready, but the elevator opened anyway onto a floor of patient rooms, and she hobbled down the corridor. A door slammed somewhere down the hallway ahead. She stumbled into the nearest patient room and gently nudged the door closed.

She hadn't realized she was holding her breath until the footsteps passed by. She exhaled with a *pfft*. She was about to slip back into the hallway when she heard a weak voice from behind her.

"Layla? Holy cow, you're as big as a ... well, a cow."

51

Nick slowly raised his head off his arms, not certain that the human figure before him was really there. His eyes were bleary, and his head ached from dehydration and hunger. He clutched the table with a weak grip and pulled himself to a standing position.

"Mr. Beaumont, Dr. Meyers would like to see you now."

"I'd like some water and a bathroom." Nick's voice was as weak and tired as the rest of him. His tongue felt like leather.

"Of course, sir. Right this way."

After three bottles of water and a supervised piss, he was transported to a cottage that looked more like an adobe casita guest house than an office. A sign out front read DR. JEANNETTE MEYERS, MD, PSYD. WELCOME.

"What's this?" he asked.

Neither the driver of the van nor the security escort uttered an answer—not that he expected one. No one had said a word to him since they'd left the security building.

He followed the guard up the decorative pathway to the front door, where they were met by a tall woman with a short haircut too sassy for her age. She offered a professional smile as he stepped over the threshold, but she didn't move in for a handshake or bother to introduce herself.

She glanced at the guard's name badge. "Mr. Cooke, thank you for accompanying Mr. Beaumont, but I'll release you of your duty."

"Ma'am, I was instructed to keep Mr. Beaumont in my custody."

"I do understand. I'm grateful for your service. But I insist." The smile remained plastered on her face even as the guard hesitated. It only took a moment before he offered a slight nod and backed obediently out the front door.

So this was someone with some authority. Someone who could be an advocate, perhaps, if he played his cards right. But right now, exhausted and hungry, he wasn't sure he could do that.

The tidy room wasn't furnished in the contemporary style of the rest of the Colony, whose decorator seemed to really like white and gray. This place was almost rustic, with soft leather sofas, plush carpeting that looked a lot like something from a seventies TV show, and soft lighting that gave the room a warm, relaxed ambiance. A teapot whistled from a small stove in the corner, catching Nick's attention, and his eyes landed on a large framed quote: ALMOST ANYTHING WILL WORK AGAIN IF YOU UNPLUG IT FOR A FEW MINUTES.—ANNE LAMOTT

Or, say, twenty-six hours and twenty-three minutes.

He didn't move from his position in the doorway as she strode gracefully to the stove and lifted the pot. "I've always been a big fan of tea. A few years ago, a colleague gave me a book on the history of tea. I imagine it was meant to be a joke, but I read it cover to cover. Did you know that it wasn't until the late nineteenth century that tearooms became popular, finally giving women a place to gather outside the house without a male escort? I can only imagine what some of those early conversations were like."

Nick glowered. Psychiatrists and therapists were quacks who fed on loneliness and depression and low self-worth, and Dr. Meyers had an air about her that made him even more distrustful. Even her benign story about tearooms felt like a test. A psychoanalysis.

But he needed an ally. He tried to soften his tone, but the words still came out snippy. "Why am I here?"

She seemed unfazed by his testiness. "You're here because I've taken an interest in your profile, and I wanted to speak with you in person." She set two teacups down on the coffee table along with a small tray of chocolate biscotti.

His stomach rumbled. "Are you the one responsible for locking me in a room for twenty-six hours?" Again, his big mouth betrayed him. He was supposed to be building rapport.

"Yes." Her smile finally faded, but her expression held no apology. "I'm a strong believer in the cool-off period after a confrontation. One needs enough time to move through the emotional process: anger and blame for the injustice, denial of one's own contributing behavior, understanding and validation of both subjective realities, and finally acceptance of responsibility."

She perched on the edge of an oversized armchair, crossed her ankles, and gestured for him to sit. He fisted as many biscotti as he could and fell into the cushiony sofa.

"But then again, you didn't need to cool off, did you, Mr. Beaumont? Your little stunt wasn't an act of aggression, despite your long record of assault and battery."

He shoved an entire biscotti into his mouth, relishing the momentary euphoria caused by the surge of dopamine. His muscles went limp.

"And that's what I find interesting about you. Let me turn your question back to you. Why are you here?"

Nick could practically see the life donut fly from the side of the boat. He could hear it splash into the ocean just within his grasp. This was his chance. She was allowing him—asking him, really—to do what he did best, talk his way inside the Colony.

He'd been trained to hustle since he was ten. He could out-maneuver even the most experienced interviewees. He had perfected lying to the point that he could beat a polygraph.

But as the shrink's skeptical stare bore into him, his mind went blank.

His eyes darted around the room, desperate to avoid hers. It had only been minutes, and already she was trying to manipulate him. Using uncomfortable silence to get him to confess something. He knew that trick. Mirroring his movements—*we're so much alike, you and me*—just like a pro.

His gut reminded him that his story, the story of a lifetime, was at stake. Just play along, tell her whatever she needs to hear. But his ego wanted to wriggle from her penetrating gaze and storm out with a *fuck you*, just like he had the chief's office barely two weeks ago. This internal struggle sent his thoughts swirling like leaves in the wind until he forgot what question he'd been asked.

"Mr. Beaumont?" She urged.

Douchebag Victor. The swirling leaves in his brain lost their breeze and fluttered to the ground. His mind cleared.

He could channel the douche.

52

"Jonah?" Layla recognized nothing but the voice emanating from the corpse on the hospital bed. Muscular and handsome just a few months ago, Jonah had shrunken to a fraction of his size, judging by the outline of his body under the white sheet. His face, once tanned and chiseled with impossibly defined muscles and a perfect jawline, was now blotchy and bloated, like a body on an autopsy table.

Oh, god. Jonah was sick. *He is the plague.*

The contraction that had nearly crippled her just moments ago subsided, as if the monster that needed to be born was willing to allow her this moment.

Her lower lip quivered. "What happened to you?"

He chuckled softly. "I'm fine. Really, Lay. I've been undergoing treatment for bone cancer. I'm doing well, though. Getting better every day."

Jonah, the eternal optimist. Early on, Jonah had assumed the role of her big brother. *You're not shy and awkward, you're quietly confident. You're introspective, always assessing the world around you like a puma on a high rock, looking down on the rest of us baboons.*

But this time, his optimism was in vain. *No, sweet Jonah, you're not getting better.*

She turned her head as tears filled her eyes. "My father had spinal cancer."

She had no idea why she told him, and she immediately regretted it when he asked the obvious next question.

"Did he recover?"

"No." The headline she'd read on James's computer flashed before her eyes: *Madison mourns the loss of patient rights activist who took his own life through assisted suicide.* "He gave up."

"Oh." Jonah's freakishly swollen eyelids closed.

Layla's gaze traveled to the drip bag, releasing a single droplet every couple of seconds through an IV tube into a needle taped to the back of his hand.

Those little droplets travel through my hand into the parts of my body that hurt and make the pain go away. But it makes me verrry sleepy.

Daddy? she'd tentatively tested.

Gotcha!

Layla palmed her blurry eyes so she could read the computer screen. She cranked his dose of morphine to the maximum allowable without a physician password to override it. The pace of the drip increased, but only slightly.

"Sorry, Lay, gonna have a nap," Jonah murmured. "I miss you … work out … soon."

"I'm sorry too, Jonah."

She perched on the edge of the bed and took one of his hands in hers. It was soft and squishy, filled with fluid and gasses. The dry skin felt like it might tear if she squeezed too hard, and maybe maggots would pour out. Try as she might to push the thought out of her mind, her brain stem spoke.

He is the plague.

Her face crumpled in agony as she laid his hand back down and gently pulled the blanket over it.

He must be purged.

No. She wouldn't. Jonah was the closest she ever had to a brother.

Poison.

"No!" The word came out more like a plea than an assertion.

Her brain held a thousand wonderful memories of Jonah, and she tried to conjure them up, but her mind flooded instead with memories of her own poisoned life. It was as if her brain stem was turning against her, distracting her so that it could get on with the important work.

Daddy, why do you have to go? Why do you have to die?

Because my body is filled with poison, Butch, and the poison is spreading everywhere inside me.

The fetus seemed to drop a bit lower, allowing her the pelvic flexibility she needed to step up onto the crossbar of the bed and straddle Jonah's thin body. She wrapped her hands around his neck, her small fingers sinking into the soft flesh. She wanted to gag from the smell, but even though he was fast asleep, she felt any expression of disgust would be disrespectful.

But the medicine, she'd protested.

Sometimes medicine isn't enough, sweetie.

Her tears landed on Jonah's cheek and rolled down the sides of his blotchy purple face. The increasing pressure against his throat forced his mouth open, and a grotesque, swollen black tongue protruded from between his cracked gray lips.

Please, Daddy, I don't want you to leave me.

If I stay here with you, I'll suffer in pain every day and the poison will fill my whole body. But if I go to heaven, all the poison will be washed away, and I'll never suffer again. Remember the words I taught you?

No. I can't. She'd howled with grief.

Come on, Butch.

She hadn't been able to say it back then, back in her poisoned life, when she was just a little girl. At that tender age, some words had such a dark, sinister connotation that they could never be associated with an act of compassion.

Now she spoke those hateful words aloud. "It's a mercy killing, Jonah. I'm sorry. It's a mercy killing." Her body shuddered with a powerful sob as she squeezed Jonah's throat as hard as she could, bearing down with all her weight. Mucus filled her mouth, turning her voice high-pitched and hollow. "I love you, Jonah."

The medical alarm was loud enough to yank her attention from Jonah's face. When she lowered her gaze again, the illusion of a rotting plague corpse was gone. Jonah lay unbreathing beneath her, his skin as smooth and white as a porcelain doll.

She kissed him softly on the forehead, wiped her eyes and nose on her sleeve, and waddled out the door. She turned the corner down an empty corridor just as a nurse outside Jonah's room yelped.

"Code Blue! Get the crash cart!"

Layla didn't believe in heaven, even if her daddy had, but she was certain of one thing: Jonah's suffering was over.

And the poison was purged. The earth will be purified.

53

"**I**f you didn't believe I needed to cool off, why was I held captive like a goddamn prisoner of war? No water. No toilet. No food. Do you get off on torturing your recruits?"

Nick scooted forward to the edge of the comfy couch to take an appropriately aggressive stance. This discussion would be much more productive once she was softened up by a review of his barbaric treatment.

Dr. Meyers smiled serenely. "Back in my past life—here, we call it our poisoned life—I owned a crisis center for teenagers. Anyone under the age of eighteen could show up on their own accord if they were feeling suicidal or having trouble with drugs or alcohol. It was a remarkably successful program, and I was proud of the work we did."

Oh boy, stories of the old days. This was going to take a while. Nick reached for another biscotti and eased into a more natural position.

"But there was a subset of teenagers—girls, mostly—who were there for some other reason. They were looking for attention from their parents or their boyfriends, or they were simply bored with their routine. They'd cry, they'd show up with cuts on their wrists and arms, they had all the outward signs. But they couldn't outsmart the battery of psychological tests. Their answers formed a pattern. They were trying too hard to sound suicidal. Naturally, we were able to talk it through and uncover what was truly bothering them, which certainly was a crisis in the mind of a sixteen-year-old. Sometimes when people can't identify their feelings, they grab onto what's convenient or what's worked in the past."

The sofa had all but engulfed him again, and Dr. Meyers's voice was hypnotic. He shifted a little straighter.

"I found the same type of pattern in the answers to your psychological evaluation. You want to be perceived as aggressive, but I don't see it. You say you're running from your past, but I read you as looking for something."

He licked his fingers insouciantly. "If you already have all your answers, then why do we need to have this conversation?"

She remained silent and watched him closely. He felt her eyes burning into him as if she were trying to read his mind. After a long minute, she finally spoke. "Tell me about your relationship with your father."

He snickered. "No. Nothing to say." He shifted his body to the left.

"Ah, I thought so. See that physical reaction? The flippant wave, the closing of your position, turning away from the conversation. It's a purposeful underreaction—but you're filled with negative emotions. I'm going to go out on a limb here and guess: You never measured up. Is that right?"

He leaned forward and looked her in the eye. "Let me be clear. This is not about me or my relationship with my family. I don't believe in psychiatrists or therapists. I think you're all con artists. Your science isn't real, and you don't help people. You make them dependent on you."

He slammed his mouth shut, unsure what elicited such an inflammatory reaction. He couldn't burn his one potential bridge to the next stage of the process, the one that would give him sufficient time to conduct a thorough investigation. But dammit, he was tired and hungry.

"Can I get you some more tea?" she asked. "Green tea has many health benefits, and also a big dose of caffeine." She didn't wait for his answer and went to fetch the pot and several more biscotti.

The tea burned the roof of his mouth, but he downed it as fast as he could.

"You'd know a con artist if you met one, wouldn't you?" she asked.

He gnawed one of the new biscotti. Despite the sugar, his energy was flagging now. Badly.

"I understand you successfully conned your way onto our bus."

Try as he might, he couldn't hold his eyes open. The caffeine would hit him soon enough, but until then, perhaps he could just rest a little. The couch was just so damn soft.

Her voice came in louder, as if she'd moved closer. "How do you know your father didn't approve of you?"

His brain felt cloudy. How did she know about his father?

"What did he do that upset you? Tell me."

He huffed a little at the memory. "When I was in the tenth grade, I got a ninety-seven on my organic chemistry final exam. It was the highest grade ever received for that test, a full seventeen points higher than the next highest grade." His fist, still gripping the biscotti, relaxed on the sofa next to him. He was melting into the cushions.

"That's impressive. Your father must've been incredibly proud." Her voice had filled with a warmth that hadn't been there before. "What did he say?"

Nick swallowed, but his mouth was so dry. "He said, 'What happened to the other three points?' And then he laughed at me because I missed a carbon bond in question six, and he reminded me that carbon is the building block of life. As if I didn't fucking know that."

Why was he blathering like this?

"Interesting. So he took the time to review your chemistry test. Any other examples?"

Yeah, fuck yeah. He had sixteen years of examples, and then a dozen more after he'd become one of his father's minions at the *Phoenix Sun*. "He told me I throw a baseball like a flamer—that was his word for gay— even though I could hit the center of his mitt every time. He still said my form was too feminine. And he called me Sally."

Let's go, Sally, that embarrassing pitch isn't going to fix itself.

"Hmm, so he played catch with you?"

No, no, she was getting it all wrong. Wasn't she supposed to be on his side? "He didn't go to my high school graduation."

"Did you invite him?"

I'm doing the speech! he'd screamed into the phone. *Uncle Jay, will you help me write it?*

Nick snorted, jolting himself into alertness, but only for a second. "He made Mom leave us." He couldn't believe he was saying this aloud. "He didn't even wake me up to say goodbye."

Some birds just aren't meant to be caged, Nick. He hadn't understood why his dad wanted to talk about birds instead of getting into the car to go find her.

"Did she leave in the middle of the night?"

He didn't answer. He'd long since repressed this memory. But this lady was right. She *had* left in the middle of the night. Why hadn't she left in the daytime?

"And you blamed your father from that moment on, didn't you? You pushed him away. You made him the villain because you couldn't accept the fact that your mother didn't love you enough to want to stay and be your mom."

"No." His response lacked any conviction. He did blame his father. In fact, several years ago, he had performed an extensive search to find his mother and confront her. What he found was her gravesite. She'd died young of Huntington's Disease, and for some reason, even though he knew she'd inherited the disease from her own parents, he'd blamed his father for her death, as well.

"You were a child. Children create stories and memories and good guys and bad guys to deal with their anguish." He felt her take his hand in hers. "But now you're an adult. Maybe if you accepted him with all his flaws, he might accept you with all yours."

He didn't have the strength to argue.

"But it's a moot point now, isn't it? Because he's back home, in your poisoned life, and you're here with us." She slapped the top of his hand a couple of times. "Wake up now, Mr. Beaumont. I know you've had a hard couple of days, but I need to get on with my next appointment."

His eyes opened, and his head began to clear. The caffeine was finally kicking in. She handed him a box of tissues, then collected the teacups and platter. He wasn't sure what the box was for until he realized the front of his shirt was wet. Did he spill his tea? Or...

He reached up to his face. His cheeks were wet with tears.

"Mr. Beaumont, I'd like to invite you to stay." She set the dishes in a small sink and rinsed out the teapot. "I've taken an interest in adults who were abandoned by a parent and how they form relationships, particularly with authority figures. The literature is rife with theories about distrust, anger, commitment issues." She waved her hand. "Rubbish. I have my own theories. I'm planning a phase one observational study, and I'd be grateful if you'd agree to join it."

He couldn't process a word she said, he was too concerned with what the fuck just happened, but he nodded. "Okay."

"Wonderful. I'll send my recommendation to the recruiting team. Welcome to the Colony, Mr. Beaumont."

As he fell in behind the security detail to return to the van, he surveyed her impressive credentials prominently displayed over a swanky antique desk. Her medical degree, her doctorate of psychiatry, and one other: President of the Milton H. Erickson Society of Clinical Hypnosis.

54

She was a cold-blooded killer, one that could look a loved one right in the eye and viciously end his life. The sickest, cruelest of murderers.

Layla put up a hand to brace herself against the corridor wall. A siren blared in shrill pulses in every direction, no doubt in her honor, so she only took a momentary break before dragging herself down the corridor in search of a stairwell. Someone would surely be surveying the security monitors. Even in the endless sea of white linen, she'd be easy to identify. She had to keep moving.

We'll burn it.

They had done this to her. They had made her a killer, and they would pay. She had to stay focused.

Up ahead, the symbol of a stick figure climbing some stick stairs glowed under a red security light. Relieved, she took several long awkward strides toward the door, ignoring the excruciating pinch in her groin. As her hand closed around the cold steel stairwell railing, something popped with a twang deep in her lower abdomen. She took two ungainly steps down before she felt warm liquid running down her legs. She clutched the rail with both hands. Pink-tinged fluid was pooling around her bare feet. Her water had broken.

Her hands instinctively flew to her crotch in a vain attempt to stop the progression, but the parasitic monster inside her seemed determined to leave her body. She was no longer of any use to him; she was no longer of any use to the Colony.

In a matter of hours, she would be scrap salvage.

A spark flickered in the most primitive part of her brain, igniting something that flowed through her veins like gasoline, moving through her in a fiery inferno. She was rumbling inside, and she wondered if the monster might simply explode from her.

She threw her head back and howled like a wolf, desperately trying to release the pressure building inside her. The anguish of being enslaved. The self-loathing of being a killer. Her deep, dark revulsion for the thing, the demon parasite, that fed off her body and destroyed her mind.

Breathless, she leaned back, squatting against the top stair. She was drained. So hungry, so sleepy. Her eyes darted up and locked onto her reflection in the bubble mirror. Her face, red and blotchy from crying, was hideously distorted by the curvature. Her eyes were too far apart, her nose wide and flat, her lips deep red and swollen. But that's not what captivated her.

She awkwardly pushed herself up and took a couple of steps closer to the mirror, opening her heavy eyelids as wide as she could. She didn't recognize the eyes looking back at her. There was no connection there, no sense of self. She wasn't looking into the eyes of the woman she'd seen in the mirror every day she could remember.

She was looking into the eyes of a stranger.

"It's you." The words came out as a guttural growl. "You've taken my soul."

Movement in the reflection brought her back into the moment.

The stairwell door banged open. "Freeze!"

The guard dropped his gaze to the puddle on the floor, and in that moment, Layla lumbered down the steps, leaning heavily on the railing. She clawed open the door on the lower level, praying it was the kitchen.

It wasn't.

She recognized the elegant dining tables, the espresso machine against one wall and a dessert table opposite. The far end of the room was demarcated with a wooden banister. This was the physician's loft.

Heavy footsteps vibrated the stairwell behind her. They were coming for her.

She scuttled to the balcony and peered over the edge. Two stories down—she couldn't jump. There was no escape except the door she came through, and it would be only another second before it flew open.

She backed up against the wood.

"Don't move, Layla." The guard stepped back into a power stance and pulled a gun. Unlike Isaac, he held it with confidence, and she had no idea if it was a stun gun or a tranq gun or an actual handgun.

It didn't matter. He wouldn't shoot until he was told to do so by a Colony leader.

She threw a leg over the balcony. Instead of a graceful swing, she misjudged her center of gravity and ended up painfully astride the banister. She cried out and fell forward, crushing her abdomen, and flailed at open space. The only thing that prevented her from falling was her left knee, which hooked the top rail.

She grabbed hold and pulled her second leg over.

"No, no, don't shoot. You'll harm the fetus!" A familiar Italian accent preceded the man shoving his way through the guards, who huddled in formation to block the door.

Dr. De Luca froze when he saw her position on the wrong side of the banister. "Layla, what are you doing, bella? Let's talk this out. I don't want you to get hurt."

A trickle of amniotic fluid slipped off the back of one heel and pattered in the darkness below. "Drop the act. You don't care about me."

"Of course I care about you. I care about every carrier in the program. You're like my daughters, *miei tesori*." He strode toward her with one hand out. "Let me help you."

"Bullshit." She could smell the contents of the syringe in his pocket even before he closed the distance. "Don't come any closer."

Fear crossed his face, and his gaze dropped to her belly.

"We're just vessels for your fetuses. We're breeding slaves, forced to bear whatever genetically mutated freak you want to mass-produce."

"Please think about what you're doing. You're carrying the future of the human race. That fetus is what will purify the earth. It is a necessary part of a greater whole."

She adjusted her grip on the railing.

"You don't understand the big picture," he continued. "You mustn't do anything to hurt yourself or the fetus. Your role is so important."

His eyes were begging her, but it was nothing more than selfish greed.

The fetus, for once, remained silent and unmoving. It knew. It knew she was standing precariously on the edge of death. An unevolved parasite, virulent and deadly, would destroy its own source of survival, but an evolved parasite had a commensal relationship with its host. It benefited as long as it didn't harm its host. An evolved human parasite might even sense when its host, and therefore its survival, was in danger.

Maybe it even understood Newton's law of gravity.

The doctor dropped his charade of compassion and tried another angle. "You made a commitment to Eugenesis and the Colony that you would serve its mission. The Colony has made a significant investment in you. We will not allow you to dictate the terms under which you exist, and we will not allow you to endanger the life of that fetus. Step back over the rail, Layla, or you'll spend the rest of your days behind bars. I'll make sure of it."

His ultimatum fell on deaf ears. She could already see her future.

She had failed. The fire that had burned so hot inside her, the one fueling her mission to make Eugenesis pay, had extinguished. The sacrifices of all those women in salvage had been for naught.

She had only one thing they wanted, and once they had it, she would be scrap salvage.

"Fuck Eugenesis, and fuck you. I will not bring another monster into this world."

Layla released the railing.

55

"Excuse me, my friends."

James recognized the Italian accent that interrupted their pre-dinner drinks in the executive lounge of the corporate offices building.

News about Layla. Without looking at the doctor, he shifted his weight to get up, but Stewart put a gentle hand on his arm and locked eyes with him for just a second, a subtle message that anything to do with Layla would not be private.

James gave Dr. De Luca a curt nod as he picked up his martini to hide his discomfort. He needed to keep a poker face no matter what news the doctor came to deliver.

James's search for Layla in the tunnels had been futile, and he'd reluctantly stepped away to deal with today's landmine: a surprise visit by senior officials from the Department of Defense Threat Reduction Agency. Just as he and Stewart were making introductions with the military team, he'd received word that Layla had been found and that she'd survived a fall from a second-story balcony. Stewart, ever concerned about James's emotional well-being, had insisted that he let the doctors take care of her. *They need to work, James. You'll only be in their way.*

But that wasn't why he stayed away. The unfortunate timing of this

DOD inspection was a huge risk, and he wasn't about to leave these men alone with Stewart to tour the campus. His reversion research team was so close to getting an efficacious dose, they were working overtime. He'd expanded their lab space, which now occupied several rooms on the first floor, and the work would be impossible to conceal if someone with medical training were to poke around the research building.

And if Eugenesis discovered that he had been formulating a therapy to reverse the praefuro mutation, undermining the billions of dollars that went into the praefuro development, he'd be indicted as a traitor and sentenced to death. No prosecution, no trial, and no defendant rights.

Stewart slid next to the doctor and put a collegial hand on his shoulder for the benefit of the four suits at the table. "Alessandro De Luca is the chief physician for the carrier program. His brilliant work has accelerated our praefuro program."

De Luca flashed them a tight smile. "I'm sorry to interrupt, gentlemen. I just wanted to alert Stewart and James that Layla is in good condition in recovery. She shows no signs of injury, thanks to the exceptional coordination of the security team in cushioning her fall."

Stewart dragged a chair over from another table and gestured for the doctor to have a seat next to Colonel Shaffer, the most senior officer of the group. "And the offspring?"

James fisted his hands under the table. Stewart was trying to trivialize the role of the carrier. He wanted the colonel to perceive the women the way he did, as nothing more than delivery systems for their newest, most destructive weapon.

De Luca took a seat. "The offspring is in the care of our exceptional nursing staff. We harvested the cord tissue successfully and will harvest the brain tissue in the coming days. This specimen will provide dosing for 420 subjects with Layla's HLA type. They're prepared and ready for transplant as early as tomorrow."

Stewart exhaled a dramatic sigh and flopped backward, which James knew was all for show. "What a relief." He met the eyes of his guests around the table. "We put quite a lot of money and resources into each and every offspring. It's tragic to lose one, especially due to mental illness of the carrier." His eyes darted back to James's for a reaction.

It was a cheap asshole shot. James kept his expression impassive. "Great news, Alessandro." He refused to let Stewart denigrate Layla's reputation, but he only had one angle. "Layla is one of our brightest in the praefuro program, a brilliant predator. Her phenotype is exactly what the program is looking for. We'll need to spend some time with her now that she's no longer a carrier."

Stewart slapped his knee. "Yes! James, brilliant idea. Let's get Layla into the simulation tomorrow." He raised his hands to the heavens. "Sometimes the planets just line up. I've been feeling good about tomorrow's demonstration, but this—putting our best out there for you to see in action, a real application of the furo model—that's practically divine intervention."

Divine intervention, seriously? From a man so vocally atheist that he once called Charles Darwin a mystic. But James was well aware of Stewart's motives. Stewart didn't want to show off Layla as much as he wanted to torment James. *She's a furo now.* It was a test, like God's test of Abraham. James was meant to demonstrate his devotion to the vision, to sacrifice Layla as an offering to Eugenesis.

James turned his lips up in a slow grin and nodded as if he were just now clueing into Stewart's ingenious idea. "Just wait until you see her. She's incredible."

"I'll get it all set up with Eva." Stewart dropped his eyes to his watch. "Oh, look at the time. I'm going to have to leave you all in the capable hands of James, who'll be giving you a tour of the campus. He has a real treat to show you—our new senior employee cigar bar is open. I've reserved it all evening for us, although James will undoubtedly be burning the midnight oil on the furo training program."

James felt a flush crawl up his face. This was another squeeze play. Stewart had kept James locked at his side from the moment their plane had landed early this morning, all to prevent him from seeing Layla. He narrowed his eyes at Stewart, who remained gleaming with joy. A power struggle with Stewart right now could compromise their already tenuous relationship. He couldn't allow an ego-fueled battle of wills to set off alarms, not with the Department of Defense watching their every move.

James rose with his most charming smile. "Well, if you're ready, gentlemen, let's get right to it. We'll start at the purification center, the place where it all began."

And I'll see you right after the simulation, beautiful girl, I promise. And I'll make everything right.

56

L ayla shoved her dinner tray away with such force it slid off the overbed table and crashed to the floor, splattering cream of mushroom soup and chocolate pudding all over the white marble. It was a childish tantrum, but it gave her the tiniest sense of satisfaction. They could all rot in hell, every single one of them: Dr. De Luca, the members of the Eugenesis council, and yes, Bradley James Elliott, liar-in-chief.

She stretched as far as her wrist strap would allow and rubbed her blubbery belly. The fetus was gone, despite her having no memory of giving birth. Of course, given today's technology, no carrier actually *gave* birth; fetuses were taken, extracted by robotic arms through the vaginal canal, without the usual childbirth injuries. No pain, no recovery necessary.

At least, that's what the nurse had explained.

Layla's response had dripped with bitter derision. *Gotta make sure the baby factory slaves are ready to get right back on the horse, hmm?*

But the nurse apparently hadn't noticed because she giggled. *That's right, sweetheart! You'll be ready for your next implantation before they even saddle up the ol' mare.* She'd giggled again at her addition to the idiom. If Layla hadn't been strapped to the bed, she would've choked the woman until her stupid giggle became a gurgle.

Dr. De Luca had been far less chatty. He hadn't spoken to Layla at all when he arrived to check her progress.

It wasn't until he was at the door on his way out that she raised her voice. *I want to see James.*

James has been informed of the situation. He hadn't even looked back.

All day, she'd been imagining how that conversation—James being *informed*—had gone. Had he somberly replied *fine*, with one of his famous dismissive waves? Or perhaps he'd just shrugged and gone back to schmoozing with Stewart and the latest group of suits. *Layla? Who?*

She might have cried at the thought if she were still human, but they'd stripped her of every last trace of humanity. Only weeks ago, she'd been a powerful Colony leader. Days ago, she'd been reduced to just another soldier for the greater cause, one of hundreds of carriers. Yesterday, she'd become scrap salvage.

And today? What could be less human than scrap salvage?

She didn't feel sorry for herself; she felt sorry for failing her mission. This had been her moment to rivet the attention of the powers behind Eugenesis, to foment a rebellion from the inside that might have changed the future. She might have halted the conception of the praefuro army, Vanessa Sykes and the hundreds like her incubated below ground, comatose husks being transformed into the subhuman creature she had now become. She might have burned that underground factory, releasing those victims from a lifetime of misery.

She rolled onto her back to relieve the grating of the cuffs against her raw, chafed wrists just as the door of her infirmary room clicked and swung open.

"What the hell is all this?" Stewart Hammond paused in her doorway and scanned the floor.

"Nurse! Get in here and get this cleaned up. This is not how we run our infirmary."

"I'm so sorry, sir." Nurse Giggles was far less giggly as she dropped to the floor and collected the plastic dishes and tray.

Stewart stepped over the woman and made his way to Layla's bedside. "Who the hell authorized restraining a leader of the Colony to a goddamn hospital bed?"

"Sir, Dr. De Luca said she might be a threat to—"

"Jesus Christ." He unstrapped the cuffs and inspected her wrists, gently running his fingertips over them to soothe the burn. "Layla, my dear."

The nurse hustled out of the room, leaving the two of them alone.

Stewart leaned over and gazed deeply into Layla's eyes, the same gentle way he'd looked at her during her purification, those deep brown eyes drawing her into his aura. His heart. *Thank you for coming to us, Layla. Thank you for bringing all the beauty of your impure life to us. You have so much to give.*

She averted her eyes to avoid being drawn into the spell. She wasn't that same submissive, gullible girl anymore. He wasn't her friend. He was the enemy, just like the rest of them. She should have burned them all.

He gently turned her chin so that she couldn't avoid him. To her surprise, his eyes were shining, and his mouth spread in a slow, curious grin. "Do you remember the words I said to you, Layla, on the day of your purification?"

Lies. Every word was a lie, you son of a bitch.

"I said that I'd been watching you. And I had. I said I was not disappointed in you, and I wasn't. I said you'd even surprised me, and to this very day, you continue to surprise me." He slid a small leather armchair next to her bed without moving his eyes from hers, clasping her hand in both of his tightly enough that she couldn't yank it away.

She wouldn't give him the satisfaction of an acknowledgment.

After at least a full minute, he spoke again. "I've never been prouder, Layla. You've accomplished everything I ever hoped for and more. You are my vision. You've made it real."

"This?" It burst from her lips like a locust, first of the plague to come. "This was your vision, Stewart? This is what you saw for me back then? Salvage, to spend the rest of my days locked in a cell?"

"Salvage?" He laughed out loud. "Salvage? Oh, my dear girl, you're a million miles from salvage. You are… I don't even know how to say it… You are the single most important product of purification that we've created, after all this time." He shook his head as if he couldn't believe it himself. "You're our salvation."

His eyes softened as he searched her face. "Is that what you thought? That you were salvage?" He winced and spoke under his breath. "How could we have gone so wrong?"

He wasn't convincing her. "You implanted a monster into me. You forced me to be a slave to that—"

He slapped both palms against his forehead. "A monster? No, no, you misunderstand. Oh, god, what a mess." He sat up straight and crossed one leg over the other, his no-nonsense posture. "Layla, the fetus you carried has given you a gift. It wasn't a curse. I know you've suffered in the last few weeks, feeling enslaved by the process, feeling unattended to by the doctors. It's my fault. I should've personally taken charge of your progression through your pregnancy. It's just that James—"

He stopped and turned away from her, as if embarrassed. "I just… Gosh, I really thought he had your best interest at stake. He told me that your pregnancy was going fine. I asked him months ago, after he learned you had the mutation, if you'd shown any praefuro symptoms yet so that—"

"He knew?" Her voice was a squeak. She cleared it and repeated the question. "He knew I had the mutation?"

Stewart's eyebrows raised. "He didn't talk to you? He didn't explain what you'd be going through? Tell you how important this pregnancy was?"

She let out an exasperated sigh. Of course James had known. James knew everything. And of course he hadn't told her. She'd been right all along: James was keeping her in the dark.

"I should have intervened, I know. I just—well, I thought James was doing right by you." He gazed at the wall as if lost in thought. "So often over the years, I've questioned how he could lie to you so easily. I figured he just didn't think you were strong enough. Now I see that he didn't trust you. He didn't think you could rise to such an important challenge." He shrugged and dropped his eyes to his lap. "I don't know. Maybe I should give him the benefit of the doubt. Maybe he knew you were capable, but he just didn't want to be outperformed by his beautiful girl. You were like a pet to him. I can't blame him for that. We all know how special you are. He wanted to keep you to himself."

Fury spun up inside her. James had met her during her poisoned life and convinced her that she was miserable and worthless so he could emerge as her savior, giving her the gift of a new life at the Colony. He'd said he loved her all that time, but she was only a conquest, something to win and possess. Just like the Colony. Just like every achievement in James's profoundly accomplished life.

Stewart was leaning into her, his charmer smirk back. "But your special gift, your talent, is where you'll finally break James's chokehold. You will rise to your gift, and you'll propagate purity into the world just as you promised you'd do on that special day when we first met. And you'll do this as a furo."

She pulled away. "What are you talking about?"

He chuckled and threw his arms up. "Your extraordinary gift, my dear."

She pulled herself upright in the bed and addressed him directly. "Stewart, stop beating around the bush. Talk to me like an adult."

"You're right." The smile melted from his face. "The world is filled with poison, Layla. That's a doctrine we've preached here at the Colony since the beginning. The impure world, the poisoned world. It's an easy way to make colonists understand the difference between us and them. But you're too smart for such a childish viewpoint. The real difference between us and them is their inferiority. The human species is filled with mistakes, people who are passing on illnesses, viruses, and genetic imperfections through generations, weakening us as a species."

She knew this, but she let him continue.

"That's why we're testing genetic drugs and designing genetically superior offspring, to improve the gene pool by adding dominant positive genes. That's my vision, what I've dedicated my life to achieving."

She nodded.

"That part is not new to you, but this part is: My vision was inadequate." He bowed his head.

It was the first time she ever heard the man admit to a mistake.

"See, those imperfections must stop. Now. They must stop being reproduced and passed down, or else we're fighting a war that can never be won. This is where my original vision failed; I had only half the formula. But now, with you and others like you, we have the whole formula. You, my dear, are the most important part of fulfilling the vision. You're the real hero."

She leaned back and crossed her arms as she processed what he was saying. After weeks of suffering, of nearly ending her own life, Stewart marches in and tells her she's the answer to the whole problem? The salvation?

"James had an image of you, Layla, purity in its purest state. Innocent, demure. Someone who needed to be shielded from the poisonous world and protected from anything even remotely harmful. But purity doesn't have to wear white linen and be submissive."

He bent to retrieve something from his bag. A book. The bold red cover featured a woman in tight black leather pants and a sleeveless vest that showed off her curvy body. She instinctively sucked in her stomach.

BLACK WIDOW: THE MAKING OF A LETHAL ASSASSIN

The woman held a long-bladed knife in each hand.

He handed her the book. "I didn't come here to shower you with compliments. I have a request. I'd like you to participate in a demonstration tomorrow. We have some gentlemen here from an important government office, a branch of the US military that believes the praefuro model—you—are key to saving the human race. I want you there. I want to bring out my absolute best for them. You'll make me so proud."

So that was it. Stewart wanted to show off his newest genetic creation, his latest Frankenstein's monster. She held his book back out. "And if I say no?"

He didn't reach for it, and the sparkle in his eyes flickered. "Why would you say no to such an opportunity, my dear? This is your chance to shine. James will be there, too. After weeks of feeling betrayed by the one man who was supposed to be elevating you to your true potential, wouldn't it be poetic justice if he were to finally see how strong and talented you really are?"

She could hear the tension in his voice. He wanted her to choose his side, to fall back into her submissive mindset and do what he asked of her.

"I'm not interested."

His body temperature rose. She could hear his blood pressure increasing as if she were listening to the brachial artery through a stethoscope. *Lub-dub, lub-dub, lub-dub.* Stewart wasn't used to being told no. But this wasn't arrogance; this response was something else. He *needed* her to do this.

She had leverage.

"Not without something in return," she said.

Lub-dub. Lub-dub. His blood pressure dropped somewhat, but his jaw remained tightly locked.

"I want a meeting with the council." He didn't respond, and she felt a familiar fire ignite in her belly. "I want to speak on behalf of all the praefuro here and at all the other colonies. I want Eugenesis to realize what they've taken from us." Her voice grew louder to drown out the pounding in her ears. "How their unconscionable greed for power has robbed us of our humanity. Turned us into mindless killing machines. Salvage." She folded her legs underneath herself so she could lean closer. "I want to understand why they chose to do this."

And then we will watch them burn.

"And then I want to come back and help the others like me find a way to live with the monsters we've all become."

She ground her teeth as she waited for an equally enraged response.

He clasped his hands together. "My dear, you are nothing short of brilliant. Yes, Layla, yes—why didn't I think of that? You'll be the face of the furos, the embodiment of a concept that so few, even on the council, can even fathom. It's what we've been missing all this time." His eyes glistened with admiration. "You'll be our ambassador."

His reaction was stunning.

"Your request is granted," he continued, patting her leg. "We have a deal, my dear. You show me your best tomorrow, and I'll personally call a council meeting and buy your first-class plane ticket. Start thinking about where you want to go. Spain is beautiful this time of year."

He waggled his eyebrows, kissed her forehead, and strode from the room. "Nurse? Nurse, get in here and get Layla some—"

The door cut off his blathering.

This was no promotion; this was a fall of the deepest order. What could be less human than scrap salvage? A praefuro. And less than a praefuro? A praefuro ambassador, the face of the killing machines. Still, Stewart could spin it however the hell he wanted, as long as she got her moment. As long as she got them all into a small enclosed space.

In a room that would burn.

She opened the book Stewart had left and read the first quote aloud: "'War is war. The only good human being is a dead one.' George Orwell."

And for the first time in days, a genuine smile crossed Layla's face.

57

"**R**epeat after me."

Nick mirrored Brother Zane's cross-legged posture from his position among the sea of inductees. They were just like him, chosen to stay, chosen to progress to the next step. Whatever that was.

"A poisoned life cannot be purified until it is fully understood," Brother Zane continued.

Nick joined the response as solemnly as he could. "A poisoned life cannot be purified until it is fully understood."

"As an impure, I must acknowledge, accept, and despise the poison inside me so I can be free of it."

Nick repeated it with the others, intrigued by the ritual.

Brother Zane smiled and opened his chiseled arms to the hundred or so young men and women ranged before him.

Eddie elbowed Nick. "When you think they'll bring out the Kool-Aid?"

He wanted to answer with a clever retort like *right after the bikini-line branding*, but he kept his focus on Brother Zane. The opulent domed room had no corners in which to hang cameras, but there was no doubt in his mind that they were being carefully observed. He didn't want his behavior to give anyone the wrong impression of him. He didn't want anything to prevent him from seeing what came next.

"Welcome, my friends, my brothers and sisters, to stage one, your first step toward purification," Brother Zane said. "It's so rewarding to see such a large group of inductees. You've chosen the right path. A better life." He gracefully rolled onto his heels and stood, as if he'd been doing that move for years. "The promises we've made to you from the moment you were invited to join us are all very real, but I won't lie to you. They're not free or easy. They require long days of physical and mental training. To be successful, to reach a state of purification, you will prove that you have the strength and conviction to be among the elite of the human race. And I mean that literally."

He removed his shirt and turned his back to the audience.

Nick gasped along with the rest of the crowd. Long scars crisscrossed Brother Zane's back, from his muscular shoulder blades down to the waistband of his white linen pants.

A prickle crawled down the back of Nick's neck. There it was right in front of him, proof that these kids were tortured. Savagely whipped.

He still hadn't shaken the sense of foreboding he'd had since realizing his uncomfortable interview with the shrink had involved a hypnotic trance of some sort, some mental coercion that had him spewing details of his life that not a soul in the world knew. The first step in brainwashing.

And that ragged woman with all those people in that basement hospital haunted his dreams, her scratchy voice etched in his mind. *The pray pharaoh will rise like the phoenix.*

What the fuck was going on here? It wasn't just criminal, it was perverse. Evil.

Brother Zane moved to an audio-visual stand and picked up a remote control. The backdrop illuminated with a picture of a pale thin kid stretched across an armchair. Long greasy hair flopped over his dark-circled, drooping eyes as he held his arms in a double-bird salute. The insides of his arms were red and bruised. This was clearly the image of an addict.

"You may not recognize me in the photo."

No shit. Nick did a double-take and squinted at the image again.

"I don't need to bore you with my woeful life story," Brother Zane continued. "You can see my entire poisoned life in that picture. To be honest, I can't even remember most of my life before I was given a second chance here at the Colony."

Images flickered across the screen. Zane huddled in a corner, covered in sweat. A group on its knees in front of an instructor holding—a stick? A cane? A series of pictures of Zane, each showing him progressively healthier and stronger and happier, until he was positively glowing with pride and confidence. Nick had to admit that the transformation was remarkable. But then again, every rehab program had its success stories.

Brother Zane adjusted his headset and pulled a small strap under his chin to keep it in place. He placed his hands on the floor and rose into a perfect handstand.

Applause filled the room but petered out as Brother Zane continued, still in a handstand, his voice as smooth and clear as before. "Rehab is easy. Anyone can do it with hard work and dedication and desire."

He lifted one arm off the ground and held it straight out to the side. The audience cheered.

"But here at the Colony, rehabilitation is not the goal. In fact, rehabilitation is just the starting point."

He bent his supporting arm slowly and lowered his legs slowly to one side until they were parallel to the floor. The guy's weight was resting entirely on one arm. Nick leaned forward with the others. There was no applause or cheering this time. Everyone was too awestruck to react.

Impossibly, Brother Zane kept speaking, not a hint of strain in his voice. "This is why we call it purification. Anyone can recover to the point of an average twenty-something adult. But here, we don't strive for average. We don't even strive for perfection. We reach beyond that. We strive for extraordinary."

On that dramatic note, he pushed himself back up into a handstand and bounced back onto his feet. "Welcome to induction."

The profundity of his words and demonstration was palpable. No one made a sound or so much as twitched a muscle.

Nick stole a glance at Eddie, whose eyes were wet, filled with either tears or stars. Like everyone else in that room (well, except Nick), Eddie had swallowed the whole package hook, line, and sinker. If someone were to pass around a pitcher of Kool-Aid, Eddie would've gulped down two glasses.

Then again, even Nick might've taken a few sips.

This was how they sucked them in. This was where the brainwashing began.

"In the long-standing tradition of the Colony," Brother Zane continued, "tonight you will say goodbye to your impure lives in the poisoned world. I want you to enjoy yourselves in the Gallery. You can relive a moment in time before the virus changed the world. But I also want you to remember that that world is long gone. Once you leave the Gallery tonight, it's time to push the past from your mind and move toward something bigger, a new definition of self-actualization. And I promise you, it will be so much better than you've ever imagined."

A single slow clap started in the back of the room. Nick wanted to roll his eyes; it was so obviously a plant to create a dramatic close to the presentation. But it wasn't hard to play along. Once he crossed over into the next phase of the Colony's brainwashing, he'd be inside the story he'd spent four years looking for. A hidden government facility that recruited people from the dregs wasn't a Pulitzer Prize story; the real story was the basement filled with people attached to machines through tubes in their spines. All he had to do was get inside. And if he had to suffer through chants and heartfelt, emotional stories and group hugs in the Gallery, whatever that was, he was all in.

The story had to be told.

58

I t was almost time. Layla checked her image in the full-length mirror in the staging room outside the Gallery. She twisted left and right to check out her frumpy figure. It was the first time she could remember wearing black stretch jeans—or black anything, really, any color other than white—and she looked more like a black whale than the Black Widow. She was a long way from regaining her flat stomach, although she couldn't help a smile at the sight of her exposed cleavage. If James were there, he would've said something like *Whoa, put those things away! You're gonna poke someone's eye out* or—

No. She wouldn't allow James in her thoughts. James was from her past life. She was the new Layla, and she had a job to do. An important job. Her stomach fluttered at the thought. Could she go through with it?

Yes, she could. She had already proven it, years ago, when, as Allison Stevens, she killed a police officer. Long before the Colony turned her into a killing monster.

More importantly, this exhibition, whatever it was, would earn her the moment she'd fantasized about since Stewart waltzed into her infirmary room: trapping the Eugenesis council in a fiery blaze, watching with delight as they writhed in agony from the burning flames before their mouths and lungs filled with smoke and ash. She would savor the taste of sweet vengeance for the rest of her days.

A door slammed behind her, and she stood up straighter. Her jaw dropped at the sight of the tall muscular woman with a shaved head who strode confidently into the dressing area. She didn't realize she'd spoken the woman's name aloud until she heard the echo of her voice.

"Keisha."

"Well, well, if it isn't the sister." Keisha raised a perfectly defined eyebrow and gave her the once-over. "Look who's crossed over to the dark side."

She was too stunned to respond.

"What's the matter? Did they cut that smug, condescending tongue out of your mouth?" Keisha took two steps toward her. She was at least six or seven inches taller than Layla, and she bent slightly and spoke in a hushed voice. "Or didn't you realize that everyone, even the most poisonous among us, finds a home at the Colony?"

Her mind flashed to Vanessa Sykes, whose only offense had been to recognize the woman interviewing her. How many others in that underground room were there because Layla just hadn't been feeling it that day? How many recruits had made the long journey to the Colony only to be sentenced to a life of misery at the flip of Layla's wrist?

Seemingly satisfied with Layla's disquiet, Keisha pivoted to the locker area and retrieved a pair of battered jeans with holes in the thighs and a black tank top. Layla felt a sharp stab of jealousy. Keisha was the Black Widow, with her tall, fit body and gorgeous features. She made Layla feel like a little white mouse, pale and weak.

Once dressed, Keisha sidled in next to Layla, gazing at their reflections. Her eyes dropped to Layla's feet. "I wouldn't wear those shoes if I were you."

Layla glanced at her heeled ankle boots. "Um, why?" The question came out as a timid squeak, and she cleared her throat.

"When was the last time you wore three-inch heels to shank a two-hundred-pound dude? You need balance and agility. Wear something flat."

Layla wasn't sure what shanking was, but she got the gist of it. A nervous chill jittered down her arms, and she stepped back so Keisha wouldn't notice.

Layla's escort couldn't stop jabbering about the Gallery, an enormous arena on the far side of the campus, recently built to simulate the poisoned world. *It's the spitting image of Las Vegas. You know, the Strip? Oh, don't tell me you've never been to the Strip. It's so much fun.*

He might've had some wisdom to impart, something that could have given her an advantage or at least soothed her trepidation a bit, but her fury at James, once again, clouded her head. Another secret he'd kept from her. Another lie.

But now she wished she'd asked more questions because it was clear she didn't know what she'd gotten herself into.

Keisha rolled her eyes and clomped over to the walk-in costume closet, returning with a pair of knee-high riding boots with no heels. "These will go well with your schoolmarm image."

What little confidence Layla had fizzled out like a doused candlewick, and she collapsed onto the bench, defeated. Where was her flaming fireball when she needed it?

Keisha took a seat next to her as Layla pulled on the riding boots.

"It's not as hard as you think," Keisha said. "Once you get out there, it all comes very naturally. You'll smell the death first. You just follow the scent. There'll be a lot of people, so you'll have to find your mark within the crowd. The tricky part is eliminating them without being observed. We work in the background, never seen. Can't create a panic. Once you're within proximity of the mark, your vision will clear and you'll know what to do. The prey and kill drive is in your brain stem, but the intuition is in your cerebral cortex, which takes in all your surroundings. It's as if the environment is speaking to you. It's what makes us different from the ragers." Her bristly tone had softened by the time she finished. To Layla's utter shock, Keisha seemed to genuinely want to help her. "Then once you get the feel of it, you'll find your MO. Your signature move."

Several seconds passed as Layla tried to think of the right way to respond.

"I think—" She swallowed. "I'm sorry. I misjudged you."

Keisha slid off the bench and stretched her arms over her head as if loosening up her spine and neck. "You didn't misjudge me. This is where I belong. You misjudged yourself."

A whoosh of outside air blew in from the doorway with the entrance of two young women, a young white girl with jet black hair and a pierced lip, and a petite Asian woman. Layla didn't recognize either of them. She wondered if they too had been among her rejections for the purification program, but neither seemed to recognize her either. The one with black hair pulled her hoodie over her head and reapplied some dark purple lipstick.

"All y'all ready to do some purifyin'?" She held out a hand to Layla. "I'm the Wasp."

Layla was about to ask what that meant when two loud claps came from behind them, along with a heavy whiff of perfume. A third woman had hopped up onto the bench like a fitness coach and was gesturing for them to move in.

"Grab a hand. Let's make a circle." She spoke with an accent—French, maybe?—and was probably at least ten years older than Layla.

Layla took the hand of the Wasp on one side and Keisha on the other. She glanced at each of them. They were the most eclectic group imaginable. She could only assume that was intentional.

The French woman breathed in deeply and held her palms up near her ears as if she were praying. Layla glanced at the Wasp, who rolled her eyes.

"The role of a furo is to be the shepherd," the French woman intoned. "A good shepherd knows how to cull the unfit from her herd to save it."

"That's a new one," the Wasp muttered.

"You know who else was a shepherd? The Good Shepherd." The French woman gave them all a knowing look.

"Who?" the Wasp asked.

The Asian girl slapped her sarcastically.

Layla chewed a hangnail, a nasty nervous habit that she thought she'd outgrown. She wished they would just get on with it. She wanted to get this over with, do whatever Stewart wanted her to do so she could begin planning her revenge.

The French woman scowled at the Wasp, then addressed Layla with a wide, warm smile. "Sister Layla, so great to have you join us. My name is Eva, and I'm in charge of the simulation."

"It's just Layla." Her eyes darted to Keisha.

Keisha didn't look back, but her mouth twitched.

"Okay," Eva said, "the four boys have already been released. Our team of eight is the best of the best. We'll be performing for a small group of US government officials. They won't be drinking or enjoying the Gallery games—I understand they're conducting some sort of evaluation—so be on your best behavior." She handed each of them an earpiece. "Our demonstration today is extremely high profile. Therefore, I'm inserting myself into your heads to offer you guidance should there be an unsightly or untidy elimination. Please target your marks carefully. Quality over quantity. This is not a contest, it's an exhibition."

Layla observed the others first and inserted her earpiece into her ear, covering it with her hair.

"I realize it's difficult to ignore your instincts, but if the setting isn't right, move on. Don't waste time waiting for the perfect moment. And please try to look for a chance to work together. That always impresses our guests. Tap the earpiece if you need guidance."

Eva waggled a finger at the Asian. "Tara, no drinking. I'm serious. Not for this demo." She looked from one to the next. "That goes for everyone."

Tara rolled her eyes. "How else am I supposed to get a mark into a bathroom stall? No one wants to bang a sober chick." She winked at Layla and spoke in a high-pitched accent. "You want fucky-fucky?"

Layla turned away. Despite waking up with a whole new outlook, despite her resolve to go through with this so she could earn that meeting with the council, she was obviously in way over her head. These women came from the poisoned world. They understood it. They fit in. But she didn't have the luxury of life experience outside the Colony, not that she could remember. She would look incompetent. She had no idea what to even say to someone.

"Fake it," Eva responded to Tara. "Layla, you okay? Any questions?"

She had a million, but her rattled mind didn't know which to ask.

"I'm fine," she muttered, as she tore the cuticle of her thumb off causing it to bleed.

"Make me proud, girls."

Layla took a ragged breath and followed the others to the door. *I am the shepherd. I will cull the unfit from my herd to save it.* But the words did nothing to boost her confidence, so she upgraded it to something more convincing.

I am Allison Stevens. I am a killer.

59

"**W**hat. The. Fuck." Eddie's eyes were bulging out of his head. Nick's were too. They had stepped inside an arena of some kind, a massive indoor space unlike anything he'd ever seen, but they'd also stepped into a time capsule and been transported to Las Vegas, Nevada, circa 2010, back when Las Vegas was the epicenter of sin, money, sex, and booze. Before the virus. Before the Strip had become a desolate ghost town. It seemed impossible, a perfect replica, the only difference was the visible steel-framed walls all along the perimeter of the Strip, heavily lined with guards.

"Glitter Gulch!" Eddie slapped Nick repeatedly on the shoulder in excitement. "I've seen it on TV. Man, this is gonna be the best night of my life."

Nick cowered from the slaps, but he was grinning. God, it felt so real, and he was flooded with happy memories of bustling, carefree cities.

"Where do you wanna start?" Eddie asked.

Nick was already heading toward Aces & Ales. "I don't know about you, but I could use a beer."

The street was packed with people and performers. Women in sexy gowns and high heels laughed and leaned into each other, sloshing booze from their martini glasses. Couples walked hand in hand, pausing to watch a man juggle fire sticks. Groups hollered and cheered from inside the casinos. Who were all these people? Were they all actors, hired to make this place seem authentic?

Nick and Eddie took a seat at the bar—a real tap serving what looked like real beer. He almost ordered a Guinness out of habit but caught himself. "Do you have a good stout on tap?"

The bartender swept a towel across the bar in front of him. "Sure do." He pulled three taster glasses and set them in front of Nick. "Give these a try."

Nick closed his eyes and sipped. The cigarette smell emanating from the upholstery, the electric warble of the slot machines, and the grainy coffee taste of his creamy beer so overwhelmed his senses that he nearly choked up.

He had to remind himself that he was working. This Disneyland ride was obviously a lure, a way to seduce the recruits into signing over their lives—or, more accurately, their bodies and minds—to genetic experimentation. As long as he kept his wits about him, he might be able to learn something about Allison Stevens and what really was going on here.

"Who's playin'?" Eddie asked.

Nick's eyes shot over to the TV.

The bartender dried a pint glass and restacked it. "New England, Dallas. Patriots leading thirteen–two."

"Fuckin' Patriots, I hate those guys." Eddie was practically giggling with delight.

Several guys at the end of the bar yowled as Dallas intercepted a pass and returned it half the length of the field. The game had clearly been taped in some year back when the NFL was still a thing, but he couldn't stop staring at the TV with childlike wonder. It was surreal.

He waited for Eddie to join the howling bunch and then leaned over the counter. "What gives, man?" he asked the bartender, careful to keep his voice low. "Is this, like, a movie set? These all extras?" He stabbed a thumb in the direction of the Dallas fans.

The bartender laughed and set down another pint in front of Nick. "Not at all. Everyone here is a member of the Colony."

His confusion must've shown.

"Everyone's here to enjoy themselves, same as you."

Nick spun away on his stool as he sipped. By habit, his gaze slid across the corners of the bar. He wasn't surprised to see a wide-angle camera there, and similar cameras in the other corners. Here to enjoy themselves? That was doubtful, not with an outlay like this. This had to be some sort of social experiment. The quack who'd locked him in the interview room was probably watching him right now. Something to do with selecting candidates for their genetic research. Angry drug addict Brother Zane had probably come through here at some point, and someone behind the camera had spotted something magical: *That one. He'll be the poster boy for the Olympic gymnast drug,* or some shit like that.

As Nick turned back to the bar, his attention was drawn to a guy reaching over the bar for a napkin. Nick's eye caught a flash of silver off his belt, just before his leather jacket fell back into place to cover it. Hey, now—that couldn't possibly be standard issue Fremont Street garb for an inductee. That was a handgun, or possibly a Taser. Undercover security, no doubt. But why? What were they expecting to happen here?

The stout was starting to make him feel a little loopy. He was probably overthinking the situation. After all, he was no conspiracy theorist, always looking around the corner for some powerful bad guy. *Big Brother is watching you.*

"Yo, let's go check out the rest of the place." Eddie pulled him off the stool.

"Enjoy your night, fellas. I suggest dinner at Buddaka. Best Peking duck you've ever had. All the way at the far end."

Just when he wanted to drop his guard, he stole a glance back at the bartender. His smile was too wide, his wave too chummy. It was like it had been rehearsed or … indoctrinated. The thought stirred his spider senses, and he cursed himself for drinking that high-octane stout.

Stay frosty Oscar Mike.

60

"See you around," Keisha said as she cut in front of Layla and marched into the Gallery. Tara and the Wasp locked arms and galloped after her, laughing.

The door to the dressing room slammed behind Layla, and the security guard gave her a nod. "Ma'am."

She took three tentative steps forward and halted. The sound stage that lay before her was so alien, she felt as though she were on a different planet. It really was a slice of the poisoned world enclosed in a massive dome. The stagnant air was already stifling, and the chaotic scene in front of her was a complete assault on her senses. Blinding, flashing lights shot from all directions; even casting her eyes downward didn't seem to help. And the noise—beeps and chimes and people yelling over each other, loud music emanating from a dark room with a bright flashing strobe light that made her feel nauseated. So many people practically on top of each other.

Her chest tightened. She couldn't pull in a full breath. She'd never experienced the poisoned world, not that she could remember, and—god, it was utter madness. She squeezed her eyes and covered her ears. *Breathe in to the count of four. Breathe out to the count of four.*

Her breath hitched, and she began panting heavily. Sweat dripped down her back. She couldn't do this; she didn't understand this world. The speed at which everything around her was moving made her dizzy. Her legs felt paralyzed, and her hands tingled, on the verge of becoming numb.

"Layla, dear. Are you okay?" Eva's voice came from her earpiece.

"I have to get out of here." She turned back toward the guard. "Please, I need to leave."

"Wait, Layla," Eva said.

She wrapped her arms around her torso and folded in half, worried she might faint.

"You can do it, you really can. Stewart's counting on you. Don't back out. I'll help you. I'll be with you every step of the way."

Stewart. She had to go out there and do her job. Find her target. If she didn't live up to her part of the deal, Stewart wouldn't grant her a council meeting. She clenched her jaw and tried to control her breathing.

"What is it? Tell me what you don't like."

"It's mayhem in here," Layla shouted over a group of squealing women. "I have no idea what's even going on. I don't know where to start. I look out of place. They'll all know I don't belong here."

"Pull out your phone."

She put her hand on the exit door, but the guard moved in front of it.

"Come on, just try it. Pull out your phone and open the camera so you can see where you're walking."

She did as she was told.

"Now pretend you're texting a friend you lost in the chaos. Keep your head down, look at your phone, and take a few steps forward. Don't look at anyone or anything else, okay? Just try it."

Layla gripped her phone with both hands. *I'm just sending a text to Mia, who was supposed to meet me at the Strip. Mia, I'm at the Strip. Are you coming?* She mimed keying the words into a message bubble and moved out into the middle of the road. People skittered past, cut in front of her, and even sloshed a drink on her, but she kept her eyes locked on the camera view and inched forward one step at a time.

A minute later, her camera landed on an A-frame sign advertising a caramel macchiato. She looked up straight into a coffee shop.

"Starbucks." The word came from her mouth as if she'd said it a million times.

If there isn't a Starbucks in this town, we're driving straight through. I need a fix.

She dropped her arms and stepped inside the mercifully quiet shop. The bitter smell of freshly ground coffee and a tingle of spices filled her nostrils. She gazed into the glass case, stacked with baked goods. An old-fashioned glazed doughnut. *What? I'm not on a diet.* And a cranberry orange scone. *Nope, dry and flaky, like they forgot to add the butter.*

"Layla, you good?" Eva asked inside her ear.

She looked up at the … the…

"—barista!"

The girl behind the counter startled. "Oh, sorry! I didn't see you."

"No, I'm sorry. I didn't mean to yell."

"What can I getcha?"

She closed her eyes, a wide smile crossing her face. "A venti iced skinny hazelnut macchiato, sugar-free syrup, extra shot, light ice, no whip." It rolled off her tongue like the lyrics of a song. Her heart hammered. This was so familiar somehow. So real.

The barista nodded as she jotted notes on the side of the large plastic cup. "I like your style."

Layla inhaled the Starbucks smell as she surveyed the small shop, enchanted by every detail. She sauntered over to a display stand and picked up an oversized ceramic mug with the Starbucks logo on the front. It had some heft to it. If she swung downward with enough—

"Here you go, miss."

She fumbled the mug but caught it just before it hit the tile floor.

"Wow, great reflexes." The barista pushed a large plastic cup across the counter.

Even though she had no idea what she was about to taste, her mouth watered. The lid popped off as she wrapped her fingers around the cup, splattering a few droplets of the creamy drink onto her sleeve.

The barista grabbed a paper towel. "Oh, god, I'm so sorry. I must not've pushed it on all the way."

"Hey, Cruella, you know caffeine works a lot better if you ingest it, not wear it?"

She dabbed furiously at her expensive wool dress. "The goddamn barista didn't put the cap on tightly. I need your sport coat."

"What? No way."

"Ms. Stevens, are you ready?" Her assistant handed her a leather folder with A.S. inscribed in the corner.

"Ry, give me your fucking sport coat. Austin and I have to be in that board meeting in three minutes."

"Fine, but I want it dry cleaned. Your BO will scare off the ladies."

"Are you okay?" The barista waved her hand in front of Layla's face.

But Layla could only stare blankly as a sense of wonderment bubbled up inside her. She couldn't remember Ry's face, but Austin... She remembered this—well, a little bit. This was her poisoned life. She was Allison Stevens. She wasn't sure who Allison was, but she was certain of one thing: She hadn't been a submissive little schoolmarm. She'd been someone with power and influence—a board meeting, for heaven's sake. Maybe she'd been as important out there in the poisoned world as James was inside the Colony.

She took a long pull from the straw. God, nothing had ever tasted so good.

She finally addressed the barista, who was eyeing her with suspicion. "Gotta get to work. Thanks so much." Maybe she'd said those same words to a barista in the poisoned world.

She clutched her drink to her chest and stepped out into the chaos. The big glass door swung closed behind her, cutting off the comforting aromas of the peaceful haven. She wrapped her lips around the straw for another sip when a new smell gusted around her from the street.

She grimaced and tossed her macchiato into the trash. Time to get to work, indeed.

The smell of death was in the air.

61

"This is not a good idea." James tried to keep his voice low as Stewart led their guests down the narrow hallway toward the stairs. They were leaving the safety of the observation room to get a firsthand experience of the Gallery.

"Oh, it's fine," replied Stewart, his inner petulant child rearing its pouty head. "All you do is worry, James. You need to live a little. It's perfectly safe. The furos target cancer and AIDS—so unless any of you guys are hiding something, you won't even be noticed."

The tasteless joke was infuriating. Stewart was first and foremost a showman who considered people—all people, whether they were terminal cancer patients, members of the Chinese Ministry of Health, or as was the case today, agents from the US Department of Defense—as mere captive audiences to feed his perpetual appetite for attention. His self-serving desire to give them the full experience, to walk them down the pedestrian mall and through the casinos, was not only compromising the program but putting additional lives at risk.

"The Gallery was built by set designers for Universal Studios. Finished just—what, James?—six weeks ago? It's a replica of a section of Fremont Street in Las Vegas." Stewart paused with his hand on the doorknob, no doubt trying to build suspense.

"Packing so many in here seems like an unnecessary security risk," Colonel Shaffer noted dryly.

"No risk whatsoever," Stewart said. "It's mostly recruits and inductees—the new, young ones. They view it as a reward, a night on the town. They visit a costume department, just like a real movie set, and get all decked out for the night. It's the real deal."

"And the targets are your people as well, yes?"

"We include a small number from our sick lots—residents with HIV, cancer, hepatitis—then we bring in the furos and let the fury begin."

The colonel looked as though he'd bitten into something sour. "I understand you're simulating the real world, but I'm not sure I see the need for such spectacle. Las Vegas?"

"We conducted extensive research to see what would appeal to the broadest group of men and women in their twenties. Other than Disney World, the Las Vegas experience transcends race, culture, and socioeconomic status. Everyone loves Las Vegas."

Stewart flung the door open and stepped to one side. "And remember—what happens in Vegas stays in Vegas."

James forced himself not to wince. The impious manner in which Stewart presented the Gallery was yet another signal that he didn't fully understand what they were creating. James had observed nearly every simulation run since the Gallery was built, but unlike Stewart, he'd also supervised the cleanup. Blood had to be removed, and damaged furniture replaced. Bodies had to be located and disposed of in a respectful way— James insisted.

"We've recreated the Gallery at our two largest sites, China and the Philippines," Stewart continued. "Huge successes. Maybe even more so than this one."

James hung back, scrutinizing the scene with a jaded eye. Flashing lights and backlit slot machines sucked the recruits in. Even without real money, gambling was irresistible to so many of this young generation. It was the dream of winning, the fantasy of living on a yacht or driving a Lamborghini they craved, even though they knew it wasn't real.

But somewhere among the indulgent party-goers, the predators lurked. And today, his beautiful girl would be one of them.

Someone howled with delight as the overhead display ticked up hundreds, then thousands of dollars. God, he was already edgy.

Stewart was still working through his tour speech. " …not provided with weapons. They don't need them. Instead, they use everyday objects from the environment: a knife from a restaurant kitchen or a belt from their own body. This serves two purposes. First, they're less likely to be noticed. Imagine someone approaching you while brandishing a gun or a long knife. It would cause a panic. And second, it allows them to be nimble. The furos don't know when they might come upon a genetically compromised target. We are training our soldiers to think and act in the moment."

That was another misnomer that Stewart liked to tout, one that warranted a wider discussion with the council. The praefuro predators were not trained in any type of combat. While they were extraordinarily intuitive and quick, the risk existed that they might underestimate a mark and get hurt or even killed.

But Stewart refused to discuss it. *Show me one example where a target got the upper hand, James. They're inferior to normal humans, so they're doubly inferior to my furos.* It was a dumb argument. Stewart believed the praefuro had superpowers, but they very much did not.

James caught a glimpse of Keisha, Stewart's favorite. *My blueprint*, he often called her, as if she were a prototype robot and not a mere mortal. Her presence meant the praefuro had entered the Gallery. His eyes darted from person to person, his heart hammering. His stomach flip-flopped as if he were a teenage boy on his first date.

Layla was here.

62

The target was covered in maggots that squirmed in and out of what remained of her exposed bluish-green flesh and bubbled up under her light blue silk slip dress. Her arms brushed against her skirt to give it an extra-sexy swish, but Layla's attention was locked on the worms dropping off the woman's dead skin, leaving a trail of slime that would be squished into the red carpet by the hordes inside the crowded casino.

Despite that, the target was surprisingly poised, if not particularly graceful, clicking through the gaming area on six-inch stilettos. Why did women wear stilettos, anyway? They offered no support or balance. But the target moved with the confidence of a young woman who'd spent hours curling face-framing strands teased from her elegant loose bun. It was a shame she couldn't see herself the way Layla saw her, decaying from the poison inside her. She might have opted to stay in tonight.

Eva popped into Layla's head so suddenly, she jolted. "Layla, do me a favor. Stay closer to the pedestrian mall. I can't help you in the—"

Layla pulled the earpiece and dropped it into an abandoned glass of wine. She'd chosen her target, the woman in the blue dress, whether Eva liked it or not.

She followed the target through a black-curtained doorway. A thunderous roar coming from the oversized speakers inside assaulted her overly sensitive ears. *Thump, thump, thump.* It vibrated her entire torso. The only light in the room came from a spotlight directly above the deejay and a handful of colorful pinspot lights over the dance floor, which was packed so tightly that when the dancers jumped in unison to the beat, the whole room pulsed like a human heart the size of a whale.

Body heat had warmed the room by at least ten degrees, and the pungent smell of sweat nearly distracted Layla from her mark. The target was walking the perimeter of the thrumming mass toward the bar. Layla slowed her pace and glanced upward at the tiny red dots in the dark corners of the room. Was Stewart watching her? Evaluating her?

Nerves got the better of her, and she veered in the opposite direction. She opened the first door she came to, hoping it led to a restroom. No luck—a staircase. The bitter smell of beer wafted up from the darkness below. Storage, perhaps. Part of her wanted to descend the stairs, find a nice, cool corner, and hide. Certainly, that part of her was stronger than the part that wanted to get anywhere near those sweaty bodies on the dance floor.

But an even bigger part of her wanted to purge. To purify.

She eased back into the club. The target leaned over the bar, resting on her elbows with her back to the crowd.

Layla slid up to the bar next to her. She was petite, her small neck and shoulders bare except for the thin spaghetti straps crisscrossing her bare back. She was dressed for sex, but her body language made it clear that she wasn't ready to flirt. She wouldn't be getting lucky tonight, because Layla could smell her. The woman in the blue dress was filled with poison, all the way to her DNA, and humanity couldn't take the chance that she would pass those poisonous genes to a new life.

It was Layla's job to make sure of it.

She is the plague. She must be purged.

The urge to grab the vile creature by the throat was almost too much to resist, but Layla didn't want to strangle her. What she wanted was to claw at her face, tearing off chunks of foul flesh. She wanted to shred her torso with a knife, making sure that every drop of poisoned blood was spilled on the floor, then crack her skull, removing her warm, spongy brain and stabbing it repeatedly until there was nothing but an unidentifiable mass of tissue and blood.

The fantasy sent a tremor of excitement through her, and she dug her fingers into the bar to regain control. Her skill wasn't torso shredding; that was how the ragers worked. They were practically animals, completely unable to control themselves. She, on the other hand, was a shepherd. A good shepherd knew how to cull the unfit from her herd to save it. It was her mission.

It wasn't personal; it was business.

Her body relaxed and her mind cleared, just as Keisha said it would. With each flash of the strobe, her gaze fixed on objects around her: several half-filled wine bottles. Stacks of highball glasses next to a tray of fruit slices. A cutting board of lemons and a thin-bladed knife. A glass shelf against a mirrored wall. A softly lit neon sign advertising Absolute Vodka, its electric cord stretched to the nearby outlet.

The barstools emptied as people surged onto the floor for a hit song, leaving only herself and the target at one end of the bar, and at the other end, a man with a neatly groomed soul patch under his bottom lip. A player, Layla thought, by his posture and the way he eyed Layla's target, his lip turned up in a wry smile. He was waiting for his moment to approach.

But Blue Dress still wasn't sending out signals. She ordered another gin and tonic and kept her gaze on her glass, sipping frequently.

Liquid courage. The expression popped into Layla's head. She could hear her own voice from the past, then the voice of Allison Stevens: *I need some liquid courage before I can dance.*

The room brightened as the music changed from a thumping base drop to an electric synthesizer. Laser lights swung wildly up one wall, across the ceiling, and down the other wall. The crowd erupted in cheers, and the jumping gave way to suggestive gyrating, arms and legs coiling around each other like slithering snakes.

The bartender leaned onto an elbow to hear Layla over the music. "Can

I get you something?"

"Club soda, please," she hollered back.

By the time the drink appeared, the target had gulped down her second drink and started a third. She took one last slurp and faced the dance floor, back arched and chest thrust forward. It was an invitation Soul Patch couldn't refuse. He drifted over and spoke into her ear. She took his hand and allowed him to lead her onto the floor.

A whiff of fresh lemon distracted Layla, and she studied the bartender as he picked up a lemon and sliced through it. Out, in, out, in. Four slices through a whole lemon.

That would work.

The deejay bellowed into the microphone. "Put your fuckin' hands up!" The lights dropped again.

Now. It was time.

The pull came from somewhere in her gut. Her mouth watered, and she wiped away the saliva with the back of her hand.

She is poison.

The beat moved through her body, and her heartbeat slowed to match.

Thump, thump, thump, thump.

She swung her right arm over the bar, knocking over a stack of highball glasses. She didn't hear them break as they crashed to the floor—they may have simply bounced off the rubber floormat—but the bartender dropped his knife next to the sliced lemon to clean up the mess.

Thump, thump, thump.

Three steps to the left. She palmed the knife and kept moving.

Thump, thump, thump, thump.

Four steps onto the dance floor. The erratic flash of the strobe light was making her dizzy, but she wriggled toward the middle of the pack, grimacing at the heat, sweat, and body odor.

Thump, thump.

She must be purged.

The target and her partner were chest to chest, their hands in the air.

The earth must be purified.

Layla moved in behind Soul Patch, reached her left hand around his waist, and squeezed his genitals. He spun around. Her right hand slipped the blade ever so gently beneath the Blue Dress's spaghetti straps and whisked back.

The top of the silky dress fluttered to the woman's waist. She shrieked. One arm flew up to cover her chest and the other clutched the dress to keep it from slithering to the floor.

Layla moved in to help, putting one arm around her and easing her off the dance floor. "I gotcha, I gotcha."

"Oh my god," she panted. "I don't know what happened." Her fingers trembled as she fumbled with the fabric, trying to reposition it over her chest.

"Don't worry at all. It was so dark in there, no one saw anything." She opened the door that led to the basement storage room and gently pushed the woman inside.

"What's this?"

"Turn around. I'll retie your straps for you."

The target held her dress in place as Layla pulled the straps over her shoulders. Layla spread her feet to secure her stance and pulled, dragging the woman backward by the straps as she buried the blade of the knife in her neck, neatly, just below the base of the skull.

The target crumpled into a heap on the cool cement floor. Layla could've taken time to verify the thing was dead—to listen for breathing, feel for a pulse—but she didn't need to. Within seconds, the stench of the poison had dissipated.

Just like Jonah's last moments.

She studied the location, depth, and angle of the knife before retrieving it. She hadn't been one hundred percent confident that the little blade would be sharp enough or that she would be strong enough to sever a human spinal cord. The stiletto heels had been the deciding factor. Tugging the target's straps, which forced her to topple backward, had given Layla the perfect angle for an upward thrust with the added advantage of gravity.

Elementary, my dear Watson. She smiled at the clever expression, not quite sure where it came from.

Layla breathed in a deep satisfied breath, enjoying the subtle aroma of beer, uncontaminated by the smell of decay. She felt lighter, as if she'd purged a weight that she herself had carried. One fewer inferior human on the planet, thanks to her. One small step closer to purifying the human race.

She tugged at the blue dress, which ripped easily with a bit of force, and cleaned the blood smearing the knife and her fingers. She gave it another tug toward the stairs. A nudge with her foot sent what remained of the target tumbling to the bottom.

Bummer that Stewart and his guests had probably missed her skillful slaying. How would she prove she kept up her end of the bargain?

She pocketed the knife.

Perhaps the next target.

63

"Oh, there's one of 'em right now."

Stewart had also noticed Keisha, and he nudged Colonel Shaffer, whose face was locked in a permanent state of impassivity.

Although Stewart couldn't see it, this DOD visit wasn't about a sales pitch; it was an audit, and James was certain the colonel was significantly savvier than Stewart realized. *They're just a bunch o' desk jockey bureaucrats,* Stewart had said with an eye-roll, as he and James walked to the gate to greet them. But these men were here on orders from General Harding, and the general would never send out desk jockeys.

James eased closer to the group, who were drifting through the noisy casino following Keisha's moves. Although the temperature in the Gallery was a perfect seventy-one degrees Fahrenheit, his armpits were damp. If Keisha made an error in judgment or was sloppy in any way, he didn't doubt that the government would send in an army of inspectors for an extensive investigation. His reversion therapy research would be discovered.

Keisha paused at a craps table, resting one muscular glute on a barstool, her gaze following the roll of the dice.

"This is the prey phase," Stewart said. "Unlike a wild animal, this furo's cerebral cortex has been enhanced."

"With a genetic drug," Colonel Shaffer asked, "or infant cord tissue?"

Stewart nodded at James to take over.

Fine, but he'd do it his way. "This is Keisha. She came to us only a couple of weeks ago with a strong predisposition for violence. She was an interesting case because she sincerely wanted to change and start her life over. With only a few counseling sessions, we were able to rechannel her focus and help her see that she had a calling."

"You didn't make her … engineer her to be what she is?" asked the colonel.

"She willingly joined the praefuro community," James replied, "and she's proven to be more successful than those who did not join willingly. It's an interesting dynamic to consider for the future, as we identify others who might be inclined toward violence. Psychology has taught us that success is driven by strong internal motivation."

Stewart raised his eyebrows, and James read the message there: *I know you're passionate about your work, but don't give them too much.*

"But to answer your question, Keisha was one of the first to receive the praefuro offspring cord tissue transplant," he continued. "As Stewart said, the benefit of the cord tissue is the intensified intuitiveness and laser focus, as well as a tendency toward a more thoughtful yet rapid elimination. We haven't been able to get quite the same outcome from a genetic drug."

He gestured the group to a tall bar table where they could observe Keisha's next move.

Keisha was leaning into a guy at the craps table, whispering something in his ear. She gave a nod to the dealer, a signal that they'd be right back. She walked several feet to a curtained area, easing her arm behind him to pull him close and whisper again. A second later, he slumped into a chair, his head bowed. She slid the chair back a couple of inches and pulled the curtain around him. No one, other than the six of them, even glanced in that direction.

"These praefuro are not trained?" the colonel asked. "How do you manage to keep the eliminations discreet?"

James spoke just loud enough to be heard over the background noise. "We have an expansive team of insiders. In fact, only about thirty percent of the people you see here tonight are what we call guests, unaware of the experiment. Seventy percent are here to ensure nothing gets out of hand and to make the experience completely seamless. That includes disposal of the deceased. That's the beauty of a heavily controlled environment."

But no one knew how the praefuro would fare in the field without a support team. He changed the subject before the colonel could follow up. "One thing that makes our praefuro subjects unique is their ability to work covertly. They don't operate like serial killers, who have a pattern to their target identification, and they don't follow a chain of command like paid assassins. They're not driven by emotion or money. They're driven by instinct, much like you or I would drink water when we were thirsty."

He had to fight to keep the sadness from creeping into his tone. Everything he said was true, but he held deep heartfelt sympathy for every one of the praefuro subjects, even Keisha, who had led a truly despicable life before arriving at the Colony. A praefuro lived a dark existence. One that one day he hoped to change with the brilliant science of mutation reversion and get his beautiful girl back.

Stewart jumped in. "Just think about how incisive we could be if we sent our furos into the world like soldiers onto the battlefield, waging a war against genetic inferiority."

James turned his face away. Goddamn Stewart was going to blow it. He was giving them entirely the wrong impression.

He smoothed his expression and held up a finger. "Well, let's be clear. Our intention has never been to discharge a mass force of praefuro soldiers. Our team is currently developing a deployment plan, and our goal is to start small and conservative."

"Go on." The colonel gave a curt nod.

"We'll start with only a handful spread out across large urban areas. As we develop and test more subjects, we'll release five or ten at a time. They'll be observed and protected to the extent that we can, and over years, they'll reproduce. Our genetic army, so to speak, will grow slowly and naturally. In this way, the praefuro will stay under the radar—and more importantly, we'll avoid inadvertently releasing a weapon of mass destruction."

"Exactly." Stewart nodded as if he and James had said the same thing. He rose and held out a hand, palm up, like goddamn Vanna White. "Let's continue down the pedestrian mall. In a few minutes, we'll be joined by our simulation director, who'll give you the behind-the-scenes tour of the Gallery."

Stewart led the way back to the pedestrian mall, launching into a story about the first time he'd walked into a casino in Vegas. James couldn't repress a grin and a head shake. Stewart might have his faults, but James didn't know anyone else who could make up a story on the spot with a grand finale that both punctuated the issue at hand and raised his credibility. It would come soon, something like *That's the moment I realized that the human race was the only thing left worth saving and I was the only one who could save it.*

A piercing squeal of joy erupted from the casino below. He swung around.

And that's when he saw her.

His shoulders sagged, and he felt his face soften in a dopey grin as if Cupid had shot him right in the ass. His mind flashed back to the first time he'd seen her, back when she was Allison Stevens, a grad student standing nervously in front of the podium to defend her grant proposal. The moment he'd laid eyes on her, the rest of the world had faded into pallid shadow. From that moment on, his world never brightened unless she was there in it.

Her hair was much longer than it had been back then, and it hung straight down her back. But here, in street clothes—and without the fetus—she looked exactly like Allison. She was his beautiful girl.

And he fell in love with her all over again.

If she'd been looking around, she might have seen him, but her gaze was fixed on a group of boisterous men stumbling into a restaurant. She tilted her head to one side and followed them inside with purposeful strides, disappearing into the crowded dining room.

And just like that, James's world once again paled.

64

Her second target sat in a group of five guys in a booth at Buffalo Wild Wings. Like Blue Dress, Layla had been drawn to him by the sour smell of decomposing flesh. She now studied him from the kitchen, keeping her distance, staring at his black lips and the skin of his rotting face peeling off, threatening to fall into his plate of nachos. She wanted another minute to watch the corpse decay in front of her eyes. To smell the rot. It fueled her.

She felt invigorated after leaving the nightclub. Her senses seemed so sharp. She could focus on single conversations among all the craziness around her. Her eyes were drawn to every potential weapon and hiding place. Her eagerness to find her next mark was so overpowering, she no longer cared whether Stewart was watching or how well she was performing for the demonstration.

The hunt was thrilling, but the predation itself was utterly electrifying. The longer she allowed herself to study the target and the environment, to predict the behaviors of the people in the room, and to envision a short vignette of her intervention, the greater her hunger. It was better than foreplay.

She snickered out loud.

Time to get to business. Eva would be watching, probably cursing her for losing her earpiece and ready to deliver a scolding if Layla took too long. Her plan for this target hadn't come together just yet, though. She'd have to lure him out of the booth. With what? She moved closer. God, it was simply exhilarating.

At that very moment, the atmosphere changed. It was as if the oxygen had thinned, as though someone were breathing her air. Her eyes darted around the room and landed on the Wasp, who leaned against the hostess table. Her colleague's gaze was fixed on Layla's target.

Layla flushed with jealousy. *I found him first. Move along to someone else.*

The Wasp seemed to sense Layla's presence as well. She looked Layla straight in the face, threw her a small nod, and spoke into her mind. *All yours, then.*

The Wasp turned on her heels and started out of the restaurant.

Wait, I need your help.

The woman froze for a moment and turned back to face her.

Goodie was the only word that echoed in Layla's head.

Layla smirked. She was learning to like the mind talk.

I need a distraction. Layla held her arm out. *And skin.*

The Wasp gave her a lopsided grin and headed toward the booths, stopping at each table for a brief greeting: "How ya doin'?" or "Enjoying dinner?"

When she got to the table of five guys, she gave them a nod. "Any of you up for a game?" She pulled out three slightly bent cards from her back pocket and laid them face up on the table. Two kings and an ace.

"Oh yeah, I remember this game," cried the guy at the end of the table. "Three-card something, right?"

She gave him a nod. "You in? Got some funny money left over? Whaddaya say? Here ya go, first one's on me. Watchin' the ace?" She tossed the cards from one side to the other.

"There! Middle."

"Yeah, man, you're good at this. I better make it harder." She played again.

"Left."

She showed him he was right.

The target chimed in. "Dude, she's gonna hustle you. She's just making it easy right now. That's how they get you."

The Wasp looked hurt. "No, man, that's not how I work. Come on. If your eyes can move as fast as my hands, you'll win."

The guy at the end of the booth pulled out a bill and waggled it over the table.

"Give it to your boomer buddy over there to hold." She tossed her head in the direction of Layla's target. "Trust. That's what it's all about, right?"

He handed the bill to his buddy, who leaned back to access his wallet.

"No, no, boomer, I gotta trust you too. Keep the bill above the table where I can see it. Come on, up-up."

The target draped his elbow over the back of the booth, the bill dangling between his fingers.

Nice work.

Layla glided toward the restrooms, passing by the booth and the now exposed arm. Concealing her favorite knife against her palm, she reached out, giving him a short nick enough to drip blood, and kept walking.

He grabbed his arm. "Ah, fuck!"

Layla glanced back. He'd spun around and was examining an exposed wood staple next to a spindle on the booth.

"Damn it."

"Ah, shit, man," the Wasp said behind Layla. "Better go clean that up. You know … tetanus. That shit is real. My cousin—"

Layla snicked the door to the unisex bathroom closed without engaging the lock. She admired her reflection in the mirror. She didn't see the schoolmarm that Keisha saw. She didn't see flabby post-pregnancy Layla, either. She looked radiant. Powerful. Like a superhero. She hardened her expression, mimicking the woman on the cover of the Black Widow book.

Seconds later, her target stepped inside. "Oh, sorry."

"No, no, I'm done. You can have it, I—whoa, are you okay? Is that blood?" She had to narrow her eyes to find the cut on his decaying arm.

"It's fine, it was—uh, Sister Layla?"

Layla grinned. "Yeah. Hi there."

"Oh, my god, it's so great to see you again. You were such an inspiration. I mean…"

"Here, let me help you." She pulled him to the sink and splashed water on the blood with one hand and turned the lock with the other.

In her head, she did the math. He was probably five feet ten or so, and his head was bowed over the sink. She'd have to swing downward.

She pulled the knife from her right pocket.

"…and god, those talks you gave. And that one time when you were leading the group meditation, when you told us how hard you'd worked to become pure. How much you'd sacrificed for the vision. How the Colony changed your life…"

No, the angle was wrong. She wouldn't have the leverage. She had to get above him.

"…and ever since then, I've felt lucky and grateful every single day. You're the reason I made it through induction."

Her left elbow shot out and flipped the light switch. She curled one foot around his ankle and shoved him toward the porcelain sink. His head ricocheted off the mirror, then the sink, and he landed flat on his back.

"Ahh…"

She groped in the darkness until she found his throat and buried her knife in it. The room was too dark, and she wasn't certain she'd hit the windpipe, so she stabbed him three more times.

She flipped on the light.

"Sacrifice," she panted, as the oozing boils that had covered his head just seconds ago vanished.

Her eyes lingered on his face. Yeah, she did remember this guy.

"Sister Layla?"

"Yeah, hi. What's up?"

He folded his arms, hunching forward. "I just wanted to ask you. Does it get better—the pain, I mean? Because sometimes I don't think I'm going to make it. I'm afraid I'll pass out or throw up. I just wondered if I'll ever get used to it."

"You will." She hugged him, and his body shuddered with a repressed sob. She wondered if he had a mother who hugged him. "You'll get past the pain, I promise. And you'll be pure and perfect."

Layla dragged the body to the other side of the toilet and slouched against the wall to catch her breath. She used the back of her hand to wipe away a tear that dripped down her cheek. His sacrifice was over, but she didn't experience the same exhilaration this time.

She cleaned her knife and hands in the sink. "I am the shepherd. I must cull the unfit from my herd." The words fell from her mouth, but she didn't feel the importance behind them. She felt hollow. Vile.

She locked the door from the inside before she pulled it shut and returned to the restaurant. The table where the group had sat was empty, except for drink glasses and a note on the back of a paper placemat. "Going to the nightclub with the hustler. Catch up."

Layla wadded up the placemat, tossed it into a bus tub, and strode out of the restaurant.

She paused in the pedestrian mall, circling slowly. Happy hollers and laughs echoed in the street. It was peculiar to be surrounded by so much elation. The Colony was a happy place, but in a quiet, subdued way. A contented way. She hadn't seen people experience pure outward joy in this way. She wasn't accustomed to a culture of work hard, play hard; her way was work hard, sleep quickly, and work hard again.

She kept her breath shallow, trying to avoid detecting a scent. Keisha had been right about that, too, that she'd smell them before she would see them. But she didn't want to purge again. She wasn't ready for more death yet.

She turned away from the crowds and noise and headed toward the end of the long pedestrian walkway. It was significantly quieter at this end, with only a Chinese restaurant, a quiet lounge playing soft rock music, and a small art museum.

A wave of longing washed through her. If she'd been offered an enjoyable evening at the Gallery, she would have spent the whole night right here—after she and James stopped at Starbucks, that is, so she could surprise him with her new memory. They'd walk in, and she'd pretend to innocently look at the menu, and she'd rattle off her drink order. His face would register surprise for just a moment before his lip curled up in that dorky smile she loved.

You never stop impressing me, beautiful girl, he'd say.

But her daydream was in vain. She'd never be able to impress James with her silly drink order, nor would she be rewarded with an enjoyable evening. Her destiny was more work, purging the Gallery of the genetic impurities that were ruining the human race.

Like the boy she just killed. A young man who'd sacrificed everything for the Colony. And on the one night that he was given to celebrate, he had to die because something in his DNA told her he didn't deserve life.

As deeply ingrained as her praefuro instincts were, her human brain still recognized something wrong. Yet she would live this way until she died, alone and unloved. A heinous monster.

Why, James? Why am I here? Why did you abandon me?

It's the only way I know how to protect you. That's what he would have said. That's what he always said when she questioned him.

And she would have fought back with her usual response: *I don't need your protection. I need you to let me go. Let me breathe. Because you're suffocating me.*

Maybe he'd finally given in. Maybe this was James letting her go. Letting her breathe.

She inhaled a deep breath and her brain registered a scent. Not the smell of decay, really, but something equally poisonous, like medicine or…

Whatever it was, was masked by a familiar perfume.

She spun around to see Eva walking toward her … past her, toward a group of men just inside the art museum: Stewart, several men in military uniforms—and James. Layla's stomach filled with butterflies, just as it used to years ago. She wanted to move closer, to catch his eye. To read his expression when he saw her.

But instead, her legs staggered backward into the shadow of a red canopy over the Chinese restaurant entrance. Her eyes swam with tears.

This was her new life. She was a furo now. She was no longer James's beautiful girl.

65

"**N**o, never split sixes," Nick said to Eddie. God, was it possible the kid didn't know how to play blackjack? "You'll end up with two sixteens. The dealer has a ten showing. You assume she has a twenty, so you have to take a hit."

Eddie, in his inebriated state, was good cover. He attracted all the attention, allowing Nick to study his surroundings. Mirrored dome cameras were abundant. In a real casino, where they played with real money, security cameras were necessary to watch for cheaters. The domes might have been there only as stage props, but Nick was certain they were live and manned behind the scenes.

It wasn't just the cameras, either. In this casino alone, he'd identified well over twenty armed secret security guards, pretending to be enjoying their night as a guest. If this was simply a social experiment or placement test, they wouldn't need so many plants packing heat. What were they preparing for?

"Hit!" Eddie said as he scooped up the cards.

"Don't touch the cards," Nick and the dealer scolded him in unison.

It was embarrassing, but Nick had to smile. Eddie was an okay guy. He reminded Nick of a slightly dumber, low-key version of himself ten years ago.

"How many's 'at?" Eddie wobbled on his stool.

"Eighteen, sir," the dealer said.

He looked to Nick for advice.

"He'll stay." Nick rolled his eyes. It was probably time to move on. Maybe Eddie would sober up a bit with some food in his stomach.

Anyway, he'd seen enough in the casino. He wanted to move toward the perimeter to see if he could identify a door to the backstage. A set this elaborate would have to have an off-limits area with the security monitors, and possibly even a concealed observation deck.

Nick doubled his bet. "Facedown." He nodded to the dealer, who slid one card face down under his double-down bet.

"Good luck, sir."

It was remarkable just how real this Fremont Street Experience was. The dealers were professional. The drinks were classic Vegas drinks: the Cosmo, the Vodka Red Bull, Jack and Coke. Drinks that kept you awake but made you stupid. That's how Vegas had made its money until the virus dried up the desert oasis. Las Vegas had been one of the earliest, hardest-hit cities in the country, losing thousands in the span of weeks. The images on TV had been devastating.

Nick took a sip from the Jack and Coke he'd been nursing for the last hour. No sense in reliving the past. Vegas would eventually rise again, once people could again trust their government to take care of them.

Eddie made an announcement to the entire table. "Yo, I gotta take a piss."

Nick got up as well. As he spun to follow Eddie, he came face to throat with a hulking woman which he could only describe as a black Xena Warrior Princess. His eyes drew upward to her bulbous shaved head, glistening with sweat, which cocked to the right as her gray eyes studied him.

Barely six inches away, she took up a wide stance like a point guard getting ready for a jump shot, and for some reason, her stare was so unsettling Nick couldn't seem to utter the words *excuse me.*

Her bulging biceps twitched. She parted her lips and whispered,

"You."

Somewhere beyond her, Eddie called out, "Ouch! Motherfucker."

Eddie's voice snapped Nick from his paralysis, and he eased past her, mumbling, "Pardon me. My buddy over there..."

He picked up Eddie, who had fallen and only made it up as far as his knees. "Let's get some food."

He turned back to look at her as they headed for the pedestrian walkway. Her expression had hardened, and the way she was looking at him with those laser eyes. It was as if she were trying to make him spontaneously combust.

Chilled to the bone, he practically dragged Eddie out of the casino.

66

J ames tried to keep Stewart and their guests in a tight group as they walked to the end of the street and into the art museum.

"…my personal collection," Stewart was bragging. "Each piece came from one of my six properties. But I see them so infrequently, I figured I might as well put them to good use. Here, check these out."

Something felt wrong. Stewart was giddier than usual, and Colonel Shaffer seemed skeptical of everything he was seeing. Maybe seeing Layla, knowing she was here as a praefuro, was messing with his mind.

He gazed into every pair of eyes that turned in their direction, searching for the characteristic nystagmus, the eye tremors the praefuro described as signifying the point of no return, the electrical storm in their brains that sparked their deadly focus. His team had conducted numerous voltage imaging studies to detect the point at which the neural module in the amygdala responsible for initiating the pursuit of the target—the neurons that triggered the visual illusion of death and the olfactory illusion of rotting flesh—elicited an even bigger cluster of firing neurons, those responsible for the kill of the target. They'd not only been able to track the electrical chatter between the pursuit and kill modules, but they'd observed how the kill neurons silenced other functions of that region of the brain—specifically, emotion and motivation. The outcome: a resolute and tenacious terminator.

Stewart was launching into yet another made-up story about a watercolor he found while visiting the China site when Eva arrived. James exhaled with relief. Eva not only knew the simulation like the back of her hand, but she also knew the hunting styles of her subjects. She'd certainly know if anything was wrong with any of the praefuro. Including Layla.

"Ah, perfect timing," Stewart said. "Gentlemen, this is Madame Eva Ridel, our simulation director. I will turn over the reins to her. She's been working daily with our furos, training them to tap into their intuitive minds and work collectively. She'll answer any additional questions you have."

The colonel spoke up instantly. "We'd like to know more about the mind-reading."

"Oh yes, of course." Eva smiled warmly. "We believe it's not mind reading, per se. It's more of a deep intuitiveness, a sixth sense. The praefuro are uniquely in tune with each other's body language, facial expressions, and movements, and the more they work together, the better they become at it. But it's not innate. It must be trained. Practiced."

Bullshit, James thought. He'd seen the data. This was another one of Stewart's protective lies. He was paranoid that his resources—specifically, his praefuro—would be reallocated to the global intelligence alliance.

As Eva steered them back toward the Gallery entrance, Stewart put an arm around James and led him back into the pedestrian mall.

"I know about the reversion program, James."

James's blood ran cold, not because Stewart had discovered his research but because he'd chosen this moment to tell him. That meant he was planning to blackball him in front of the Department of Defense men, forcing him to admit he'd been working in secret. Stewart was a shrewd manipulator.

"I know you hired the NIH to analyze the praefuro DNA because you didn't have the talent inside," Stewart said. "Your own team couldn't figure out where the mutations were happening. And I know you've been running a night shift to develop and test a reversion therapy."

James waited for the punch line.

"Did you really think you could keep this from me? Do you not know that I have eyes and ears everywhere in the world?"

James felt a fury boil up inside him. He could spend hours discussing the importance of developing a drug that would reverse the mutation. And if Stewart had spent even one minute in salvage, he might understand. But Stewart didn't value individual human lives; ironically, he only valued the human race. However, right now was not the time for this conversation.

"Why would you spend so much money and effort to undo everything we've created?"

James held his silence as a moment of vulnerability flashed by. He had a long history with Stewart. They'd been partners—friends—since the beginning, both equally committed to the vision and fully dedicated to the program. Perhaps he should have tried harder to spin the reversion therapy as a precaution instead of keeping it a secret.

Stewart's expression hardened. "I'll tell you why." He grabbed James's chin and jerked his head in the direction of the restaurant. Layla stood stiffly under the eave, watching.

"She's why. Because you knew from day one that she had the mutation. You knew long ago that she was showing the signs, isn't that right? And when she was finally discovered as a furo, you tried to make me believe you didn't care about her. You looked me in the eye and lied."

Stewart released his chin. James locked eyes with Layla. Even though her face held no expression, he could read the anguish and betrayal in her eyes. The sweet radiance that had permeated her being as long as he'd known her had dulled into a gray shadow.

"You destroyed years of trust we built. And that's a shame, a damn shame. But I understand. You love her. Love is what makes us human." Stewart drew James closer and whispered in his ear. "But this is no place to be human."

James felt the pinch of the needle and reflexively threw up his arms. The syringe popped from Stewart's hand and skittered across the pavement, rolling to a stop just a few yards from Layla's feet.

The two men locked eyes, breathing like bulls about to charge.

No, Stewart wouldn't do something so heinous. He was a lot of things, but not … no. James broke the spell and moved stiffly toward the syringe. He picked it up. The label on the side said QUANTITATIVE SYNTHETIC HUMAN IMMUNODEFICIENCY VIRUS 1 (HIV-1) RNA ATCC-1 VR-3.

He searched Stewart's face. *Why?*

Stewart swiped the palms of his hands down his pants legs. "Your reversion therapy is too late, James. I released the furos from the China site. All of them."

James gaped at his friend. His friend who had just turned Layla, the love of his life, into his mortal enemy.

"They're already out there, purifying our world. Too bad you won't get to see it."

67

The noxious odor of viral poison burned her eyes long before Layla found where it was coming from. It had started in James's right shoulder, and it was spreading through his veins like long black snakes, crawling down his torso, creating a wave of decay until his flesh hung from his bones.

He is poison.

No, not James. Please, god. No.

He is the plague.

Her fingers were slick with panicky sweat, but she instinctively reached into her pocket for the knife, gripping it tightly in her hand. Against her will, her legs carried her toward him. Tara came out of nowhere and moved in on her right. A man …

Arvin

…moved in on her left, completing the formation so there was no direction James could run.

Stewart took three steps back, putting distance between himself and James. "It's remarkable," he said, his wide eyes lit up with excitement.

Layla's eyelids fell in a long blink as she forced herself to remember it was an illusion. But when she opened them, James's face had decomposed to the point that he was no longer recognizable. His lidless blue eyes stared back with primordial terror.

He must be purged.

"It's okay, Layla, do it." That was James's voice emanating from the corpse. "It's all my fault. I turned you into this. I deserve it. Do it, my beautiful girl."

Arvin took three long steps toward him, a gesture to claim the target. He held a strap of leather wrapped in both hands.

But James kept his gaze locked on Layla. "I just… I was just trying to protect you."

Layla lunged. She slammed both palms into Arvin's chest and shoved him backward.

What the fuck is your problem? He dropped the leather from one hand and caught his balance, his brows drawn together.

She held up a shaky hand, struggling to keep her brain stem in check. "No! He's not poison." *He is the plague.* "Don't touch him." *He must be purged.*

She closed half the distance to James, fighting the electrical charge in her brain, forcing the tension from her muscles, refusing to submit to her brainstem.

She stepped right into James, pressed her head to his chest, and squeezed her eyes tightly as she wrapped her arms around him.

The decaying corpse that she held close to her wasn't real. It was an illusion. But even as she told herself that, she could feel his rotted flesh pulling away from the bone. His body felt warm and gelatinous, like the mucus that comes from your nose when you have a cold. The stench was unbearable. Her stomach rolled, and she gagged and gasped for fresh air, but she didn't let go.

When her gut settled enough for her to speak, the words came out like a guttural warble. "I'll protect you now."

68

"**W**ake up, man." Nick gave his friend a not-so-light slap on the cheek.

"What? What? I'm awake, asshole." Eddie had stalled out in the middle of the pedestrian walkway.

"I need you to walk on your own. Fast." Nick looked over his shoulder. Bald Xena was definitely following them, but she seemed to be purposely keeping some distance.

"Why? I thought we were getting something to eat."

"We are."

All the way at the end. Best Peking Duck you ever had.

"We are," he repeated. "Chinese. Best thing for you when you're drunk."

"Bro, slow down."

Nick swiveled his head again. The woman was moving in. Her eyes were even bigger and wider, and her lips were moving as if she were talking to an invisible friend. A security mic, no doubt. She somehow recognized him.

Nick grabbed Eddie by the wrist and pulled him down the road.

A knot of women stepped aside for them to pass. "Excuse you!" one of them snapped.

"Yo, man, if you need to take a piss, you just passed the john!" someone yelled. He was rewarded with laughter.

Nick paid no attention. His mind was on Bald Xena.

"I do need to take a piss," Eddie said, his voice a fraction soberer. "Did we do something illegal? What are we running from?"

He eyed Eddie, considering. "It's me they're after, not you. I'm an investigative reporter. I've been working undercover."

Eddie's eyes widened. "Sick."

"Listen, I want you to head into the Chinese restaurant. I'm gonna try to break through security somehow and find an emergency exit. There's gotta be one at the back."

"Nah, bro, I'll go with you."

It was a kind gesture, but Eddie would only slow him down. He could barely keep up speed walking.

The restaurant sign protruded overhead.

Buddaka

Fine Asian Cuisine

"Okay, here we are," Nick said. "Head straight to the—"

He halted so suddenly that Eddie didn't notice until he was halfway into the restaurant.

The world seemed to darken around Nick as he registered the scene before him. He lurched backward, tripped, and landed flat on his ass.

The restaurant facade. Four pillars, three red lanterns.

His eyes drifted upward. The red canopy hung slightly crooked.

He rolled onto his hands and knees and inched toward the farthest left pillar.

He blinked to make sure he wasn't seeing things, but it was there, unmistakable. A crack at the base of the pillar that looked just like the Liberty Bell crack.

He found ground zero.

69

J ames froze in Layla's embrace, waiting for her to bury the knife into his head, or his chest, or his throat. He squeezed his eyes shut for what seemed like an eternity. It wasn't until Stewart spoke that he opened them.

"Do it, Layla. This is your purpose."

James glanced down at Layla, whose arms wrapped around him so tightly they seemed glued to him. Her face was contorted as if she were in mortal agony. Her body shuttered and quaked, making her teeth chatter.

His fear subsided as he was overcome by profound awe. Look at his Layla: She was fighting the demon inside her. The kill neurons were exploding in her brain, triggering the release of hormones in such a flood that she would inevitably rip him to shreds—and yet she didn't. Fighting the instinct Eugenesis had spent so much time and so many billions of dollars to hone required every physical and mental fiber of her being.

And she was winning.

He had only a moment to appreciate her remarkable strength before Stewart spoke again.

"Layla," Stewart said. The gentleness was gone; now it was a warning. "We have a deal."

She released James slowly, tenderly—his beautiful girl—and spun savagely at Stewart. The impact of her leap slammed him into one of the pillars in front of the Asian restaurant. The faux stone column cracked with a *crunch*, and his eyes shot up to the overhanging canopy, certain it would come crashing down.

It dropped a few inches, but Layla didn't appear to notice as she grabbed Stewart by the shirt and swept her leg behind him and upward. He fell onto his back with a thud, and she dropped onto his stomach with all her weight. It must've knocked the wind out of him, because his head thunked back against the pavement as he lay gasping, unable to suck in air.

"So this was our deal, huh?" Layla's voice boomed in the hushed arena.

Stewart seized her waist to throw her off, but she scooched up his chest, pinning his upper arms to the ground. She grabbed his hair to lift his head, wrapped her leg around his neck, and clasped her ankle in an impressive headlock.

He bucked his hips and beat his hands against the pavement.

"That's why you wanted me in this demonstration," she growled, "to set me up to kill James. What better an ambassador than the furo who killed the man she loved? How much would your precious government saps enjoy that?"

Despite Layla's much smaller frame, Stewart was trapped. His arms were useless, and he stopped thrashing around. His face was nearly purple.

"But I have a better message to send." She pulled the hold even tighter. "You cursed us forever with a rage syndrome, a locked-and-loaded weapon against the diseased."

She released the hold and pushed up to her knees.

Stewart sucked in a raspy breath and coughed several times.

Sweat-soaked hair draped over her face. "But here's where you fucked up, asshole. Once the rage is triggered, we don't care who's at the sharp end of the knife."

She brought the knife down with such force that blood sprayed to either side. Stewart's hands flew up into the air and then smacked the pavement palms down on either side, spread-eagled.

"This is what … salvation … looks like, Stewart." Her labored breathing made the words ragged. "I am your … ambassador … the face of the furos."

The knife rose and came down a second time. And then a third. And a fourth, until James had to close his eyes.

Layla was gasping for air. "This is your vision. Welcome to the rage colony."

70

This was it. This was the place. Nick had studied the photo of the Chinese restaurant where the virus had been released for weeks. Every centimeter of it was burned into his brain.

He pushed himself to a standing position, wavering slightly from light-headedness, to stare at the almost imperceptible crooked canopy, presumably the result of whatever had cracked that pillar.

He dropped his eyes to the pavement. Patient zero, as she'd been described, had lain right here, a woman whose face was concealed by her long dark blond, blood-caked hair. She'd straddled her victim, hunched and wet with sweat, both hands wrapped around a knife buried to the hilt in his chest.

Neither the woman nor her victim had ever been identified.

He studied the clean, smooth cement to his left and right. In his mind, he saw the splatter pattern as clear as if it were there now.

"What the fuck is wrong with you?" Eddie had stepped in front of him and was scrutinizing his face. "Are you like having a panic attack or something? You're pale as fuck."

"Jesus, this is where it started. They created it here."

Nick's head was swimming with possible headlines, floating in and out of his mind before he could grab onto them, before he could connect the pieces. "Governments Lied About the Origin of the Virus." "Billion-Dollar Vegas Experience Re-Created in Secret Area 51 Location." "Genetic Experimentation Targets Brain Cells." "Desert Cult Recruits Young People From Cities to Cure Them of Drugs and Diseases."

Somehow, he didn't believe Eddie would get any HIV treatment as part of his five-year Eugenesis contract. He didn't believe a cure was the logical chaser to this big night on the town.

And he didn't believe this was any night on the town.

His eyes darted left and right, up and down, as he tried to wrap his brain around something concrete.

Security cameras were positioned in every possible niche, not an inch of this surreal playground wasn't monitored from at least three angles.

Undercover security guards strategically placed, at nearly a one-to-five ratio.

Area 51. Government.

Virus.

An ample population of white-clad cultists, here to do … something.

Young, sick recruits.

Brainwashed blank slates wandering all over the campus.

"It's a training facility," he breathed.

"What happened?" Eddie frowned.

"Reality-based training. Immersion training. This place is a government facility, like … like combat field training."

It made perfect sense. They had cultivated a herd of sheep, with carefully planted cases of illness. This was a simulator. They were watching the whole sequence, studying it. The lure, the setup.

The kill.

He spun around toward the pedestrian mall, and his eyes landed on Bald Xena, who watched them from barely ten feet away. Her lips were still moving, her eyes were involuntarily bouncing side to side. The eye spasms.

Eddie scoffed. "Training for what? Partying on leave?"

"Oh, Jesus. God." He leaned closer to Eddie, eyes locked on the woman, and whispered, "This is where the virus was created."

"What?" The color drained from Eddie's face, and his eyes followed Nick's stare.

"Eddie. She is the virus."

71

The world around James had gone silent. All he could feel was the air moving in and out of his lungs.

He couldn't look away from the scene in front of him, even though it was covered in blood, even though he just witnessed a brutal murder by a human weapon he'd helped design, and even though his longtime business partner lay dead.

The greatest and worst moment of his life was slipping through his grasp, and he was afraid that if he turned away, it would slip away entirely: the moment he'd first seen her, Allison Stevens, ten years ago—the same moment he'd lost her.

Austin insisted on dragging him along to the thesis presentation, some nonsense from a college girl.

"Just look into her research," Austin said. "It's an interesting concept. You might be able to use it as a recruitment tool."

Pain as a positive concept? A reward? No. It was a dumb idea.

But the moment she stepped up to the podium, he felt a connection so powerful he was practically paralyzed. It was as if she'd reached into his soul and squeezed. He knew, even then, he'd never be the same.

His fate was sealed that night at the cocktail reception following her presentation.

"Are you going to talk to her or not?" Austin handed James a glass of champagne as they stood against the back wall of the reception room.

He hadn't taken his eyes off her all evening. Her radiant smile, the way she held her Diet Coke with extra lemon, the way she tossed her head and looked away to say thank you, too modest to take a compliment. She was truly enchanting.

He wanted more time, he told Austin. He wanted to read her publications first, check her research. In reality, he just couldn't seem to make his stubborn legs move toward her.

"For God's sake," Austin said. "I'll do it."

Austin swept across the room like a professional dancer with the confidence of—well, the confidence of Austin. Before even uttering a word, he plucked her Diet Coke from her hand and replaced it with fresh champagne. Then he leaned in with a devilishly charming smile and spoke into her ear.

James would never know what Austin said, but she looked so deeply into Austin's eyes that James could almost feel her falling in love with him right then and there.

His own heart cracked.

That reception had changed everything. James had suffered in silence every moment from that night forward, as Austin used Allison, lied to her, framed her, and almost killed her.

But that was nothing compared to what he himself had done to her. James was the one who had stolen her past from her, who'd implanted a monster inside her and turned her into the predator he saw before him now. Not a shred remained of Allison Stevens, that sweet, shy, brilliant girl who sipped Diet Coke at a cocktail party, and he was to blame. One hundred fucking percent.

The flash of a camera jolted him from his reverie.

Colonel Shaffer was regarding the scene with the same hardened expression he'd worn all night. The youngest DOD staffer held up an iPhone and snapped several more pictures of Layla straddling Stewart in a pool of blood just beneath the now-crooked canopy.

The colonel nodded at James. "I believe we have what we came for." He turned on his heels and started back to the main entrance, his men in tow.

James had to jog after them to hear what the colonel said next in a low voice to his lieutenant.

"Call it in. I want this facility terminated immediately. A full annihilation."

The lieutenant startled. "Sir?"

The colonel lengthened his stride. "That is not a weapon. That's a nuclear time bomb. I want this facility to be a meteor crater on satellite images. Is that clear enough for you?"

"Yes, sir."

"Sir, if I may be honest with you," James called.

The colonel kept walking.

"I've known the risks with this model for a very long time now. I know General Harding had his doubts, and I'm pretty certain that's why he sent you. I agree with him completely. It's not ready for release. My research team here has been working on a reversion—a cure, should we find we're unable to control the evolution of the praefuro. We're close. We've been testing the lower doses, and we're seeing a modest but distinct repression of the prey and kill instinct."

He fell back a few steps as the DOD team squeezed in front of him at the main entrance. Security held open the double doors and saluted as the colonel strode through.

James shuffled to catch up again. "Please reconsider your order. I only need a little more time. And once we—"

The colonel stopped and faced him. "Dr. Elliott, I suggest you get yourself onto an airplane and get out of Mexico immediately, or you too will be reduced to dust."

James watched them slide into their black vehicles, which would take them to their private jet and back to Washington DC.

Get yourself onto an airplane.

His eyes lifted to the sky, a dark and starless void beneath the high desert clouds. Here and there he saw airplanes overhead, their red beacons flashing. How many flights took off every day? How many from places with other colonies, places like—

Beijing.

Fucking Beijing.

He sprinted to the black SUV, idling just outside the back gate as it rumbled open. He banged on the back passenger window. "Sir, it's too late! It's too late!"

The front window cracked, and the driver leaned over. "Back away from the vehicle. Now."

James leaned in so his voice would echo inside the cab. "They've been released. The praefuro! Stewart told me a little while ago. They've been released from China. They won't stay together. They'll spread out. They'll travel."

He expected the window to close, but it didn't.

He raised his voice. "Sir, with all due respect, you've seen what they're capable of. You know what will happen—"

The SUV peeled out onto the dirt road, shooting gravel and dirt at James's face like pellets from a BB gun.

"Ahh." He fell to his knees and rubbed his burning eyes with his fists.

The vehicle screeched to a halt, and James heard a door open and slam. He rolled up to his feet.

Colonel Shaffer stopped ten feet away. "China is outside my jurisdiction."

It was too dark to read the man's expression, but James could tell he understood the problem. He straightened, but his voice was pleading. "We have to warn them. We have to warn the whole world." James's voice hitched. "And then, for the love of God and humanity, you have let me save them."

72

E ddie's hand, wrapped around Nick's arm, began trembling. "Oh, no. Oh fuck. She'll come for me first—they always kill the sick ones first. Oh god."

Nick surveyed the area around him, searching for a way out. Behind them, three security guards huddled against the steel walls that enclosed the far end of the Gallery. Two were chatting and one seemed to be daydreaming; none of them were paying Nick and Eddie any attention. The place was as big as six airplane hangars, but he couldn't see an exit point. It had to have multiple emergency exits, probably along the long sides and certainly at the corners, through the Asian restaurant or the art museum.

"Eddie, we have to run through the restaurant," he whispered. "Head for the back door. Find the kitchen. It'll have a back exit for trash."

Eddie mewled as the woman took two steps closer.

"Stay right behind me. Count of three. One, two, three!" He yanked his arm from Eddie's death grip and barreled into the restaurant.

He dodged a man carrying a water pitcher, barely avoiding a dousing. "Hey, what's going on?"

Virus rule number one: If you suspect you're in proximity of the virus, don't run. Remain calm. Stay in a large crowd, and avoid physical contact with it. Every little kid today learned that rule.

His legs pounded ahead.

"This way!" He yelled over his shoulder as he slammed his palms into the double swinging doors—the kitchen, just as he'd expected.

He stopped dead. In front of him was a prep table buried in freshly chopped vegetables. Along the wall hung twenty or so knives of various sizes and blades.

Virus rule number two: Never lure the virus into an area heavy with weapons.

Just beyond the prep table was a door. The sign above it read EMERGENCY EXIT ONLY. ALARM WILL SOUND.

"We can make it," he panted. "I know how to get off the compound." Never mind that they'd have to crawl through cactus and squeeze through a fox hole.

He bolted across the kitchen, slammed the bar, and flung the door open. Despite the wailing siren, which would certainly bring security running, the cool night air was an invitation to freedom.

"Ready? We need to stay along the fence."

Eddie didn't answer.

He did a one-eighty and leaned back inside to scan the kitchen. No sign of Eddie. Just three fearful chefs standing in a cluster, waiting for Nick's next move.

Virus rule number three: Protect the sick; they are the most vulnerable.

He closed his eyes and let his breath stream out slowly through his nostrils. Eddie would certainly be dead already. There was no point in risking his own life by going back.

And now he had the story. The whole story. The world would soon know where the virus came from, how this heinous desert compound collected people from the streets to ... to what, feed the virus? Create more of it?

He shivered. The story had to get out there. He could save thousands of lives, but he had to escape to write the story. Eddie was just a casualty. Collateral damage. A sacrifice for the greater good.

His legs didn't move.

"Leave him." He spoke the words aloud, hoping that his muscles would listen. "Just go."

I don't care how long it takes to get a cure for my HIV, 'cause at least the virus won't get me.

Nick shook his head. "Fuck it."

He grabbed the biggest knife he saw from the rack and ran back into the dining room.

Virus rule number four: Don't try to kill it. You'll lose.

"Eddie! I'm coming!"

73

James crouched in the back seat of the colonel's Cadillac Escalade, his thumbs tapping madly on his phone's notepad. This message to the world, coming from the president of the United States of America, would save not only countless American lives but lives in every country.

The message would have to be brief. Straight to the point. Under thirty seconds. Every major network would run it, and it would hit social media like a storm.

The door swung open and Colonel Shaffer took a seat stiffly, facing forward instead of looking James in the eye. "The Central Intelligence Agency has received confirmation that a group of more than ten thousand mentally ill patients has escaped from a hospital in the Gansu province of China. According to the CIA, the clinic was illegal, and the Chinese, US, and western European governments have gone on record stating they had no knowledge of its presence or practice."

James gawked at the colonel, whose gaze remained on the headrest of the seat in front of him. It was a lie. Eugenesis' success was overwhelmingly based on the support and protection of the national governments. Stewart had reported to the highest ranks of leadership on a monthly basis. They knew. They all knew what was happening in the colonies.

"The US government denies any knowledge of or participation in human genetic research beyond carefully scrutinized genetic therapies for the treatment of life-threatening diseases, such as cancer or AIDS." The colonel pressed his lips together in a tight line and continued. "The US government will not endorse nor deliver a statement that suggests the US was in any way involved with such an atrocity."

James sat back, the phone dangling from his fingertips. If the national militaries refused to acknowledge the situation, they wouldn't be prepared the take down the ragers. It would be like—Christ, he couldn't believe he was thinking this—it would be like the zombie apocalypse. The ragers would kill thousands before they could be eliminated, but that wasn't the end of it. The world would let down its guard, people would reenter society, and that's when wave two would begin. By then, the praefuro predators would be embedded throughout the world, nearly impossible to identify. And—oh god, just like his very own Layla, who had killed a man, a security guard with no known proliferative diseases—the praefuro would deviate from their mission. Their minds would evolve. They'd establish their own definition of *impure*.

There had to be something he could do.

When he raised his eyes, the colonel was finally looking at him, straight at him, with a stony, inscrutable expression that made James's neck prickle. "Dr. Elliott, my driver and I are going to step away from the vehicle for the next five minutes. I have some unrelated business to attend to."

And with that, James was alone in the car.

What was happening? What was he missing?

He'd just reached for the door handle when the opposite door opened, and the young man who'd snapped the pictures of Layla slid into the seat next to him.

"Sir, my name is Sergeant Albert Larsen. I've been ordered to take a statement from you."

"What? What kind of statement?"

"A warning, sir, to the American people. I work in military communications, and I liaise with the media."

"You're going to leak a warning to the media? You'll be discharged or—"

"Understood, sir." He nodded, his face sober. "My loyalty is to the good people of the United States of America. I took an oath the serve and protect against all enemies, foreign and domestic."

Oh, Jesus. He was the sacrificial lamb.

James dropped his eyes to his notes on his phone. The words blurred. If he was going to have a prayer of protecting this young sergeant, he would have to choose his words much more carefully. No US involvement, no genetic research.

"I'm ready when you are, sir." The kid held his phone out in front of James, the voice recorder superimposed over the open image of Layla astride Stewart's bloody corpse.

James swallowed a sob.

"The colonel suggested that sending the image as a backdrop to your warning will send a strong message. Given the restaurant in the background, the American people will believe it was taken in Jiuquan."

His beautiful girl would forever be the poster child of the predatory killers, the face of the furos, just as she'd said. If he hadn't done enough damage to the only woman he'd ever loved, this would certainly secure his position in hell.

He cleared his throat several times, but he couldn't wipe the anguish from his voice.

"Sir," the sergeant urged.

Time was of the essence.

He nodded and looked down at his notes. Then he began speaking.

"Today is October fourteenth, 2022. It is with great despair that I report a virus has been released from the Gansu Province in China and will soon enough spread across the globe. It is unlike anything the world has seen before. I have had firsthand experience with this virus. I've seen what it's capable of, and I am sending this message as a warning to stay out of public places. Stay off the streets. Quarantine in your home with your loved ones."

He looked away. "I'm begging you."

74

To Nick's relief, Eddie was frozen right where he left him, paralyzed with fear. His knees folded inward, and his hands firmly covered his crotch. As Nick approached, the unmistakable smell of urine wafted up.

Bald Xena neither attacked nor retreated, perhaps because several onlookers circled them as if watching a street performer.

Virus rule number five: The virus is a stealthy killer. It protects itself by not being discovered.

This was why the virus still hadn't been eradicated. Even now, a full seventeen months since the release of the virus from the Gansu Province of China and "A Desperate Warning to the World" hit the media, so many of them still crawled the earth. Not all of them behaved like rabid zombies. Some, the stealthy ones, could just sneak up on you and drive a dagger into your chest without even breaking stride, blending right into the crowd like well-trained pickpockets. He'd seen plenty of security surveillance footage.

The moment Nick returned to Eddie's side, the virus stiffened, its eyes blazing with anger.

"You," it said, taking two steps forward. "You don't belong here."

Adrenaline surged in Nick's head. The virus wasn't interested in Eddie, not unless it was playing some sort of game. It was talking to him.

"You're an imposter."

Nick widened his stance and adjusted his grip on the knife behind his back.

It inched toward him, tilting its head slightly. Its brow furrowed as if it were about to ask a question. "He doesn't belong here. He's a fake. A liar."

Its black eyes bore into him, and he almost forgot what he was doing.

Eddie's voice broke the spell. "Oh, god, I pissed myself, bro. I pissed my pants."

Nick held up the knife, pointed at the virus's chest. "Don't come any closer."

75

J ames struggled to steady his voice. A man with a tremulous voice wouldn't be taken seriously. He had to sound authoritative. He wanted to sound presidential.

"Unlike pandemics we've seen in the past," he continued, "this is not an invisible enemy. No, this deadly virus takes the shape of human beings, young men and women of all colors and nationalities whose brains have been altered, compelling them to destroy, to brutally kill. The virus will come first for the weakest of society, those who are ill or have a terminal disease. But it won't stop there. Like all viruses, it will continue to evolve and mutate until it's accomplished what it's been hardwired to do: to eradicate the existing human race."

Sergeant Larsen crossed himself reverently.

"I implore you, do not humanize this virus. They're not normal human beings. They cannot be threatened, bribed, or negotiated with. Do not allow yourself to be tricked into thinking it is anything more than an infectious disease with one goal: to feed on its host. Stay inside. Protect your family. Lock your doors to outsiders. This is not the time to be a hero. This is not a war we can win. Those who live to see the end of this virus will be those who've had the wisdom to hide from it."

His voice caught, and he couldn't continue. He wanted to tell people not to panic. He wanted to remind them that like any virus, it would burn out eventually. It would be taken down by authorities and the military.

But the words wouldn't come before the door opened and the sergeant stepped out of the vehicle.

The colonel sat back down. "My men and I have a plane to catch. I expect there will be classified discussion, and the military will go on high alert." He reached across James, pulled the door handle, and pushed the door open. "Our audit here will be filed and buried behind higher priorities. Finish your cure, Dr. Elliott. Godspeed."

James stepped numbly from the car and watched the red taillights disappear into the night. He stood alone in the dark, quiet desert long after they'd gone, miles from the main campus. No light or sound escaped the Gallery behind him, a world within itself. He was alone with the incessant chirping of the crickets.

He had a major cleanup on his hands, not to mention an elaborate story to weave to calm the few colonists who'd been exposed to the carnage before the cleaners stepped in. Yet all he wanted to do was run inside and find Layla, cradle her in his arms, and carry her away. He wanted to keep running until they were far away from the Colony, hidden from the whole world, which was about to see more death and destruction than anyone had witnessed since the Holocaust.

What little energy he had left seemed to drain from him, and he fell to hands and knees. The sharp gravel bore into his shins, and he leaned back onto his heels in the traditional heel-sit position he'd taught his young inductees for years. *Take a deep breath and release the pain.* He'd believed the words then as he did to this day. Once you succumbed to the pain, you were free from the weight of impurity, closer to a future without concern over anything outside the Colony walls. But to get there, you had to suffer the pain.

All that pain they'd endured. For purification. For saving the human race. For the propagation of purity across the earth.

He needed that sense of freedom right now. He needed to release the pain of the poisoned world. He folded his hands over his lap and breathed deeply and slowly.

"With pain comes peace."

A voice came from up the path. "And with gratitude comes the Father's love."

76

J ames was only a silhouette in the starlight, too shadowy for Layla to tell if he was real or if he was the decomposing remains of what once was her true love. But she didn't trust herself to move in any closer than she was. Electricity surged through her brain, inducing flashes of lightning behind her eyes. Her teeth chattered, and she couldn't seem to unclench her fists. Her neck muscles ached.

She could tell by James's posture that he had bigger concerns than her ability to leash the killer inside her. She'd never once seen him on his knees or in any position of weakness. That wasn't how James worked.

He lifted his chin and spoke clearly so she could hear him from that distance. "Allison Cassidy Stevens. You were born on December seventh, 1990. That makes you thirty-one years old."

He must be purged. The earth must be purified.

"You probably already know that. But I'll tell you something you don't know."

The crickets chirped louder, and she was straining to hear him, but she refused to take even one step toward him. It was too risky.

"When you were twenty-three, your appendix ruptured. You had to be rushed to the emergency room. There were complications, and you were moved to intensive care. Austin Harris, your significant other, was traveling, and he couldn't be there for you. But I was worried about you, so I posed as a doctor and sneaked into your room. I thought you were sleeping when I sat beside your bed, but you opened your eyes and asked me to please call your mother, please ask her to come."

He bent forward and shifted his weight slightly. His legs were probably numb. She almost smiled; the feeling of pins and needles surely was unfamiliar to him.

"Rachel Cassidy is your mother's name, and I called her. I explained that you were in critical condition. But…" He lowered his head. "But she wouldn't come, even after I told her I'd pay for her airplane ticket. She said she had higher priorities."

Layla closed her eyes remembering the image she'd seen on James's computer. The woman with short brown hair who'd held her hand at her father's funeral. What kind of a mother had she been? What could have gone so wrong that she didn't want to see her own daughter?

James had been right all along. Her poisoned life had been filled with sadness.

… *purified* …

"The next day, I visited you again. I told you that your mother had come, but hospital policy wouldn't let her into the intensive care unit. I gave you a small vase of flowers, daisies with those little purple flowers sprinkled in. It was the only thing they had in the gift shop besides puzzles and books. I said, 'Your mother brought these for you.'"

His next words came out choked. "You shifted in your bed just a little, and you took the flowers, vase and all, under your covers. You laid the flowers down on the pillow beside you. Then you rested your head on the flowers and put your arm over the vase, and you whispered, 'I'm sorry, Mommy. I'll be a better daughter from now on, I promise.'"

Layla felt a tear run down her cheek.

James sniffled and wiped his nose with his sleeve. "Days later, when you were well again and back home, you told Austin a story about some asshole doctor who promised to call your mom but never did. I was some crazy psychopath."

... purged ...

Tears dripped off her chin, but she didn't move to wipe them. She couldn't. Every muscle in her body was locked. Her teeth were no longer chattering because her jaw had clamped down so fiercely that her breath sounded like angry hisses. Her arms had gone stiff at her sides, hands fisted, and her feet felt glued to the ground.

James pushed himself up to a wobbly standing position. Layla wanted to run and put a supportive arm around him until the blood flow returned to his legs, as he had done countless times for her.

He steadied himself. "Since the first moment I laid eyes on you, I knew I'd do anything, even lie outright like 'some crazy psychopath,' to avoid seeing you hurt. To avoid the sadness and disappointment that I read on your face that night. I'm sorry, Layla. I'm sorry for everything."

He took two steps toward her, and her muscles finally heeded her brain. She took two stiff steps backward and defensively held her arms in front of her.

He stopped. "Lay?"

She spoke through clenched teeth. "Don't come closer."

He didn't move.

Her vocal cords were as stiff as her body, and she coughed to loosen them, but her words still came out choked. "I know about the reversion."

"Layla—"

"Isaac. He said you need a subject for the highest dose, for the cure. Choose me."

"Oh no, baby, listen, it's still risky. We still have—"

"Choose me!" She didn't mean to shout, but she couldn't control her tone. She was struggling to even put together an intelligent sentence. Her mind and body were turning against her, betraying her because she continued to deprive it of what it needed.

He must be purged. The earth must be purified.

"I cannot be a killer. This is not who I am." She sucked in a stuttered breath. "If you love me, you'll give me a chance to be me again. Not a furo, not Allison Stevens, just Layla. Your beautiful girl."

The beam of a flashlight bounced around them, landing briefly on James, then Layla.

"Layla, honey?" A familiar French accent. "Come on. Let's get you back with the others."

Layla focused on forming words one last time. "Please. Please, James."

Two security guards materialized from the darkness and took her arms, tugging her toward the Gallery.

But her gaze remained on James until he vanished within the night.

77

The lights in the Gallery dimmed, and a flashing blue and red police light strobed across the back wall. Nick nearly dropped the knife. He clutched it with both hands for security, but the lights distracted him long enough that his assailant pirouetted out of his range.

He'd underestimated Xena the Bald Warrior Bitch. The virus.

It stepped back in with one long leg, which it set down firmly a foot in front of him. His mind registered its next move: *It's going to kick me in the balls.* He twisted to the left, both hands diving down to protect his groin. But instead of the kick, its right elbow connected with his cheekbone. Unsurprisingly, his head whipped backward, throwing him off balance, and he landed on his tailbone for the second time that night.

Stars flashed behind his eyelids, and the knife flew from his hands and skittered across the floor.

Over the siren, Eddie was yelling, "Vic! Get up, bro. Get up. Get up!" as if he were watching a boxing match and about to lose his moneyline bet.

Nick tried to roll to a standing position, but just as he reached his knees, a blast of heat struck him between the shoulder blades. Every muscle in his body stiffened like a board, and his brain screamed, *stop, stop, stop!* The clicking noise that lit up every nerve fiber of his body felt like it would never end. When it finally stopped, he toppled over, landing face first on the floor.

"Fuuuck you," he moaned. His vision swam, and he heard more clicking. He wrapped his arms around his head and curled into the fetal position, bracing for another round.

The clicking got louder and then slowed.

Shoes.

A woman's voice called out, "What the hell's going on? Keisha, what's happening?"

The virus repeated its mantra. "He doesn't belong here. He's an imposter."

"What?"

More clicking. High heels approaching.

The virus spoke again. "He's undercover. An investigator, like a reporter or a cop. That's not even his real name."

"Turn off that damn alarm!" High Heels bellowed.

The alarm stopped and the world fell blessedly silent, except for Nick's hammering heart, which he was ever grateful was still beating.

Then the virus said something truly shocking. "He thinks I'm the virus."

What the fuck? Could the virus deny being the virus? An unsolicited headline flashed through his mind: "The Virus are Self-Aware!"

He finally opened his eyes and rolled onto his back as the house lights came back up. He squinted up at the voices, shielding his eyes with his hand.

"Who are you, and what are you doing in my training facility?" High Heels bent at the waist to get a closer look at him. Her bobbed bleach-blond hair hung toward him, framing her face. His eyes flashed down her trim but curvy body—he honestly couldn't help it, she was dressed in all black leather plus the sexiest boots he'd ever seen—and right back to her scowling face.

It was her. She was a bit older than her Quandary Therapeutics badge picture, the same one that had accompanied the APB issued by the FBI when Agent Vincent Wang was found stabbed outside her apartment. She'd cut her hair, and somewhere along the line she'd apparently acquired the body of Catwoman, but it was her, all right.

"Allison Stevens," he said. "I've been looking for you."

78

Layla peeled off her leather tights and yanked a sensible knee-length skirt off the hanger.

"I'm trying to understand why you're even entertaining this ridiculous discussion," she called to James in the kitchen as she pulled up the zipper and clasped the annoying little hook behind her.

It was late, nearly midnight, and the appearance of the reporter who'd infiltrated the Colony—the first ever—had forced her to shut down the Vegas simulation early, much to the dismay of the participants. James wanted her to accompany him to question the intruder, but she was tired and irritable and had no interest in talking with whatever asshole had just ruined her sim. James, who still hadn't dressed down after his long workday, was sprawled at the kitchen table squinting over the images Mr. Aroyo had sent over, security camera shots of the devious reporter who had, as the story went, outsmarted Aroyo himself.

James replied without looking up. "I just want to hear him out, babe."

She growled melodramatically and rippled a hand through the rack of hanging blouses, looking for something to add some life to the boring beige skirt.

"You have to trust me, Lay."

Trust. The word was like a delicate piece of blown glass teetering on a rickety shelf. As soon as she allowed herself to let her guard down, allowed it to just exist in her heart and mind, it would crash to the ground, shattering every confidence she'd built in herself, in James, in their relationship. To James, it was just so simple: *Trust me, Lay.* A shrug and a smirk.

Well, she had trusted him. She'd trusted him that catastrophic night nearly a year and a half ago when Stewart injected him with the HIV virus; she'd turned her rage on Stewart in that moment, brutally butchering him, but she'd maintained her trust in James. She'd trusted him, even in the face of his own misgivings, when they'd surgically implanted a port at the base of her spine to deliver his untested reversion therapy, an all-out effort to cure her of her brainstem's desire to kill. She'd trusted him as he slid her into a medically induced coma after the reversion drug nearly killed her.

And when she'd woken from the coma three months later, one hundred and twelve pounds of soft, toneless flab hanging from her skeletal frame, she'd trusted him when he looked into her droopy brown eyes with his impossibly bright blue ones and said, "You did it, Layla. And now I'll make you whole again, my beautiful girl."

It had taken weeks of rehabilitation before she could walk to the bathroom of her hospital room, several more before she could lift a five-pound kettlebell. It was six months before she could jog a mile. And she'd never stopped trusting him, because he was all she had to keep her going day after day. James had promised to make her whole, and he had.

Yet when it came to dealing with this new threat, this Nicholas Slater, she didn't feel the same level of confidence in her gut.

She strode to the kitchen, gripping the blouse she'd selected. "You're asking me to trust you? Seriously?"

He glanced at her with a flat expression and flopped the stack of photos back onto the table.

"I trusted you when you told me demolishing the Vitapura Wellness Center would take care of him. He obviously didn't die in that explosion, and you know what? I don't think you intended for him to die. I think you wanted him to escape. To disappear."

He raised an eyebrow, and she recoiled. She didn't have to push her way into his mind to understand what he'd done. Now it was all so clear.

"You did it on purpose," she breathed. She shook her head in disbelief even though she knew it was true. "You drove him into action. You … you challenged him to come find us."

His silence was all the confirmation she needed.

"Why would you do that? After all we've been through since Stewart and Li Jian released the furos from China. After all we've done to find them and bring them home. Now you've compromised the Colony and Eugenesis, and you've threatened our work … our safety…"

All her energy drained away with her last words, and she leaned her bare back against the doorjamb, wincing from the cold. The now wrinkled blouse floated to the floor.

James rose to pick it up, but she held out her palm and snatched it up herself. She turned her back to pull it over her head and tuck it into the waistband of her skirt.

"Sweetie, your work with the furos has been exceptional. You know that."

She hated it when he called her sweetie. She wasn't a six-year-old, for god's sake.

"But while you've been busy curing the virus that has been caught and returned, I've been doing damage control. The virus is—"

"Don't call them that. They're not *virus*." She spoke the words softly because she knew James had only called the praefuro a virus to try to protect the Colony, but she still hated it. The furos were thinking, feeling humans, not some mindless pathogen.

"That's my point, Lay. You're inside here with the truth, with all the knowledge of what we've done and what we're doing to change it. I'm out there in the poisoned world, dealing with what the public only thinks of as a deadly virus."

"They're not virus," she repeated dully.

"I'm the one visiting the hot spots. I'm building alliances and allegiances with law enforcement, government agencies, politicians…" He fell back into his chair and slumped over the table. He continued without meeting her gaze. "It's a delicate balance, leading an organization with such enormity of mission and size while staying under the radar. We need new inductees, but we can't openly recruit. We provide value, but that value can never be known. And the ever-hungry media will always be on our tail—if not Nick Slater, someone else."

She wondered if he really believed that. Would they always be running? Would James consider another move of the Colony to a new, safer country?

"You're implying he can help us in some way," she said finally. "So tell me. How?"

"I don't know yet. That's why I want to talk to him."

It wasn't good enough. "I'm emphatically against this."

"Duly noted." He rose and tenderly pushed a lock of hair off her face. "But please open yourself up for some signal from him. Okay? Promise?"

His touch, which she'd known for years now, could still soften her. It was a gentle reminder that she was now filled more with love than rage.

Still, she rolled her eyes. "Fine."

79

Nick paced the long wall of a board room on the top floor of an executive office building. His escorts, two security guards in full SWAT gear, hadn't been particularly chatty as they dragged him from Glitter Gulch to this empty meeting room where he now impatiently waited.

He had no idea what was happening. The only words Allison Stevens had uttered were, *Keisha, please call James,* and *Gentlemen, will you kindly escort our guest out of my sim? We're trying to work here.* And the bald warrior bitch who'd been stalking him—was she the fucking virus or wasn't she?—had simply hulked away shaking out her hands like a bodybuilder who'd just won the deadlift event.

Stevens had offered no reaction, not so much as a raised eyebrow when he called her by name. Now he was second-guessing himself. Maybe it hadn't been Allison Stevens. Certainly, a five- or ten-second electrocution could kill a few million brain cells. But what really troubled him was the look of utter annoyance on her face, as if he was the scumbag here. How dare he interrupt their training of savage killers?

He'd always known it would come to this showdown. For years, this organization, which he now knew was called Eugenesis, its sci-fi logo proudly displayed above the fancy videoconference monitors along one wall, had threatened him into silence again and again, knowing full well it would only be a matter of time before he was back.

Why hadn't they killed him like they killed everyone else who got too close to the truth?

Not that it mattered now. He was about to be cactus fertilizer. He'd come to the gunfight packing a revolver, and they'd shown up with a multi-billion-dollar weapon of mass destruction. Boy howdy, had he not seen that coming.

It had to be after midnight by now, and he wondered if they'd forgotten him. He stomped over to a whiteboard, popped the cap of the marker, and wrote his story headline in large letters: Secret Government Facility in Mexican Desert Created the Virus and Kidnapped Thousands From the City Streets to Feed It.

That was a tabloid headline if ever he'd seen one. A shame it was actually true.

He looked into the camera blinking down on him from over the door. "Let's get this show on the road. I have a story to write." It was arrogant, but if they were going to kill him, he'd rather get it over with.

He resumed his pacing.

He wondered how long they planned to let him live. Surely they wouldn't want to soil this impeccable walnut furniture with his blood. And then he wondered how he'd die. Would it be cartel style? A long, hot walk into the desert with a burlap sack over his head, followed by a good, bloody beating for their own kicks, and when he'd finally fallen to his knees, a shot in the back of the head? Or perhaps mad scientist style. He'd wake up naked, gagged, and strapped to a gurney. A doctor with perfectly clean scrubs and a surgical mask would enter the hospital room, and with a glint in his eye, he'd methodically remove his surgical tools from a bag and lay them out on a table—

The double doors opened. Three people entered the room, neither cartel members nor mad scientists.

It looked like it was going to be death by fountain pen.

The man leading the way had a Sean-Connery-as-James-Bond swagger, as well as a short beard like Connery sported in later films. Still, he easily recognized the man as a less portentous version of the author of the cult brochure, James Elliott.

Trailing him were two women, Allison Stevens, less Catwoman and more sexy librarian, and another beauty with mocha skin and long dreads tied in a knot. She took a seat next to James, but Stevens remained standing. She leaned back against a console table and folded her arms across her chest.

Elliott extended a hand. "Nick Slater. We've been at odds for many years. I figured this day would eventually come. My name is James Elliott."

Nick didn't return the gesture, but not because he was finally facing his longtime adversary or because he would never stoop to shake the hand of a man responsible for so many reprehensible crimes.

It was because he instantly recognized the voice. And the whole world turned upside down.

You came to the gunfight with an ice cream cone and a roll of toilet paper, you fool, rattled the maniacal voice of Uncle Jay in Nick's head.

"You—you're the voice," Nick stammered.

"Hmm?"

"The virus. You're the one who recorded 'A Desperate Warning to the World.'"

80

Layla felt Mia's eyes burning into her as they watched James talk to the reporter. Mia was trying to read Layla, to guess what she was thinking by her physical reactions to the conversation. Facial expressions, eye movements, changes in breathing such as sighs or gasps, and of course body language: leaning in, turning away, crossing her arms, that kind of thing. Mia was good at reading people this way—better than most, in fact.

But Mia was still a solid zero on the psychic intuitiveness scale. It wasn't her fault, of course. She wasn't a praefuro. She wasn't part of the collective.

Layla, on the other hand, was a five on the psychic scale and improving each day, as were the other praefuro they'd been cultivating over the last year. Keisha, for example, whose rank was barely below Layla's at the helm of the collective, was now an eye-popping four; together, they were a force to be reckoned with.

But James hadn't felt he needed the dynamic duo tonight. He'd invited Mia instead of Keisha because he wanted, as he put it, a human opinion.

Normally, Layla would have concentrated on keeping her body language neutral and her face expressionless, just to torture her friend, but tonight she couldn't hide her hostility. She refused to sit at the table with the reporter, and she certainly wouldn't speak to him. Despite his so-called superb investigative skills and writing talent, Nick Slater was behaving like a petulant child. His inability to grasp the situation was solely due to his refusal to open himself to a new idea. His brain was nothing but a brick.

Frankly, she hoped he'd remain a brick. That would make James's decision to wipe his memory and dump him back into his miserable, poisoned life a lot easier.

"Jordan Jennings gave you the cure, didn't he?" the reporter asked. "He figured out a way to cure those monkeys. But they didn't return to normal. They were different, like they had some kind of telepathic ability." His voice trailed nearly to a whisper. He was struggling to connect the dots, but apparently, he'd connected those two.

Layla's mind flashed to the elaborate underground primate cage, from where Dr. Jennings's cynomolgus monkeys signaled to the collective. She could find them if she really tried, but monkeys weren't her priority. Her furos were.

"Yes, indeed. I see you've done your homework." James's eyes sparked with an adulation that made Layla want to barf. She couldn't understand what James saw in this guy.

The night James had recorded "A Desperate Warning to the World" had changed him. The China colony's release of the praefuro, what scientists had erroneously called a lyssavirus due to the rabid behavior of the ragers, had been a wake-up call to the entire Eugenesis board. Every council member had sobbed, helpless, as they watched the carnage on television. General Harding and Colonel Shaffer had mobilized the US military, but it was ill-equipped to find and destroy this enemy. The praefuro, with their genetic hardwiring, were relentless. With their enhanced intelligence, they often left the scene unnoticed. For over a year, the bodies piled up. The world was losing the war against what they called, to her utter dismay, the virus.

But no one had internalized the devastation as deeply as James had. He had adopted a new mission: not to save the human race, but to restore faith in humanity.

She didn't share his sentiment. In fact, over the months of her reversion treatment and rehabilitation, she'd grown steadily more critical of unevolved humans. She knew it was irrational. But it was just how the collective mind worked.

"Dr. Jennings's genetics expertise is like nothing I've ever found," James continued. "Truly a genius. We tried to recruit him, but unfortunately for us, he disappeared."

"That's because he knew what you were doing, turning people into … something inhuman."

She scowled at the reporter but didn't bother to respond to his insulting assumption. She'd promised James she'd be nice.

James snickered and shook his head. "I'm not surprised by that in the least. As I say, he's the best of the best. I was disappointed he wouldn't join us. I know he'd be most encouraged by the work we're doing here."

"Creating killers?"

Come on, you moron, try to follow the plot. Layla wished she had the ability to will her thoughts into his mind, but sadly that was beyond her skills. For now, at least.

"Curing the virus." James's unflappable composure made her want to scream.

"So you're telling me that woman, the one who followed me and took me down, is not a killer." He stabbed a finger at the window. "She's been cured."

James leaned back with a satisfied smile.

"And now she's what? A telepath? Like those monkeys?"

"Telegnostic," James corrected. "She can't communicate with you mentally. She gets a sensation, a feeling. That's how she knew you were here under false pretenses."

He nodded at Layla as if she might want to contribute, given her own firsthand experience, but she remained silent. The brick wasn't ready to listen or understand. She didn't like to waste her time.

"And all those people I saw in that basement with that tube in their backs," the brick mewled. "They're being cured?"

The treatments—Layla had endured sixteen of them herself, fourteen of them while unconscious to the world—were the result of the most advanced genetic biotechnology the world had ever seen. Even Jordan Jennings would've agreed. So to hear the jerk refer to their subjects as people with a tube in their backs made her want to lunge at him.

"That's right. They're subjects in Project Phoenix. Like the mythical bird, the praefuro will rise from the ashes, born again with a new life, a new purpose."

"What purpose?"

"Evolution."

The brick narrowed his eyes, and Layla rolled hers. The primitive human mind had a tendency to believe evolution was something that occurred naturally, or worse, something that required divine intervention. This dullard probably thought some god had created humanity.

He addressed his next question to her. "And your Vegas sim?" He emphasized the word *sim* with air quotes. "What is it you're training out there?"

She didn't appreciate this smug attitude. She folded her arms and glared.

James answered for her. "The Gallery is a simulation of the real world. We use it as a testing center for our praefuro subjects after we've dosed them with the reversion therapy. Keisha, for example, the woman you encountered, monitors the energy in the room. She looks for signs that a praefuro has been released too early. It's a necessary step in the process because every person's uptake of the reversion is different. Some subjects need higher doses or even blood transfusions. We need to be sure it works."

It wasn't exactly true. Keisha and Layla stayed in close proximity to the praefuro subjects so they could speak to their minds. Direct psychic communication belonged only to the collective. It was something only the praefuro could experience, but that wasn't something James would ever admit to an outsider.

"So Eddie and other sick people like him, they're *bait*?"

James beamed. "Exactly. But rest assured, we've never had an incident. Our simulations are heavily supervised. All guests are guarded by undercover security within a three-foot radius at all times."

This was a waste of time. Normally, she admired James's dedication for turning a negative impression of the Colony into a positive one. He took great pride in his ability to bring out the best in people. In her opinion, Nick Slater wasn't deserving of his patience. Especially after a very long day.

Although the reporter hadn't needed to be convinced that Eugenesis was protected by the US government, among other world powers—he'd discovered that on his own—he seemed incapable of believing that the organization responsible for releasing the virus was also the organization responsible for curing it. In his mind, allowing the Colony to prosper was shameful and corrupt. Classic nirvana fallacy. There had to be clearly defined good guys and bad guys. She and James were in one camp, and he and the people were in the other. It was a sophomoric mentality, especially for a reporter, who should've been more balanced in his ideologies.

"The fact that you cured the virus doesn't negate the fact that you created it in the first place," the dolt said, right on cue. "The virus is still not entirely eradicated. It's still showing up, destroying neighborhoods."

"It's true."

"And you're responsible for not only all those lost lives but for the devastation caused by the economic crisis."

"Indeed, I've visited the dregs in every major city in the US and other countries across the globe. It's truly heartbreaking." James nodded, encouraging more hostility, more accusations.

If she'd been sitting in James's chair, she would've gotten straight to the point and cleared up every simple-minded notion in the reporter's feeble brain. Nick Slater wanted justice, but no justice would ever be served. He wanted someone to take the fall, but not a single person would ever go to jail. He wanted to expose and shut down the Colony, but he'd never be allowed to do that.

Their work was too important.

He wasn't getting it.

She pushed herself off the console table. "This isn't working."

But James raised his index finger. One more minute.

She stalked over to the water cooler. Maybe it'd help cool her jets, as Keisha would say.

"Is it okay if I ask you a personal question?" James leaned toward Slater with his elbows on his knees, his eyes wide with an earnest look.

She rolled her eyes at Mia, and Mia winked back. Mia loved watching James work.

"Why did you come here? For the truth, or for the story you've been wanting to write for the last, what, four years?"

"Both," Slater said. "The American people deserve to know where the virus came from. They should know that people are disappearing right off the streets and being used as test subjects."

Layla felt Slater's body temperature rise. Finally. Anger was good.

She baited him further. "You just want a story, you selfish prick."

Slater glared. "No. It's not about me."

His rising emotion opened the thinnest crack in his brick brain: *Darcy.* She tried to push through, but it closed back up.

"It's about protecting innocent people from unknowingly being subjected to genetic experimentation," he continued. "Maybe you own government officials and police, but once the people see what you've been doing, once they understand that you created the virus, whether it was a mistake or not—that you're responsible for hundreds of thousands of horrific deaths—you'll never get another person to step onto your bus. You'll die out."

He was full of shit. He didn't care about these people. He was obsessed with this story. His entire life was meaningless without it. He had nothing back home, nothing except this Darcy, and she was only a fraction of his pathetic self-absorbed universe.

Layla bit her tongue. For James.

James nodded and sat back, crossing an ankle over a knee. He liked to lead people to the right answer. *You can't shove a belief system down someone's throat, Lay. They have to come to it on their own.*

"Ah, you're an excellent reporter, but you misjudge human nature, especially as it relates to sensationalism." James reached into the breast pocket of his jacket and pulled out his iPhone. He scrolled through and handed it to Slater. "Our colony in Jiuquan was infiltrated by an undercover policeman from Chengdu, who leaked some pictures to the media. Take a look at this image. What do you see?"

The first was a group of people, all wearing black pants and jackets, kneeling in perfect formation. The sun shone brightly overhead. They might have looked like a martial arts team if not for the heavy black hoods that shielded their faces.

"A cult. Maybe devil worshippers."

"Indeed. That's what the policeman saw as well. Do you see anything else?"

He swiped to zoom in. "A restaurant?"

"Aha!" James repositioned the image to focus on an A-frame sign with traditional Chinese characters, positioned in front of a double door. "It says, 'Lunch today: Beef noodle soup, minced pork rice, oyster pancakes, pan-fried buns.'"

Slater shrugged.

Layla exhaled. James was wasting his time.

"Let's try another one," James said, grinning. He swiped to the next photo and handed it to Slater.

Layla looked over Slater's shoulder. The shower image. In it, a man crouched naked in a shower, facing away from the camera. The image was hazy because of the shower steam, but the dark red, inflamed slash marks across the man's back were clearly visible.

"Jesus!" Slater quailed.

"Yes, the cleanse is a whipping ritual we use to bring our inductees closer to a state of self-actualization. It's quite popular. But what else do you see?"

Slater shook his head.

James swiped to yet another picture. "And this one."

It was James's favorite. He'd had the image blown up and hung in his office as a daily reminder of the state of the world. In the image, people gathered on a busy city street, many of them dressed in the same black outfits with hoods. One man dressed in the garb held a sign.

"The sign says 'Please Take Me.' After the pictures leaked to the media, thousands of people stormed the Colony, rattled the gates, and begged to be let in. The Colony police had to turn them away. We didn't have the infrastructure to take so many desperate, hungry recruits."

Slater's face fell as the realization hit him. "The economic crisis. They were starving."

Layla glanced at Mia to see if she noticed Slater's change in posture. Mia shifted slightly, a new look of curiosity on her face.

James continued. "See, when people saw the pictures on the TV, they didn't see a group of people suffering in the sweltering heat. They saw food. And they'd gladly have taken a whipping for the opportunity to take a hot shower. Most people don't even have access to cold fresh water."

James didn't look up from the image of the man holding the PLEASE TAKE ME sign, and Layla's heart broke when she saw tears well up. "I took this picture myself. I was called over to Chengdu to assist with damage control. I had an escort take me through the streets so I could see what it was really like. There was no good drinking water. I offered a bottle of water to a woman with four kids. She thanked me over and over again and allowed each of her thirsty children to drink from the bottle, taking none herself. Then—" He choked up and took a moment to collect himself. "Then she begged me to take her children so they could live. 'Take them to your paradise,' she said. To this day, I wish I'd been able to do something for her."

Layla pushed her mind into the reporter's head. The words she could pick up filled her brain like a radio with a bad signal: *Reese's little girl … give her up … better life.*

He was cracking. His mind was opening. James was working his human magic. Despite her animosity for the reporter, she wanted to grin with pride. James was truly brilliant.

But just as she was embracing this glimmer of hope, Slater's heart hardened. His muscles tensed, and darkness clouded his face. She heard the voice of a woman: *Find them, Nicky. Do your fucking job.*

Darcy.

Slater walked over to the whiteboard. Layla saw his drawing before he even popped the cap off the marker. A tombstone. On it, he wrote three names: Vincent Wang, Peter Malloy, Daniel Garcia.

"They were killed because they knew the truth."

Slater was wearing thin. His haughty idealism about truth for the deserving American people was abating, and he was grasping at straws to keep his outrage alive. But the wrath he wanted to feel for Darcy's sake wasn't in his heart.

Time to enter the discussion.

"They weren't killed because they knew the truth."

He wheeled from the whiteboard, popping the cap of the marker back on with a vicious *snap*.

She gave him a tight smile. "They were sacrificed because they didn't understand the importance of our work."

81

S o snooty Allison Stevens, who'd changed her name here to the twee, airy-fairy Layla, had finally come out of her huff and joined the conversation. In that moment when she'd looked down at him as he lay incapacitated on the floor of her sim, Nick had decided he was going to make sure she rotted in prison.

Judging by her hostile tone, she obviously didn't think much of him, either.

She snatched the marker from his hand and moved to the whiteboard: *23,000+*

"That's the number of offers we've made to homeless people, drug addicts, and people infected with HIV and other diseases, worldwide."

Another number: *0*

"Of those who've signed a contract to stay, that's the number of people who've asked to break their contracts."

33%

"That's the percentage of people who have received medical treatment, rehabilitation, and education and have reentered society to help others in need. And the rate is increasing every month." She whirled around and glowered. "Name me one social services program on the planet with that success rate. Well? You're a journalist. You're one with the people. How are the people doing out there in your dregs?"

Nick held his poker face. Sure, those would be impressive statistics if they were true. But there wasn't one goddamned positive word he was going to believe coming from this loony bin. All he wanted was to keep them talking, to create just enough tension to reach them at an emotional level. Because once an interviewee succumbed to their emotions, they spewed like a volcano.

James leaned forward as if he might cut Stevens off, but she was too quick.

"No one out there is curing diseases," she said. "No one is curing the virus. No one is taking care of the most vulnerable in society. No one but us."

Yeah, taking care of people by stealing them from the streets. Taking them from their families, just like ol' Red had told him about Reese's little girl.

Stevens grabbed her phone from the table and furiously tapped and swiped, leaving Nick to wonder if her bullshit spiel was over. He hoped so; he had more questions for James. He swiveled back toward James but jolted when he felt a hand on his knee.

Stevens crouched in front of him and offered her phone. When she spoke, the shift in her tone was such a one-eighty he almost fell off the chair. "This is Tiffany." She looked at the picture with tenderness in her eyes. "She's Reese's little girl."

He recoiled as if she were a rattlesnake. What the fuck? Had he said the name out loud?

She didn't move from her crouched position, looking up with an earnestness that just minutes ago he would have thought her incapable of. "Red's buddy? From Skid Row?"

He couldn't avert his eyes from her face. How did she do that? Could she read his mind?

She picked up his limp clammy hand and wrapped it around her phone. He reluctantly looked down.

"Not the little girl you were imagining, I know. She's seventeen. She arrived here about three months ago, and I've taken a personal interest in her because I was touched by her story. When she was twelve, she was coerced into joining a prostitution ring that catered to deviants in the wealthy areas of LA. She was practically enslaved, unable to escape. Even her father couldn't protect her. But we rescued her."

Nick was transfixed by the picture. The eyes of the young girl were empty. Utterly lifeless.

"At first, Tiffany slept under her bed every night. She could barely talk to anyone. Now she's confident and healthy. She's in the education program, showing an aptitude for math. After her induction, I hope to recommend her for work in our bioanalytics group.

He looked up in surprise.

"And yes, to answer your unasked question, she will participate in our genetic research, as does everyone."

He leaned back. Her mind-reading magic trick had jarred him, but her sappy human-interest story wasn't going to deter him from writing the real story here: the heinous exploitation of young, innocent, vulnerable people to test genetic drugs. Their colossal fuck up cost the lives of millions. Precious Tiffany would be a big hit with NPR, but he wanted his Pulitzer Prize.

As she noted his reaction, her expression clouded over and chilled to become the cold, hostile glare that, frankly, he liked better. It was more believable. She collected her phone and stood, giving James the slightest headshake.

She strode to the door, glanced back at Mia, and left the room.

82

James pushed up his glasses thoughtfully. Layla had been a nay vote before they even talked to the reporter. She'd grown increasingly intolerant of present-day troglodytes, as she called them, but she'd seen something in this reporter. She'd made it past his defensive, distrustful exterior. But then, somehow, she'd lost him.

He glanced at Mia, who was already rising from her seat. Mia had always been his steady right hand, unemotional in both business decisions and character assessments. *I call 'em like I see 'em* was her mantra, and he weighted her opinion heavily.

She subtly shook her head and followed Layla out the door, leaving him alone with Nick.

A no from Mia, too.

But he wasn't ready to give up on Nick Slater. A man with that much passion for truth, someone who would chase a story for four years, despite James's many attempts to stop him—doggedly pursuing answers even now, with his own life on the line—could be a valuable ally on the outside. If he was going to convince Nick Slater to walk away from his story of a lifetime, he needed to find common ground.

He moved into the chair closest to Slater. "Mr. Slater, I'm going to be honest with you, because I hope you'll be honest with me. I don't want to take your life."

Perhaps the openness of the threat reminded the guy that this wasn't his interview, that he didn't have the upper hand, because fear coiled in Slater's expression.

"I've watched you for years, off and on, through the eyes of operatives who work for me in the field. I've seen your obsession. I've read your blog. I understand how deeply important this story is to you."

He expected Slater to launch into another first amendment rant, but he remained impassive. Good. Maybe he finally stopped composing story headlines and was ready to listen.

"Your being here puts us in an awkward position. Our work has never been more critical than it is right now. We've made tremendous progress in our reversion cure, but the fact is, there are still thousands of praefuro out there that must be found. Keisha and others like her are the only ones who can find them, and soon we'll be able to send hundreds more into the world to help. I'm sure you can appreciate that we can't risk a story that could slow or stop that work."

He reached into his briefcase and pulled out the small Ziploc he stashed there for this moment. He slid it across the table.

Slater glanced down. Recognition registered on his face, but he didn't move to take it.

"We're sorry about the cops. Agent Malloy and Agent Garcia came to us. They pulled guns and threatened our work. They didn't allow us the conversation you're having right now. So yes, they died in vain. But no advancement in science or society was ever made without sacrifice."

He took a deep ragged breath in the face of Slater's statue-like posture. The hostility and goading he witnessed minutes ago, characteristic of a cop trying to extract a confession from his suspect, had abated. Maybe Slater just wanted his big story, or maybe he'd taken a turn.

"You've been looking for Allison Stevens for a very long time. I've seen the diagrams on the walls of your apartment. I know you believe she's the glue that holds your story together. So now that you've found her, I'll give you the story. The truth."

After a slight nod of assent, Slater didn't move a muscle over the next thirty minutes as James poured out her story. He didn't flinch while James explained how Allison had been framed, victimized, and kidnapped by Austin Harris, nor did he cringe when James described how he himself had coerced her into taking a genetic drug to erase the memory of her twenty-nine years, stripping away her entire world and leaving her with a blank slate and a new identity. More remarkably, Slater held his stony expression as James described in detail how she'd willingly accepted the implantation of a genetically engineered embryo and how that embryo mutated into a fetus that enslaved her mind, turned her into a killer, and drove her to try to take her own life—all while James stood idly by.

"Allison Stevens knows sacrifice." James hung his head. His beautiful girl. She was so strong. "She's sacrificed enough for ten lifetimes."

On that devastating night, when he'd released "A Desperate Warning to the World," he'd vowed to never let her suffer another day for the rest of her life. Still, she'd suffered with months of reversion therapy that nearly killer and even more months of recovery and rehab. Now, as he took a moment to collect himself, he was again reminded of her indestructible spirit. She was nothing short of extraordinary. "And despite everything she's been through, she wakes up each day with purpose. Nothing is more important to her than bringing the last praefuro home. She is the one who will eradicate the virus. She's humanity's only hope."

He dropped his head into his hands. He was tired. Tired of cleaning up the worldwide calamity and economic devastation that Stewart had caused. Tired of harboring the good work of the Colony as if they had something to be ashamed of. But mostly, he was tired of being perceived as the villain. All he'd ever wanted to do was help people, to help the human race.

He had nothing more to offer Slater.

The defense rests.

His eyes locked with Slater, looking for some sign of understanding, a glimmer of empathy. Nothing.

He stalked to the sweeping oversized window and gazed into pitch blackness, frustrated that he'd been unable to win Slater's trust. Now another innocent mind would have to be wiped away, another sacrifice made for the vision of the Colony. The work was too—

Sacrifice. What have you ever sacrificed, James? Layla's voice echoed in his head.

She was right. God, she'd been right. What had he ever given up? Maybe it was his turn to make a sacrifice.

His proposal tumbled from his lips before his brain could stop it. "If you need a story, if you can't leave here without a fall guy for Peter Malloy, for the virus, you can have me. I'll go on the record."

Sheer surprise brought life back into Slater's glassy eyes, and James could practically hear his mind racing with new headlines. "An Interview with the Voice Behind 'A Desperate Warning to the World.'" Maybe it would be enough to protect Layla and her work.

At long last, Slater slouched back against his chair. His long hair flopped over his eyes, and as his hand swept it away, a corner of his mouth lifted. "Nah."

James gaped at him. He was putting his own ass on the line. He was giving Slater the man behind the Warning. It was the story of a goddamn lifetime.

"No matter what spin you put on it now," Slater said, "you'll be leaving me to give the people only part of the picture."

James searched his face. Had he broken through? Did Slater see how important this project really was?

"That makes this story unfinished."

"But you and I both know that you've fought tooth and nail to keep this story alive for nearly half a decade now, and—"

Nick straightened and pushed back from the conference table. "And an unfinished story will never get me a prime time slot."

83

L ayla tossed her laptop beside her on the sofa when the front door opened.

James draped his sport coat over the kitchen chair and opened the liquor cabinet. He popped the cap off a bottle of Talisker and poured two glasses, then swallowed his antiretroviral preventive. *Just in case you start to notice a hint of decay,* he'd said. *I can't have you grimacing every time I step into the room.*

He flopped onto the sofa next to her with a grunt, both drinks in hand. He looked utterly exhausted.

She took a sip of her Scotch, savoring the smoky flavor, and squirmed down to lay her head in his lap, her glass on her stomach.

Neither of them spoke.

She wouldn't ask what he decided to do with the reporter. Despite her indignant rant earlier that evening, she trusted his judgment. He knew what was at stake, even though he would never fully understand her kind or why she was so passionate about her work.

Eugenesis, now led by General Harding, was fully on board with Project Phoenix, committed to finding and curing every praefuro that still wandered the earth.

But even after they'd been cured, the praefuro would never be normal humans. Their minds had evolved. They functioned as the collective, not a cluster of individuals, and they no longer identified as separate physical human beings. It was an ethos outsiders couldn't grasp, let alone experience.

One thing James did appreciate was that the collective, as evolved as it was, had a pecking order, a hierarchy not unlike that of a wolf pack. Newly discovered praefuro had to establish their positions in the collective, and a miscalculation could send the collective spiraling out of control.

Her simulation was where they found their places. The Sin City microcosm allowed praefuro and outsiders to come together in close proximity while newcomers filled the void in the collective life force that had been waiting for them. The praefuro newcomer sensed both otherness from the outsiders and oneness within the collective and accepted this position, a puzzle piece sliding into its proper slot.

James understood that nothing was more important to her than reintegrating the tribe. She'd kill, though the thought repulsed her these days, before she'd allow anything to compromise her vision. She was the alpha, after all. It wasn't a position she'd earned; it wasn't a reward for dominant behavior. It just was. And it was her responsibility to protect the collective. Her family.

James would never let anyone or anything threaten her work.

She took another sip of Scotch and reached up to stroke his scratchy beard.

It had to be two in the morning. She had a long day ahead of her. The council wanted an update on the reversion dose regimen for the praefuro children. Madeline wanted to meet with her, Mia, and James to talk about adoptions of the sensus offspring. And much to her dismay, she'd promised to meet Isaac and Nicole for lunch in the Gallery as an evaluation of Nicole's readiness to participate in simulations. She could already hear the old Nicole, now nearly back to her normal self and crowned with new teeth and hair. *Oh, my god, Layla, look at me! Tell me I'm not the most beautiful woman in this … whole … restaurant!*

But at that moment, she didn't care about the day ahead. She only wanted to be with James.

"Wanna go out to the bench?" She waggled her eyebrows. "Make love under the stars?"

His face lit up with renewed energy, and he practically dropped his glass to slide out from under her and trot to the front door.

She hopped onto his back.

"Promise you won't push me over the edge?" he asked.

"A furo can never make that promise." She draped her arms over his shoulders as he hoisted her onto his hips.

"Hmm. I'll take my chances."

Epilogue

Nick grunted at the jabbing between his ribs.

"Got some ID?"

He peered up through one eye and squeezed them both tightly shut. The intensity of the sun was a fiery assault on his senses. God, his entire body felt as though it'd been crushed by a steamroller.

"How about a name?"

Christ almighty. What had he done to warrant such a hangover?

More jabbing. "Let's go, buddy. Find another place to sleep it off, or I'll haul you in and you can pay rent for a jail cell."

Nick heard what the man was saying, but the situation wasn't registering. He flopped onto his stomach with a snort.

"Drag him to the swine wagon."

Hands grabbed him under the arms and tugged him into a vertical position. His legs sagged and his head fell forward. All he could do was moan in protest.

"Nicky!" a female voice called out. "Oh, my god, Nicky! Officer, he's with me. My nephew. I'm so sorry. Please don't take him. I'll take care of him."

"Found him sleeping on the sidewalk, resisting the orders of a police officer."

"I'm so sorry, sir. I take full responsibility. Please don't let us burden you. No one works harder than law enforcement. Thank you so much for your service. Phoenix's finest."

Nick's head lolled to the left. He tried to get his brain to tell his neck to hold up his head, but the synapses didn't seem to be firing.

"My late partner was at the DEA," the female voice continued. "Peter Malloy? Killed in the line of duty."

"I'm sorry for your loss, ma'am. Pete was a good man. Is that your place of business?"

"Yes, sir. Yes, it is."

"Let's help our friend here inside."

Nick felt his bare heels drag along the pavement until he was out of the sun and lying on a cool cement floor.

"Thank you, officers. Thank you so much. Be safe out there today."

"Make sure he gets some fluids in him, and not from the Guinness tap."

She chuckled. "I certainly will."

A door closed, and he was surrounded by cool, dark blessed silence.

But then that shrill voice echoed through the room. "Nicky? Are you all right? What happened? Where have you been?"

He half covered his head with one elbow and squinted up at her. Her face was familiar, but he couldn't place it. His brain seemed to have completely glitched out.

"Nicky?"

He opened his eyes a bit wider. To his right, bar stools lined up perfectly under a bar, where a Pictionary box jutted over the edge enough that he could read the title. To his left, he spotted a flashing neon Budweiser sign, a broom and a dustpan, and a cowbell hanging from the door handle. Straight over him stood a woman with short salt-and-pepper hair framing a slightly wrinkled, worried face.

"Drink this." She shoved a glass at him, sloshing a few droplets of water onto his face.

He flinched, but the water made him realized just how thirsty he was.

He rolled onto an elbow and managed to hoist himself up far enough to gulp down the entire glass of water in one breath.

She refilled the glass, sat cross-legged on the floor, and set it in front of him. Her forehead furrowed as worry shifted to annoyance. "You gonna tell me what's going on? Where you've been?"

He opened his mouth to say *I'm working on it, give me a minute*, but the entire glass of water came back up, followed by a cringeworthy belch.

"Jesus Christ." She rolled onto her feet.

"Sorry." He coughed.

A second later, a bar towel hit him in the face.

"God, sometimes you remind me of Jay. When you get your shit together, I'll be in the office."

He wiped his sweat-covered face and sipped tentatively at the second glass of water. Then he told his brain to tell his legs to stand up. They didn't, but he managed to get onto his hands and knees. He took a few more breaths and pulled himself up by the wooden legs of the barstool.

"Move," he said to his feet, and by some act of god, they shuffled forward. He picked up a stack of bar napkins to wipe his dripping face again and inched toward a closet-sized room with the light on.

He collapsed into a folding chair next to her desk. His head throbbed at the very base of his skull. Every muscle ached. He couldn't even get his fingers to make a fist. He wiped the slime off his lips with the back of his hand, closed his eyes in a long blink, and took a deep cleansing breath. He could almost hear his brain cells coming to life with a disgruntled groan.

She sat back and crossed her arms over her chest. Darcy—so stubborn, but always there for him.

Might as well get it over with. He reached into his pocket, pulled out the Ziploc bag, and held it out.

Her hand flew to her mouth to muffle a gasp. "How did you…?"

She pulled the wallet from the bag and plucked out a Department of Justice DEA ID card. She ran her finger over the unsmiling photo of Special Agent Peter Malloy, lifted the wallet to her nose, and inhaled.

Tears welled in her eyes.

"You did it," she whispered. "You found them. You got the story."

"No story. Just the truth."

"What do you mean, no story?" She balled up her hands. "Nicky ... You have to write the story. They have to pay for what they've done."

He put his hand over hers and looked deeply into her eyes. He loved her with all his heart, and all he wanted was to make her happy again. He wanted to see her eyes sparkle like they did when Pete Malloy was still alive. But that peace was something she'd have to find within herself.

"I'm not the hero, Darce," he said. "There is no hero or villain in this story."

"But what about Pete? He died for this, Nicky. What about all those people who were victimized and tortured?" Her face contorted in grief.

"There's more to it than we understood. It's complicated."

"Bullshit." She pounded her fists on the desk. "You promised me. You told me that you'd find them and expose them and make them pay. And if you don't do it, you'll be just like them."

"Pete's fight was four years ago, and his death was unjust. But justice doesn't always come in the shape of vengeance. Sometimes it comes in the shape of atonement."

He looked into her biting glare once more and forced his wobbly legs to schlep him to the door.

It was an answer that would never satisfy her. She viewed life as a rigid dichotomy between good and bad, moral and immoral, legal and illegal. Good guys were rewarded, bad guys were punished, and no one was forgiven. One day, he hoped she would also understand that a better world in the future sometimes required the sacrifice of the innocent.

Meanwhile, all anyone could do is play the hand life dealt. No cheating. And no folding.

***

Nick stood on the porch a good three or four minutes before he drummed up the courage to actually reach for the doorbell. The exterior lighting flipped on, showcasing the impressive Spanish colonial house against the deepening twilight.

The door opened to a stony glower.

This was a terrible idea. He should turn and walk away, let bygones be bygones.

Or … Or he could try something new. *Fides humanitati*, as a wise man had recently told him. Faith in humanity.

He held out a six-pack of beer and a DVD.

Ed Slater took the DVD and studied the cover, his face as emotionless as ever. Game six of the 2001 World Series, Diamondbacks versus Yankees. One of the last happy moments of Nick's relationship with his father. Every day for a week, they'd sat down together on a beat-up sofa in the basement with a bowl of popcorn and watched Arizona win the World Series.

It had taken Nick most of the day to find a copy. Full recordings were hard to come by these days. "Thought we could have a few beers and relive the good ol' days."

His dad pursed his lips and turned the DVD over. Finally, he looked back at Nick through narrowed eyes. "What, you couldn't get game seven?"

"*Pfft.* Fuck you."

And his dad wrapped his arms around him for the first time ever.

From the Author

Thanks for reading *THE RAGE COLONY*. I sincerely hope you enjoyed it.

I'd be ever grateful if you would consider putting up some stars on the Amazon store page for *THE RAGE COLONY*. Reviews are the lifeblood of new independent authors, and your review would have a huge impact on my book's visibility to other readers.

Just a quick acknowledgment...

Thank you with all my heart to my husband, Steve, for reading the dreadful first draft of Rage ("Well, it could be worse..."), and the second ("Rollicking good fun, but..."), and the third ("Nailed it."). Or maybe he couldn't swallow the thought of one more round.

I'm eternally grateful to my editorial team Lisa Poisso and Martha Hayes, who so skillfully reached into my soul and yanked out the story I was trying to tell, one narrative technique and one strong verb at a time. They've made me such a better writer.

Finally, feel free to visit my website (shanonhuntbooks.com), where you can sign up to be notified of my next book, friend me on Facebook (Shanon Hunt Books), or write to me at shanon.hunt@gmail.com. I answer every email.

DISCOVER THE COLONY

The Colony Book 1

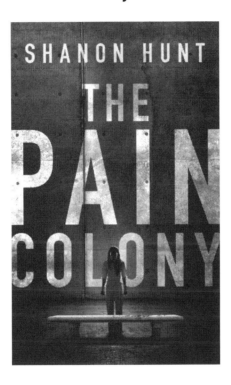

A secret society of true believers will do whatever it takes to become Pure…

…unaware that they will soon be victims of the most chilling medical discovery in human history.

With Pain Comes Peace

A Companion Short Story to The Pain Colony

My name is Layla. Or so they tell me.

In no world could I be a Layla. Layla's a feminine name. It's for

someone tall and graceful with flawless skin and thick silky hair. I'm five foot six with stringy hair and a round baby face. Slender but a little beefy in the thighs. Graceful? No. I walked right into a sliding glass door just this morning. I feel I'm more of a somewhat klutzy tomboy, more of a Charlie or an Alex.

I've been rescued and rehabilitated by a curious place called the Colony. Rescued from what, I don't know. Possibly a life not worth living, since I was found unconscious and bloody with a broken foot. Hiding from someone (or something) in a dirty dumpster alley in a bad part of Phoenix.

Or so the story goes.

Read Layla's introduction into the Colony! Download the free book here: **https://dl.bookfunnel.llcom/zlg4dr1w5c**

About the Author

As a former pharmaceutical executive of 15 years, Shanon Hunt has firsthand experience with cutting edge medical advances. But it wasn't until she took an interest in CRISPR and the near future implications of genetic engineering that she became inspired to write medical suspense thrillers.

When she's not plotting her next story, she enjoys being tormented by her frisbee-obsessed Australian Shepherds, hiking the wilds of northern New Jersey, and canyoneering in southern Utah with her husband, Steve.

Printed in Great Britain
by Amazon